A LOVE
LIKE HELL

A LOVE
LIKE HELL

FRANCESCA FRATAMICO

The Book Guild Ltd

First published in Great Britain in 2023 by
The Book Guild Ltd
Unit E2 Airfield Business Park,
Harrison Road, Market Harborough,
Leicestershire. LE16 7UL
Tel: 0116 2792299
www.bookguild.co.uk
Email: info@bookguild.co.uk
Twitter: @bookguild

Typeset in 11pt Minion Pro

Printed and bound in Great Britain by 4edge Limited

ISBN 978 1915603 890

British Library Cataloguing in Publication Data.
A catalogue record for this book is available from the British Library.

Nan and Grandad
and
Nonno and Nonna

Caro Signoro Maestro,

I have done something unforgivable.
I have done something sinful.
I have done something terrible.
Truly terrible.
I have removed the crucifix from my neck today.
My fingers had been clumsy and clammy, for it sounds strange, but I was scared, frightened by the powerful childish fears and phantoms which encompassed this removal of faith.
My cold fingers curved and uncrinkled the chain, causing the crucifix to dance upon my cold prickled chest, as if Jesus found a sick jest and joviality in my thrashed faith.
The clasp had been stiff, unreleasing, for it had strangled my neck for many years, like a leash, and therefore it was unwilling to leave my body without a fight.
My cracked, quivering fingertips slipped and struggled over the clasp, pushing my fragile state of mind over the edge.
I swore loudly, profusely, viciously, like a dog baring his teeth.
I slammed my fists against the frostbitten wall, like a monkey trying to break into a coconut.
I clenched my teeth, grunted, grabbing the necklace, I tore it away from my neck, snapping the clasp, and letting the cruel crucifix clatter to the floor.

I am free. I am free. I am free.

I am lost. I am lost. I am lost.

And in this loss of faith, I have had to find another old, bearded man to confide in.

This is why I write to you Signoro Maestro.

Congratualtions, you are the newly appointed God of the sky, and now I must ask you some tough questions. You have watched me persecuted on this pedestal of punishment. You have listened to my tormenting testimonies. You have smelt the sweat of shame on my clothes, and now it is your turn to be trialled for your crimes against humanity as the new God.

Firstly, why would you sacrifice your only son for mankind, God?

Why would you allow his blood to stain pillars and posts for the cruel kind of men?

Why would you want his bones and skin to be pierced with rusted nails to save the disease of men?

Why would you allow men to clamp your son's body in death? A death to save these very men.

It is a preposterous idea! The very meaning of madness, for mankind are the villains which stalk this earth.

God, are you blind? Do you not see the treachery of men? Do you not see the blood on their hands, the blood on their spears, the blood in their eyes?

God, are you deaf? Do you not hear the murderous cries twisted from women's throats, and the foul cries they torture from their fellow brother's?

God, are you unfeeling? Do you not feel the sadness, the destruction, the violence, the fear squeezed into every man and woman, like a calzone?

God, can you not taste? Can you not taste the salty tears of a woman? Can you not taste the metal of blood? Can you not smell the burning? The burning of grass? The burning of wood? The burning of flesh?

God, in my humble opinion, sacrificing your son was worthless, for you have allowed mankind to run wild and mad, breeding brutality and cracking consciences, like shelling walnuts.

And I know this man who you have saved, who walks the streets, who eats delicious dishes, who drinks the finest wine and fucks the fanciest whores, but I cannot understand why you let this man walk free?

Not guilty, they had concluded.

NOT GUILTY! NOT GUILTY! NOT GUILTY!

How could you allow this? That man had guilt riddled through his bones and blood, like cancer. His shadow is blood red in the streets, his spit is blood red on the fork, his lip stain on the glass is blood red and his fingermarks on his whores are blood red. How could you set a man like this free?

I remember how that man had faced me in that dingy, dark courtroom. Proud in his isolation. Righteous in his wrongdoings. Defensive in his deadly despair.

His face had been a cold, unfeeling shield, as they discussed the flames thrown up from the grass.

His eyes had been clear and cut, like flints, at the mention of the smoke smothering her lungs.

His lips had quivered with a smug smile at the thought of her hollow, helpless screams.

He had been a man, emotionless, fixed and frozen by his fight for freedom.

And he had got what he had wanted, like he always did.

The burly, blue officers dragged my fighting body from the courtroom. My last picture of that man was his rich lips smirking, his rich hands shaking other rich hands, rich sighs of relief exchanged with rich voices of congratulations mocking me, like the tinkling of coins.

Why was I so shocked by this result?

Perhaps I had naively believed justice and faith would prevail, but how foolish I had been, for money always wins.

Money rules the justice of the law. Money rules the conduct of society. Money rules the games of love. And now, I believe, money has even corrupted the philosophies and policies of the old God.

The rich will always hang the poor by their necks, like chickens, one wrong move, one misplaced word, and a sharp knife will cut their life short without mercy.

This, my dear Signoro Maestro, is why I have appointed you as the new God, for you always seemed fair and judgeless in your living days, and why should this have changed?

After I rid myself of that awful necklace, I circled it, like a lion uncertain of its prey's strength. Round and round and round I stomped, my frustration fizzing and frothing, fizzing and frothing. My body combusted, bursting with this boiling energy, and I stamped and stamped my foot upon the metal. I ripped my shoe from my foot, and continued beating the crucifix, bashing and banging it until the evil within me had been exorcised.

But then I stopped.

My foot had hovered in the air, frozen, as the fury emptied from my soul, like an unclogged sink, leaving my body cold and sensitive to that vision.

I crouched to the floor, strong and afraid for what I had seen. I scooped it between my fingers, and pinched the head of the crucifix turning it to face me.

I had gasped, and I couldn't let the breath go.

I had closed my eyes, whispering, begging, pleading for what I had seen to be true.

I opened one eye and then the other. I then gulped, trying to force the hard lump down my throat.

The figure of Jesus was no longer that figure.

It was her.

The tangled dark gold hair was hers, the starved, untoned belly was hers, the slim arms were hers, the tilt of his head was her head resting on my shoulder, the closed eyes were hers sleeping soundly in my arms.

I kissed the crucifix, and tightly closed my eyes, tears leaking from the corners uncontrollably. She had cast her spell, sending me away from that dark, dismal cell back to the valley. I could see the flies dithering and dreaming. I could hear the breeze tickling my ears with its lullaby. I could feel my pores overfilling with the sun's sweetness. I could see the grapevines, weaving a maze through the land, like my dreams, and I followed their lines obediently. The widespread leaves rustled, the grapes were swollen, unable to move with the wind, the tendrils creaked.

The wind, the grapes, the vine leaves, the tendrils, the grass tickling my ankles, the wild flowers smiling, tilting their heads to the sun watched me.

I ran on faster and faster, the colours spilling and colliding into one another, the holy blue of the sky, the gold, the green, the yellow, the brown, the purple, the red, the indigo, the violet, the maroon, and then her eyes stopped me.

They hid on the other side of the grapevines, the colour shocking my senses.

Blue. A beautiful, brilliant blue. They teased me. They tormented me. They tortured me. But I could not stop loving them. I was addicted to their magic. I was addicted to their mystery. I was addicted to their misery.

Reaching my hand through the gap, I wanted to grab those eyes and lock them in my heart, but she turned and ran. Her hair slipped through my fingers as she fled, and I thought this would be a mere moment of loss.

But then I had opened my eyes back on the cage of my reality, my fingers had held the crucifix of her so tightly, it had left indents in my palms.

How could you God? How could you? Signoro Maestro, you taught me The Parable of the Sower in those fields, so why must you persist in teaching me these lessons in this cramped, grey cell? What good are they now?

'...as he was scattering the seeds, some fell along the path, and the birds came and ate it up...'.

Is this some kind of sick joke?

Am I the soil or the sower? I feel the pain of both. Yes, very funny, and she is the seeds, like the grapevine seeds, and I am the soil wanting to hold them and nurture them forever, as I did my dreams and her. But you are the bullying birds, or maybe it is that man, eating up my dreams and desires without a care, and even in this desolate place, you still have to lecture me, stealing away those precious memories, as if they belonged to you and that man.

'...They hardly hear with their ears, and they have closed their eyes'.

Is this what you believe of me?

Well, God, Signoro Maestro, you are very wrong. I can see what you see, and I can hear what you say.

I shall speak what you want me to think. This crucifix, once Jesus, but now her, is a symbol of sacrifice. A man was not sacrificed for mankind, but it was a woman. Despite the new age of technology and gender fluidity, women are still being sacrificed to atone for the mistakes of men. Innocent women burnt on fires, anchored beneath the water, used as bait for a man's career, or used as swords and shields in a battle between two jealous men; it has never ended, but merely taken a different form.

She had been the sacrifice of two men's jealous and arrogant hearts. She had sacrificed her hair for ash, her lips for frazzled crisps, her eyes for black burnt bulbs, her laughter for the pitchfork screams of darkness. Her heart, alone and empty, sacrificed for nothing.

Why God did you sacrifice her? Why did you make her suffer for the mistakes of two men? Why did you set her body on a pyre? Why did you let her die alone for nothing?

Why have you punished her, and now me, for I loved her, and still do?

Why have you permanently paused my life for who knows how long? Why have I lost the only girl I could ever love to the merciless hands of that monster? Why was she taken from me? Was it my fault?

No!

No, it certainly was not my fault.

I open my hand, and see the crucifix of her. She stares at me in silent judgment, but I can hear laughter, sobbing and shouting in that silence, like the jury in the courtroom.

My neck feels bare and cold without that small slip of metal, which now intertwines itself around my fingers.

I stare into her eyes and speak. Do you fear me? Do you weep for me? Do you hate me? Do you believe me? Could you even love me? Do you believe I deserved this cruel fate? Do you even think about me stuffed away in this grey, freezing shoebox?

Only that silence, the voices crying and shouting the words: GUILTY! GUILTY! GUILTY!

No, it's not true, please believe me.

I promise you Signoro Maestro that I am not guilty. I have not committed a single crime. I have done nothing wrong, despite the overwhelming evidence against me.

I am an honest man, and though you may doubt me, I will never surrender myself to this accusation.

Tell my girl, your sacrifice, that I am NOT GUILTY!

Write back and let me know there is one soul in this whole world who believes in my sanity and innocence.

Yours sincerely,
Domenico

ONE

Giacomo's palms grew damp against the black, sticky steering wheel of the bus, as he leaned closer to the large, dirty windows.

He felt anxious, even paranoid, as he squinted his large platinum-blue eyes up and down over the dents and lumps of the illogical, grey road ahead.

Pressing his foot on the stiff clutch, the monstrous corner of the mountain came into focus. His moist left hand slid over the gearstick, wet and unyielding, but it was not enough, he had to apply force. Gripping the stick, sweat trickled from the creases in his palms, as he forced it from fourth to second with a grating sound that set his teeth on edge.

The bus jolted, and the revs diminished, but Giacomo could not reduce focus at this point.

The corner was sharp and near, causing Giacomo to slow his big, dark blue bus almost to a stop. His clammy hands expanded, the fat of his fingers now taut and rigid, as he gripped and turned the wheel slowly and carefully and consciously around the narrow corner. He maneuvered the huge body of the bus, needing to avoid the sharp claws of the mountain wall on his right, yet equally avoiding the sickening death drop of the empty valley on his left.

He needed to be meticulous. He needed to be methodical. He needed to be mathematical. The day had not yet begun. The road was a dark, sinister shade, and the sky was pale and ill. The perfect moment to die, unheard and unseen by any other soul.

Life and death were not subjects many had to grapple with in their morning routines, but Giacomo did not know any morning without it.

Sweat snuck from his navy-blue cap, like candle wax, making his face feel tight and irritated, but he had to ignore this. He did not dare brush them away, for he feared losing all control of the road, bus, and monstrous corner.

He bit his pig-pink bottom lip.

His dark, hairy nostrils flared as he inhaled a huge breath of air, as if it might be his last.

Adrenaline electrified the dense black hairs of his body, for no matter how many times he made this trip, the thrill of death so close sparked something like fireworks in his dismal heart.

His eyes were locked, unblinking, on the road, and he felt the very movements of the worn, dusty black wheels creak and angle themselves just so, to succeed in this mission of survival.

The silence within the empty bus was palpable, chaotic and kinetic with the tension of this old, boring bus driver.

Giacomo felt as though the very threadbare, violet seats had sat up straighter, alert and invigorated with the fear their boss imposed on them.

Suddenly, the bus rattled, and the engine grumbled, low and menacing.

There was a crash of the right wheel. The left wheel screamed. The seats violently shuddered.

Giacomo's lips crinkled, and he wiped the sweat from his chubby face with a victorious smile, for he had made it around that impressively scary corner.

Life flooded from his body in small, chuckling hiccups, reddening his cheeks, for he laughed in the face of danger.

His laughter grew stronger and stronger as he thought of all those old young fools, who had condemned their reckless existence to the unforgiving valley beneath.

But Giacomo was smart; a god of the road.

The bus hummed, relaxed and loose, as did Giacomo's own body. His strong back and torso slumped, his chest caved over the steering wheel, and his thick hands loosened their tight grip on the wheel, allowing the bus to move faster and smoother over the broken, irregular road.

Moving around another bend with ease, the town, which was the centre of his life and love, came into view.

The beige, rocky town was spread lazily across the mountain, shaped like a crocodile, snapping its jaws open and devouring any person who dared enter its mouth.

Giacomo slowed instinctively, as his small, fat fingers touched his thick-lined forehead, his hairy chest, his left and then right shoulder. He always crossed himself with a religious importance, for that very mountain was the church, and the town snuggled in the shadows was the priest that had baptized his dreams and confirmed his nightmares. The large, domineering black pine trees, sheltering high above in the mountains, were the dark angels, who had haunted his childhood with scary stories of bloodthirsty beasts and roaming wolves. Beneath the village, tumbled the land and livelihoods of farmers, like a well of life, like the pot of hell. The farmers' dwellings were the homes of the devils, and the farmers with their pitchforks were the very figures of Satan himself. They ploughed and rooted the land with seeds of evil, growing and developing distorted alien limbs, which bore intoxicated, sumptuous dark fruits.

And the town of Castelmauro was the setting of purgatory, the waiting room of death. The dark angels trembled with their conversing and mutterings, like a jury at a court, disagreeing as

3

to who should be sent to the sheltered heavens of the mountains. But was this heaven truly safe? Once you entered this kingdom, by day and night, you were watched and inspected by the guards, who, like wolves, would chase any merciless sinners away. Would you not spend all your days in anxious anticipation of being tossed down to hell?

Giacomo shivered, and he tried to shake these foul thoughts from his head by turning his attention to the scenery. He no longer focused on the road, for he had travelled this stretch many times, and now his feet instinctively moved across the pedals, like an old organ player over a beloved hymn.

The morning sun had risen, yet it was not dazzling, but sweet and sleepy, like melted butter, as it brushed over the valley, like pastry, muffling and moistening the crisp grass. In the mountainous trees, the sun softly streaked the dark ground, like spotlights to lost lovers on a dance floor. The sky was an old, cotton baby-blue, faded with the gentle sun, and worn away with loose ribbons of watery, white clouds, like the veil of a drowned bride in a lake.

The valley was a picture of old tradition, where farmers worked hard for a small price, yet gained great satisfaction in their small successes. Giacomo could see the small moving figures of multicoloured three-wheelers zigzagging through the maze of grapevines, olive trees and vegetable patches. He was suddenly reminded of his departed father, grandfather, and great-grandfather, who had shaped that valley with their own bare hands. His eyes grew misty, yet he was comforted by the thought of their spirits still wandering the land, watching him travel past their world every day. What people failed to realize was that these men did not merely work the land, they were part of it, and they would remain part of that land, like the very crops they sowed. Nothing could remove them from this fated place, for this is what they were and what they would always be.

Perhaps their spirits were the very thing that protected him from falling to his death each morning, he pondered, as he

4

continued along the cracked, bumpy road, beaten and bashed by the harsh rain, and the landslides which succeeded these storms.

To his right steeped the stealth like bank of the mountain, dark and bare, like naked skin, except for a few sparse dead shrubs, which clung to the bank for dear life, afraid to fall as their fellow friends had done. This dense black wall built by nature could not be destroyed by human hands, for it was as strong and unbreakable as a diamond. But nature was stronger, and it had weakened the futile soil, gutting and ripping and hollowing its area, so that even plants did not dare go near it. Landslides, especially in winter, ravaged these banks, making phenomena facts. Could you ever believe a tree could move?

Well, Giacomo had to smile as he recalled a long, lost memory of his childhood.

He remembered how the village had been heavily dosed in rain, and his father had dragged him down to this very highway to inspect the damage of the banks. His father and Giacomo had chattered away, but then he had silenced him with a severe urgency. He had watched his silent father watching the bank, and he had liked the way his ears twitched at each sound, like a cat. Suddenly his father had grabbed his small hand and yanked him away. Giacomo could still to this very day remember the sound of nature, living and breathing and moving, like a disgruntled beast awakening from hibernation. But this beast was furious, mad, and malicious with its entrapment, and it did not withhold its feelings. Rocks had sinisterly clattered down the side of the bank, bouncing upon the road before they fell silently to the valley. It was only a few at first, like the first droplets of rain ushering the cows to sit in their fields, and it had brought the same alarm to Giacomo's father.

After the first rocks had fallen, like the lonely voice of a trumpet, the rest of the bank erupted with an accelerating force, like the crescendo of an orchestra. Rocks of all sizes tumbled faster and faster, and the noise was deafening and foreboding. The noise had made his young ears ring with its raucous and roaring tune, like the grumbles of thunder before a storm, like the stampeding gallop of a hundred horses, hopping and rolling to their deaths.

And then the soil stirred. It rose and crawled creepily, squelchy, and young, as if it was a herd of a million black spiders. His father covered his small ears with his own large hands, for the soil seemed to almost howl and rumble with its efforts, collapsing and separating. This weak, wet soil bubbled like lava, dragging trees, shrubs, and flowers with it, unforgiving and brutal. The trees snapped from their roots, the shrubs crunched and crackled, and the plants took their death silently, but the torment was loud and slow and painful, like a bullet to the stomach. The soil bullied and shoved these innocent creatures of God into the road, like some cruel twisted sacrifice. Pulling and pushing was all one direct motion, for the laws of physics held no existence in landslides.

Finally, the soil, the heaviest mass of wet mud, laboriously collapsed on the road, inches from his feet, smothering the already dead artefacts of nature with a tumultuous thud. This staggering event had been a shock to the young, innocent Giacomo, but the silence that had followed was the main sound he could remember. The solemn and sombre silence had shaken his heart, for he had been lucky to not know of bombs and wars and the silence of death which followed these destructive explosions. The magic of the soil had scared him, for nature only had minutes to live and move as humans, yet the soil had betrayed its fellow friends, sending them to their deaths. It had felt like a biblical story in action, for had these trees been sacrificed by the Lord for a crime he had not known? Or had the soil been arrogant in its evil powers, like in a fairy tale?

Giacomo shook his head at these childish recollections, whilst cursing the poor teaching of science behind this destructive magic, which had injured and killed many. But maybe it held no importance to know the equations and explanations of landslides, for people would still lose their lives to the powerful, merciless soil.

Accelerating slightly, he moved faster and faster from the painful memories of childhood to only meet another. Giacomo passed a shield of trees, usually streaked and marked with the blinding white lights of the football pitch behind. Young boys' dreams were nurtured, nourished, and treasured at this place, yet equally dashed, destroyed and decimated by the nightmares of adulthood. Giacomo was another of the many boys to become a victim of fairy tales. Bitterness swelled from the saliva in his mouth, like the stale aftertaste of a cigarette, as he recollected his own sweet dreams of screaming fans and grass-burnt knees, which he had childishly savoured like the sweetest chocolate.

But where had those dreams got him? What had those dreams done for him? Why had he idealized the smiling, serious posters of football teams? They now mocked his memories, for his dreams had been rich, and his family had been poor, if only he had known this then. Why had he skipped dinners, parties and fun to train and polish his skill, when fate knew he would never be granted this wish?

Giacomo remembered, with reluctance, the race of adrenaline through his veins as his feet pounded across the uneven pitch towards the threadbare, grey goalpost. He remembered how his face had streamed with sweat, his eyes had narrowed with concentration, and how his heart would drop as he kicked the ball towards the goal. He remembered how the breath would be taken from his body, waiting, as if for hours, for the ball to hit the goal. And sometimes it would, and his heart would electrify with life, thudding, pounding and punching as he let out crazy delighted screams at his smiling team. They would run, leap and jump towards him, shouting his name, like he was a rockstar. Sweaty hands would ruffle his sweaty hair, or slap his sweaty back, a wet, smelly greed of success.

When he was a child driving past these lights, they would brighten, as if they were the very eyes of God glowing with a prideful hope at his future career. Suddenly that old pain shot through his chest, was it loneliness? Worthlessness? Disappointment? Perhaps it was a mixture of all three, for when he saw those lights now, they were the glaring, piercing eyes of God, reminding him of the boy he used to be, searching for this boy lost somewhere within this strange old lump of a man. The boy who was reckless. The boy who was a leader. The boy who would have driven around that corner without caution, only risk, defiant in death. But that boy no longer existed. He was lost to the past, and as dead as his own father in the ground.

Was he unhappy in this life? Giacomo questioned.

No, not necessarily. He found numbing contentment in his boring life, and though his peers did not admire him, he knew they mutually respected him. Giacomo knew he was not an unpleasant or unkind person, and he hoped this was enough to preserve his spirit for heaven. Yet as his eyes met the rear-view mirror, his appearance contradicted his thoughts, for his face was contrite and pale, and his long, messy eyebrows clenched, as if he did not believe himself.

Giacomo forced his mind away from these questions, as he tensely clasped the stiff gearstick, shifting it into fourth. The bus jolted at the unsmooth exchange of these gears, yet it continued to rattle and hiccup along the road.

Giacomo shuffled uncomfortably in his leather throne, for the heat was already becoming such a force, and it had the power to sour his mood considerably. His right hand scratched roughly and irritatingly around his groin, suffocated by his tight black trousers. Yet, he struggled to satisfy the itch, for his belly bulged and bloated across his lap, only adding further to his sweaty discomfort. Grabbing his lukewarm water bottle, he drenched his achingly dry throat with this delicious drink, richer than champagne, and more awakening than brandy.

His discomfort eased, as he reshuffled his body, reawakening his concentration to the white sign ahead, welcoming in black scratched letters the rare visitors to the Commune di Castelmauro.

A sign that had bitterly welcomed him home many, many, many times. In all these years Giacomo had been a bus driver, the sign had not changed, perhaps it was slightly less polished and dustier, but so was he. Giacomo sighed.

Giacomo turned his attention to this community, which shivered precariously on the edge of Monte Mauro. Castelmauro was a town that had not aged or moved away from old traditions, and consequently many of its inhabitants had fled for the modern world, without its rigid traditional eyes, and fearful religious regimes. The town was spread higgledy piggeldy across the mountain, constructed with crumbling houses, crumbling businesses and broken brittle streets. Yet through this town, rumours riddled every small alley, road and step. Nothing in this town could be kept a secret, for nosy ears listened intently to gossip, as if their minds and bodies would be starved without these stories. Did they question if what they heard was true? Of course not, for without the grapevines of gossip, the town was a dead and empty shell, hollow in amusement and dull in dreams. The twisting tongues of dwellers created worlds destined for Greek plays. In this town, fact and fiction were the same difference. Even the dullest rumours could become the most elaborate tangle of truths and lies, like the result of a very complicated game of Chinese whispers. Giacomo guiltily delighted in the fake news of the townspeople, yet he did not judge and condemn these characters, unlike others. What people did in their own lives was their choice, and his silent judgement would not change their actions. He disliked people's involvement and interference in the lives of others, for he had witnessed how untamed gossip could ruin the lives of men and women. The results were mixed, some turned to drink, some turned to another town, and some ended their shameful lives, lonely in their distrust and lost in their sin.

However, this town, parked high on a hill, was set, like cement, in its ways. You had two choices, accept its quirks for what they were or leave.

And many had done the latter.

As Giacomo passed the signpost, the first 'tourist attraction' of the town was on your right, a running and dying car mechanics.

The gentle white of the house was now threaded with exposed grey cement, like the hair of an aging gentleman, and the museum did not start within the house, for battered, bruised cars were scattered in the foreground, dusty and beyond repair. At this time in the morning, only a small snippet of sunshine flickered across the smeary windows, yet it did not manage to awaken its owner from his bed. However, nature revelled and rejoiced in the early morning sun, untainted by the hot heat of humans and their complaints. Flies and paper-white butterflies fluttered freely through the dry, pale grass, whilst a large black and brown Alsatian rolled around in the drive with the joviality of a puppy, creating sun-glittering clouds of dust.

Beyond this building stood another pair of tall, cream-coloured buildings, one perhaps uninhabited, for the windows were smashed, and the balcony wobbled in the wind. Despite the firmly shut dark oak blinds, the other building displayed signs of human life, for washing waved gently with the tickling wind's breath from the yellowing balcony bars.

Giacomo softly pressed his foot upon the break, as he saw the still, heavy bright blue sign of the IP petrol station, with the hope for coffee. He slapped his lips together with the sweet excitement of that dark, bitter drink.

Pulling into the nearby curb, he stopped the bus, and turned the ignition off with relief. Jumping from the bus, he slammed the door shut, and ambled towards the place of his hope. There were no cars plugged against the oily and greasy petrol pumps, but this did not deter him from his mission. It was quiet, the crickets were still sleeping off their hangover, and so were the humans, therefore not another soul disturbed this serene, chemical-scented place.

However, as Giacomo came closer to the small, white, abandoned building, like a massive fridge, his heart sank.

The windows were jet black, and shielded by thick, red blinds, like sausages, and the red warning sign of closure halted Giacomo's slamming feet. He swore beneath his breath at the consistent unpredictability of Alessio's opening and closing times. That man lived by the ticking clock in his head rather than the summons of the church bells, Giacomo thought bitterly.

Luckily, Giacomo was in a good mood, and he forgave this mistake. Secondly, he was grateful to just stretch his rigid, aching knees, and breathe the fresh, nostalgic air of this town.

Gazing around, Giacomo lifted his trousers by his belt and sighed. He knew his stomach was expanding more and more every day, for the hooks of the belt were worn and close to snapping from where he had fought against the pressure of his large belly. He did not care too much, for he would certainly never be the jewel of a lady's eye, and he did not want to play those stupid, irritating games that women played. Yet he worried his stomach might betray his greed to God at the gates of heaven.

As Giacomo stared at the valley, and the distant mountains, his mind was soothed, for the sun cast a spectacular spell of sublime reverence across this view. The sun veiled and disfigured the far-off mountains in a transient display, as if they were hidden beneath a million thin, paling yellow daffodil petals, making the mountains look lost, lonely and lovely, untouched and innocent. These mountains seemed adoringly mysterious, soft and approachable in this heavenly fog. Giacomo was eased further by this sumptuous scene, for the weak, golden lace made his imagination stir. He could imagine thousands of angels clustered in that mist, conjuring sceptical visions of peace and singing of beauty, like the luring songs of mermaids. Yet Giacomo knew that once the mist cleared, the singing would stop, and you would be met with a patchwork of land, poor by the people and poorer by the weather, like a sailor diving into the sea only to meet his death.

Shaking his head, a smiling Giacomo strolled back to the bus with a tender heart, swollen with childish prayers. The engine rumbled with a start, and the familiarity of his constant companion brought him away from his pure religious imaginings.

Pulling away from the disappointing IP petrol station, Giacomo continued through the entrance of the town. In a short space of time and distance, he witnessed how much this town had been degraded by its backward boundaries, for houses, once full of life, sat on the side of the road, decrepit and derelict with laughter and happiness. Old farm equipment was abandoned to the side, rusty and worthless with their modern replacements. Some had lost their use at the death of their original owners, like a food chain cut of its most vital component.

Slowly the bus creaked and crackled, as it crept past the old, grey solid prison with its emotionless, black boarded windows and blood-red roof, like the hands of a murderer. A tall burgundy iron gate surrounded the perimeter of the prisoner's freedom, shut tight against the false free world outside. A sly, yet large black camera stood on top of one of the gateposts, waiting and watching, ready to snatch its next victim, like the statues of a stately home. But prison would never be a home for the rich, only the poor belonged here, hidden and harmed in this place monopolized by money and power. Large, solid pine trees sparsely bordered the outside of the fence, like policemen, guarding the fathers of children, and daughters of parents with handcuffs, never again to feel the warmth of a hand that had truly loved them. Its spiky, untouchable leaves added a severe and sharp warning to the misled youths of the town to think twice, think twice about their social conduct.

Giacomo shivered as a memory of his early childhood washed through his brain. An image of his fierce mother being escorted from the prison by a huge, horrible policeman rose before his eyes. His mother was a passionate woman, and these violent attacks of her heart led her countlessly in and out of these gates. Giacomo remembered how scared he was of his mother, for one moment, she would be sweetly docile, smiling and twirling her ginger ringlets around her fingers, and the next, her eyes would boil red, fangs would snip her smile, and long, sharp claws would deform her hands. He was grateful to have taken after his father, a placid man, guided by the strong hands of God, rather than the vicious, volatile, vengeful heart of his mother. He always remembered how his father had described his mother's switch from angry to happy, like the two taps in their old bathroom, one was freezing cold, and the other was burning hot, with no happy medium.

Continuing a small way, he tried to navigate the large olive-green rubbish bins, which littered the roadside, like huge stray dogs, whilst he tried to not trample the wild and untamed shrubbery of the roadside, sharp and brittle, dehydrated by the heat of the long, long summer.

The first glimmer of life in this dead village came in the form of well-kept dishevelled houses. They were a variety of colours, daisy whites, light brown gritty stone, pink, like women's lips, sky blues, plum purples and grey, like gravestones. Though the town was still slumbering, you knew life existed, for there were many, many, many cars. A fellow friend of Giacomo's once said there were more cars than people in this deserted town, and he had to agree. However, many of these cars had not flown down roads for years, for they were old, abandoned and broken with scratched leather seats and black, thick cobwebs, like mourning lace.

Street lights stooped over the road, white and intimidating, like a dentist's lamp, investigating purposefully for something and anything of fault. And in this place, you did not need to look far.

Giacomo squeezed the large blue bus through the barricades of tarnished, broken buildings, which had stood as old as time, so that if you were to travel through this street 100 years ago, it would still be the same. These houses did not hide this fact, and they showed off their scars with a careless pride, like the faces of the elderly ladies who owned them. In this town, the houses seemed designed for risk, either they were hung precariously over the steep drop of the valley, where to drop a peg would be unretrievable, or on the other side, they were built so close to the road that to step from your front door would end in squashed toes, like pancakes. Some buildings, like old people, showed their age differently. Some had tiny, blocked, secret doors next to the front doors, as if it was an entrance for elves. Others held brittle balconies, which cracked the walls, and creaked frighteningly loudly if so much as a mere feather should fall upon it.

Many modern-eyed visitors might turn their phone-buried noses up at these houses, yet they held character and testimonial stories of long-lost families, who had once lit these homes with love and joy. Another characterful feature of this old town was the many twisting, dark, secret alleys. They were as narrow as a lady's shoulders, as steep as their heeled boots, and as secretive as their hearts. But they were integral to the social conduct of the town, where secrets could be kept secret with no brandished shame. Children hid from fuming parents, and men drunkenly slept, before seeing their sharp-eyed wives. No one knew why these tunnels had been created, for they circulated and mapped the whole town. Was it for hiding? Was it for escaping? But surely, they were the same thing, contemplated Giacomo.

He shook his head, and guiltily swore, as he attempted to not run over the haphazardly discarded cars by the stone wall. The bus shrank against the balconies of homes on the opposite side, whilst it limboed under the low black telephone wires. He always feared one day he would become entangled and choked by these deadly wires, like a black mamba.

Between these terraced homes came moments of relief, for small chinks of the dry, dark valley were exposed, but this only made Giacomo sigh, for the heavenly mist of earlier was already dissipating.

Crossing over the slightly wider bridge, he accelerated, for nothing of great importance ran beneath this bridge, only another dusty, broken road, and more dwellings, some blessed with life, and others broken with loneliness.

Finally, Giacomo reached his usual stop, and he braked quietly, for he did not wish to disturb the snoring drunkards with a heart attack. In his childhood, he had harassed the drunk and deluded enough. He recalled hiding and waiting in alleys with his friends to throw cold bags of water over the drunks, who would swear and uncontrollably swing their arms around with anger. As a child, Giacomo had always seen the drunks as the most humiliating of men, especially in the winter, for the unconscious drunks would be carried home on a ladder used to carry the dead pig carcasses. He chuckled now as he remembered how the bearers had slipped and slid in the icy streets, sometimes falling to the ground in a pile of groans and curses. He owed these men some peace after his unthoughtful childish actions.

Some slept on the doorsteps of their homes near the bar, which stood small and sly opposite the bus stop, but others, who could not stomach the journey home, passed the night under the dirt-smeared bus shelter. They slept precariously against the dark, green shelter, like damsels in despair. Yet, these damsels were not fairy tale ladies with long flowing golden hair, but skeletal middle-aged men with sleeves marked with lumps of stray sick, and dehydrated tongues lolling upon their chins, like dogs, whilst saliva flaked across their cheeks, like the trails of a fat slug.

Ever since he was a child, Giacomo had found endless entertainment in watching these drunks, and he could sit there for hours watching these men. But he would never step from the bus, for he feared these sleeping men, who held wild animals trapped inside their souls and bodies. When he was nine, he had followed a drunk home, and even into his house, he had staggered and swayed, but when he heard the furious voice of his wife, this man had pulled a glinting, sharp knife from his pocket, alive with murder. Giacomo had snuck away from the house, afraid, to learn only the next day that this man had killed his wife, slitting her throat, like a Hasselback potato. He never followed another drunk again, but it still entertained him to watch these men from the safety of his bus.

Some snored so loudly it would attract the attention of their wives, who would fling the door open with a crash, robed in a dressing gown and gripping an old, dirty broom. They would slap their confused, stray husbands all over, swearing profusely. These men would groan, and peel open their wrinkled eyelids to reveal eyes bloodshot with their intoxicated conviction. But Giacomo knew that if you looked deeper into their eyes, somewhere you could see a sadness sinking and swirling within their black, shrunken pupils. These men were lost in a dark tunnel of misinformed beliefs, leading a life of search, yet no discovery. They believed that the light liqueurs of the night would recapture the light and hope of their youth. These men awoke colder, confused, and more lost than before, and further from that promise the night before had claimed. The night had breathed promise of escape, yet they were still trapped in this dark tunnel, racing and running around and around and around in circles, desperately trying to find this addictive light. The light of reasoning to their miserable existence, but they drove their stomachs to sickness and their minds to madness. It was an endless cycle, like running through the alleys of the town to escape, yet only returning to the spot they had left.

Giacomo must have been early, for the wives had not awoken, and the drunks had not even stirred at his approach.

This bar was a historic and prestigious monument of this town, crouched in the corner between two tall, white buildings. Sheltered beneath the brow of the blue and white canopy, the bar was the ears and eyes of the villagers' secrets and sins, and it was the very beating heart of the town. Friendships were sanctified and foes were matched. Clink, clink, clink was the rhythmic baseline of the bar, the laughter the chords, and the stumbling speech the melody, which held this place together. Men gathered under the protection of dark cigarette smoke, as they grumbled about their wives picking their pockets for new clothes at the shop next door. Yet they seemed completely ignorant, or in denial, of their own lavish spending and greed.

Sliding away from the unresponsive drunks, Giacomo continued his morning trail, passing houses, a brightly coloured clothes shop, a dark, sombre shoe shop, a clean, compact hairdressers, and a few others, which could hardly be described as healthy businesses. On the right of the main road, and hidden in the dark, disturbing corner of the Via Annuziata, the light of the basil-green pharmacy flashed and flickered like a warning, for menacing, medicinal magic spells were being conducted, like a witch over her cauldron. It was a strange place for the pharmacy to attend to its weak and feeble villagers, for it stank of dog faeces, and blocked, eggy gutters. Walking past the pharmacy was enough to make you feel sick and wretched.

Beside the small, creepy pharmacy stood a house riddled with large, black holes, like bullet shots. It seemed appropriately distanced to the pharmacy that Giacomo found it hard to believe it was a coincidence. If you believe this house to be the worst invalid in this town, you will be shocked to find another house staggering in front of the pharmacy's watchful eye. Giacomo was not sure as to whether you could describe this house as standing, for it barely did this. He was not even sure if he could truly call it a house, for it was merely a sad jumble of rocks, which would have once been called home. Giacomo's heart grew despondent at this destroyed home, for this house would have protected a family, cradling, nursing and attending all the happiest and saddest moments of its dweller's life. But in return for this loyalty, it had been left isolated, bullied by the wind and rain, pelted by rock hard hailstorms, smothered by snow, and burned by the sun. Bruised, battered and broken, this house seemed to symbolize something greater to Giacomo. It symbolized the fall of this thriving town, and the descent of disloyalty to traditions and heritage. This town was emptying fast with the death of the elderly, and the frustrated new generation, who could not live without their neat Wi-Fi packages and plasma homes. They had no respect for long-standing family positions and were willing to sacrifice this all for the delicacies of the modern world. Giacomo sourly knew society did not have the patience to appreciate the traditions of the old world, for now, things could be bought and sold within a day, delivered from far lands in tainted plastic bags. It seemed in this modern, material world that things were not bought to last, for they broke easily and were replaced quickly, as if the past had never existed. Giacomo found humour in this concept, for people lived longer and longer, yet materials did not match this extension of life, whilst the old world made things to last, generation after generation.

Giacomo lifted his black speckled chin with pride, for he had not forsaken his family's name to the fast modern world.

Giacomo continued and arrived at the centre of his Castelmauro. This was the place where he had crawled, walked and run, and with the sight of these mismatched houses, the most vivid memories came back to life with every detail he saw. The hidden crooked stairways and roads were no mystery to Giacomo, for he had sprinted up these roads, tripped over all their uneven cobblestones, and found his most vital and life-changing moments in these places. He knew where every path led, and he knew all too well the joy and melancholy of finding these places. He remembered throwing himself down the stairway with his friends, skinny, muddy, and smiling, destined for adventure and discovery. He remembered the hidden path that had witnessed his first sloppy, awkward kiss with Juliet, her braces noisy and bubbling with saliva. He remembered plodding up that hidden stairwell after his father's funeral, as he dragged the heaviest and blackest grief with him.

The houses also warmed and soothed his heart with their cosy familiarity. Giacomo loved the way the houses were misshapen, some were as tall as giants, whilst others were dwarfs, snuggled between their peers, like frightened children between their parents. He loved how these houses were joined at the hip, and snaked together by the rusty metal pipes, like a ribbon around a present. These houses could not be described as merged together, for none of them were the same. Individuality is what made these barricades of houses a feast for the eye, for not only were the houses a variety of colours, but if you looked closer, the very details of these dwellings were different. Yet in these details were the structures of social disparity, for one house might hang thick blinding-white sheets, perfumed with expensive washing powder, whilst next door might hang sheets as thin as tracing paper, which smelled weakly of damp. Some had plant pots of the most beautiful and exotic flowers perched on the front doorsteps, whilst others had pots filled with purposeful herbs from the land. Some had snappingly expensive shutters pulled tightly over the windows, whilst others were naked and reflected the light. The rich and poor of poverty was a subject of inverted snobbery, for those who had money believed they were film stars, boasting of their wealth with doorbells, whilst the poor hated them, knowing full well they were born of the same bread and bones as they themselves were.

Despite this, Giacomo smiled like a child, for a comforting joy welled his simple, sentimental heart.

Suddenly a movement attacked his attention and snapped his smile, as he tried to decipher who and what it was. Giacomo slowed the bus to a crawl, as he leant his broad upper body over the steering wheel, narrowing his heavy-lidded eyes at the strange moving creature.

It looked like a child with long, long legs sprinting around the bend of Via Calvario, passing the crooked steps leading next door to the newsagent and the small flower patch, which Signora Morderna had adopted as her own private garden.

This child was waving its hands madly above its head, was it trying to attract his attention? Giacomo wondered.

Giacomo stopped the rumbling bus near Fango's Grocery store, and he continued to inspect the child, who sprinted down the street with its oddly long legs. However, as the thing grew closer and closer, the child transformed into a man.

The long legs were still long, but not odd, for his body fell into a proportionate frame. The shoulders opened wide and strong and broad, and the torso held firm beneath his flapping moss-green checkered shirt. The arms, which had been thin and puny with tiny doll-like hands, grew, like a magic trick, into long, solid arms, finished with strong work-hardened hands.

The face was still unclear.

Giacomo snapped his engine off. Within the silence of the town, he could hear the long, black shoes slamming and slapping quickly against the road, like an applause. The busy, bushy dark hair bobbed in time with his body, yet his face was still a fuzzy mess.

Giacomo looked down, and leant against his squishy leather seat, exhausted with the effort of thinking and inspecting. As he rubbed his heavy eyes, Giacomo felt that new worry rob his breath and squeeze his chest tight, ridding the happy, childhood memories of earlier. He was becoming old, maybe he was already old, how could you tell? How could you define a precise moment you became old? He did not know this, but he knew his body and eyes were aging and breaking with the slow insistent motion of time, ticking off his life's descent to the grave, like a shopping list.

Suddenly a loud tapping sound shocked Giacomo from his depressive thoughts, shaking his body, as if death himself was knocking on the door.

Turning to the dusty, finger-smeared glass door, the vague outline of a man's figure stood in the frame.

Giacomo opened the stiff, squeaking doors, and waited for the reveal of this annoying man.

Stepping onto the bus was Domenico Fango, and Giacomo's grimace turned to gladness, as his eyes fixated on the small, black flask gripped in the thick, veined fingers of this promising young man.

Coffee! Giacomo's mind cheered with delight.

"*Buongiorno* Signoro Ficcanaso, how are you?" Domenico asked between gulps of breath, as he leant his heaving body against the door frame. The voice always shocked Giacomo, for it was deep, dark, and rich, like the mellow tones of a jazz singer.

Giacomo glanced up; his attention unwillingly drawn away from the nearness of coffee.

A face he knew very well watched him, and Giacomo smiled. Domenico's darkened olive face was flushed a deep, nectarine red. His face was narrow for a man, and the puffing and sinking of his cheeks heightened the strong, defined cheekbones cut high in his profile. Stubble peppered his thin cheeks, pinched chin and sharp, sweeping jawline. His thin crimson apple-coloured lips were moist and parted, exposing chinks of white teeth and healthy pink gums, like salmon flesh. His nose was narrow and pointed, like a scarecrow, and perched upon the bridge was the thick, black frame of his glasses, which branched across his temples and looped neatly over his long, pointed, elf-like ears. Sweat clamped clusters of dark curls against his smooth, unlined forehead, like twirls of dark chocolate, dribbling droplets of sweat into his thickly combed eyebrows.

Domenico Fango had a reputation within the village, one that was rich in promises and full of future success, unlike his brother, who was a troublemaker. It was the well-established belief that Domenico was destined for great things in life, as he was intelligent beyond understanding and repair, like those fancy new smartphones. He was the son of Giorgio Fango, who had been a couple years younger than Giacomo in school, and not particularly successful in dating or studying. It seemed unbelievable this lanky, intelligent boy was his son.

Giacomo felt a sting of jealousy, like the nip of a wasp, for this young man was bursting and bountiful with health, hope and optimism, whilst he was being tightened into the straight jacket of old age. It seemed unfair, even cruel. However, Giacomo quickly reproached himself with the satisfaction of Domenico's blighted eyes and boring beauty.

"Yes, I am well, Domenico, and yourself? How is your family?" responded Giacomo brightly, yet falsely, for he did not care to hear about his monster of a mother and bully of a brother, who had tormented his bus journeys with seats sticky with gum and muddy footprints, and curse words and crude drawings smeared onto the window in felt tip.

"I am fine, and my family are still… well, you know my family."

Giacomo chuckled softly, before responding: "Yes, I do."

A wide toothy grin broke over Domenico's face, drawing and deepening the permanent dimples in his cheeks as he sniggered.

"Do you want my coffee? My mother added sugar, and I won't drink it," offered Domenico, as he extended the flask to Giacomo.

Giacomo's lips wobbled with a tempting and terrified smile, for this young man was strange, he seemed to be able to read people's minds, as if they were books. Unlocking the blue door of his cubicle, Giacomo reached out and accepted the flask with a nod of gratitude.

Unscrewing the lid, the pungent aroma of sweetened coffee made his mouth tingle with saliva, and his chest heaved with thankfulness, ridding the stale stench of sweat and bad breath from the claustrophobic air of the cubicle.

Domenico stepped away with his face lowered to the ground, and Giacomo noticed how the young man's ink-smeared hands twisted nervously together.

"Did you want something, Domenico?" queried Giacomo gently, his eyes softening, like ice cream in the sun, at the young man's boyish shyness.

"Yes, this will sound strange, but in a few weeks, I have my exam at the Universita di Bari, and I am catching the train from Termoli at 11, but the timetable at the bus stop is smudged, and I couldn't see when the nearest bus time would be," explained Domenico.

"Oh yes, I know, I have tried to get them to put out new ones, but it seems to go in one ear and out the other. The closest bus time would be the 8:40am, you might get there a little early," informed Giacomo, anxiously glancing at his watch, reminded of his own lateness.

"That will be fine, thank you, but I wanted to check, and I saw the bus coming as I was walking down to the shop, so as you saw…" Domenico trailed off sheepishly.

"Yes, you would be better at sprinting than studying," Giacomo observed.

"I doubt that but thank you for stopping. I should probably get to work," Domenico muttered, as he glanced towards the shop, where his father shuffled outside to set up.

"Yes, you better," Giacomo eagerly agreed, as he snatched another look at his watch.

"Hmm," Domenico assented, as he stepped off the bus reluctantly, for it was no secret that he resented his family's trade.

"Have a good day, Domenico and thank you again for the coffee."

"No worries, I will see you soon, and promise me on that day if I'm running even 10 minutes late you will wait, it's really important," Domenico earnestly called.

Giacomo's heart softened with pride, and the comforting feeling of being needed and wanted by someone greatly soothed his lonely heart, and he responded with the greatest sincerity: "I promise."

The grin firmly returned to Domenico's lips, and Giacomo felt satisfied in helping this young man, perhaps he might even mention his important role in Domenico's Noble Prize for Science speech. His whole body tingled at the thought of such grand recognition.

"Have a good day Signoro Ficcanaso, goodbye," Domenico shouted, as he waved his large hands at Giacomo.

He smiled as he waved Domenico off, for he liked this young man, as unlike the other lazy youths around the town, he always addressed him with a formal recognition of respect, which satisfied Giacomo's ever-growing need to feel important.

Closing his small cubicle door, the warm humming of sweetened, smoothed coffee bleached his mouth with a comforting radiance, which elevated his mood, as he shut the doors and ignited the engine.

Pulling away from the curb, Giacomo forgot the surroundings, as his mind indulged in thoughts of selflessness and contentment.

Giacomo had always wanted a family, especially a son, and the dependence of Domenico strengthened that bitter regret with sweetness, as if it had fulfilled a secret wish that had never been granted.

Entertaining the thought of a family, Giacomo thought to himself that he would have liked to have a son like Domenico, but without those dreadful eyes.

Those dreadful eyes.

Giacomo shivered, repulsed, yet guilt swamped him, for Domenico was a generous and intelligent young man, but his eyes would deter anyone from loving him.

Those eyes were hard to explain or understand, like the soil of a landslide.

They were peculiar, dangerous, dislikeable, and death-like.

They were unpredictable, like the wild, grey movements of that drunk man.

They were uncontrollable, like the swift, silver knife of that drunk man.

They were unexplainable, like the eyes of the murdered wife.

Suddenly the loud, unrhythmical church bells crashed through his thoughts reminding him of time's never-ending journey to what or where he dreaded to know.

Giacomo turned the radio on, trying to forget those eyes, like his own future gravestone, but he could not, and the sweet taste of coffee turned bitter and black in his mouth.

TWO

Signoro Fango studied his son, Domenico, with sceptical, hazel eyes, as he stood within the huge, blue bus talking to Giacomo, the bus driver.

A man Signoro Fango despised.

He saw Giacomo as a bullying bullshitter, stuffed full of selfish pride, pointless arrogance, and heartlessness. He marched around the town like a sheriff, hands in pocket, as if a gun was hidden there, ready to whip out for protection. Ha, as if! The only thing that man whipped from his pockets were candy bars, and the only person he would ever protect was himself. He would sacrifice his own dead father before himself, and he would trample and crush anyone who held a different opinion to his own. He was arrogant in stupidity, he dictated his creed of goodness and kindness to anyone he should meet, yet he did not follow his own directions. He spied out all the secrets of the villagers, shoving his large nose in all businesses that did not concern him, only so he could use it against them in the future. He made people's lives a living hell, spitting on the way they lived their lives, and punishing their actions with cruel isolation from everyone in the town. He thought that Giacomo believed himself to be some sort of religious revolutionary, finishing and defining the jobs of Matthew, Mark, Luke, and John. But in fact, he was a revolutionary snitch, a revolutionary blackmailer, and a revolutionary prick.

All families within this village were faithfully devoted to the church, yet it seemed to Signoro Fango that Giacomo saw himself as Jesus Christ, self-sacrificing and a working man of miracles, turning water to wine, and tying himself to a cross to save humanity.

Ha! A man too alone to be criticized for his deluded mind, diseased by foolish values and stumped by diminishing old traditions. That man was the least self-sacrificing man to be met, for he ties himself to his bus, gorging on donuts, pastries, cakes and sweets, like an oversized child, and the only miracle this man performed was the ability to bypass diabetes, heart attacks and death.

He was not a good man, not at all.

His ears pricked, as he listened to their voices from the bus, deep waves of murkiness, which seemed unable to travel further than the bus, to his dismay.

Signoro Fango continued dragging items from his shop, baskets of blue, clean mops, thickly, combed bristled brooms, tall baskets of multicoloured footballs, and more and more, until it masked the plain, grey, gloomy building of the shop. Once he lumbered the last stack of items from the shop, Signoro Fango paused, stretched his back with a snapping sound, and breathed hard. Looking towards the long-standing family shop, he saw time's sweeping presence upon the white paintwork, which was now grey and mottled with green mould, whilst the white wooden borders were scratched, exposing the cheap, dark wet wood beneath. The entrance of the shop wreaked of cat piss, like the entrance to a public toilet. The windows had not been cleaned in months, and now they were laden with thick dust, blurring his family's name and making the inside of the shop look vague and visionless. And perhaps that is what it was, a place degraded by its failing and falling position, and Signoro Fango cursed the new shop further up the road for robbing him of customers and money with its bright, red laser signs of SALDI, SALDI, SALDI.

Signoro Fango felt exhausted as he shuffled his shaking hands through his cluttered black trousers in search of a cigarette. He thanked the shade, but he bitterly knew it would not last. Trickles of sweat already trailed down his thin, wrinkled face and stained his grey shirt with wet shadows, as he slipped the smooth cylinder of the cigarette between his cracked, dry, thin lips.

Lighting the end, it crackled satisfyingly. Signoro Fango found little happiness in many things, except for this delightful noise. It was the sweetest and dearest music to his ears, for it hailed a moment of peace and release. A release from many things, especially his burdening family. Whenever he smoked, Signoro Fango tended to step backwards and forwards and walk around in circles, his eyes firmly plastered to the floor, so that no one would speak to him. An agitated habit, which had developed after marriage.

And who could have blamed him, considering the monster he had married?

Signoro Fango stopped himself from thinking about that beast of spite, which claimed his life, for it would truly ruin his day. He turned his face to the sky, and savoured the deliciously dusty, dirty smoke, which claimed his lungs and heart with a poisonous promise that death would come soon.

Squinting his eyes, Signoro Fango envied the pigeons, the rats of the sky, flying their fat, grey bodies through the air above, for they could escape whenever they wished. They could never be caught, for they were too far out of reach for the brutish, broad hands of his wife. He was jealous of the sky. A place you could escape. A place you could never be trapped. A place of refuge. A place of no responsibilities. If he was a pigeon, he would fly low, shitting in the eyes of his wife and stealing the food from her hands, even if he was not hungry.

He took comfort in the sky, for it always changed, like the pictures in a movie, nothing was permanent, and he wished life could be the same.

His favourite sky was one stuffed full of dark grey, clouds, murky, mucky and muddy, like piles of dirty laundry. As a child, he used to stand in the street for hours watching the sky, for he was fascinated by rainfall. How was it created? Where did it come from? Why did it happen? These questions had plagued his childhood, and he used to believe there was a great act to create rain, chemical potions leaked from the moon, a fizz of secret electricity from the sun that burst the pipes of the sky, like water sprinklers in a field. But one day, a boy in his class had said the rain was God's tears, and as a young child, Signoro Fango had been confused, for how could a man that had everything, who could do what he pleased and create what he wanted ever be sad?

Signoro Fango recalled how he had wanted to test this theory, and one day he had stood in the street all day beneath the dark, cumbersome clouds, waiting patiently for that first droplet, for he believed he would see the real God, the mysterious man, who knew so much about everyone else, yet no one knew a single thing about him. But his eyes had begun to ache, and he had grown frustrated, and then an idea had occurred to his young mind. Whenever he had cried, it had been at the expense of boys bullying him with abuse, and so surely this would do the same trick. Standing face to face with the clouds, he had shouted and screamed abusive insults: "you're not real", "you are mean", "you smell", "no one likes you", "you're stupid", "you're poor", "you are weak". Suddenly, a tiny raindrop had smacked his forehead and trickled down his cheek. Fury had blazed through his veins, for he had not seen anything, not even a flash of a man, how could this have been? This thing he could feel on his hands, cheeks and head had snuck up on him with the invisibility of a skilled thief, and so had his mother, who grabbed him by the ear, dragging him indoors, furious at his blatant blasphemy. He went to bed with no dinner, but he was happy, triumphant, for he had made God cry, like the bullies had made him, and the bizarre beauty of this power excited him beyond imagination.

However, these confused and curious ideas had been crushed by his scary, intelligent middle child, Domenico.

Signoro Fango turned his tired eyes to the lean, strong stature of his son, and he inhaled a deep breath of the silky smoke.

Picking a bit of tobacco from his yellow, rusty teeth, he spat it to the floor, like a grape pip, his saliva wet and bubbling upon the dusty, stained pavement.

It was strange, Signoro Fango observed, for his middle child looked most like him, tall, lean and topped with curling dark brown hair, yet he was so different inside. Sometimes, Signoro Fango felt he was gazing into the past at his younger self. This only blackened his jealousy further, for his own body was now crippled by an undesired and unsatisfactory life. His dark curls were now limp, thin and ribboned with silver, his bony shoulders huddled over his body without confidence, collarbones strutted out in waves upon his hairy chest, whilst his belly bulged slightly, bloated by the beers he survived off. His neck sagged with loose, unpinned fat, like a chicken, whilst his thin, furry legs were like sticks, bulging at the knees and wobbling beneath the weight of his worthlessness.

Despite the likeness of their features, they were polar opposites in personality, except their curiosity, but even this differed. Signoro Fango was curious, yet he did not care enough to truly understand the meaning behind things, for he preferred to imagine his own science and theories behind the mysteries of the world. But Domenico could not accept curiosity, he had to know every little detail, every little reasoning, every little cause and consequence, every little explanation to every single little thing. His middle child was as curious to Signoro Fango as the rain in the sky, for he could not understand his son's dizzying thirst for knowledge. Domenico had read every book in the school library rather than playing football. He had studied plants and insects rather than setting death traps for them like the other boys. Domenico was a boy who was not satisfied to taste facts, he had to devour the whole understanding of things, otherwise it was pointless.

This desire for learning and constant hunger to know things had driven Signoro Fango mad, for each question unpinned his pride, and denuded his title as father and leader. Ever since Domenico was a child, he had asked question after question after question, never tiring of learning and knowing and understanding. He could never answer his son's questions, and if he tried, his son was not afraid to contradict him with his own knowledge, which would only infuriate him.

Signoro Fango had a queer outlook on his middle child, for he detested him, yet equally admired him. He used to hate it when Domenico ran home from school, spewing facts about science, history, and space. He used to hate watching his son's fingers flicking through the sticky pages of a textbook, scratching and scribbling notes in the side lines, always ending them with a question mark. That boy seemed to be one big question mark, his skin tattooed with question marks, his eyes shaped like question marks and his heart pulsed like a question mark. He hated how his son knew more than he did, especially when he was a child, and sometimes it would drive him so mad, he would send his only clever son to the cold, dark basement to eat his dinner. But most importantly he feared his son. He feared all the things he could see that could not be seen. He feared the world his son had entered that he could not enter. He feared his son, and he feared that question.

Oh, that question had made him drunk many times. That question had plagued his sleepless nights. That question brought misery beyond belief. That question had made him hate his son, and himself.

"Did you know that Dad?"

That simple, innocent question was punishing and painful, like a knife to Signoro Fango's heart, for he never knew the things his son talked about. Domenico had a superior knowledge to himself, and no matter how hard he tried, he could not stop the resentment that ripped his confidence to shreds, and eventually he gave up trying to fight this feeling.

Maybe this is why he had done what he had.

Resentment, anger, jealousy, loathing, self-pity had been the reasoning for his careless and selfish punishment towards his son.

But Signoro Fango did not blame himself, if Domenico had been more like his older brother, Matteo, who was lazy, stupid, and foolish, he would never have done what he did. Matteo did not hold a promising future, he stole from the till, he did not turn up for work, and he persecuted his home with the endless sounds of his love life. Both of his sons were the reasons for his sleepless nights and exhausted days, for they both irritated him, one for his greedy stupidity, and the other for his invading intelligence. The only ray of hope and happiness in his life was his beautiful and sweet daughter, Bianca.

Throwing his finished cigarette to the ground, his lips creakingly tilted into a smile at the thought of his youngest child. Bianca had been a blessing all his life, for she was innocent, generous, and infinitely happy and content with her life. Signoro Fango always thought Bianca resembled him the most, for she never wanted more than she needed, and she was always willing to help others, even at her own expense. Her heart seemed larger than her whole body, and she held no prejudice to who she allowed into it. But mostly, he loved how Bianca doted on him, and he doted on her, buying her ribbons for her hair, and cuddly bears for her collection. Bianca was the pride of his heart, and he held her past and future, like a medal around his chest. Bianca had always been his comrade and dearest companion, and even though she had a boyfriend, Alessandro, he was merely an extension of her. Signoro Fango had huge faith in Bianca, for ever since she left school, she worked hard in the local hairdresser, and always behaved respectably with Alessandro. They were his future, his goal to see each day out. Luckily, Bianca had not taken after her mother, for he could have hated her more than his sons.

Suddenly, his thoughts were disturbed by the grumbling of the bus as it pulled away from the curb. Giacomo drove away without acknowledging Signoro Fango, choking his breath with the black, dirty fumes of the bus.

Damn his bus! Damn his job! Damn his life!

Ambling towards the shop, Signoro Fango stood upright as Domenico approached with a bounce to his step.

"*Buongiorno* Papa, how are you this morning?" Domenico inquired, his unsettling grey eyes gleaming, like silver pistols, whilst his thin olive tanned cheeks flushed a deep pink.

"Fine, why were you talking to that idiot?" interrogated Signoro Fango, folding his weak, sickly arms across his heaving chest.

"I had to ask him a question, also, do you mind if I leave work early today as I need to go to the farm," Domenico responded, before picking some dirt from his fingernail with his teeth.

Another slash to that unhealing wound in his mind. When would this wound ever heal? When would this guilt ever leave? Would he have to die to get some peace?

This farm was another pest of his past, for Signoro Fango had dealt the heaviest punishment to Domenico. Years ago, when Domenico was only nine, he had sacrificed his son to repay a debt he could not afford. He had gambled that night, a lot of money, and once the money had gone, it was a choice between the shop or his son, and he had picked Domenico. And now, even the result of that night still pervaded the present, for Domenico had been lumbered with acres of land to work, alone.

"Yes, yes, of course," Signoro Fango muttered hurriedly.

"*Grazie*, Bianca and Alessandro are going to come and help," Domenico prattled on, as he adjusted the ugly, thick, black-rimmed glasses on his nose more comfortably.

"Yes, fine, look after Bianca," warned Signoro Fango, as he moved his sluggish body towards the door of the shop.

"OK."

"What question did you need to ask Giacomo? He can't answer your science stuff, he barely knows his own name," grumbled Signoro Fango, as he forced the stiff, white door to open, disturbing and rattling the signs behind.

"Nothing, I didn't know the bus times for my university exam as the ones at the bus stand are wrong," explained Domenico, a sulky expression crossing his thin lips, for he knew Domenico's dislike of name-tagging a person as stupid.

"I see," Signoro Fango concluded bitterly, flicking his eyes to the ground, and far away from those shining, silver glass eyes, which would only reflect and expose his own deep spikes of spiteful jealousy.

The church bells trembled through the unblemished sky, as father and son entered the dismal shop in silence.

THREE

The morning passed like every other Saturday, quietly and slowly.

Signoro Fango and his son spent the solitude of those awakening hours reading. He read the newspaper, flicking his yellow, crusty thumb between the thin sheets with a snap, as he attempted to understand some of the more complex articles. Whereas Domenico leant over the till, studying some strange and thick book about plants, which he could see intrigued his son, for every so often, those thick tightly drawn black brows would release as he understood something, before he rapidly scribbled notes down the margin of the page.

The shop was quiet, a low purring of the fridges and freezers filled the dense silence with noise, yet it was not enough, for Signoro Fango became more and more infuriated by the scratch, scratch, scratch of his son's pen, and the flick, flick, flick of the turning pages. He quickly withdrew from the shop to the cluttered backroom to count the earnings of yesterday, the tinkling of loose coins and the swish swish of notes restored a sense of calm and control to his life.

Whilst these two men kept their heads bent over their reading material, the outside world was subtly and slowly changing with each new minute. The sun crept into the village without a sound, weaving its awakening threads of gold into the dark alleyways, unpicking the shadows of the night, as if they had never existed. The sun's fingertips combed through the dark shutters of homes, hailing the drifters of dreams to seize the day before them. Some answered this call and emerged from their homes in thin, pastel heat-combating clothes, whilst others pulled their pillows over their eyes, denying the sun to break their blissful sleep. But the sun did not care, it was carefree and full of liberty, dancing and twinkling along the steel frames of balconies, like fairies, refracting the light just right to create little, gleaming rainbow slits. Whereas other rays simmered and sizzled within the damp clothes of washing lines.

The light of the sun managed to transform this gloomy, grey town into something welcoming and beautiful, filling the empty, abandoned homes with gold, like empty pastry cases filled with the sharpest, tingling lemon curd.

But the two men would never have noticed this change.

The clock was about to strike nine, when the two men's attention was snatched by a deep, barking and bullying voice from outside the shop. Instantly, Signoro Fango threw his newspaper in a random cupboard, and clumsily flung his white plastic apron across his body, whilst Domenico shoved his huge book onto the floor with a crash, before stacking the cigarette cupboard.

Suddenly the clanging ding dong of the church bells rang through the town, yet the voice continued to crash and bash from the outside, overpowering the bells and rattling the feeble windows with its brashness, like an animal trying to enter. A meeker voice tried to argue against this blasting, bruising voice, but it was no match, for that voice was destructive, demolishing and damaging, like an earthquake.

Luckily, it gave the men time to recover their breath, and dull the redness in their flushed cheeks.

Suddenly the door was flung open by the fierce, formidable and frightening woman of Signora Fango.

Signoro Fango gulped nervously as he made himself look busy behind the meat counter.

Signora Fango tore her narrow black eyes around the shop, like the eyes of a boar, as she examined the work of her useless son and even more useless husband.

"*Buongiorno* Mama," greeted Domenico quietly, adjusting the heavy frames of his glasses.

Signora Fango grunted in response as she squeezed her huge, sweltering body around the door. Cramming the last of her pastry into her large, round painted coral mouth, she tutted her head, for these fools were cluttering the entrance with more shit.

Signoro Fango watched his huge wife waddle and squeeze herself through the door, her large, fatty belly jiggling and jumbling beneath the bursting seams of her dress, as if it were a moving, vile jellyfish. Her body was undefined and tiered like a flabby, melting wedding cake, her hips were like huge, inflated rubber wings, her stomach was like a huge bag of unmoulded flour, her breasts were dragging and dense, resting heavily upon her stomach, whilst her chin was swallowed by the thick folds of fat, people called a neck. She was expanding every day, like a balloon constantly being inflated, he only wished he could stick a pin in her and she would pop and disappear forever. How could she not see how disgusting she looked? His wife repulsed him, disgusted him, sickened him, for she was like a humongous slimy toad. Her spit was poison, her words putrid and her breath black with grease and sugar. Her heart was horrible, poisoned with age and bitterness, like the smelliest, odorous curdled cheese, pumping blue mould of meanness through her veins.

Signora Fango huffed, and grabbed her second pastry from her bag, her arms jiggling with the search of this precious food. She glared at her husband, who was staring at her with those vague, lifeless brown eyes. He was a sheep of a man, following the crowd, confused and lost by his own empty mind. His body creeped her out, for he looked like a skeleton that had crawled from beneath the grave, and his breath, she could smell it from here, rotten vegetables. Signora Fango gagged and tried to extinguish her husband's revolting body and breath with the sweet golden pastries.

Standing in the doorway, Signora Fango blocked the sun from entering the shop, making the room dark and more claustrophobic with the density of her large stature, as she stood and interrogated her son's work. Lumbering her body around the till, flaking pastry crumbs across the cracked white tiles of the floor, she investigated the cabinet, and her eyes flashed like red warning lights. Her thin, crumb-laden lips were sucked into her mouth as she readied her fury to be expelled upon the men.

Signora Fango marched closer and closer to Domenico, who backed further and further away from her, squirming, as if he feared her.

Whipping her stuffed face around, Signora Fango glowered at Signoro Fango's cowering face, his lifeless lips wobbling with fright.

"Why is there a packet of cigarettes missing? It's a filthy habit and..."

She stopped speaking. A low growl of fury rumbled through her throat, rippling the loose fat, as she noticed the book beside her son's long, feminine feet.

She was at the end of her nerves and patience, she really was. Why could these men not do as they were told? Why did men need instructing all the time? They were worse than children, worse than dogs. Why did she always have to instruct them on every little thing?

And Domenico, she really found him irritating and tiresome. People in town always congratulated her on having such an intelligent child, but she could not see it. Domenico was stupid and selfish, and far too sensitive for a man. If he was really so clever, he would go to university to study law or medicine and save his poor-stricken family from destitution. But no, she could not even be granted peace, luck and security with this wish. He wanted to study plants. Plants? Really? Why? What was there to know about plants?

They grew in the summer and died in the winter, and that is all you needed to know. But no, her son was going to study plants. She had made these points to Domenico, and he had thrown a tantrum, like a toddler, and why? What more was there to know? Honestly, Signora Fango prayed day and night that Domenico was not one of those men who did this and that with other men. The shame would be unbearable, and her chocolatey spit turned dry and bitter at the thought of other women whispering behind her back about her son kissing and loving his own kind. He surely would not do this to her, for it would be the cruellest revenge for her long, laborious years of mothering.

She thanked God, day and night, for her faithful and manly son, Matteo, that boy would bring her hope and grandchildren to this failing family. He had always been her saving grace, for without him, she would never have been able to tie down her foolish dithering husband, and save her parents and herself from the starving, unsparing streets.

"Why is Domenico reading this shit, Signoro Fango? That boy should be working. Do I have to do everything in here? You should both be ashamed of yourselves. I have cared for both of you, and this is how you repay me. You are both a waste of space and time, I would get a better job done from the stray dogs in the street. Fucking useless, if my mother could see the pain you two have caused me, she would turn in her grave. Get back to work," shouted Signora Fango, flapping her thick-cut arms around with furious gestures, like huge gammons.

Opening the till with a crash, she grabbed a handful of notes, before slamming it shut, as she waddled away, her thighs squeaking with the friction and heat.

Signoro Fango witnessed this scene with lips trembling with fury, his eyes twitched crazily as he watched his cumbersome, cold, cruel wife steal money from his shop. He was immensely proud of his small shop, which had fed the town of Castelmauro for three generations, and he believed his father would have been pleased by its progress and profits. But he could not stomach his wife taking and touching his precious money with her fat, greasy fingers, as if it belonged to her. His father had loved money, and he had always been found counting and calculating the silvery coins with trembling fingers of happiness, and he had developed the same blind respect for money. To be taken by a bestial woman gutted his heart and cut his memories of his father into fragments, for she had no respect for his family's name and empire.

"Why don't you work before taking that money?" bellowed Signoro Fango, as he sharpened his knife against the whetstone, the long scratching sounds soothed his mind with fanciful murder.

Signora Fango's fingers froze over the thin, teasing notes, as her punching black pupils dilated with a fury as white as ice.

"I do work. I work more than you or your father," retorted Signora Fango, placing her round sweaty sausage-like fingers on her fleshy hips.

Signoro Fango threw his knife upon the counter with a crash, making Domenico jump at the sudden sound.

"Don't fucking say you work more than me or my father. The fucking bags of flour do more work than you."

"Ha-ha, you need medical help, I am sure of it. The men in the white coats need to take you away to the fucking crazy house. I work, day in and day out for this shit hole without receiving a single penny. I have raised your three ungrateful children without any help—"

"Raise them? You have driven them away—"

"What do you mean by that? I have—"

"You have made Matteo a vampire of the night. That one wants to run away to Bari, and even my sweet Bianca has left to work in a hairdresser—"

"That is because you are a shit father, who craps all over other people and cannot accept responsi—"

"Responsibility! You are going to lecture me on responsi—"

"Yes, what father lets his son be traded to cover debt and—"

"What mother eats like you. Those children would have starved to death if it wasn't for me, you greedy, fat cow."

Signora Fango froze, speechless, flummoxed for words to match this blatant, insensitive insult. But then suddenly the fury erupted within her heart, and she barrelled her body towards Signoro Fango, her breasts bouncing violently, sweat trickled between her groin, making her thighs squeak louder with the sticky, stale heat.

She stopped before the meat counter, her wide hairy nostrils flared, as she breathed hard, in and out, in and out, her dark, button eyes flashed insanely, whilst sweat trickled from her moustache onto her coral lipstick-stained lips.

Signoro Fango leant his thin, tense hands on the counter, gripped hard to stop himself from reaching for that very knife and slitting her throat in half. His eyes were wide, almost tearing the twitching lids open, whilst his lashes, like dusty, dead spider's legs ferociously beat against each other, like an old woman beating the dust from her curtains. He inhaled gulps of air through his parted lips, and exhaled a splattering of spit across his grey, prickly chin.

She stood solid and unmoving. His body shook from the nervous, irritating jitter of his left leg.

They were in a lock of time and tricks, examining and searching and scanning for weaknesses, like a bull and a man, who was the master? It was impossible to say.

There was no love. There never had been.

Only fury.

Only detestable hatred.

Signoro Fango could not understand how he had been tricked into fucking and marrying this hairy, slimy, fat, painted woman, the love child of a gorilla and a toad. Had he been drunk? Had he been blind? Had he been stupid? Had he been desperate? No, for he had been tricked, terribly tricked by her poisonous and vile plans, which had trapped him for eternity. Had she always been this ugly and overbearing? He could not remember, for if there had been any love for her, it had been bled from his memories, like water from a broken radiator.

Signora Fango bitterly regretted the day she had put her plan into action, for why had she married this thin, weak scarecrow of a man? She wished she had defied her parents' anguish and started a new life for herself. She could have been admired and free to pick and choose her men, like sweets in a sweetshop, but instead she was pitied and jailed to a man, who drank her happiness away to only piss it out into a nearby gutter. Love had never existed in her life, only the economy to survive, and she had barely succeeded at that, despite the huge price she had paid for her sacrifice.

"You have ruined my fucking life," hissed Signoro Fango, leaning closer to terrorise his wife.

"Ruined your life? Ruined your life? What do you think you have done to me?" screeched Signora Fango, spitting in her husband's vile face.

He staggered back, and wiped her brown-tinged spit from his face, as if it was pigeon shit.

"Don't ever fucking spit in my face woman—"

"Don't woman me—"

"Don't fucking tell me what to do you ugly pig—"

"*Buongiorno*, Signora Antico. How are you today?" Domenico's deeply serene voice cut severely through the tension of his parents', like the ringing of church bells.

The parents halted their argument, the tension suspended, as they greeted Signora Antico, a sweet, old lady, and luckily slightly deaf, but she did not acknowledge them.

"*Buongiorno*, Domenico, I am well, thank you, busy as always I can see," remarked Signora Antico with her quiet, purply blue eyes and modest smile.

"Yes, I guess, can I help you with your shopping?"

"What, Domenico? I couldn't quite hear you?" questioned Signora Antico, leaning her left ear closer to Domenico.

"Can I help you with your shopping?" accentuated Domenico slowly.

"Oh no, don't worry, dear. I just need a packet of biscuits for my granddaughter," explained Signora Antico, smiling gently at the eager, handsome face before her.

Suddenly the noise of shuffling feet and hissing curse words caught her attention, making her eyebrows knot together with displeasure. Turning, she noticed the husband and wife, and her smile quickly diminished.

"*Buongiorno*," she greeted with her fragile, age-fractured voice.

"*Buongiorno*," one barked and the other whimpered.

"You look like you're up to no good," lied Signora Antico, for she could see the false, tense smiles, foretelling the argument about to erupt.

"No, we are doing the accounts," responded Signora Fango. What a nosy donkey, she thought.

"I see, very good," replied Signora Antico curtly. Rude cow, she thought.

Signora Fango had had enough with civil, meaningless chatter, irritation had birthed many insults within her head to use against her husband, like a litter of puppies, and her tongue, mouth and lips were hot with the need to explode these curses. Heavily marching into the backroom, the door slammed with her disappearance.

"I am sorry, Signora Antico. I hope to see you soon," apologized Signoro Fango, as he rubbed the back of his hot neck.

Signora Antico waved a nonchalant withered hand: "Please do not worry, Domenico will take care of me."

Signoro Fango weakly smiled, and dipped his head in thanks, before disappearing into the room his wife consumed. Signora Antico feared for him, as if he had entered a cage with a big, bloodthirsty bear.

The argument began as a hissing and whispering battle of accusations, before the voices fizzed and grew, exploding every so often, like a deadly science experiment. This was the music that accompanied Signora Antico around the shop.

Signora Antico began her journey through a maze she knew too well. She knew what she needed, a packet of chocolate biscuits for her granddaughter, who was visiting, a delight to the lonely woman.

Once you entered and turned right, your eyes were greeted with a domino effect of yellowing-white shelves, stacked neatly row upon row. She knew that the only way to leave this maze was to weave your way through each small, squeezing isle.

The first shelves that greeted you into the maze were cluttered and stacked with toiletries and cleaning products. Signora Antico idly scanned the creamy white shelves stacked with a variety of essential toiletries. She bent her hunched body closer to the shelf and examined a bottle of glittering, Barbie pink nail polish. She smiled; her young granddaughter would love it!

Signora Antico's misty wet eyes surveyed the narrow aisles, and her eyes lighted on the towering packs of toilet roll and kitchen roll balanced precariously, like skyscrapers, jolting her forgetful memory. Reaching her thin, wrinkled arm out, the slashing sun cut her skin into pieces of dark and light as she grabbed a pack of toilet roll. Behind the towers, the sun lit up the dark corners, thick with dust, and exposed the white, fractured tiles, smeared and streaked with the motions of a mop.

Hobbling around the shop, Signora Antico turned her eyes to the back wall, where a large shelving unit stocked fresh, colourful fruits and vegetables, perfuming the air with the earthy scents of garlic, bitter aniseed and hair-shrivelling oregano. This place overwhelmed Signora Antico's senses with the extremeness of their colour and scent, and she found it hard to know where to look, but then her eyes settled on an old, large, chipped pot, which managed to throw her senses completely.

Signora Antico's heart sank slowly, and that inconceivable grief, which grips many widows, took a firm hold of her. Picking up the fresh, green cucumber, she could smell the work of the sun and soil upon its body, and she was reminded of her departed husband. She still found it difficult after ten years to shop for herself. She still found it strange to not consider buying certain items to please her husband, like this very cucumber, which he used to love so much in the summer.

Due to her deliberations and the thrashing shouts of Signora Fango, she did not hear the second customer enter the shop and greet Domenico.

Popping the cucumber into her basket, it soothed her aching heart, for since her husband's death, his spirit had almost become the other half of her brain, he walked by her and would have scolded her for not making the most of the fresh produce. It might sound scary, even freakish to others, but she loved hearing the lost voice of her husband whispering in her ear and reminding her that she was never alone. But sometimes his voice would become invisible, and she would try to trick her brain into bringing it back by doing things or buying things to make her believe he was still there. This would bring a strange joy, but then as soon as she entered her home, the grief would attack her with a greater force, as if it were a punishment for her delusions. But the temptation to relive the tiniest memory of him made her do it over and over and over again, a recycling of pain.

Entering down the next aisle, her eyes were bombarded by the display of dry stock. On the right, the shelves were weighed to the point of collapse by cans of tomato sauce, anchovies, beans, tuna and glass bottles of olive oil, vinegars and more. Whereas the left shelves were overcrowded with pasta and rice in all its forms, from tagliatelle, spaghetti, orecchiette, penne, linguine, rigatoni, farfalle, conchiglie to risotto, followed by boxes of sugary colour-coated cereals, loaves of tasteless breads, which never sold, and finally the biscuits.

Just what she needed!

Flying passed Signora Antico with a quick greeting, she was enveloped in the seductive, caramelized rose scent of Signorina

Morderna. Signora Antico smilingly responded, yet her smile did not meet her eyes, which were pale pools of disapproving disgust, as they moved slowly and inspectingly up the body of that woman. From the vibrant red heeled sandals with gold winking clasps, to the cream tight hugging skirt, which clung around that woman's curves, like a banana skin. And the top. What an awful, hideous blouse for a woman of that age, she scolded. This top looked as though it had been crafted for a prostitute, sheets of red lace layered, yet not enough, she thought bitterly. The horrendous red lace blouse fitted tightly around her breasts, so that they burst from the gap, prominent and proud, and not leaving much room for the imagination, she tutted. She flattened her own pale pink blouse with a self-righteous pride, for she severely disapproved of women who did not dress appropriately for their 'age'.

Signorina Morderna was on a mission, but she still felt that scolding, snarky gaze of Signora Antico burn holes in her back, as she suffocated in her potent lavender scent, probably used to cover up her pissed pants. Her full lips, carefully lined with the deepest red, quivered with a mischievous smile, for those disapproving glances had been thrown at her by many people, and she no longer cared for how these people saw her. She held a reputation for being the greatest flirt in town, yet who could resist this woman? Sensuality spewed from her pores, like burst pipes. The art of sex was in her every movement, from the flick of her finger to the swinging of her hips. Her eyes smacked a man with passion, and the smooth, dark skin of Signorina Morderna made men hungry, craving to taste the exotic oils of her skin with their own tongues. Men delighted in her smile, foreign, yet friendly, difficult, yet easy, distant, yet close, so close, so tantalizingly, teasingly close. She knew men, she knew how far you could push them, before pulling them back in, like a skilled fisherman. She never made the game easy for them, for she loved the game, the chase, the excitement, the sexual thrill of a new man. She knew what people said and saw, and many had the audacity to claim her unhappy, but this was far from the truth. Some said she had made herself dirty and vile by her act of defilement, but in truth, she loved herself, and she loved that others loved her for her. She never pretended to be something she was not for a man, and if they did not like her, it was no loss for her, excepting one man.

The mission Signorina Moderna needed to complete was for an intimate dinner date with a man she had been pursuing for a long time. She needed her dinner date essentials – cheese, cured meats, bread (from the bakery – already accomplished!), and bottles of red wine.

Coming to the last aisle of the shop, two counters stood unguarded, and Signorina Moderna could clearly hear why.

The blasting row of Signoro and Signora Fango boomed through the shop, like a radio, but she ignored this as she inhaled the deep pungent fumes of the cheeses. Huge bulbous white mounds of Caciocavallo, crumbling, salty Pecorino, stretched ribbons of Stracciata, and further afield were the blue veined hunks of Gorgonzola, the heavenly creamed yellow blocks of Parmigiano, and the aged creamy sharp slices of Provolone. It all made her senses water. She used to hate cheese, any dairy products really, for it turned her skin into a red mountain range of humiliation. But her hormones had done her justice in her forties, and to make up for her long-term sacrifice, she gorged herself on cheese, like a greedy mouse.

Pulling her longing, lustful eyes away from the cheese counter, she investigated the boulders of cured meats: the light purple sheen of Capocollo, the small thin spicy Salsiccia and the spotted flesh of Mortadella, which curled by the front like cats by a fire. The thinly sliced pale pink sheets of cured pork loin were already weighed and wrapped in a thin, brown tissue paper, smeared and sweaty, like two lovers' sweaty bodies against the bed sheets.

Leaning across the finger-smeared-glass counter, Signorina Moderna seductively bent her body across the aisle, her skirt crackling with the movement, as she called: "Oh Signoro Fango, I'm waiting."

A call no man could resist.

There was a diminishing of voices, hushed poison, and then a scuffle of weak footsteps across the back, like the scrabbling of rats.

Signoro Fango emerged with a flushed face of violent annoyance, which grew deeper as he beheld the stature of Signorina Morderna. His head buzzed loudly, even louder than the soft rumbling of the fridge behind that wistful woman, where uncooked meats, butter, yogurt, cream and milk watched, like a crowd at a play.

Sucking in his breath, he could not look at her playful smile, bouncing dark eyes, and delicious curling hair, for it brutally reminded him of his wretched teenage years. They had been in the same class, but Signorina Morderna was the queen, and he, well, Signoro Fango was a nobody.

The ice-cream freezer aggressively shuddered, strengthening the strained, awkward tension between them.

Why was this queen as nervous as this nobody?

Why did this queen find companionship in men for one lonely night?

Why had this queen never settled?

The answer stood before her in all his awkward, bashful beauty.

Suddenly a rustle and the disapproving tut of Signora Antico awoke the pair of misguided lovers, trapped in lives they wished they did not exist in.

They began their meaningless chatter, as Signora Antico rounded the last bend of the aisle, her mind mulling over the loss of morals, yet she felt triumphant in her foundation of old-fashioned ideals. She could not understand all these stories of divorce, if a man and woman had stood before God and married, surely, they loved one another, and why should that love ever die? But what she neglected to remember was that she had lived a life of luxury in the way of love, for she had always been loved by her husband. Yet, she still felt it was utterly selfish of people divorcing and parting from lovers when the uncontrollable force of death had separated her own body from her beloved husband's.

And as for Signorina Morderna's ideas on love, they were full of shame and insincerity. The only person that woman loved was herself, and she clearly needed this love to be constantly approved by man after man after man.

She passed the racks of wine and came to the last shelf, neatly containing bright packets of crisps, sweets and chocolates, a last temptation for the pennies. Signora Antico idled over the sweets, like a child, for she needed something, anything that would turn this bitter bile of grief to honey.

Settling on a selection of candied fruits, she made her way to the till, focusing on the careful words of Signoro Fango and Signorina Morderna.

"Hello, Signora Antico, do you have everything?" Domenico asked softly, as she placed her beige wicker basket by the checkout.

"Yes, thank you, Domenico," Signora Antico confirmed, fumbling in her dark leather bag for her purse.

The beep, beep, beep of the scanning machine and the deep, guttural laughter of Signorina Morderna broke the nauseating memories of her husband.

Two boys entered the shop crashing and bashing into her elbow, further awakening her anger.

These young people have no respect these days, she thought bitterly.

Except Domenico.

She watched his hands rhythmically move. The fingers were long and thin, like a pianist, but the fingernails were short and gutted with dirt, like a farmer. The side of his left thumb was cut deep with a scratch, whilst the rest of his hands were marked with little scratches. Some were healing, whereas others were small, red pockets of infection. A quick glance of his palm told a tale of hard work in the fields, for the lines were cracked and defined by the rough grassland and trees. She liked to see this, for it reminded her of her husband's hands, and without touching, she knew exactly how these hands felt, rough, ragged and ruinous. Yet, the thought made her feel content that the hard work of past generations was not being destroyed and neglected by the screen-mad youths of today's world.

Those deep olive hands had placed all her items gently in the basket, and she pulled her battered black leather purse from her small handbag.

"How much do I owe you?" Signora Antico inquired, her shaking fingers fumbling over the small pennies, made this way for her inconvenience, she believed.

"€8,59, Signora Antico," responded Domenico low and discreetly.

A loud shout from one of the boys shocked the poor Signora Antico, whose limp, grey curls shook with her fright.

"Sorry, my brother believes he owns the shop," apologized Domenico.

Glancing up, she placed the coins on the counter with a slight slam as she said: "I believe he thinks he owns the whole town."

She noticed Domenico's face break into a huge, humorous smile, pressing his long cheeks with deep dimples.

"Yes, very true, here is your change."

Grabbing the single coin, Signora Antico chuckled at the companionship of mocking smiles. She had not had an accomplice for years.

"Thank you, Domenico, have a good day!"

"Yes, take care."

Shuffling from the shop, Signora Antico enjoyed the warmth of Domenico's laughter, like a sweet medicine for her lonely heart. Yet, she feared to look at his eyes. A silly thing, perhaps, for those eyes were soft, blurred and vague, yet they were equally cold, hard and haunting, like the eyes of a ghost.

Those eyes were unidentifiable.

Those eyes were shocking in their tragical translations.

Next in the queue was Matteo and his friend, laughing and cursing, as if they were the only people in the shop, thought Signorina Morderna, as she patiently awaited her turn.

"Hey brother, busy?" jostled Matteo, his impish, twinkling dark eyes brightening with thoughts of mischief and mockery.

"*Buongiorno* Matteo, are you going to pay for those?" questioned Domenico, his voice gruff and low, it reminded Matteo of his old annoying maths teacher.

His grin widened showing teeth defiled by cigarettes, candy and alcohol.

"Hey Matteo, why is your brother wearing those spastic glasses?" mumbled his friend, feeding the bate of Matteo's mockery.

"I don't know, Massimo, let me ask him. Domenico, why are you wearing those glasses?" Matteo asked, examining Domenico's chest, which heaved with sighs of annoyance.

"Because I can't see," Domenico replied dryly, as he opened another packet of cigarettes for the cupboard.

Matteo's bait was not working, why was his brother not budging?

"Are you doing it to impress girls?"

"No."

Domenico's face was kept bent towards the cigarette packets, which infuriated Matteo, for he did not even look up, diminishing his superiority as older brother.

"If you need advice on getting girls, just ask, nothing to be embarrassed about," Matteo patronized with a snotty snigger, as he interrogated his brother's face for the tiniest flinch of a reaction.

Nothing.

"I mean, I'm not boasting, Domenico, but you only have to ask half the girls in this town for a reference," teased Matteo, his ears rising and falling with the movements of his mouth.

Matteo pitied his brother for his weak, ugly face, unlike his own. Matteo believed he had a face people, especially women, could not resist, healthy and full, rather than blind and skinny. Matteo believed his red lips to be the leash to a woman's heart, which he could connect and disconnect as he pleased. Though his brother was taller and leaner, Matteo complimented himself with his upper body strength and thick-cut thighs, which shrunk the slight tubbiness of his belly. He always styled his hair to the newest trend, and for now, it was cut short at the sides, but full, dark, and floppy on top. His eyes were dark and high on horniness, he looked at women, as if he were undressing them in his mind, and he was. He licked his lips, like women were joints of roasting, grease-dripping meats, and his body was constantly shifting this way and that, as he tried to hide his boner from obvious view.

But Matteo was adamant these features added greatly to his charm and sexiness. No question about it– he was the clever and beautiful one of the family, and his mother had always praised him for this.

"Why would that be boasting, Matteo? Half of the girls in this town hate you," muttered Domenico, his lightening silver eyes whipping Matteo's mind with the abrupt shock of them, for he had not expected this answer.

"What?"

"You would be better at giving me advice on losing girls than gaining them. Signorina Morderna, how may I help?" gestured Domenico, his eyes moving away from Matteo's face.

Short! Sharp! Final!

Matteo glared at his brother, and then at Massimo, who chuckled quietly at his elbow.

Why did Domenico always make him, the older brother, feel like an idiot? Why did his baby brother insist on having the last word?

He hated Domenico and all his stupid intelligence.

Slamming the door behind him, Matteo marched into the street, chewing on a sticky strawberry lace, like a cow.

Signorina Morderna ignored Matteo, who was the selfish offspring of a selfish mother. She could not stand that boy, but she delighted in the knowledge that his future was cursed with unhappiness, that unlike his mother, could not be cured with an 'unplanned' pregnancy.

Placing a hand on her wide hip, she impatiently waited for her essentials to be scanned.

Any man, no matter how committed to his wife, and no woman, no matter how morally constricted, could deny that Signorina Morderna was a beautiful woman for her age. A childless and husbandless life had proved to secure far more beauty and sophistication than any of her peers. Some men had whispered her body was shaped and curved like the statue of Aphrodite, and her heart was that very statue, cold and unyielding, for she never let anyone near it.

Why?

She knew why, and she was embarrassed and made fragile by the unconscious betrayal of that man.

"Did you want a bag?" interrupted Domenico.

Signorina Morderna snapped her head in his direction and nodded.

She watched Domenico put her items into a white plastic bag with care, and she could not help thinking that he was very much like his father, dashing and dark in his deadly silence. Glancing up, she realized that if she stood on tiptoes, she would never reach the top of Domenico's head.

But she was grateful for this, for she did not have to look into those dead eyes.

Signorina Morderna never sought to look into those eyes.

They were queer.

Strange.

His eyes were opaque. A blur. A mystery, like the moon. Something that seemed so close yet was deceptively far away from any real understanding. When she stared at his eyes, they seemed shallow, a scrape of the moon's surface, yet they were deeper than that, far deeper than anyone dared to explore.

"Are you ready to pay?" interrupted Domenico, slightly impatiently.

"Yes, yes, sorry, here you go Domenico. I must be off," Signorina Morderna exclaimed, as she gathered her heavy bags and left the shop.

Domenico counted the money that had been hurriedly left on the counter within the silence of the shop and realized she had paid more than needed. The till snapped open as he tipped the clattering coins into their pockets, before slamming the draw shut again!

Picking up his book from where he left off, he began to analyse his notes.

"*Buongiorno* Domenico," said a voice. A warm, welcoming, and sweet sound, like vanilla custard.

He knew the owner of this voice, and he knew, without looking, the way that pink, wet mouth moved around the words, and how the small tongue would slip around each curving syllable, like licking ice cream. This voice, no matter where he heard it would be home…

…and the owner of that voice knew, without looking, the way Domenico's silvery eyes would light up with thoughts as he read, the way his characterful eyebrows would strain and release in concentration, and how his hands would suddenly snap down an idea, as if it would leave him as instantly as it came.

Lifting his gaze, he found her there, the owner of that voice.

The person he called home.

Meeting his gaze, she found his eyes, the owner of her happiness.

The person she called home.

"*Buongiorno* Chiara, how are you?" Domenico asked flustering, as he gently closed the book with his right hand.

Those books, they held a cage over Domenico's heart, shutting himself away from other people's feelings and his own, Chiara regrettably thought.

"Fine, fine, fine, can I buy a packet of Dunhill International cigarettes?" Chiara asked, pulling a €10 note from her chocolate-coloured leather purse.

The rich, designer clutch, perhaps Gucci or Prada, a clamp on her heart and dreams. Domenico knew this to be true, and he wished she knew this too.

"Sure, you know he is the only person who buys these disgusting, expensive cigarettes," Domenico blabbered, as he chucked them on the counter with disdain.

A soft giggle escaped from her downcast face as she took the change from Domenico's hand, enlivening her heart with the old, tired emotions of love…

…which plagued him daily, finding small bursts of relief in the touch of her fingers against his own, but…

…why could she not fight this feeling? Why had an engagement to another man not deterred her from this one? She could not stop loving him, yet…

…why could he not fight this feeling? Why had his heart not been defeated by her defiance? He still longed for her, day and night, and…

…no, she did not love him, she instructed herself, as she fiddled with the diamond studded engagement ring on her finger.

Domenico was her best friend. She had known him since she could walk and talk. Domenico was a person from her earliest memories. She had depended on him, and they had done everything together, but now there was an obvious distance between them.

She knew Domenico was not keen on Vincenzo, yet it should not create problems within their friendship, unless…

…he did not love her, Domenico tried to convince himself, yet the logical side of his brain taunted him with these illogical denials, for his days were spent in constant thinking and wondering and questioning about her.

Chiara was his best friend; someone he had known since he could walk and talk. Chiara was the earliest person from his memories. He depended on her, and they had done everything together, but now there was something separating them.

Domenico knew what it was, and "it" was a man called Vincenzo, who he disliked for many, many reasons.

"What are you doing today?" Domenico spoke, trying to tear his thoughts away from the deepest love and deepest hate that cruelly stretched and stabbed his heart, like a medieval torture device.

"Not much, I am going to Termoli with Vincenzo to sort out wedding stuff, but I should be back by 5, if you still want to go down to the farm this evening," responded Chiara, her voice expanding from low to high, from burden to brightness.

"Are the cigarettes for you or Vincenzo?"

Chiara broke into peals of laughter, as she pocketed the box into the back pocket of her light blue denim shorts, which squeezed around her shapely thighs, rounded bum and cinched waist. A white crumpled blouse hung over her body, yet the top button was open, exposing the bronze of her smooth, flat chest. The gold crucifix, a fashion trend of the villagers, rose and fell heavily with each breath, the sun glinting, making the figure glow brighter.

Domenico was daunted by her beauty.

No, she was plain. She had plain brown hair. She had a plain body. She had plain skin. She had plain clothes. She had plain...

Domenico's thoughts were instantly bombed from his brain, for she looked up, stealing all the life within him. He always forgot how all the life within her soul lay in those burnt, aqua blue eyes.

Beauty broke across her face from those very eyes, they made her skin glow, her straight, dark hair shine, her dark lashes curlier, her lips pinker and her face fuller with the purity and poignancy of her pain.

Stop! She is your friend!

Only your friend, Domenico instructed, but his thumping heart was not convinced.

"Domenico?"

Chiara watched his face, inspected his eyes moving up and through her clothes, softly, carefully and kindly, his short eyelashes fluttered over her bare, bony chest, and his eyebrows screwed and tensed over the loose button.

Chiara rejoiced in his affectionate adoration of her body, but her thoughts were completely disturbed when she met his eyes, for they sucked the breath from her lungs, and held onto it until she thought she would faint. She always forgot how those eyes pulled the gravity from the earth, sweeping her into clouds of glittering silver mist.

She wished she could forget them, move away from their spell, yet, just as the grapevines grow away from the ground, it was impossible to cut this connection between the soil, for they were bound together by their secret journey.

"Yes, sorry?"

"What is wrong with you today, Signorina Moderna's in a trance, and you, all I will be left with is Vincenzo," Chiara laughed bitterly.

"Sorry I was thinking," apologized Domenico, his face flushing at her words, making his glasses steam, and blur the vision of Chiara.

"About?"

"About later today, maybe we could pick up some pizzas for this evening?" lied Domenico, as he took his glasses off and rubbed them slowly against his shirt.

"Yes, sounds nice."

He glanced at Chiara, yet she was a blur, like looking at a bunch of grapes, unable to identify each individual one.

A loud blaring of expensive horns disrupted her thoughts, as she glanced towards the loud, ostentatious red sports car parked adjacent to the shop, revving, growling, ordering her to leave.

Vincenzo. A murderer to their happiness.

"I'm sorry, I have to go, but I'll see you later," Chiara said anxiously, as her lips faded, and her eyes fell to the ground.

"That's fine, have a good day," Domenico offered, though he did not mean it.

"Yes, you too, see you later," shouted Chiara, as she rushed out of the shop, slamming the door behind her with a force.

The silence returned heavily to the shop, except for the barking bruises of Vincenzo's voice scolding his Chiara, telling his Chiara to get in the car, shouting and reprimanding his Chiara for taking too long.

The church bells began their hourly melody, but they were suddenly cut off by the violent revving of his expensive engine, tearing the small, old town of Castelmauro into shreds with its modernity.

Chiara disappeared.

Domenico returned to stacking the cigarettes on the shelves, excited with the promise of the evening with her, yet made miserable by the long minutes that lay between them.

FOUR

The battered navy-blue three-wheeler tumbled down into the valley, like a rickety roller coaster.

The girls shrieked with wide-open pink mouths, their young breasts bouncing over each deep pothole or large rock.

The man gripped his black work cap as they flew down the steep, petrifying valley corridor, whilst his teeth gritted together with fear.

The pizza boxes were pushed and pulled, to and fro, bashing and smashing the weak cardboard boxes, as the reckless driver twisted sharply around bends. The man hoped the precious food would not be destroyed by its travels.

The girls' cheeks were ablaze with colour as the fast, cold force of the three-wheeler tore through the valley, whilst they shielded their eyes against the grinning sun's rays, so that it would not steal the colour from their irises. Their noses engulfed the sun's new scent, polluted and dusty with dry grass, crisping leaves and every so often, the salivating scent of pizza.

The man knew they were driving too fast, for the dry, golden country around them was a blur of empty fields, small, friendly olive trees merging with other dying trees, and tiny weeping flowers. It was all a splatter of colours and scenes, like an impressionist painting, a million stories forced through colour and light and madness.

The noise was furious in their ears, the gruff grumbling of the old engine and the zipping wind, spitting flies in the sticky faces of the young people, who pulled these little smashed black bodies from their lips and cheeks with disdain.

Despite the unbearable heat of the afternoon, the three young people were completely unaware of its power, for the pressure of the wind was a cool colliding force of relief, only the man's face was smeared with a sheen of fearful sweat.

They laughed and shouted at each other, but the noise was sucked into a vacuum of the wind, like a hoover, and this was a fortunate thing, for in the village above, it was quiet and lifeless with the snoring and sleeping of old and young.

It felt strange to Chiara, for way up above her, the sky was silent and a still blue, like a frozen fresco, yet down in the valley, the three-wheeler was disturbing the ground, coughing up clouds of dusty soil and crunching the rocks beneath the wheels.

Chiara treasured the rich tones of joy blasting through this lonely wilderness, like a radio on an empty dance floor, for it unfroze the icy glaze from her eyes, untwisted the knotted droop from her lips, and rubbed away the lines of worry from her forehead.

Gazing around, she noticed how the light bounced and bumped upon the edges of the three wheeler, like little fairies, but it made her feel sick, as she was bluntly reminded of the afternoon she had spent trying on rich necklaces that strangled and pulled her humble neck lower and lower. She thought it would have lifted her spirits, made her feel powerful and beautiful, but the necklace had been a chain of degradation and darkness, for it was a trap. All of this was a trap. A trap of decadence, a trap of luxury, a trap of wealth, but she had been the one to lock herself in this beautiful cage, and now she could find no way to rework the locks. Poverty had made her run into the cage, like a starving mouse at the scent of cheese, but now she was in the cage, she wanted to be released back to the poor and humble life she once knew.

Today had been a day full of little annoyances caused by her fiancé, Vincenzo, and like milk left in the sun, the annoyances had grown and fed off one another, like bacteria, curdling and turning the grand and wealthy image of Vincenzo lumpy and bad.

Despite the sun and the speckless bright blue sky above, Chiara still felt uptight and constrained from the day's excruciating excursion.

Crawling across the back of the three-wheeler, she battled the wind, falling against the glass frame of the back with a thud, yet she held on, despite the jolting movements of the vehicle.

Peering through the glass, Chiara felt the weight of the sun press on her exposed head and back, as she waited for her sun-blighted eyes to adjust to the darkness of the van. Eventually Chiara could make out the back of Domenico's dark, shaded head, whilst the rest of his body jumped and twisted with the movements of the three-wheeler.

He did not see her approach, and for a moment she stared at him, that man who had grown from child to adult right by her side. Suddenly, she had a thought that belonged to an elderly woman, for where had all that time gone? It had slid away from her, like a sandcastle collapsing with the hours of the day, and now they were stuffed into these costumes of adults, pretending to be this and that, when in reality, they were still children seeking to find out what they wanted and who they were. Time could steal many things, but it had also given her the gift of knowing this man's face as if it were her own. Though she could not see his face, Chiara could sketch it from memory, from the faint scar torn from his temple to his ear after he had fallen down the stairs at school, the tiny white marks, which had remained on his face from his first shave, and the mosquito bite that had become a permanent resident under his right eyebrow, occasionally becoming inflamed if he rubbed it.

She could place her finger in exactly the first place he had grown his first teenage spot, she could tell the story behind his lost lashes, which disappeared at the end of his left eye, and she knew the red raw mark his glasses left on the bridge of his nose when he took them off. She knew the expressions of his face, from the cutting line between his brows when he thought, the sarcastic tilt of his lips when someone challenged him, the way a blush would erupt from the centre of his cheek and spread all the way to his temples when he was embarrassed, and the dimple that darkened and deepened in the fold of his left cheek when he laughed or smiled. All these things she loved and treasured, for it reminded her of his never-ending support and steadfast love he sacrificed for her. But beyond those dark, curling, thick whips of hair, she no longer knew him like she had once done, for his mind was hard to explore, and even harder to read. Chiara wondered as to what he was thinking about. She thought she could hazard a guess, but even she could not truly say, for his thoughts were untrapped and at liberty to do as they pleased, unlike herself. They probably ventured all territories of great and small, intelligent and stupid, exotic and ordinary, but no one would ever know, for he was as silent as a summer breeze. Chiara wondered if he thought about her, if he thought about other women, if he thought about love, if he thought about sex, if he thought about his loneliness. Would he miss her when she left? Would his life be unchanged by her disappearance? Would he not care? Would he even notice?

She wished she could be more like him, but her mind was a claustrophobic space of anguish, which seemed to be closing in on her, cramping her mind with the proximity of that future she feared. Her thoughts were like sheep to a sheep dog, following the daily course of her life without query or question as to whether the direction was safe or a cliff drop of death.

Chiara needed to rid these thoughts from her mind, for they were full of sickening poison, which only made her stomach unsettle and her throat tighten.

Knocking on the glass, Domenico's eyes looked up into the rear-view mirror and met her own with a loving affection, which she cradled when sorrow squashed her. Those eyes had saved her so many times from despair. Her mind was heavy, like the grapevines, weighed down by her persecuting past and fearful future. But his eyes were always there, infinitely supportive, like the soil, nurturing and loving, allowing the grapevines to flourish, exposing their beauty, whilst sharing the burdens of her mind. Yet she knew her dependence on him would be her death, whether it be her soul or heart, she knew it would kill her eventually.

Chiara had heard others whispering of his strange, cold eyes, but it was not true. His eyes were magical and mysterious, like mercury, independent and different, working in ways other eyes did not. Whenever she looked into those silver, glittering eyes, they filled her whole heart, soul and body with a warm affirmation, for in those eyes there was tenderness, time and eternal love. She had not found this in any other eyes, for Domenico's eyes held something special.

Trust!

Those silver pools bled the deepest trust, and filled her with confidence, like the wet soil to a dying flower, like a silver penny to a beggar, like a silver mirror to the beautiful, like those silver glass eyes of her favourite childhood doll. Within Domenico's eyes, like her doll, she felt a familiarity and love, for both those eyes had witnessed her pains, her happiness, her sorrow, her confusion with undying support and stability. His eyes offered her comfort, like her favourite doll, which she had curled and cuddled as a young child, crying herself to sleep when she realized her mother would never return, when her dad became as motionless and emotionless as a chair, when she had left school, and when Vincenzo had first struck her. Those eyes were frozen silver lakes, firm in their friendship, fondness and freedom.

Domenico's eyes were the ones she looked for in her darkest and brightest days. They were the eyes she saw before she fell asleep and the ones she saw when she awoke. But no, she had to stop thinking of his eyes, and think of Vincenzo's eyes. Yet, no matter how hard she tried, she could not see his eyes, and for all the life within her, she could not say what colour they were.

"Are you ok, Chiara? Should I slow down?" shouted Domenico over the grumbling of the noisy engine, snapping her imaginings.

Domenico had been stealing glances at Chiara, as she unconsciously gazed at him, but he could not look at those eyes for too long, and he was thankful to be driving. Those eyes, God, those eyes killed him, suffocated his senses and pummelled his heart with bruises as black as squid ink. Those eyes he treasured more than anything else in this world, for one glance was worth more money than a thousand diamonds, more treatment than all the medicine in the world, and more happiness than any drugs could offer. He survived off her eyes, like it was food for his soul, and he knew these eyes would be taken from him, and the thought terrified him, for surely, he would starve without them. He lay awake at night thinking of those eyes, the way they reacted to the world around her, and it gave him a glimpse into her very mind. He could see her eyes in the darkness of the night, staring at him with their questions, with their weakness, with their strength, with their untold secrets, making his stomach knot and his penis throb hard against his pants. In the lonely fields, he thought of her eyes, the way they brightened, like a glint of sun on a wave, the way they calmly watched, like an endless blue sky, the way they flashed with passion, like the hottest blue burst of a flame, the way they wept, like heavy dewy bluebells. After looking into her eyes for too long, they held a spell over him, making him see the world in blue swirling patterns, like walking out of the sun into a dark room, distorting and darkening his vision. They were his water, his life source, his heaven, his sanctuary, his home.

But now they were distant, unattainable, for he could not look into those eyes without seeing Vincenzo's spiteful gaze. He had stolen their colour, and banished their sparkling hope, and for this, Domenico could not forgive him or her.

"No, go faster, much faster," Chiara suddenly instructed, awakening him from his painful thoughts.

Domenico nodded, and revved the engine, making the three-wheeler shake and rattle as they zoomed faster and faster down the rocky path.

His eyes were gone as he focused on the road, and Chiara closed her eyes, allowing adrenaline to become her only compass. Every sensation was now awake in this dark rushing space, she could feel the wind bashing past her face, tangling her dark hair, catching her breath and shrinking her lungs with its power.

She could barely breathe, but she liked this feeling, and devoured its energy, like it was the only fuel to see her into the next day. She could hear Bianca and Alessandro shouting, shrieking and swearing, and she gripped onto these sounds, smells and sensations to keep her hope alive.

Suddenly her body was being pulled and pushed, like a fish in a raging cross current, as Domenico swerved sharply from left to right, left, right, left, right.

Her eyes snapped open, her stomach clenched, and her heart raced with wild adrenaline, and for once she enjoyed the reason for this feeling, as normally she felt this way when worry woke her nights with nausea.

Bianca and Alessandro tumbled across each other, their legs knotting together, their hands clutching parts of their bodies where she had never touched Vincenzo, and their laughter bounced between their mouths, like the lyrics of a love song.

Chiara could not help envying them, for though they were her closest friends, she could not fight this feeling of jealousy, as they had something she could only dream of having, love. They had been together two years, yet the love had only grown rather than diminish. Why did she not have that? What had she done to deserve her future partner? Was she too ugly? Was she too unlovable? Was she unapproachable? Was she destined to love Vincenzo forever? A man who pushed her aside and pulled her in when it was convenient to him, like the sharp swerving movements of this very vehicle.

She clung to the side alone.

Finally, Domenico started to slow the truck down, and Chiara could see the countryside unfolding its blurred distortion into the pixelized view of a camera. The soft trees became hard and strong, the flowers became brighter and bigger, the grass became more static and pointed, the houses grew firm from their Play-Doh muddle. The world zoomed in, growing and clarifying, cutting the vague beauty of this place to shreds. The sun's heat was now hot against her face, the wind was gradually dying, the caramelized smell of the sweet dry grass grew stronger, and the distant sound of crickets burned her ears.

The three-wheeler stopped beneath the only group of shaded trees in this barren countryside, coughing and spitting and spluttering with exhaustion, grumbling with a need to rest.

Chiara thudded against the glass as the engine jerked the three-wheeler with one last effort, before it was silenced for the afternoon. She could hear the distant murmuring of Alessandro asking Bianca if she was OK, and again the jealousy bit her heart with a savage torment, for Vincenzo never asked her these questions.

The world of nature seemed to grow in volume at the extinction of all modern life, and its beauty was only highlighted further by the breathless wind and the shakily silent sun.

A slam of the door, the slim black shadow of Domenico, and the crunch of dry grassland beneath instructed the others that it was safe to leave the vehicle.

Chiara did not move at first, and she watched Bianca stand to her feet collecting the pizza boxes and chip bags, as if she had not been disturbed by the journey. Chiara felt her resentment deepen as she analysed the beauty of Bianca, for she had the face and body that every girl dreamed to have. She was small, but everything seemed to fit perfectly within her yellow floral dress, for it clasped her small waist, bloomed over her wide hips, skimmed her perky bum, and tightened across her large breasts. Even though Bianca was three years younger than herself, she had already developed the face and body of a mature woman, for her chest was slightly broad, yet balanced by her large breasts, her arms and thighs were perhaps thick, yet they were equalized by her curvaceous figure. She seemed to move differently to other girls, as if this new female body empowered her walk and stance, making her an image of sexualized strength. Even her hair was womanly, for it was thick and almost black, tumbling down her shoulders and back in curling rivers, tidy and neat, even with the journey. Her face was wide and welcoming, her cheeks always held a small hint of pink blush, her forehead was clean from worry, her nose was sweet and unnoticeable, her lips were round and rouge, and her eyes were dark and velvety like melted chocolate.

Chiara could have hated this girl with the jealous vengeance of a self-piteous heart, but when Bianca smiled, which was often, that dimple, just like her brother's, would burst from her cheek, and she could forgive this beautiful girl for any fault or flaw. Yet, Chiara could not help feeling empty against Bianca's beauty, for she hated her own body. It was the shape of a teenage boy's, and her beauty was as bland and basic as a slice of bread. Why did she not have curves? Where were her large breasts? Where was her perky bum? Why did she not walk like Bianca? Why did she have sticks for legs? Why did she have a lopsided nose? Why did she have thin, unkissable lips? Why did she have skinny arms and long hands? Why did she have a face older than her years? Why was she ugly? Had her mother's disappearance made her ugly? Or had her mother disappeared because she was ugly?

"So how did you all find the drive? What are the reviews?" questioned Domenico sarcastically as he leaned on the side of the truck, a mischievous delighted smile spread wide across his lips.

Alessandro jumped from the truck with a couple of pizza boxes, and shook his long head, before he said: "You are an awful driver."

"Domenico are you trying to get us all killed?" shouted Bianca between hiccups of laughter, as she went towards the edge of the truck where Alessandro held an outstretched hand to her.

Gazing up at Bianca, this woman, silhouetted by the shadow of the trees, was the love of his life. In this moment, Alessandro wanted her all to himself, pulling away her dress and kissing all the fractured pockets of sunlight, which tickled her face and body. He wanted to hold her against the tree and fuck her hard, fuck her deep, fuck her true. He wanted to feel her pointed nipples brush and tease up and down, up and down his chest, as their bodies moved with the love they gave one another.

Laying her fingers in Alessandro's grease-streaked hands, Bianca felt a tingling sensation beneath her skin, for those fingers had touched her in places she had only touched in the darkness of the night. Those fingers had burned invisible tattoos upon her skin, scorching their passionate path from her neck to her breasts to her waist to her hips to her bum, and her vagina, which even now, grew moist with the love he had pursued in her. She loved him more with the loss of their innocent love, and the new reckless, dangerous and dizzying love they now indulged in. She tried to punish herself with guilt for disobeying the laws and sanctions of religion, but her passion overthrew these bullying commands, for religion knew no love like this. Bianca now wished there was no one else here, only Alessandro, with his naked body pressed against her own.

Bianca sighed and smiled secretively as she leapt from the truck. The pizza boxes were tucked tightly under her arms, whilst her fingers grasped the greasy chip bags as she landed safely upon the grass, which crackled at the weight of her feet. She giggled and turned her dark eyes to Alessandro's darker eyes, both aflame with the secret desires of their hearts.

He bent down and kissed the top of her head with a luxurious promise of more.

Chiara pushed her body from the dirty, scratched truck, gathering the remainder of greasy chip bags, cold, oily and dusty from their long journey, and she felt the same. The sun had already made her body feel damp and uncomfortable in her denim shorts, and the white blouse was wet against her chest. Wiping her brow on her thin wrist, sweat made the light hairs on her arm become slick and dark with the pressurized heat.

Moving to the edge of the truck, she saw Domenico standing proudly with his hand outstretched to her, mimicking Alessandro, who sniggered at this re-enactment.

"I was much more romantic than that," defended Alessandro, shaking his head with annoyance.

Bianca laughed and cuddled closer into Alessandro's arms, who squeezed her bum discreetly.

Smiling, Chiara placed her hands in his work-riddled palms, and slipped from the truck with ease, crushing the dry grass beneath.

"Why would he be romantic Alessandro, she has a fiancé," argued Bianca winking at Chiara, who smiled uneasily.

"Bad driver, bad at romance, maybe your stupid brother has a point," laughed Alessandro teasingly as he skipped away with Bianca giggling and tripping behind him.

Chiara watched Domenico roll his eyes, and she suddenly realized how tall he was compared to Vincenzo, and how broad his chest and shoulders were, as if they were made to protect rather than harm.

"Really? Well, if you think that Alessandro you are insane, have you seen my brother? Not just passed out drunk, even him eating is enough to make me vomit," Domenico dryly commented, his hand still holding Chiara's soft, slim fingers.

A cackle resounded from Bianca as she buried her head closer to Alessandro's, as if they were whispering secrets to one another.

Slowly, Domenico's eyes met Chiara's from above, and a smile spread across his dimpled cheek, exposing his characterful, crooked teeth, and Chiara's face melted with a warm smile.

"I don't like it when you are taller than me," joked Domenico, as compared to him, she really was tiny.

Chiara pulled her hand away and smacked his thick-cut arms with the chip bag, before marching away, desperately trying to conceal her giggles. She could hear his slow footsteps following her closely behind, and his humorous laugh slowly dissolved, like a sherbet sweet.

Domenico watched Chiara leave his side, and his hand felt empty without her fingers, despite their petiteness, the loss of them felt like a huge presence was missing from his life. As he watched Chiara move away from him, he stopped laughing. A sudden fear overwhelmed him, crushed him, killed him, for in a couple of weeks he would have to watch her walk down the aisle to marry that man, and then watch her walk out of his life forever.

"What are you guys laughing at?" Bianca called from afar, her high-pitched voice carrying loudly within the quiet music of the countryside.

"Nothing," Domenico shouted from behind her, his voice low and mellow, melting into the dry grass, like rain.

Bianca peered around and said: "You are as mad as people say you are."

Chiara burst into fits of laughter, and Domenico's face clouded slightly, for in all honesty, he hated the sound of Chiara's laugh. It was loud, high pitched, almost evil, like a hyena, and quite frankly it irritated him, unless she was laughing at something he said. Luckily, she didn't laugh very often.

Suddenly Chiara felt a large hand clasp and curl around her narrow shoulder, stopping her steps. The hand spun her around, like spaghetti on a fork, so that she faced Domenico, whose eyes seemed to gleam and glare in one swift emotion. Those eyes were solid, steel bullets, wounding her heart with his freedom and carelessness. She only wished she could feel like this, free from others' emotions, free from her own emotions.

She wanted this freedom more than anything in the world.

"I'm not mad, am I?" Domenico tested; his left brow comically risen in puzzlement.

"You are not mad, if I'm not short," challenged Chiara, her wide blue eyes glittering with a teasing danger, like the rippling tremors of the sea.

His smile twitched, and Chiara loved the effect of her words upon his face, which flushed and flickered with the entertainment of this idea.

"That's not fair, you are short, you can't even reach the top shelves in the shop," sulked Domenico jokingly.

"Well then that must mean you're mad," concluded Chiara, pulling away from his hand as she walked defiantly and victoriously away.

"That's not how they usually diagnose madness," argued Domenico as he fell into step beside her.

Chiara felt his large body sheltering her from the sun's stinging rays.

"And that's not how they diagnose shortness."

Domenico chuckled, and a bittersweet warmth filled his mouth, for he loved how quick and clever Chiara was, yet he hated that she would waste her thoughts on a man who did not seem to own one.

"I mean it is if you can't reach the top shelf and—"

"Domenico, you are so mean," Bianca suddenly scolded between bubbles of laughter, as she watched the pair with a sadness. Bianca loved the idea of love, and she knew in the depth of her heart that her brother and Chiara belonged together, but why did they make love look so complicated? Bianca sadly questioned.

"No, he isn't," interrupted Alessandro turning his face towards Bianca disapprovingly.

"Yes, he is," retorted Bianca and Chiara together, before laughing at their simultaneous thoughts.

"Chiara, all I am going to say is that it would have been better to pick a man more like Domenico than Vincenzo. He is only a bit taller than you," laughed Alessandro, alone.

Bianca chuckled uneasily.

Chiara's face erupted with heat, and her heart began to gallop unsteadily.

Domenico fell out of step with her, and he turned away, keeping his eyes glued to the road ahead, trampling the long grass beneath him without a care.

Chiara looked away, tears pricking her eyes, for she hated Alessandro's cruel comment, it had crashed through their innocent, carefree joy, like a bomb. This small, insignificant comment had completely disturbed the distance between herself and Domenico. She had felt so close to Domenico, as if they had been fifteen again, but now he felt far away, unreachable.

Closed off.

They continued to walk silently along the track, except Alessandro, who whistled loudly and tunelessly to the uncrowded countryside, piercing the tension further with his happy ignorance.

All three heard the crisp grass, crackling and crunching, like chips in a deep fat fryer. All three heard the sneaky scuttling of mice and rats, hiding within the long grass. All three heard the trees creaking and crippling with the heat.

All three saw the pale olive trees, like frozen distorted dancers. All three saw the small, wildflowers smiling weakly. All three saw the distant farmhouse, almost fuzzy and vague with the heat.

All three felt the sun, exploding bombs of light and heat, making the fields feel like fire, and the dreams of those who wandered ash.

But most importantly, all three felt within their souls the impact of those words, like daggers and bullets to their childish dreams. Life was changing, and with that comment they were all reluctantly accepting this hated transition from youth to adults, hope to despair, without a fight, for who were they fighting? Each other? Or themselves?

Finally, the group reached the old, decaying farmhouse, where the wild, rusty orange and dirty white chickens rushed around in disarray, fluttering and fussing at the arrival of these new guests.

Bianca beheld this place with mixed feelings, for this place had held her brother hostage for many years. In some ways, she felt happy for Domenico, as this place had birthed his dream, passion and goal, and with this place, if everything went according to plan, he might actually achieve his childhood dream. Yet, she could not ignore the fact that this place had captured her brother's childhood and broken his body into a man, maturing his mind before it was necessary. Her brother's wrecked childhood was the only thing that blackened her beloved Papa's image, for he had been a drunken fool, making a fatal decision to save his whole family from sinking into the grave of poverty.

At the time of the incident, she had been too young to recall what had happened, and much too young to form an opinion about her father's actions. But even at that young age, she had understood the effects of this decision with the selfish, vicious and cruel memories of childhood confusion and sadness. She could remember how she would walk home alone from school as her brother was taken to the field. She could remember begging Domenico to play a game with her, but he would get grumpy and push her away as he went to the fields. But she could also remember how she would sit cross-legged on his bed, sucking her thumb as she listened to the entertaining stories of the animals, plants, fields and old tales of Castelmauro. He had opened her young eyes to the world of the past, where dead men and women were as alive as the living and breathing people she met day to day, but despite this, her life was hollowed by the invisible place of her older brother.

When she was twelve, she had asked her father, yet he had swatted her away, as if she was an annoying fly. Finally, her mother had recounted the story, lavishing the past with a brutal, bitter image of her father. According to her mother, her father had been in a foul mood, and he had gone to the bar to recover his spirits. Men were playing cards, and her drunken father had decided to battle the legend of the card world, an old man called Signoro Maestro. Her drunk father, bullied by the other men, rose the stakes higher and higher, so high even he could not see them, let alone afford them. The ultimatum was that if Signoro Maestro won, Signoro Fango would hand over his shop and livelihood, but if Signoro Fango won, Signoro Maestro would pay him a substantial payment, so that her father would no longer need to rely on the income of his poor business. Signoro Maestro had won, and the payment could not be made, and so her father had sold his son to this man for free labour. Domenico was nine, forced to work the fields day in and day out with Signoro Maestro, an unsmiling and unhumorous man.

She used to think this old man was cruelly kidnapping her brother, so that she was unprotected against the bullying abuse of Matteo and his friends. But now she believed that this old man and his land were the birthplace of her brother's dream, for Signoro Maestro taught him the science of plants, and helped him understand the biological warfare within the valley. She knew their relationship was deeper than employer and employee, for they seemed like father and son. This theory of hers was made conclusive when Signoro Maestro died, for it had been the only time she had ever seen Domenico cry, and it was not a shock to the village that he inherited the land. Many believed Domenico would let it slip away into decay, but Bianca knew this would never happen, for Domenico had laid out a plan schemed with sentimentality and success.

Bianca stood before the old, decaying farmhouse with a heart bursting with pride, for she believed in her brother's dream. He would achieve this dream and move away from the village that trapped so many dreamers, like snowflakes in a snow globe, smashing and mashing all these individual dreams into one big pile of shit, like a rubbish dump. Yet, she also felt comforted that this small house built with a mismatch of beige and dark stones, lopsided sky-blue roof, glassless windows and shutters hung precariously from their hinges, would still be standing, waiting for him to return if life did not go according to plan.

Stepping carefully through the front courtyard, the stench of the chicken shit and large rotten seeds of peaches and plums made their noses crinkle with disgust. The chickens fearfully fanned away, as if these guests were the kings and queens of the land.

The group of young dreamers trod through the dusty, rust-coloured courtyard. Bending around the corner of the house, they reached a place darkened by shade, yet occasionally the excruciatingly hot rays of the sun dappled its gold randomly on the grass, trees and house.

"Right, let's eat," decided Alessandro, his stomach growling ferociously.

"Yes, let's eat, I am so hungry," Bianca cried marching towards the small, rickety picnic bench, which was wedged beneath two almond trees.

"Can we wait, I just want to look around first," said Domenico casually, as his large body began to move through the sea of growing salad, vegetables and fruit.

"But Domenico we are starving," moaned Bianca, her full, red bottom lip drooping sulkily.

Domenico shook his head mockingly irritated, but he could not hide the slight smile which twisted the corners of his lips.

"Bad decision Domenico, there will be nothing left for you," Alessandro replied, shaking his head in mock despair, further antagonizing his best friend to shirk his duties.

Chiara could see Domenico's face trying to fight the smile, which played with his mouth, yet his left cheek had already betrayed his weakness, for his dimple deepened.

Alessandro fell upon the moss-infested picnic bench, before yanking Bianca down beside him. She fell with a thud, making the worn picnic bench collapse slightly on one side.

"Well, Bianca it looks like we are going to have to eat all this pizza to ourselves," teased Alessandro, flinging each pizza box open with a lavish bullying display of joyful greed. Alessandro further added to his ridiculous tease by licking and smacking his lips together, pulling a piece of pizza from its circle, twirling the almost frozen cheese around his finger, before licking it slowly clean.

Domenico did not budge, but Chiara could see his mouth split into a wild smile, before an infectious, loud roaring laugh was flung from the deepest depths of his body to the quiet trees and countryside. She was in love with his smile, but she was even more in love with his laugh, which seemed to change him into another man. A man who was not stooped by seriousness and studying. A man who did not care what happened. A man who could feel every word and touch every thought. It mesmerized her, for how could such a simple thing change someone into something brand new and different?

"I'll risk it," Domenico added, ignoring the oohing and aahing sounds from Bianca and Alessandro, as they devoured another pizza slice, their fingers shiny with grease.

"You are an idiot, tell him Chiara, he only listens to you," giggled Bianca, slipping the cold, floppy chips into her mouth, leaving an oily trail upon her lips.

Domenico turned all his attention to the small figure of Chiara, and he knew whatever followed from those thin, pink grinning lips, he would not be able to resist. He could understand many things, from the smallest microorganisms to the tallest, infinities of the sky, yet he could not understand this obsession she unconsciously insisted in him. Why did he hang on her every move? Why did he hang on her every word? Why did he hang on her every breath? She tormented him, but it was cruel in its unconscious intention, for he knew she did not know how deep this obsessive love for her chained him, jailed him, tortured him to the point of death. He felt drowned by this love. He felt suffocated by this desire. He felt wretched by its unrequited response...

...and she did not know what to think or feel when she looked up at the staggeringly tall figure of Domenico. When she was alone, Chiara felt she was convinced in her actions and secure in her thoughts. She would marry Vincenzo. But when she looked into those silver pools, her thoughts lost control, running wild with imaginings she only wished were true. Why did she feel lost with this man? Why did she feel unsure with this man? Why did doubts devour her sane thoughts when she was with him? It felt like she depended on him, but to depend on him was to depend on something completely uncontrollable and unpredictable, like depending on the forecast of an English summer. Would she find happiness or sadness at the hands of this man? Chiara knew that he did not know of these feelings, nor the depths of their darkness, and maybe this was for the best.

"Chiara tell him, otherwise there won't be anything left for either of you at this rate," shouted Alessandro, his mouth full of mushy pizza dough.

"Come on Domenico, we can't let them eat everything considering you paid for it," laughed Chiara, taking Domenico's large, warm hands within her own.

Domenico's body slouched, defeated, a small smirk bubbling from his mouth as he allowed Chiara to drag him towards the table.

Bianca and Alessandro mockingly clapped and cheered, congratulating Chiara on wearing down their stubborn, serious friend.

Once they were all seated on the old, crusty picnic bench beneath the dusty, white almond trees, they devoured the remainder of the cold pizza and chips hungrily.

After they finished, the valley became a well of young laughter, shouts and arguments, so loud, even the chant of the church bells could not be heard. The four young people talked, chattered, and gossiped about this and that, filling their precious time with unprecious thoughts and ideas, which would expire as soon as they were voiced.

Domenico, after a while, stood to his feet and began to walk among his patchwork of salad and vegetables, examining the crops for disease and death. His hard work seemed safe, for luckily the wild boars had not come with their crushing brutality, ripping his land to shreds with their unforgiving snouts and hooves, decimating the dreams which were becoming so tantalizingly close to reality.

Suddenly, he felt another person following his steps, and he turned to find Chiara, whose plain face was speckled by the slowly fading sun, which glorified her plainness, like adding rich butter to boiled potatoes.

Chiara held her breath as she beheld the rows of vegetables and salad bursting with a raw, earthy life, and it felt almost wrong to be walking among them, like walking over a grave. The voices of Bianca and Alessandro sounded drowsy and distant as Domenico excitedly guided her through his hard work. Chiara listened carefully as she trod past beautiful, bouquets of lettuce heads, the leaves a vibrant green, speckled with flecks of dry soil and chewed unevenly around the edges by small bugs. She marvelled at the glorious colours, the blood-red fangs of chillies balanced precariously from their tall, dark green stalks, long, dark green cucumbers dangled from paling, weak stalks, dotted with little, bright yellow flowers. The small heart-shaped red peppers grew sparsely from their stems, like jewels. Dark green courgettes lay languidly across the ground, bound to a large leafy bush that protected the dull, dusty yellow flower heads from destruction. Olive trees and fig tress bordered the patches of vegetables, one in the early stage of its fruit, unpleasant and bitter, whilst the other fruit was ripe, full and fleshy with its secret squelching decadent purple jam. But at the very end of the patch was the triumph of his labours, the tomatoes.

Chiara stood for a moment in silent awe, for they had been constructed so carefully and correctly that the red fruit thrived. They were positioned precisely and perfectly, so that the sun sobbed its transformative powers on and through the fruit, the flesh firmer, the seeds absorbent, the juice moistening, sweetening with the warmth. Triangle-shaped wooden borders held the dark, green branches together, and from them dripped the bright, bursting red tomatoes, sinking the poor, weak stems with their heavy, pregnant bodies of rich life.

"I've picked most of them, but I still have a few more to go," apologized Domenico, his dark curling hair glossy as it tossed the sunlight between each strand.

Chiara watched him inspect the plants and fruit, his eyes were like silver tweezers, as they focused and picked apart the very structure of the plant. She knew his eyes saw more than colour and ripeness, for he could see the unseeable. She knew that his brain and eyes could see the very individual cell structure of each tomato, he could see the plants absorb the water and carbon dioxide from the soil and air, he could see the sun's kinetic heat change this fuel into glucose and oxygen. Chiara knew that Domenico saw these plants as more than food, for they were living things, creatures he could empathize with, creatures he could talk to, creatures he knew listened to his words. Domenico belonged to this world of soil and sun, and Chiara only wished she could belong.

Chiara went to stand beside him, treading carefully and lightly, fearful that any pressure would collapse the whole ecosystem of these strategically placed fruits.

"Is your *Nonna* making her infamous tomato sauce?" Chiara asked.

Domenico removed his glasses, and rubbed the smeary lenses on his shirt, making his eyes seem small, unspectacular and insignificant.

Chiara was a blur, a distant mystery, a foggy light in this unfocused world of Domenico's vision.

"She has begun, but she takes longer now. Bianca and I help when we can, but she loves doing it, always has," chuckled Domenico, placing his glasses upon his face. Chiara felt relieved, for he looked like himself again.

"I know, I used to love watching her when I was little, I can help her if she needs a hand?"

Domenico turned his gaze upon Chiara, and the soft, golden sun fell upon his face, his glasses sparkling and alight, reflecting the rays, as if his eyes were the sun, blinding her own eyes with its harsh spotlights.

"Yes, she would love that, she has always had a soft spot for you, she talks about you all the time," revealed Domenico, his face shifting with a generous smile, the dimple slipping in and out, like a dolphin surfacing the waves.

"Really what does she talk about?"

Domenico twisted his face towards the vines, and lightly touched the wooden frame, his fingers fidgeting nervously with the growing silence between them. Chiara moved, turning her body away from him, as a familiar paranoia made her cheeks grow hot with shame. Ever since she had become engaged to Vincenzo, people had gossiped, and most of what she heard was bad. She tried to ignore it, pretended as if those hurtful words of others did not exist, but they wiggled their way into her sensitive, influential mind, upturning her thoughts, like boars through a vegetable garden.

"Things. Try a tomato, tell me if it tastes OK?" offered Domenico in compensation, for guilt grew uncomfortably within his chest when Chiara turned her face towards him. It was dark and shaded, full of secrets, whilst the sunlight glowed thinly around her body, like a cape to heaven.

Chiara nodded, and examined how Domenico's large, tough hands gently encouraged the tomato from its grip without force or strength, as if it wanted to be taken. Vincenzo's hands were not like this, thought Chiara. They were boned with brutality, snapping, ripping and stealing the gentlest things from their homes, as if they belonged only to him, like a machine yanking the grapes from the vines, damaging and bruising the very fruits.

Handing the red, plump tomato to Chiara, his scratchy, dry hands slipped lovingly through her own cracked, scarred fingers. Both hands were alike, broken by laborious jobs, one soiled by washing dishes, and the other cracked by ploughing the land. Domenico watched Chiara take a bite, juice spurting across her cheeks and chin, like jam from a donut, whilst the shiny sheen of the juice left a gloss within and upon her mouth and lips. He could not look away, and his thoughts spiralled out of control as he thought about kissing her on those very lips, sharing the same succulently sweet juice together.

It is strange, for the juice seemed to possess seeds of magic, transfiguring Chiara's wet, pink lips into a wide smile, showcasing a set of cream-coloured teeth, except her left canine tooth, which was plastered with the red tomato skin.

Chiara noticed how Domenico stared at her, there was something in his face, and most importantly within his eyes. Was it lust? Was it love? Those silver, familiar irises were unrecognizable, for they were almost lilac in their adoration, and this only made her more self-conscious of her appearance and her own desires.

They were silent, watching, wondering, desperately trying to understand what one another wanted, needed, desired.

Each of their breaths seemed suspended within the hot, hazy summer afternoon. They seemed paused, a standstill in the movement of time, yet the world around them moved. Flies whizzed with loud purrs past their faces, and ants marched importantly across their exposed toes, nipping their flesh and tickling their hairs. An animal rustled nervously within the bushes nearby, and the light mutterings of Bianca and Alessandro continued. In the distance, the muffled church bells rang shyly.

The sun, the tomatoes and them were the only things frozen, trapped within this tight, invisible cage of expectancy.

Something was happening, and they could both feel it shifting in the ground and in the air. An understanding was trying to be understood. A longing was being longed for. A thought was being talked through their eyes.

However, a realization stormed upon Domenico's mind with endless, antagonizing questions of confusion and cruelty. How could she stand before him like this, when she had another man waiting for her? How could she stand there knowing she was tampering with the moralities of her engagement? How could she stir his soul without even speaking? How could she electrify every hair on his body without even touching? How could he keep doing this to himself? How could she keep punishing his mind with this pain? How could she keep bending, breaking and burning his heart with her unrequited love?

A bitter anger stole through his veins and heart, for this woman he loved was selfish, playing and pampering her vanity with this destructive game of love.

He had to stop playing the game, and with this, he tore his eyes away from Chiara's swimming serene blue pools, safe from their spells of sexual suspense.

Domenico cleared his throat, and wiped a slightly trembling hand across his flopping, curling dark hair, as he moved away from her.

Chiara tightened her grip around the half-eaten tomato, the leftover juice spilling down her wrist as she watched Domenico place that fucking big barrier before her once again. She hated him. She hated how he seemed to want to make this as hard as possible for her. She hated how he controlled the distance between them. She hated how his eyes had explicitly displayed his dislike for her. But most importantly, she hated herself. She hated how she tried to cling to him. She hated how she wanted him. She hated how much she loved him. She hated how little power she held over him or her own emotions. She hated how selfish he was, playing his cruel and foolish games, as if her feelings were nothing, reeling her in with friendship, before expelling her with her own black guilt.

Her throat tightened, constrained and stuffed with a sexualized sorrow, which she wanted to expel from her chest, as if it were poison. She turned her body away from him, folding her arms across her chest, and keeping her eyes to the ground.

"Domenico, Chiara do you want a beer?" wailed Bianca, her high-pitched voice shocking them back to reality.

They followed her command at a distance from one another, silent, as frustration fuelled each of their steps.

Alessandro ambled towards the old well, and pulled the heavy metal bucket towards land, revealing four beer cans dripping cold. Grabbing the beers with his left hand, he let the bucket slide back into the well, before sealing it shut.

When he arrived back at the table, Domenico and Chiara had returned, but it seemed different. His beautiful Bianca was anxiously watching her brother, Domenico kept his eyes on a loose splinter he was unpicking from the table, and Chiara's eyes were in her lap.

"You all look miserable, did someone die?" Alessandro joked, as he handed the beer cans around.

Domenico and Chiara laughed weakly, but Bianca shot her boyfriend a scolding look, which he immediately noticed, silencing his laughter.

They clinked cans against one another, and burst the caps open, froth bubbling from the open mouth with relief.

The sun was beginning its slow descent gracefully, extinguishing the brightness of the blue sky, preparing its canvas for the soft explosions of sunset pinks, bronze shields and ferocious reds, like bath bombs across the sky.

Alessandro leant contently against the cool wall as he gulped down the beer, watching the chickens stuff their bodies with corn.

Chiara's small body hunched over her knees, which were folded tightly beneath her chin, as she sadly spotted the appearance of the pale, banana-shaped moon above.

Bianca sat upright, as she twisted her glossy hair around her fingers, glancing every so often at her brother, who seemed suddenly sombre and depressive. But she could not understand what it was about.

Domenico heavily leant over the table, as he read the side of the can, analysing the chemical ingredients, clinging to words which were familiar and safe.

"Chiara, when are you going to buy your wedding dress?" Bianca inquired quietly, desperate for a relief in this stale silence.

All eyes turned to Chiara, and she looked between them, ignorant dark brown, soft, excited hazel eyes and the momentary flicker of those emotionless silver pools, which briefly reflected her own panicked blue eyes. They all attacked her with questions, and beneath these eyes, she felt overwhelmed, sinking and drowning in her own denial, lies and tangled web of woe.

"I don't know, soon," Chiara replied casually, hiding her eyes behind her beer can.

"Well, of course soon, your wedding is in three weeks," scoffed Bianca with a gentle smile, for her innocent sixteen-year-old mind, so rich with new-found love, could not understand Chiara's undecided and reluctant attitude.

"Is it that soon? Time is passing so fast," Chiara commented quietly, almost to herself.

Domenico crushed his finished can and tossed it across the table.

"Make the most of it," warned Alessandro, also crunching his empty beer can between his fingers, the last droplets falling to the ground, and dappling the dust with little spots.

"What do you mean make the most of it?" Bianca cried, turning her eyes on Alessandro, who smirked at the fierce beauty of that gaze.

"I mean, when she is married that will be it. Do you really think Vincenzo will let her come here? Do you think Vincenzo's rich arse will sit with us?" provoked Alessandro.

"I won't want him down here," murmured Domenico, darkly.

"Stop being mean you two, honestly Vincenzo's nice and it's not fair to say if he is bad as we don't even know him," interjected Bianca, with a worried glance towards Chiara's paling face.

"Why are you defending him, Bianca? He is a prick, and everyone knows it," Domenico argued bitterly, as he clicked his knuckles noisily.

Alessandro and Bianca met each other's eyes with concern and confusion, for they could not understand what was going on with Domenico.

An uncomfortable silence followed, making Bianca fidget nervously as she flashed a glance at Chiara's flushed, downcast face, and then Domenico's cold, critical silver eyes.

One of the chickens shrieked loudly, and an engine rumbled close by, becoming a mere whisper as it grew further away.

"Well, I won't be tying the knot yet, so don't look at me with those whimpering eyes Bianca," Alessandro scolded jokingly.

"Don't worry Alessandro. You can barely tie your laces, let alone the knot," retorted Bianca, flicking her dark hair behind her, whilst her eyes became a dangerous and defiant adventure for Alessandro.

Everyone laughed, except Domenico, who looked unsettled, almost anxious. A new and strange emotion, which Bianca had not seen before.

There was a moment of silence, the crickets were thick-throated in their husky song, and the birds whistled low and close to them.

Chiara shivered slightly, for the closing evening had dropped the temperature, and she felt goose pimples rise from her skin, as if it were a barrier to protect her against the conversation, which had not finished, though she wished it had.

"Are you excited?" broke Domenico, his silver eyes flashed in Chiara's direction.

Chiara shuffled uncomfortably, yet her harsh blue eyes did not bend or budge to the unkindness of Domenico's illusions.

"Yes, it will be a good day," Chiara answered holding her gaze steady, as his eyes ravaged her lie to pieces.

Domenico rolled his eyes, blinked, and looked away from Chiara.

"Of course, she is excited. Wouldn't even your cold, unfeeling heart be excited for your wedding day?" Bianca questioned excitedly, as her eyes alighted with the visions of her own wedding day to come.

The group watched Domenico rise and pluck an almond from the tree, the flesh was creamy and smooth, like milk, as he placed it between his teeth and chewed thoughtfully.

Chiara felt torn. She wanted him to remain silent, and keep his wretched thoughts to himself, yet equally she needed to know what he thought of her, even if it was degrading and dismal. She needed to know how he saw her. She needed to know his opinions on the future life she was going to sign herself away to.

Bianca inspected her brother's face for any evidence to defend his hurtful manner, but his face was nonchalant and inflexible. She observed how his brows knotted closer and closer together, a line becoming implanted between them, as if her stupid question stumped his complicated and uncommunicative brain.

"I would be excited if I was marrying the right person," Domenico finalized, his voice low and grave, as his eyes focused on the smooth, bright lime green leaves of the tree.

An awkward silence followed, sinking and strangling the group with tension.

No one moved.

Alessandro blew out a whistle of shock and turned his eyes to Bianca for guidance.

Bianca glared at her brother, hoping he would see her disgust, but he did not look at her. She turned her gaze to Chiara, and her generous heart melted.

She sat small and isolated, her fingers gripping her shins, embedding her nails into her skin, tattooing the pain of his words for all to see.

"He didn't mean it, Chiara. How does he know what love is? He has never felt it," comforted Bianca softly, extending her delicate hand to Chiara, but she did not take it.

Those words of Domenico had been beyond cruel, for instantly he had managed to isolate her from the group. He had throned her as a criminal, someone to be avoided at all costs. He had branded her as a fool, someone to not be trusted. He had degraded her by her own truth.

Chiara needed to leave. She needed to scream. She needed to curse Domenico with a lifetime of pain. She needed him to know how deep his words had cut her.

She needed to escape.

She needed space.

She needed peace.

She needed herself, and only herself.

Chiara stood to her feet, and glared down at the sweet, oval face of Bianca, who smiled encouragingly. But this gave her strength to be mean, for she saw that same dimple which plastered her brother's face, and she did not care if she hurt Bianca, for hurting Bianca would hurt him.

"He did mean it Bianca, don't fucking flatter me with your lies," growled Chiara, before marching away from the group with arms wrapped tightly around her body, conscious of her shaking ugly limbs.

Chiara felt sick and dizzy with fury. She despised Domenico for how he used words so cuttingly and cunningly that it made her body a disease of desolation, bleeding her heart to death and numbing her mind to any other thought or person around. How could Domenico stand there and read her mind aloud to everyone? How could he betray her darkest thoughts, which even she did not really know, to everyone? How could someone she loved so much hate her enough to embarrass her, harass her, hurt her? Did Domenico think he was better than Vincenzo? Did he see himself in competition with him? Did he want to beat Vincenzo in this game of love?

Chiara already knew who had won.

It was Vincenzo. He was rich, well educated and cultured. He was a man, who a girl like herself could only dream of ending up with, like Cinderella and Prince Charming. He descended from a rich Milano family, who owned a huge clothing company, whilst she was the daughter of a missing mother and an unemployed shoemaker. It must have been fate, for chance was not this giving. They had met at a wedding. She had been serving, and Vincenzo had been one of the guests. She remembered how she had watched him carry himself around the room with such an elegance, as if he was always waltzing to a secret tune. The evening had turned to night, and Chiara had been heading home when Vincenzo had called her over, and she had gone willingly. She had believed herself to be in trouble, but instead he was drunk and began to ramble on about many foolish things, which she had laughed at. When she left, she thought she would never see him again, but the next day he met her in the store, and he had presented her with a small gift to thank her for listening to him. It had all been a whirlwind of romantic royalties, for Chiara found her vanity growing with the shower of gifts he indulged her with, fine clothes, polished purses, and more, which she had never had. How could she have resisted? All her life she had been poor, living with a father who did not seem to see her or care, but then Vincenzo came, showing her what money could do, how it changed people to do exactly what you wanted, and she unconsciously had been his victim. But now, she wanted to hurt people with money, just like he did.

Suddenly a low scurrying sound from the ground caught her attention, and when she looked up, she found her gaze submerged in a sea of long grapevines, like drunken line dancers. The setting sun was beginning to deepen its shade and blemish the sky above with patterns of dark yellows, autumnal oranges and cotton candy pink clouds. The spikes of orange sun bent the black shadows of the vines across the paths, messing with her mind and muddling her eyes.

This was Domenico's dream, and how easy she could destroy it in this moment. Yet, it would be impossible, for these vines were also her dream. As she stood before these grapevines, she saw all the paths that were open to her, all the alternative lives she could live or not, but how could you know which one was the most fulfilling? Was it the one hung heavy and black with juicy grapes? Or was it the sparse grapevines with the smaller, red blush grapes, unique with their sweet juices?

Without thinking, she ambled down one of the many paths, forgetting all her fears of what was right or wrong.

"Chiara," whispered a voice from between the large, green puzzle-shaped leaves.

Domenico saw a fragmented Chiara from between the vine leaves and clusters of robust, dark red grapes. Suddenly he smiled, for the sight of these little grapes made his heart swell with pride, for many years he had worked these vines, ploughing, planting, protecting these temperamental plants from disease and death, and now, he was so close to succeeding. He picked a grape, and placed it in his mouth, the sharp, sweet juice squeezing out at the crush of his teeth, just like they would at the press. He was eating his profits and future, and he revelled in its taste. Chiara was very similar to these plants, for he had spent years protecting, caring and loving her, through all her highs and lows, he had been there. But unlike these grapes, he did not want to let her go, he never wanted to stop loving her, no matter who she was or where she was.

Suddenly his thoughts were awoken by a soft sigh, as he heard her footsteps move away from him.

"Chiara, I'm sorry," Domenico repeated, following the trailing sound of her light feet crushing the brittle grass beneath.

Chiara did not speak, her thin bottom lip was drooping, like a hooked fish.

"Why are you being like this?" Domenico asked, picking a grape from the stalk, before examining its properties.

The footsteps stopped, and Domenico stopped.

"Why are you being like this? I have every right to be like this. You insulted my fiancé in front of my friends. You hurt my feelings and most importantly you don't even care. You don't care that this is what I want. You don't care if this is best for my family. You don't care about anything except this stupid farm and your dream. You think that if you don't strive to be someone important then your life is meaningless. I can do what I please and I don't need to be ridiculed and judged by your words. Believe what you want, but I don't care," shouted Chiara, her voice growing stronger, louder and more forceful with each new word.

Domenico was silent, and Chiara heard him spit the pip of the grape from his mouth.

"Chiara just let me say something. I am sorry about what I said, it was mean, but I just don't think Vincenzo deserves you and he won't give you the life that you might want. You are better than him, and he will trap you—"

"How do you know this?" Chiara interrupted, her blue eyes flickering and meeting the silver eyes on the other side.

"Because he already treats you like shit," Domenico murmured into the leaves, his confused heart breaking slightly with the weight of this confession, for it only proved how far she had deluded her brain into this fantasy of 'happily ever after'.

Chiara drew in a sharp intake of breath as she prepared to contradict him, yet the words did not come. Those words were difficult to hear, and even more of a struggle to fight, for this was the terrible, terrifying truth.

"You are wrong."

"Maybe."

"So, why did you say it if you are wrong?"

"Because I care about you, and I don't want you to get hurt," Domenico quietly disclosed, his throat tightening over the last word.

Chiara stepped closer to the vine and inhaled the woody aroma of the leaves and branches, relieving her head, which ached and pounded with an emotion she did not want to comprehend.

"Friends?" Domenico offered, sticking his hand between the leaves, and waiting desperately to feel her soft hands in his.

Chiara looked at the hands sceptically, her throat tight with emotion.

Eventually, she slipped her hand into his large, engulfing fingers, and held onto it tightly. Turning her face away, she hid the tears which were filling at the base of her eyeballs.

Chiara gripped his hand, craving its safety, yet she felt separated from him, separated by his wall of dreams...

...for in that lonely, lightless valley, it seemed as though they were as close as stars in the night sky, yet Domenico knew they were really a million miles apart.

Caro Signoro Maestro,

Why do you not write to me, God?
Why do you not answer my questions?
Are you scared?
Are you ashamed?

No, sorry, Signoro Maestro, I forget you are dead, buried deep beneath the earth, worms devouring your brain and bugs slurping up your intestines, like spaghetti.

Spaghetti! Oh God, I am so hungry, starving for food, which actually looks like food. I watch day in and day out the large, fat security guards stuffing their faces with glorious food; sandwiches vomiting slippy, creamy mozzarella, stringy mortadella, the white embroidered flesh of perfectly grilled fish, green cartwheels of oil-laden courgettes, and pasta shielding the smoky gems of aubergines or the sweet, pink tuna chunks. Sometimes the torment would simply be a buttery pastry, flaking crumbs onto their lips and beards, like old, peeling wallpaper. They would stand sipping the hot, exotic espresso shots, enriching the filthy air of my cell, making me feel light-headed and dizzy with the delirious memories of food.

It is pure torture, for sometimes I believe I could reach out between the black bars and snatch their sandwiches, cramming every last crumb into my dry, ravenous mouth. Even writing this letter is causing saliva to rapidly form in the corners of my mouth, like dew drops on a flower. Yet I am a caged monkey, chattering and performing to a lonely and empty audience, and those who do hear either pretend they can't, or they give me a flash of their sardonic smiles before pounding my face until my mouth is choking and frothing with blood.

God, I still have to rant about religion, for I am not satisfied with its services. I mean, if the old God had always intended those who are good to be praised and those who are bad to be punished, why did all this happen?

Why am I confined to the four small corners of this squalid cell, smelly and filthy with the odorous memories of long gone prisoners, who like me, waited tortuously for their time to come to an end?

Sometimes, I believe death is close, and I welcome its face like an old friend, yet like old friends, they filter in and out of my life, inconsistent in their promises. Yet, every time I recover from my close encounter with death, I promise myself to keep my mind a stranger to my memories, for it is best they do not meet. I fear if they should become better acquainted, a savage conflict should erupt, causing another collapse of my sanity.

However, the crucifix of her is uncovering my memories, like a squirrel digging its nuts up from hibernation. I want to run from them, but it is impossible to restrain myself.

I have no control over my mind or body. I lash out, shaking the bars, banging my fists against the walls, growling at the ground, like an animal, especially when my mind spasms with the electricity of those memories.

I lie in bed at night, cradling the cross, begging her to take me back, take me back, take me back…

…but she never does.

If God was truly fair, I would be trailing through the paths of those majestic grapevines that you and I made together, and I would feel the sun stroking my cheeks, lips and chest. I would find my back aching with the weight of books and work. I would live forever in the endless tangled, straw-like grass with her beside me. Our backs scratched and roughened, like sandpaper, yet our eyes, lips and faces would be moist and soft with sweat.

No! Stop! I must stop dreaming, for dreaming would be my destruction, my death.

God, I cannot understand what I am doing? I do not believe in this false fantasy of good and bad, heaven and hell, for if only life was that easy. If only the good went to heaven and the bad to hell. But there is no such thing, for heaven is hell, and hell is heaven, the brightness is the darkness, and the darkness is the brightness, just as shadows are born from the sun, and the brightest moon is born from the blackest sky. Good and bad cannot exist without the other.

I believe our lives are a game of poker, suspicious of the honest men, trusting in the liars, gambling recklessly with the people we want to believe in. But the wins and losses are as bad as each other. Remember, Signoro Maestro, you gambled with my father, and won me. But it was me who killed you. Remember Signoro Maestro, sorry, God, the landslide killed you, how funny! You, who pledged your life to soil, nurturing its ecosystems and loving its seedling was the very thing that killed you. How awfully ironic! How awfully betrayed you were! The very thing which should have protected you was the very thing that killed you!

Do you remember the rain on your death day? I remember it, you left me in the farmhouse and I had waited hours for you, cowering from the thunder and lightning. But on your heroic mission to save me from the merciless valley, the soil had slid from beneath your three-wheeler, chucking you down the steep embankment, before the soil and rocks collapsed upon you, strangling the last breath from you, framing you as a fossil. What a funny way to die, killed by your own comrade!

Who would have believed this same fate would have happened to another?

But it did.

I know why she was killed by those flames. I was the reason for her death, for she had done the same as you Signoro Maestro, she had gone back to the farmhouse to be with me. But this time I was not there.

What if I had been there? Could I have saved her? Or would I have been engulfed by the flames of that fire, like my dear Chiara?

Oh that name kills me!

Chiara means clear, but even with these glasses, I have no clarity within my thoughts, for they are as muddled and messy as the landslide which killed you.

However, I promise you, God, that I did not kill Chiara.

I wish I had been there if only to prove it was that man who killed her.

If only to prove my innocence.

If only to never know of a life without her.

'...Some fell on rocky places... It sprang up quickly, because the soil was shallow. But when the sun came up the plants were scorched and they withered because they had no root'.

God, do not preach at me the fucking Parable of the fucking Sower again, for you can say what you mean in simple words. Yes, perhaps, I, like the soil, was shallow and selfish, desperate to have the seeds within me, bound together with the invincible communications of love. But, you make a mistake, this only proves my innocence, for the sun killed the seeds.

Don't argue against me, the sun killed the seeds, case closed.

OK, yes, the sun killed the seeds, but the soil only made this death worse, for there was no deeper stability between them.

What are you trying to say, God? That I killed Chiara? How could you suggest this?

He killed her, but he killed her long before her actual death. He burned her happiness. He burned her youth. He burned her hopes and dreams. He burned her confidence. He burned her future. That man loved to set fragile things alight, watching them burn, burn, burn, until there was nothing left of them.

That man had a twisted sickening desire for flames, for he is Satan, dancing and singing in the fires of hell.

He killed Chiara.

CASE CLOSED!

Signoro Maestro, sorry, God, I need to stop writing the guards are shouting, swearing and hammering at my door.

Write back soon!

Ha! Sorry, I forget a real dead man cannot write like I can, for I am DEAD!

He killed me too when he killed her.

Yours sincerely,
Domenico

FIVE

Chiara knelt upon the small, ash-coloured balcony, dosing her plants with little sips of water, as if they were babies. It was quiet, except for the little chirping bleats of the baby pigeons, which nested in the opposite windowsill of another abandoned home. Chiara stopped watering and watched the little birds, their small, yellow and grey patched bodies, immovable beneath all the heavy baby fluff that time would shed, freeing them to fly far from the grasps of home. Chiara felt saddened by this sight, for her baby feathers had shed long ago, yet why, oh why, was she still trapped and tied to this place, which other's called home, but she could not? When would she have her chance to fly? Would she fly alongside Vincenzo? Of course not, he might move her cage to the mighty metropolis of Milan, but he would cut her wings off, snap her legs in half like twigs, and tape her mouth shut, unfree to speak, unfree to move, unfree to live. She wished she was more than these sweet, yet insignificant chicks, but in reality, she was worse, for they had hope.

The little sharp, high-pitched bleats of the chicks began to nestle under her skin with annoyance. Turning her attention back to her flowers, she focused on these small treasures. Pots of small, red chillies, peppery, emerald basil, innocent white daisies, lopsided purple irises, and more unnamed flowers flourished in hues of deep blues, brilliant yellows, and hung from the balcony were baskets of little, crimson lipstick buds close to breaking. But Chiara's most beloved possession was her sunflower, which grew tall, proud and dusty yellow, always smiling at her, like an old friend.

Her breathing calmed, and she set the watering can to the side, inhaling all the mingled scents of Sunday lunches, which sailed from the open windows of homes, whilst cigarette smoke and car fumes rose with fighting spirit from the ground. Yet the sun only intensified these stale scents, merging it into something disgusting and dismal.

This small balcony was her haven, her sanctuary, her escapism. The only small part in this vast world where she did not feel lost or trapped. Ever since she had been a child, she would tend her pots of flowers and herbs with the greatest love, for she felt this was the only place she held any control over her uncontrollable life. A place where she was only a servant to herself, and no one else.

She remembered how she had learnt her hardest lesson when she overwatered all her plants, causing them to die. It made her realise the more you cared and loved someone or something, the more likely they would disappear or die, just like her mother. She kept herself isolated from the village, ashamed and embarrassed by her father and their poverty. She did not like her own company, but over the lonely years she had learnt to accept her lonely, isolated life. These plants had become her companions, better than people, for they listened to her opinions without overshadowing her ideas, yet these temperamental plants had also taught her some hard lessons. She had learnt to not depend on things, to not love too deeply, and to keep her heart at a distance to all things that could change. Chiara believed people were like these very flowers, unpredictable, unattached, uncaring. A pessimistic view for a girl her age.

The only exceptions of her heart were God and Domenico, for they had been the only constant and unchanging elements of her life. She could always depend on both to love her and support her through the days where depression seemed more natural than happiness, and she clung to both people as real and mystical as one another.

Chiara found her thoughts, so silent in the company of others, would suddenly come to life in this peaceful place. Her mind would erupt with questions, explosions of thoughts would upturn her neat brain with mess, and upheaved her disciplined ideas with wild wanderings and impulsive imaginings. In the presence of people, she would keep her mouth locked, afraid to expose the deepest part of herself to judgement, yet the pressure of these thoughts would grow with strength, bashing and smashing against the inside of her skull, like hundreds of prisoners wanting to escape. Without thought, she would quickly whisper her darkest secrets and fears to the plants, whose faces were invisible with judgement and bland with curiosity, bringing a clarity and calm to her mind, if only for a moment.

Originally, this place of sanctuary had belonged to her mother, but when she disappeared, Chiara had taken it upon herself to attend to these little plants, so that when her mother returned, she would not be disheartened by their deaths. Sadly, years went by, and Chiara had concluded her mother would not return, and she allowed the plants to die, just as she had done the memories of her mother. However, Chiara found a new focus for the plants. At the time, she had been learning at school how certain plants and herbs were remedies for specific pains and problems, and she grew pots of flowers and herbs, brewing them for her depressed father with the hope they would magically transform his position into what it was before her mother left. Yet this was another failed plan, for he shirked her kindness by burning and killing all those sweet remedies with the dark liquors of the bars, and with time he grew worse rather than better.

Through all these trials and failures, Chiara refused to use the flowers to care for others, who did not care for her, and in this decision, she had found a place where the outside world did not exist, a palace of inner peace. Without this place, Chiara believed she would have been unable to endure the pain and punishments of her life, for in the flowers and fruit, she found a happiness, which whipped through her life, like sugar added to egg whites, turning something disgusting into something delightful. If this place was to be taken from her, she knew her soul would starve and die, her heavy heart would drag her body into the ground, and her crazed mind would spasm and convulse, like a dog with rabies.

At a young age, Chiara had given up all hope in both her parents, and to her, they had both died and disappeared, leaving only the vague, fleeting smiling ghosts of their past. She still did not know the reason as to why her mother left. She had heard hushed rumours that her mother had run away with another man, yet she did not wish to believe this, for it tainted the dreamlike image of her mother. But after years of being saddled with her father's depression and dullness, she could not deny the reasons and rumours for her mother's disappearance, and Chiara only wished she had gone with her.

Her father, at first, had locked her in her bedroom, but as his intoxication grew stronger and her body grew out of her childhood guises, he began to lock her in the basement or out in the street, crying and screaming her mother's name, for he had believed her to be that woman. Chiara had painful memories of sleeping in the cold, dark unused basement, listening to the scuttle of mice and rats, or cuddling up on the doorstep, attempting to sleep, as the ghostly wind moaned around her. But the worst part was the next morning, for her father would have no recollection of his actions, and if she tried to remind him, he claimed her to be crazy, like her mother.

The greatest comfort had been Domenico, who would come out and sleep beside her, for his mother never allowed her in the house, for she believed Chiara was a witch, a child of the devil. She had many memories of Domenico carrying blankets and cushions outside, topped with biscuits and water. She remembered how they had snuggled close, holding onto each other's warmth as they whispered about futures, which at the time had seemed so far away, but now sadly were present. She remembered the warmth of his body beside hers, and strength of his arms around her, shielding her against the cruel world.

She did love Domenico, and always had, yet she knew her life could never be intermingled with his, for he had always dreamed of studying, progressing, making a change to the world, and she could not afford to even entertain these ideas as her own.

Chiara did not have many dreams, but one, and this she shoved forcibly into the back of her mind, locking it tightly away, for it was useless to dream when dreaming was full of futile impossibilities. Instead, she poured her energy and hope into Domenico's dreams, for she loved listening to him talk of plants and cells, fascinating phenomena, which it seemed only his eyes could see. There had been many days and nights that kept her heart afloat with love and happiness, days of walking through the woods above the town picking out flowers and foliage, nights sitting on the steps beside the newsagent testing Domenico on his knowledge, and days when dawn and dusk drew them together in Domenico's farmhouse, content in each other's silence.

Chiara's childhood had been bursting to the brim with poverty and pain, earning small pennies in random small obscure places; babysitting neighbours' children, massaging the old, rheumatized fat feet of elderly ladies, cleaning houses, sweeping the church and more. She did these small jobs unwillingly, affording to feed herself and her father with scraps of unsavoury food. She had never been taught how to cook, and even now her food was prepared for survival rather than to delight the taste buds. When she was only thirteen, she got a full-time job as a waitress at Parco della Stella, a long walk from school, but a much-needed position to keep their small house and her precious balcony. She left school at 14 and was burdened with more hours at the restaurant. When she received her first tips from the restaurant, all those hours had been worth it to see the light in her father's dead eyes when he saw the glittering notes in her small, girlish hands, soiled by hard work and responsibility. But she had never shown her tips ever again, for every last penny of her hard work had been spent in the bar, drinking her father's liver and soul to death. Chiara was not a revengeful person by nature, but on that night, she had locked her father out of the house, and the revenge had tasted sweet, delightfully sweet, especially when she could hear her father grunting and shouting, slamming his uncontrolled body against the door.

On this holy day of Sunday, her father slept loudly, snoring in the room above the balcony, the oven and stove hummed with her lunchtime dishes, for Vincenzo would arrive soon. Vincenzo did not care for her brain or thoughts, and so she wanted to solidify her skills as a housewife by proving that she could cook and clean, for it was the only way to hold onto him. But he would not arrive for a while, and so she finished watering the baskets of flowering herbs, which dripped the excess water into the empty, narrow street. Once this was done, Chiara sat cross-legged on the balcony, and began to diagonally snip the dead heads from the plants, her mind content, warmed by the thin slits of soothing sunlight.

Next door, she could hear the chaotic shouts and laughter of the Fango's house, spilling their joy and humour, like buckets of paint, colouring the dark empty streets with the united noise of a family. She could hear Bianca's high-pitched voice racing through the staircase as she teased Matteo, who responded with false violent threats. She could hear Signoro Fango muttering and grumbling as he watched the loud, blurry TV. She could hear the barking tones of Signora Fango from the top of the house instructing her husband to stop secretly smoking from the top balcony. She could hear the splashing of tap water, the clattering of soapy dishes being washed, and the quiet gossiping of Domenico and his sweet grandmother.

Chiara stopped snipping the heads, and curled her legs beneath her arms, resting her weary head upon her knees, listening longingly to the conversations and laughter that soiled her quiet with happiness. It felt almost disorientating, for her eyes followed the deadly silent streets, where not a soul spoke or moved, yet above her there was this percussion of voices and domestic sounds, which rebounded through her body, grieving her heart with her loneliness. She sometimes could not help envying Domenico for his crazy and chaotic family, for there was love that bound them together, and a silent understanding of strength, knowing they could defeat whatever troubles came their way. But who was part of her team? Who was her army to protect her from trouble? No one. She had to face all her trials and tests alone. But it was not even the protection that she craved, it was the desperate need to know that someone else was there, alive and breathing, listening and loving you, despite all your faults or fame. There was a hand to hold against the hate, and a kiss to dull the darkest days. There were memories linking and binding all of them together, like grapevines, one beating heart, nurturing their journeys wherever they may go.

But Chiara was isolated, and it felt as though she lived across the street in the eerily abandoned houses, alone and lost to the world, watching with a desperate envy the shared happiness of others.

Suddenly Chiara's lonely thoughts were awoken by the sound of shuffling, heavy slippered feet limping towards the Fango's balcony. The elderly Signora Fango, who everyone called Nonna, arrived, before flinging out an old raggedy dishcloth across the limp, dusty line. Nonna was the only grandmotherly figure she knew, and she loved how this woman accepted her as one of her own grandchildren, sharing biscuits and sweets, as if Chiara was one of the Fangos. She continued to associate Nonna's features with happy memories, from her soft furry face, like the skin of a peach to her invisible eyebrows, thickly layered eyelids, and gentle hazel eyes, like Nutella. Chiara recalled how she used to hug the round, soft belly of Nonna with a hunger for safety and love, how she had cried into her soft, scratchy black mourning dress for her mother, how those billowing, wrinkled fat arms had squeezed her so tight she thought her eyeballs would burst out of her skull. Chiara recalled untangling the gold chain of her glasses from the rusty gold chain of the cross, and putting them over her own eyes, dizzy and delighted by the fuzzy world Nonna saw. She loved the large, gentle softness of Nonna's hands, like the fluffy old paws of a cat, yet she had heard brutal tales of those hands. In the town, Nonna's hands were not notorious for their safety, but for their savage strength, which was rumoured capable of snapping all the bones in a man. But Chiara found this hard to believe.

"Chiara dear, I did not see you there! How are you?" inquired Nonna shaking the red-faced Chiara from her thoughts with embarrassment.

But Nonna had seen her and had been watching this child with a desolate, depressed heart, for this was not the girl she remembered from a few years ago. This girl was skinny, weakened by her weariness, like a mother wearied by her child, who ate her soul from deep inside, but what was eating at Chiara's soul? She knew all too well who it was that destroyed this sweet girl, and that was the posh prick from the north. Ever since he had come onto the scene, Chiara's healthy beauty had deteriorated, her dark hair was thin and raggedy, like a stray cat, her bones seemed to jut out, her eyes were red, swollen and bug-like, whilst her lips drooped permanently with self-pity.

"I, I am well, thank you, and you?" stammered Chiara, hurriedly jumping to her bare feet.

"Well, I am getting older, my back hurts more these days,"

moaned Nonna, placing a large, age-spotted hand at the base of her back, like a pregnant lady.

"I am sorry to hear that, but you certainly don't look like you are getting older," soothed Chiara honestly, as she uncreased a wrinkle from her pale blue dress, for Nonna had always looked this way.

Nonna giggled softly, her trembling, upturned lips crinkled her cheeks with lines and deepened the crow's feet around her wise, wasted hazel eyes.

Chiara smiled and brushed a hair from her lip.

"You are sweet, child, though I don't believe a word of it," chuckled Nonna, her fat, sagging neck, like a cushion, jiggled at the amusement of Chiara's words, as laughter erupted from a place deep within her heavily bosomed chest.

Chiara smiled fondly at this old, familiar sweaty face who still addressed her as child with an unpatronizing air, for Chiara believed Nonna saw anyone who was below the age of 40 as a child.

"Why are you laughing, Nonna? Who are you talking to? Is dinner nearly ready as my show starts at one and I'm not going to miss it because of your gossiping," growled Signora Fango from the balcony above, her voice rough like the warning grunts of a bear.

Chiara saw how Nonna's misty hazel eyes rolled backwards with an exaggerated dislike.

"Who are you talking to?" bellowed Signora Fango persistently, the deep voice boomed closer as she leaned her heaving body over the balcony.

"Myself," replied Nonna with a wink towards Chiara.

Chiara clapped her hands to her mouth, stifling the laughter beneath.

"Nonna, don't mock me, humour does not become a woman of your age. Really? What example are you setting? Not just for the children but the whole village. We have a name here, and if we want to keep our customers, it would be better if we didn't look mad."

"It would be better if you actually smiled at the customers rather than scowling," dismissed Nonna with a flap of her hand.

Chiara giggled apprehensively, for she knew the two women could quickly turn from dismissive anger to dangerous fury in a flash, and the results of the latter could be severe.

"What is all this noise? Can you not fucking sleep in this village anymore?" grumbled Chiara's father, his voice croaky, groggy and scratchy with the whisky he drowned his sorrow in.

"I'm sorry to disturb, but my mother-in-law is testing my peace of mind," responded Signora Fango sweetly, for she was not scared of many things, but Chiara's father frightened her, for she knew his aggressive nature knew no limit, and could be expelled upon anyone.

Nonna lifted her head in the direction of his voice and glared at the space where he sat, like he had sat every day, letting his daughter work her life to ruin to save his fucking, self-piteous arse. She hated Chiara's father, despised him more than any other soul in the world, for he had killed any future for his daughter with his selfish, careless actions. He was no father, barely even a man, and he had proved it over and over again. He did not care if Chiara lived or died. He did not care if she starved, slowly and painfully to death. He did not care if she set the whole kitchen and herself on fire whilst cooking a dinner she was too small to understand. Nonna wished he would do them all a favour and take his last breath, for he was useless.

Nonna suddenly stopped her furious thoughts when she saw the red, downcast face and the nervous knotted fingers of Chiara. Loudly Nonna huffed and rolled her eyes again, causing Chiara's embarrassed face to smile, as she attempted to swallow her giggles, like a disgusting medicine, which she only wished to expel from her mouth.

"Well, keep it down Signora Fango, my peace of mind is being tested by your fucking—"

Suddenly Chiara's father stopped speaking, and within the silence, she could hear her father sniffing the air, like a dog, before he coughed gruffly.

"I can smell burning," grumbled Chiara's father, more irritated.

"So can I," Signora Fango agreed, as she aggressively sniffed the air.

Nonna inhaled deeply, and snuck a look at her stove, but all was fine.

Chiara followed her movements, and suddenly recalled how she had left her meat in the oven on a high temperature.

Nonna saw the panicked expression in the young face of Chiara's, and her heart swelled with compassion for this child, captured and chained to this house, like a prisoner.

"Chiara do not worry child. Do you and your father want to have lunch with us? I have plenty of food," encouraged Nonna, her tone soft, barely above a whisper.

"No thank you, I would love to, but my fiancé is coming round very soon, I'm sorry I have to go," said Chiara worriedly, before she dashed into her home. Nonna heard the crack of an oven door, as Chiara attended to the burnt items with a fallen heart.

Nonna tutted her head, lamenting Chiara's lonely life, cursing her dreadful father and wishing beyond all wishes that she had never met that vile fiancé, who called himself by the name of Vincenzo.

Remaining on the balcony, Nonna selfishly took comfort in the sounds of her home and family, the scraping of chairs, the sizzles from opened coke bottles, and the gentle bubbling of wine being poured. Slowly the church bells cascaded their docile tunes across the town, ushering those, who were not already, to their dinner tables.

Tottering back to the kitchen, Nonna smiled gladly at the laid table, the white cloth, a shroud, pinned down by the silver cutlery, smeared water and wine glasses, which twinkled in the beaming sunlight, chipped flowery plates filled with fresh ravioli she had prepared. A family favourite, ricotta and spinach smothered by ladles of fresh tomato sauce, who could resist? All her memories of family were wrapped within the dishes she cooked, and the very smells of these dishes reclaimed a moment of sweet happiness. She could remember cold winter nights serving her children, and then grandchildren, bowls of cabbage broth cooked in garlic and oil. All their hands would dip the stale cornflour bread, shaped like a squashed sponge, called Pizza Fatdei, into the large serving dish, savouring every last speck of their meal. Nonna was devoted to her family, and she would cook all day sometimes, especially her bean casserole, which she prepared in a dish with tomatoes, pasta and pork skin. A winter family favourite!

Her crooked smile grew wider at the sight of her chattering grandchildren seated, a sight she had seen many times, yet she never tired of it. They were no longer children, but adults, who held dreams and desires which might whisk them away from her, and then this scene she loved so dearly would only become another memory. All she would have left of them are those old dishes, which with each taste would reclaim their vanished figures and conversations.

Nonna treasured this sight in the deepest hole that her departed husband had left, filling her soul with safe contentment and gratitude for the fresh faces of the future.

Gazing around the small old kitchen/dining/living room, her mind was pulled and pushed through the tides of the past and present. She had lived in this house since she had married her husband at 16, and it had barely altered, except for the new technology of domestic life, like the grumbling fridge and freezer, the little radio, and the TV, which seemed incapable of silence. The old, dark wooden cabinets of the kitchen were still the same, harbouring old and new pieces of kitchenware, but their colour had never faded, for the sunlight could never reach this part of the room. The walls were still the same pale yellow of her early married years, fading into a pastel cream of time. The small, signature paintings had hung upon those walls for so many years, she believed they were even submerged in the very walls, unable to unpick with even the hardiest tool. The faded chestnut sofas were "new" by 20 years, slouched and softened by the weight of many bodies, who had slept through the hot summers or cried beneath a blanket beside the dark, empty fireplace for comfort. The departed Signoro Fango's old leather brown armchair was still pressed against the back wall, as if he had never left it, and facing this was the small TV tainting the sweet Sunday lunch with news of bloody crimes and cruelty. She felt old, as she gazed around the room, for there were cobwebs and dust as thick as butter in corners and above cupboards, yet she could no longer reach these secret places like she used to.

Sat opposite and near the balcony doors was the old dining table, wobbly and creaking with age, and here, in this specific bit, was the place she called home, for most of her memories could be drawn from this very table. Maybe this is why she had always been so stubborn to change this piece of furniture. She could remember early days of sitting alone with only her husband's eyes for company, before each seat was filled with her own children, but all had moved away to new adventures, except one.

Her only child left sat there, devouring his second glass of red wine, staining the corners of his mouth with purple, and her heart crumbled. It always did when she saw Giorgio, her son, the father of these three children. Over the years, the only thing within this house which had changed significantly was Giorgio, who, after years of being mistreated and robbed by his tyrannical wife had withered and weakened, for she knew it was not only his body and face that had aged, but his eyes. They had once been dark, like black buttons, twinkling and gleaming with promises of the future, but now they were dark, frozen and frigid, like black ice, completely dead with hope. He no longer looked her in the eye, for she knew he was embarrassed by the change within himself.

Shuffling into her seat beside her granddaughter, Bianca, she kept her eye on Giorgio, who poured another glass of wine with a trembling hand, as the loud, thumping footsteps of Signora Fango marched slowly down the stairs with foreboding. Nonna felt her heart ache for both her son and Chiara, for they were both trapped in lives they did not deserve, punished by the pain that others caused. Her son had been severely punished by a foolish youthful mistake, banished to a marriage which held no love or warmth. All the love this home had nurtured was gone, stolen by the woman most hated by Nonna, the very thought that they shared the same name turned her stomach inside out.

And that dreadful woman entered with her dreadful greedy mouth, her dreadful fat, thieving hands, and her dreadful, sneering pin black eyes.

Everyone at the table immediately stopped talking, waiting patiently for that lady to heave her body past the narrow gap between the balcony and the table. She collapsed into the weary, cracking wooden chair, casting a large shadow across the table.

All eyes turned from the form of Signora Fango to the soft gentle face of Nonna as she spoke the words of grace.

"Amen," chorused a range of voices, some solemn, some sleepy, some smiling, but all dripping with saliva, as the tasty smells drifted from the plates of ravioli.

Signora Fango observed Nonna open her eyes and her hands, but there was no peace or purity in those age-foggy eyes. Signora Fango hated those eyes, for they had looked at her, since the day she had first met that woman, with superiority, suspicion, and detestable condescension. She had never been accepted by her children's grandmother, rebuked and rebuffed for taking her precious son. Those old, sniping eyes always glared at her with the eternal message of "you trapped him".

And yes, Signora Fango smiled to herself, she had trapped him, and so easily. But she would not be punished for Nonna's dithering, stupid son, who had fallen so easily into her trap. Would a farmer lift up a fox he had trapped by the tail and let it go because its mouth was full of blood and his eyes were close to death? No, he would not, and therefore why should she feel guilty?

With antagonism and animosity tensing the air, the Fango family began their holy Sunday lunch with relish.

First was of course the ravioli, which all devoured quickly and hungrily. The filling was squelching and full of sour ricotta and spinach, which knotted between the teeth of all. Matteo, as usual, was the first to finish, and whilst he waited, he licked his bowl clean, like a dog.

Quiet descended upon the room as they unpicked the ropey, green spinach from between their teeth.

The TV continued to the next programme; the false, artificial voice of a female presenter forced the family from their silence.

The plates were cleared and piled in the sink.

Signora Fango belched and rubbed a white crumpled napkin across her tomato-stained lips.

Signoro Fango opened another bottle of wine, his flushed face almost as purple as the wine he drank.

Matteo watched the TV, his slumped back turned away from his family.

Domenico and Bianca helped their *nonna* clear and wash the plates, casting irritated glares towards Matteo.

Nonna placed the next course upon the table with a thud, sweat slipping through her wrinkles, like a burst river, swamping every crevasse with that clinging, salty moisture.

They all turned their attention to the huge bowl of curling pasta, shaped by Nonna's well-trained fingers, swimming in a thick tomato sauce, chunks of minced spicy sausage meat giving off an aroma of chilli, adding further heat to the room.

The plates were filled, parmesan dusted upon the top, the steam from the dish melting it quickly into a white plastic sheen.

They ate, faces dripping with sweat, for the sun had crept and passed the balcony, dominating the table with its supernatural power, like an unwanted guest, whilst the spicy sausage tried to equal the heat of the sun from within them.

There was a music to this dining experience, sounds of scraping and clattering cutlery, gurgles and slurps of drinks, the creaking movement of Nonna's teeth as she thoughtfully chewed the pasta, the sound like a creaking fence in the wind.

Matteo had another helping.

Signora Fango mopped the sauce with a slice of old, stale bread, her teeth chomping quickly, like a rabbit.

Bianca could not eat anymore, her stomach felt strange and uneasy, a feeling abnormal to her.

Signoro Fango watched his daughter with concern, for she had not eaten any more than a couple of bites.

Domenico quickly gulped a large glass of cold water down, wiping his wet chin, before he helped himself to seconds.

Nonna chewed the pasta with her few teeth and thought of her own mother and grandmother.

Matteo had another helping.

Once everyone was finished, and the meandering discussions had been concluded, the pasta bowl was removed and replaced with a variety of meat; beef meatballs, chicken legs and more spicy sausages, all smothered again in the tomato sauce, topped with a little dry oregano. A large salad, picked from Domenico's land, stood alongside it, the pungent sharpness of the red wine vinegar clearing the nostrils and throats of all those around.

Matteo helped himself to a bit of everything, except the salad, for he believed lettuce was for rabbits not humans. He wished it had been a bowl of greasy chips.

Signora Fango placed a whole meatball in her large open mouth, as if it were a sweet, chewing with puffed cheeks, as greasy meat juices dribbled from the corners of her mouth.

Signoro Fango ripped chicken meat from the purple bone, before his broken, brittle teeth gnawed away at the chewy fat, until the bone was clean. When he was done, he chucked the polished bones on the plate with a clatter.

Bianca took a little salad, her face turning paler and paler as her stomach rocked uneasily, like an eerie rocking chair.

Domenico ladened Nonna's plate with a little mixture of meat and salad, explaining about the land and its progress.

Nonna watched her grandson's eager grey eyes patiently explain to her the science of the land, detailing things that she had never heard or seen before, but it was all done with a careful respect, so that she could grasp it without feeling like an idiot. Nonna did not have favourites, but she did admire Domenico, for his eyes and mind held an integrity born from his intelligence, and he did not abuse his clever nature to put others down. Her grandson did not snigger or sneer at those who suffered with stupidity, but respected them, for his strong faith in God helped him help others. He seemed to recognize, despite all his science, that there was a path and pain individually patterned for each person, like the individual landscapes of a country, and he did not condemn people for this. Her middle grandchild may not have been gifted with great beauty, like his brother, but this only added to his humble nature, for even in the ugliest things he found beauty. Unlike her eldest, who used his beauty to bully others, and his confidence to control those who were weak and shy.

The meal came to an end.

The heat had intensified, drying and sticking the remains of the sauce and food to the plates and cutlery.

Discussions were in full swing, except Bianca, who focused her attention on her ailing stomach.

Signoro Fango had started and finished his cigarette quickly, flinging it off the balcony, before stumbling drunkenly back into the room, trying to avoid touching Signora Fango's chair, as if it might electrocute him.

Signora Fango closed her eyes, smacking her lips together with tired satisfaction.

"Matteo did you try your brother's salad, it was so fresh, very good for a young footballer like you," encouraged his Nonna kindly.

"Gross, if you don't want me to look as flimsy as Domenico, I think I should stick to pasta and meat," retorted Matteo, leaning back in his chair with a wretched smile of comical antagonism.

"If you don't want to die of heart disease like me, you would eat something green," interjected Domenico, resting his head on his hands.

"Don't be rude to your brother, he is older than you, and knows more than you, you should listen to him," barked Signora Fango gruffly, her eyes still closed.

"Being older means shit," slurred Signoro Fango spitefully, as he poured himself another glass of wine.

"Don't be fucking rude, Signoro Fango, your opinions mean shit," shouted Signora Fango, her eyes still closed.

Signoro Fango rolled his eyes, and drank another glass of wine, dulling his fury for a moment.

"You are both clever in different ways, and should listen to each other," advised Nonna compassionately, though she was not convinced by her own mediation.

Domenico and Matteo glanced at one another, blatantly disagreeing over their *nonna*'s advice.

"Nonna, do you know how hard it is to have a social loser for a brother, it is degrading—"

"Do you know how hard it is for Domenico to have an arrogant prick for a brother," challenged Bianca, her lips pale and trembling, for this nuisance conversation was turning her stomach over and over, like burgers being flipped on a grill.

"Bianca, you are a girl, and therefore have a brain like a fish—"

"What?" growled Bianca, her eyes flashing at Matteo.

"Also, it's not arrogance, it's confidence," corrected Matteo casually, his smile wicked.

Domenico shook his head, smirking behind his hands.

"Whatever it is it's not a nice thing—"

"Well Bianca maybe you should ask your friends as they would disagree—"

113

"What?"

"Your girlfriends seem to really like my confidence—"

"Are you joking?"

"Yes, he is joking, Bianca," Domenico interjected with a sigh.

"Don't listen to him, ask them and find out for yourself."

Signoro Fango snapped his dull eyes from the television and glared at Matteo.

"Do not talk like this in front of your sister and grandmother," Signoro Fango scolded unenthusiastically.

"Signoro Fango, without Matteo, Bianca would be a social misfit with only Domenico," explained Signora Fango lazily, as she rested her hands upon her large spilling belly.

"Exactly, you should be thanking me Bianca," Matteo ridiculed spitefully.

"I think Bianca would have been able to be her own person and have her own friends without either of us," Domenico spoke quietly, yet with force.

Bianca glanced gratefully at her brother, and he smiled sympathetically at her.

Crash!

Signora Fango's eyes snapped open.

Signoro Fango spilt wine down his shirt.

Matteo sat up, and instantly switched the TV off.

Bianca whipped her head around to the opposite wall.

Nonna observed Domenico's gentle eyes sharpen and search the wall behind her.

No one spoke, but each listened carefully, even Signora Fango had forgotten her TV programme.

The exchanging voices from next door were hushed hissing sounds, like two cats about to attack.

The family's eyes slowly moved from right to left, as they followed the volumizing voices of the man and woman in combat.

"Why didn't you tell me?" shouted the deep, gruff voice of Vincenzo, his accent strange and powerful in his anger.

"Why do I need to tell you? You don't tell me where you go!" retorted Chiara calmly, her voice strained and high pitched.

"I don't sneak off to fields with strange women, do I, Chiara?"

"Neither do I."

"Well, why do I hear from some guy in the bar near the bus stop that you were seen going to the fields with that *terroni*," bellowed Vincenzo, rattling the thin walls that separated each scene.

Nonna watched Domenico's face deepen in colour at that statement, and he removed his glasses, rubbing his eyes aggressively with resentment.

"That guy is a friend who I have known for a long, long time," trembled the voice of Chiara, as if her nerves were strained to the point of breaking, like a pulled violin string.

"He is a creep; I don't want you by yourself with him—"

"I wasn't with him by myself, his sister and her boyfriend were there."

There was a pause, and the family leaned closer towards the wall with suspense.

"Oh yes, his sister, pretty thing, shame she has a weirdo for a brother, otherwise I would marry her," broke the deep, wry voice of Vincenzo.

There was a stunned silence suspended on both sides of the wall.

Bianca's face turned as white as paper, as if she was going to vomit, and her stomach was made more uncomfortable by this thought.

Nonna watched how Domenico's face deepened into a horrifying red, his eyes were like the points of a needle, sharp and piercing. His thin lips were cut across his serious face, so that you could not see the dimples that usually sat there.

Matteo smirked and shook his head.

Signoro Fango's fists curled around his wine glass with fury, as he shot Matteo a look which silenced him.

"Why would you say that?" sung the weak, whimpering voice of Chiara.

Nonna's eyes welled with tears, for she had a fragile, sentimental heart, and the voice of that poor girl only abused this feeling.

"Because it's true," shouted Vincenzo, his heavy steps thudding closer to the balcony.

"Well, why are you going to marry me?" inquired the tender and glass-like voice of Chiara.

"I don't know. Stop! Stop! Fucking stop! You little fucking bitch, I know what you are doing, stop diverting the real reason as to why I am at this shithole," yelled Vincenzo, his voice growing rougher with volume.

"I thought you came to have dinner," shouted Chiara, impatiently.

There was a slam, like fists upon a table, followed closely by the crashing sound of cutlery and plates smashing upon the floor.

"Well, where the fuck is my dinner?" roared Vincenzo, a sound of fists thumping hard against the table.

Smash!

A glass must have fallen.

"It is in the oven; we have been waiting an hour for you to join us."

Suddenly there was a loud bang, making the whole family jump, before another wave of smashing, breaking and crunching followed.

"He's pushed the table over," whispered Matteo eagerly.

The family glared at him.

There was a crunching of glass, as Vincenzo's heavy feet moved closer and closer to the Fangos' wall.

The family, except Domenico, leaned back, frightened Vincenzo would break down the wall.

Suddenly there was a high-pitched shriek, followed by the strangled pleads of "let go, let go, let go".

Domenico leapt from his chair, and ran over to the wall, pressing his ear hard against it.

"You will always wait for me, you little witch. When we are

married the fucking meal will be on the table understand?"

"Yes," gasped Chiara, as if the hands of Vincenzo were torn from her throat.

"Also, when we are married and until that day you will not see that creep, that *terroni*, from next door," threatened Vincenzo, his voice like the cruellest poison.

"You can't make me promise that, we have been friends for years," begged Chiara, her voice crackling and crumbling, defeated.

"Chiara that *terroni* is obsessed with you, he follows you around everywhere, like a fucking dog, it's as if he is waiting for you to see him – it's pathetic," Vincenzo stated scornfully.

"No, he doesn't, we are friends."

"Not anymore, do you agree?"

"No."

"No?"

"No!"

"If you don't agree, I will make you suffer. I will, I really, really will. Say you agree! I want you to fucking beg for my forgiveness," terrorized Vincenzo as vicious and vile as a wolf.

"No, you can't make me," shrieked Chiara.

There was a brief moment of tormenting silence.

Footsteps thundered through the room, there was another scraping bang, as they thought they heard a chair thrown across the floor. There was a ricocheting noise of smashing glasses, splitting the eardrums of all those around.

Chiara's terrifying screams interrupted the noise of breaking destruction.

Suddenly there was another crash, as the balcony doors were flung violently open, and then violently shut again.

The family gathered closer to their own balcony door, except Nonna and Domenico.

Nonna watched his frantic grey eyes listening to the cries of Chiara. He must have been standing in line with her, separated by only the thin stretch of the wall. His body shook, and his hands trembled quietly against the wall.

Nonna wiped away the tears, which were gathering and falling fast onto her cheeks, as she observed her grandson's eyes fill with helpless tears, whilst the agonizing pleas of Chiara cried: "Stop! Stop! Stop!"

Suddenly there was an eruption of feral dark amber light, which crept small and sinisterly through the door of the Fangos' balcony, growing bigger and brighter in the blood-curdling sun.

The heat also snuck and snaked through the door, warming Nonna's leg, yet her heart was pressed with a cold, cold fear. This heat was not comforting like the sun, but sinister and evil with its savage heat, like hell.

"No, no, no," they could hear Chiara crying, screaming, slamming her body against the locked doors.

There was the slam of a door, and then another, and then another, before there was the loud revving of an engine, zooming away from the place of his crime.

An eerie silence followed this noise. It sounded chaotic, unlike any other silence. They could hear the tap rumbling and splashes of water being flung across the balcony, before it fell heavily on the pavement. They could hear the fast pattering of footsteps growing quiet then loud, quiet then loud, as Chiara ran in and out of her house.

Eventually the orange glow and the heat faded from the Fangos' balcony, as if nothing had happened. But it had, and Chiara's heartbreaking sobs only reminded them further of the darkness this future marriage held.

The church bells solemnly rang out, like a funeral, but despite this, they could all still hear the sobs from Chiara.

Nonna brushed the tears from her eyes and gazed around the room, but she could not find Domenico, and then she heard the purring engine of the three-wheeler.

*

The sunset was upon the town of Castelmauro, which was awakening after the heavy Sunday lunch siesta. The glowing fireball red sun shifted and dissipated colours of coral pink, tangerine orange and indigo purples across the hazy blue sky. The small insipid clouds that drifted idly through the sky were lit up with glowing baby pink lights, tinted occasionally with a flash of the ferocious red sun.

But Chiara saw none of this. All she saw were the black fried fragments of her treasured flowers set to die beneath the flaming wrath of Vincenzo. All she saw was his face, black from the shadows of the fire, zooming in and out through the slats of the balcony doors, like the face of Satan.

She had not moved since the afternoon.

The blood on her knees had clotted, the smears of snot and tears had dried and webbed her sticky lashes together, tightening the skin on her cheeks and making the liner of her lips dry and crusty with past sorrow. The balcony was now bone dry and the wet mass of dead flowers was now dehydrated and damned. It seemed as though time held no care for the pains of the present, which were already becoming the past.

The place, where she had remained, was already dark and possessed by the shadows of the night, a small, cooling breeze sneezed through the streets, blowing and drifting her once nice dress with it.

Chiara shivered, and she tightened her arms around her legs, collecting all her heat into one place.

The kitchen was still in a violent mess of smashed glass and broken furniture, as if it was her very heart.

Her father had disappeared from the house without a word of comfort or sympathy.

She remembered after Vincenzo had left, she could hear the whisperings of the Fangos' house, yet not one of them had come round to see if she was alright. They had left her alone with her sorrow and pain.

She remembered after Vincenzo had left how she had heard the loud purring engine of the three-wheeler disappear.

Domenico had disappeared. Her dearest friend in the whole world had even left her to suffer in silence.

Alone.

A word so familiar to her, it seemed to have multiplied and mutilated its meaning and forms so many times. It seemed loneliness held no end to its wicked disguises.

An elderly lady, who knew of her engagement, had advised her, "to always be an obedient and dutiful wife… give your husband what he needs and don't argue". But Chiara could not, nor would not, accept this fate. She was not arrogant or self-righteous, but she knew her worth was more than a single man's instruction.

She hated men, all of them, even Domenico. But mostly, she hated Vincenzo. When she first met him, he made her feel special and lucky in love, so when he asked her to marry him, she could not resist the temptation of being loved by this powerful and wealthy man. But Vincenzo was like a shark, his skin and manner were smooth and easy to touch, yet if you brushed him up the wrong way, his skin became harsh and abrasive, cutting your skin into fragments. She was now starting to learn the truth about power and wealth, and the forfeits which were made when taking a man of this kind. With power came control, and with money came blackmail, what could Chiara do?

Men, all the men in her life had set her in a trap she could not escape, like the grapevines in the valley. Her father had created her, and Domenico, like the soil, had held her hostage, imprisoned, dependent on his love. But Vincenzo was by far the worst, for he stole her dreams, smashing them beneath his feet, like the grapes, before morphing the mess he had made into whatever he desired. Yet still he would not be satisfied until he had completely engulfed every inch of her old, unrecognizable self, dead, a shadow within his new perfect production.

There was no way to escape this life these men had caged her in, for her father's poverty had made her accept a proposal she did not want, but why had she done this? Was it to prove something to everyone? Was it to take revenge on the schoolgirls who had made fun of her? Was it to prove something to herself?

However, the worst man was Domenico, her dearest and bestest friend was her greatest enemy, for if he did what she was sure his heart wanted, she could be saved, but he was silent and self-absorbed in his studies.

Once again, the tears began to rise within her eyes, and her weak chest heaved painfully, for it felt as though the barricades of her life were crushing her to death.

Each man in her life seemed to be eating away at her soul and body, like fruit flies, destroying even the most private places of her life, like this very balcony, and nothing could salvage their damage. She did not care for apologies or cuddles or presents, she just wanted men to leave her alone to live her life as privately or exclusively as she should choose.

"Chiara," whispered a quiet, familiar voice.

Turning her head to the Fangos' balcony, she wiped her damp eyes with the back of her hand, but instantly winced as the salty tears reopened the bloody cuts.

"Go away Domenico, I don't want to talk to you," Chiara tiredly replied, as she heaved her languid body to her worn feet.

Domenico observed Chiara, and he felt a surprising emotion take over the instant shock and sadness of her appearance, it was anger. No, not anger, but a mad fury. How could she let that man degrade her to this? How could she let that man use his power to cut her up? How could she buy into the money he flaunted and covered his fucking mistakes with? How could she love a man like this?

He wanted to go to her. He would have leapt this balcony only to hold her in his arms and whisper away the worries that carved her face into a picture of misery. He wanted to lick clean all the cuts of glass upon her limbs and stitch all those wounds together, so that nothing could harm her again. He wanted to let his hands run through her hair, soothing away all the tangles of her life.

Yet, equally, he did not want to do any of these things. Sometimes, he wanted to bash her head against a wall, drown her body in ice cold water, or electrocute her head, anything to make her wake up from this deluded and dangerous Cinderella fantasy. He sometimes did not want to hear her whining, for as much as Vincenzo was evil, she allowed him to be evil. She allowed herself to lie down beneath his feet, obediently following any orders he gave. Beg, and she would beg. Stand, and she would stand. Fuck, and she would fuck. She needed to realise that her weakness was not attractive, but pathetic and painful to only herself. He would have fought Vincenzo, but what was the point, for the fight was not with Vincenzo. The fight was a battle raging within Chiara, and she was the only one who could decide her victory or defeat.

"Wait, don't go, I have something for you, go to the edge of the balcony closest to me, and then close your eyes and hold out your hands," instructed Domenico eagerly, as he removed his glasses, hiding the secrets within his eyes, and hers.

"No, I just want—"

"I know, but I promise it will take less than a minute, please," Domenico pleaded, holding and shaking his hands together in fervent prayer.

Chiara sighed and obeyed his instructions.

With her eyes closed, she waited for something to touch her hands. She could hear a crinkling sound, like a plastic bag, rattling towards her, but she did not care what stupid game Domenico was playing, she just wanted him to leave.

Domenico checked that her eyes were tightly shut, before he precariously leaned over the balcony and handed her the bag with a small smile of excitement.

She felt the strong hot tips of Domenico's fingers touch hers, as he placed the bag in her hands.

"Open your eyes!"

Chiara did and gasped.

Every herb and flower was bundled in the bag, like they had all been reincarnated back into the world. At first shock stilled her emotions, but then they came with an immense force of bewildered love. Why would he do this? Why was he so patient with her? Why did he...

...care, for Chiara was all he ever wanted. Even though she was making a huge mistake, he cared for her too much to stay away from her. He wished he didn't care, it would make things easier for him, yet it was impossible. Caring for her was his addiction, loving her was his hangover, and the hours between were empty without her. He intensely watched her face as she...

...devoured the intense aroma of the dirty soil, and the sweet fragrance of the wildflowers, she found herself growing angry, for he made it so hard for her to stop loving him. But perhaps it was because she could not stop, whether he was near or far, perhaps she would always love him.

"Thank you, Domenico, when did you get all of these?" Chiara questioned, as she delicately stroked each leaf and petal with love.

"I got them this afternoon, I went to the woods for the flowers, and to my land for—"

"This must have taken so long," Chiara softly interrupted.

"No, it's hardly equal repayment for what you said," justified Domenico sheepishly, stepping from left to right with nerves as he recalled the argument.

Chiara's face grew hot with the remembrance of her words.

"I meant it we are friends and that will not change, I need you in my life, annoyingly," giggled Chiara, the smile odd and tight on her waxy face.

"I know but I don't want to make things worse for you," argued Domenico, but he already knew that whether he was there or not, this relationship would still be poisonous for her.

Chiara could see that he meant it, for his face had lost its dimples and his mouth and jaw were firmly set.

"I know, but I am happier knowing you are in my life than not, sounds silly," Chiara replied lightly, yet her heart felt heavier.

Domenico could see that she meant it, for her hurt face shifted into a small smile, yet he wished he could see her eyes, which would confirm her words.

There was a still and expectant silence as they both looked upon the abandoned houses in the opposite street.

"I know exactly what you mean and it isn't silly," spoke Domenico gravely.

Chiara turned her gaze slowly towards him, and saw that his eyes were fixed on her own like magnets, and she could not look away...

...for she held him spellbound in those bright blue eyes, reflecting all the happiness they had shared, and the future...

...she wished they could have together. Chiara regretted all the times they had lost and wished for them back, but mostly she wanted to know they would never lose any more...

...time together was numbered, Domenico knew this, and all he wanted to do was change this fate they were trapped in.

Suddenly the street lights below flashed a bright white catching their attention and blurring the stars that were beginning to form above. The light was exposing, making each face revolting to one another.

Glancing back at the flowers, she smiled, until the sinister twinkling of her engagement ring provoked her eyes from seeing anything, except for those clever captivating crystals.

The tears began to form, and her throat tightened with fear. This was the rest of her life. A life dominated by Vincenzo. A life where Domenico would not exist. The same loneliness, but far worse. She wanted to throw her ring from the top balcony and into the chimney pots opposite, like they had done with pegs as kids, but how could she?

The church bells were soft, almost muffled by the heat.

"It will all be fine," comforted Domenico.

Chiara nodded, but within her heart she was repulsed, deflated and angered by these unfeeling, unknowing words, for how did he know?

Did he even understand?

Did he even care anymore?

SIX

Signorina Morderna sat upon the old stone wall opposite the church, and allowed the sun to touch her body, just as she allowed men to do so. The week had passed quickly and with little changes. The ending of August was rapidly upon them, and the heat was gathering and heaving its burden upon the town, and Signorina Morderna could feel it.

Gazing up at the sky, the clouds seemed too fearful to be close, and some hung in the air motionless, like old, white rags, the sun's violent heat shrivelled those fluffy clouds to almost nothing. The sky was a virgin blue stretching for miles and miles towards the Adriatic Sea, so that when she looked out from her balcony this morning, she found it hard to decipher which was which. She turned her eyes towards the dark, crowded mountains, which stood relieved, for the coolness of their height still allowed trees and flowers to grow, but the valley was sore and dry, mouth open and cracked, begging for water, pleading for rain. Luckily, one thing that farmers, including Signoro Fango's son, could be thankful for was that the nights were cooler, and left the dew of their presence upon the deadening grassland and surviving crops. But only the farmers knew of this midnight magic, as by the time she awoke, the dew had vanished, invisible, like fairies in the night.

It was Sunday, and the town was in an eerie silence, for most citizens were to be found contrite in their prayers. The only building inhabited by the eager sinners of the town was the small desolate church, as they searched for forgiveness to secure them a place in heaven. But Signorina Morderna did not trouble her mind with thoughts of heaven and hell, for she hated religion and the whole social structure built around it. How could any women enter that church and listen to that filthy male priest preaching the filthy male stories about a filthy man, who sacrificed himself for humanity. What lies! What shit! A man who sacrificed himself for the benefits of others was as fanciful as Prince Charming. Men on earth were selfish, greedy and grabbing, taking what they believed belonged to them without any regard for the people they hurt. Men were animals, without morals or magic or mercy.

Why would she fill her ears with these stories? Religion was a home built by men; booby-trapped with ways to make women frightened if they did not obey them. Men had built a cage, using flowery metaphors and heart-warming stories to punish women, to torment women, to isolate women, to cover men's cruelty. They used it as a weapon to blind and deafen women, so that they could cover their tracks of sick and twisted desires with the words of God.

God! Ha! What a joke he was. He snooped on the secret lives of his people and preached to them ways in which they could improve. It was taught that God accepted all his children, but to Signorina Morderna, he only wanted to change them. He was no better than Giacomo Ficcanaso. Also, why should a woman listen to God's word? How could God understand what it was to be a woman? Did he know the pains of period cramps? Did he know the tearing destruction of birthing another one of his precious children? Did he know the tropical flushes of the menopause? Did he know the ways his sons hurt women? Did he know the violent ways his sons assaulted women's bodies, using their fingers to grind, grip and grab? Did he not see how women could not walk home late at night without worrying about his perverted sons? How could this man possibly sympathise with women? How could he possibly advise them? And why would these women trust him, for unless he got down from his pedestal and walked as an ordinary woman amongst ordinary women, how could he know the pain and pleasure they felt in this short life?

Signorina Morderna turned her irritated thoughts towards the church, a poignant artefact of this town, and another reminder to the elderly of how life was changing, morphing and becoming something new which they no longer felt they belonged to. Signorina Morderna was thankful for this change, yet she could still remember as a child how the houses closest to the church had been bursting with families, who guarded and kept that place clean. But now, whose hands had it fallen into? No one lived in these homes, except the fat black rats scaring meek mice from these lonely, lost houses, pigeons snuggled in the windowsills, and spiders replaced the curtains with laced webs of their own making. Scrawny, scraggly cats stalked the area with blood in their eyes and teeth snared, for they could smell the grease of the rats' slimy bodies. Hunger can make a skittish cat patient, very patient and sneaky, waiting in the shadows for the scuttling creatures to appear.

The fiery heat of the sun intensified the deathly stench of those houses further, swamping the humid space outside the church with filthy flies. They buzzed and buzzed through the knotted tangles of her hair, hissing and whispering words into her ears, like the gossiping ladies of the town.

Signorina Morderna moved away from the wall, swatting the swarm of flies from her face as she crept quickly up the stairway, cut, fitted and bent into the corners of where the church stood. She sheltered in the shade of the simple, cedar brown building of the narrow bell tower. A small clock sat at the top of the church, whilst the narrow cross balanced precariously on the roof instructing the villagers of morality and mortality. The bells were silent and still at this hour of the day, for the villagers were already inside worshipping, and those, like herself, who weren't, were not worth the effort of the bell ringers. Below the tower stood a narrow, long archway, portraying an ugly view of a white house behind it, whilst cable wires were zigzagged across the street, like laser beams, protecting the property, but damaging its picturesque humble beauty with the chaos of modernity. On the left side attached to the bell tower was a small squat building, built with a mismatch of white and brown stones, large and small, cemented together for religion, for this is what religion could be, a place for all those different and individualized by society to pray together. But how ideal a world of dreams is. This simple building held two heavy, dark oak doors, shut and unwelcoming at this hour, a pane of stained glass stood between the two doors, dark and filled with shadowy figures, unidentifiable from the outside eyes of visitors.

Sunday service was in full swing, and the voices of men, women and children sang loud and far filling the deserted quiet streets and her tuneless ears with harmonious noise. The soulful, sleepy voices of these religious students rattled the weak stones of the houses and scared the flustering pigeons from the rooftops. The sun thickened these poignant notes and words of God's love, and the organ's untuneful, minor chords were held for longer in that eerie, hot silent day.

Signorina Morderna could not stand this false noise any longer, and with an irritated turn of her heeled sandals, she marched away from this place of wasted worship.

Within the church, the song had ceased, and the congregation in that humble, cold church were seated, awaiting the words of the priest.

Inside this church, it looked exactly like it would have done hundreds of years ago. The light sketching and colours of the stained glass were reflected with the shimmering sun, leaving a wavy, ocean-like carpet of colours upon the floor. The walls were a cold, cream-coloured stone, and the only colour was one tiny, painted square, faded and rough, depicting an old religious story. Yet, it was hard to decipher this story, for time had diminished its power and importance. Wooden beams stretched high and wide, supporting the stem of the church, like the wood used to support a tomato plant. A shy, rickety, wooden organ sat cramped in a corner, aged and worn with religious fingers and feet, whilst broken statues of saints and angels were an unsettling sight for the eyes. They emerged and flew from the walls and pillars, cemented and frozen in the stone, like a punishment. Rows upon rows of dark wooden benches stood to attention facing the creaking, wooden pulpit, the steps faded with the many generations of footsteps trod upon it, and here stood the priest, bible splayed across the intricately decorated, wooden stand. The weak, ill-looking priest stood with pride, clearing his gungy throat, like he did every time before giving a sermon. The villagers shuffled uncomfortably in their seats, relieved for the coolness of the church, yet they were already cold with the guilt and sin that this holy place broke them with. The weak wooden crucifix made even the most steadfast and unashamed catholic criticize their way of life and love.

Many averted their gaze away from the confessionary; a small, dark cabinet cramped with sin and self-destruction with only a small black and barred window, like a prison, to remind them of the outside world. It was a place of powerful and punishing revelations. It was a place where faithful blackmails and upturned beliefs made those who were bad, good, just so they were saved from an eternity of burning, burning, burning.

One young congregation member was being reminded of her sin, and that pale, youthful face would every so often glow red with the memories of her wickedness. Bianca could not hear the voice of the priest, for he was far away, talking of words and wisdom that held no place in her heart. The crucifixion of Jesus did not install fear or fame in her soul, for her eyes were gazing at something far greater in its importance.

The statue of the Virgin Mary was Bianca's formidable fixation. The Madonna swaddled in garments of blue and white held close a baby Jesus, the pair a picture of divine innocence. An innocence which did not exist in the real world of men and women.

Bianca felt her stomach thump with fright and sadness, making the sickness that had awoken her at strange hours of the morning more real than it had been. Her heart fluttered wildly, and her womb felt heavy with its burdensome secret and sin. Bianca believed that love was something of luck and chance, something that was unpredictable and improvised, something that could leave as quickly as it came. It was not inhibited by time or religion, it was free, moving and mocking as it pleased. Therefore, wouldn't any sane person take the first chance to dabble in the desirous art of love? But why must this love be sinful? Why should it be sinful to express love in the most natural way? Why was it sinful to receive this love? Bianca questioned sadly.

She was young, so young, yet she could be condemned to a life of eternal hell for wanting to love. It was impossible to understand. Why did a union of marriage prove that you loved one another? Most people, like her parents, were married, but they were certainly not in love. For the first time in Bianca's young life a cruel realization came to her, she loved Alessandro, and she did not need the blessing of a fucking priest to confirm this, and if she had lived anywhere else, she would never dream of marrying. But here in this village, she had to be signed off by God to do all the things of love with Alessandro, like a contract of work. She would not feel condemned by God if she lived somewhere else, but here in this town, God walked and talked among the citizens, and religious morality became the job of social propriety. Love could not exist in any other way than marriage, but Bianca knew in her gut that this could not be the only way.

At first Bianca had scrutinized the stone cut eyes of Mary with an imploring gaze, damp clasped palms praying for guidance. But as she inspected Mary further, her eyes shifted into spiteful mockery and condescending cruelty. Mary was meant to be the purest figure of an ideal woman, not only in religion, but also society. Yet this was all wrong, Bianca thought. Jesus was not born from a place of love, but cold, lonely isolation, and surely this was more wrong. Poor Mary, she represented everything a woman should not have in life. Why would any woman want to be her? A woman cut deep with the wounds of loneliness, too divine to understand love and too respected to be shown the acts of love. Bianca hated and pitied Mary in that moment, for women surely should not be suffocated by their sexual needs. Bianca believed that if a woman was in love she should sneak away to the darkest corners, touching, holding, pushing, pulling, sweating, throbbing, breathless, doing all things women were instructed not to do.

Bianca smiled weakly as she felt that "new" familiar surge of sickness draw her mind and body cuttingly back to reality. She inspected the statue of Mary, and a new thought came comfortingly and worryingly to her. She examined Mary's divine face, which gazed down at her baby with a maternal gentleness. Despite Mary never feeling the truth of a man's love, maybe the love of her child was enough for Mary to feel content and loved. But if the worst was the worst, could Bianca feel this same happiness?

Without her knowledge, Alessandro had been watching Bianca with keen worried eyes, for it had been the first time he had seen her since the day at the farm. he had seen her in fleeting glances. Her face glowed with a pale radiance, her lips trembled, and her eyes nervously flickered. What was going on with her? She had kept her distance from him all week. It had started with her timidly dodging the usual places he walked, but now it seemed she was shutting him out of her life completely. But why?

Alessandro's chest heaved with a depressive sigh, for he loved Bianca more than anything else in the world. He loved how safe he felt in her arms. He loved the security of those small, silky neat fingers. He loved the words which burst from her lips like popping candy. He loved the way her body cemented against his own. He loved the way her dark hair entangled him in her life. He loved her calm, bright eyes, which looked up at him with this fiery, tempting independence. Day and night, sneaky fears would creep upon him, especially this week for his soul had been possessed by a maddening jealousy. What if she had found someone else? A better lover? Alessandro's eyes grew heavy, and his fingers began to nervously tap against the cover of his bible. What could he have done? Did he do something wrong, or had she stopped loving him? Why was there a deep-set distance between them? Who was this new lover? He would slit his throat. He would cut his hands off if this new lover so much as touched Bianca. He would staple his lips together if this new lover even whispered the words of love to her. Not even this divine place could rid him of these violent thoughts, for the only thing he truly knew was that he loved her, and he was not ready to lose her to someone else.

Suddenly, as if Bianca had heard his thoughts, she glanced behind her and met his eyes. Alessandro's heart stopped for a split second as they held one another's gaze. Her eyes were dark, throbbing with a new life he did not understand, whilst her flushed cheeks only added to her beauty.

Bianca gifted his lonely, violent heart with the smallest, sweetest and safest smile, before she turned her face back towards the babbling goat-like priest.

Alessandro's chest heaved, bursting the butterflies from his heart and extinguishing its angry thoughts. He looked down at his hands, a content smile creeping across his lips, and for now, this was enough, if she needed time or space, he would give it to her willingly.

Though this display of love brought huge relief to those two lovers, another lonely soul noticed this act of love with a bitterness and coldness, which was more appropriate for a divorced middle-aged woman.

Chiara wanted their love. A love so full it would burst and break every border and boundary with ease.

Chiara believed that love was a predisposed fate that sought out the weaknesses in a person's mind and using this weakness, love manipulated your mind into believing you love someone when you actually don't. Her weakness was her poverty, and this is where love found the wealthy Vincenzo. Her weakness was like the weeds growing between the grapevines, and Vincenzo was the weed killer, *La Truchiniel*. But the weeds did not die, they only grew back stronger, and more spray was needed, but if the merest speck of spray touched the grapes it would turn them black with death. It seemed this love was more damaging than the weeds, but the weakness was stronger, unable to die, even with the promises of prosperity.

Gazing down at her engagement ring, her thoughts heard the soft, low tones of Domenico, "it will be fine". She tried to find comfort in them, but they only twisted her thoughts with repulsion. How could he say that? Domenico had no idea of her suffering heart, which seemed unable to stop loving him. Why would he never say what he wanted? Domenico's mind was like the soil, boring and basic to look at, yet deep down it was teeming with life and ideas, which no one could see or understand, but she desperately wanted to pick apart his thoughts, for this was the only way to know the true Domenico. All he talked of was plants, science, and the farm, never his own heart, which seemed locked and silent, like a captive, unable to speak or escape. But maybe this is because he did not love her as she loved him. She must freeze these thoughts, for she was engaged, and Domenico would be gone soon, and maybe then she could begin to love and dedicate all her love to her new husband, Vincenzo. Chiara tried to think of him and all his goodness, and perhaps he was right not to let her see Domenico. Despite how stupid Vincenzo was, he seemed to know her heart better than herself. Sometimes she thought it was a good thing that Vincenzo was so protective, for it showed he cared, loved and respected her a lot, far more than Domenico.

Chiara was reminded of the soon approaching celebrations of the Madonna della Salute on the 7th of September, where they dragged the 300-year-old statue of Mary from the cemetery, parading her through the streets, a procession of music and men behind her. People would stand on the sides throwing money and gold at her with the superstitious belief that forgiveness and freedom would be granted. Chiara felt like she was this very statue, for Vincenzo threw money, gold and clothes at her, blinding her judgment and his violence with his wealth, prostituting herself for the protection of his sins.

Gazing up at Vincenzo, who sat beside her, she saw that his attention was elsewhere, what was he so fixated on? queried Chiara. She peered at the slim face and proud shoulders of Vincenzo, and then she saw it.

Her.

Bianca.

Chiara's heart fractured and fell apart in small chunks, and her insecurities strangled her throat for breath and caused her bottom lip to quiver nervously. Folding her leg over the other, Chiara smoothed her shaking hands down her neat, lilac Sunday dress, as she tried to hide the tears which gathered quickly in her young bright blue eyes. Her dark lashes fluttered madly to contain them, and she wished her hair was not pinned back tightly in a bun, so that she could hide her shameful face and stupid tears from the eyes of others. Why was he staring at Bianca? Why did he love blatantly tormenting her? Why did he want Chiara to suffer? She thought when he had admitted those feelings last Sunday it had been done to only antagonize her, but now it seemed that those feelings had come from a true place.

Once Chiara had gathered control, and her tears only shook in her eyes, like glasses filled with water, she turned her attention back to the priest, and listened earnestly to his words trying to rid what she had seen and find comfort in the familiarity of those holy words.

"It will be fine."

"It will be fine."

"It will be fine."

Domenico's words were torment, tragic and taunting in their easiness, but they chanted through her head, like a spell. Casting her eyes to that man, his head was bored and beautiful in its ignorance of love's pitfalls and peaks, for he most likely saw love as he saw his plants, a methodical order of growth and death, and nothing more.

Another man who was ignorant to this woman's grieving heart was Vincenzo.

He sat up tall and straight with pride, for Vincenzo believed himself to be of a higher kind compared to these southern Italians, poor and puny in their significance and secrets. Gazing around the congregation of ragged Italians, he brushed a smooth hand through his luscious, conditioned blond hair, like gold, and inspected his clothes, neatened with the stitches of designers, Gucci, Prada and more of Milan's greatest artists. His religious beliefs were flexible, modern and deconstructed like the city of his birth. His thoughts travelled back to that cosmopolitan town where everyone was fashioned as if it was their last chance to impress, suits and ties a regular sighting, beautiful dresses clinging to curvaceous women, as if they were designed for each unique body without a pain for the material's price. Even the building had been fashioned with the grandest designs, tall and overpowering, beautiful to behold, and captivating to capture through the lenses of a camera, crisp and clean were their finishes. Milan had been his city, but a city many others returned to and visited religiously, like a pilgrimage of romance, fashion and modernity. His city had moved away from the medieval ways of Castelmauro and was in competition with cities like Paris, London and New York. His city had been dazzling and dizzying, whilst this place was dark and depressive. His city lived with extravagance and exuberance, whilst this town lived to survive. His city never slept, but this place never woke, dead in its time warp. His city had wealth and power, and this town was penniless and weak. His city was busy and modern, but in this place, they clung to the past and the traditions which came with it.

How had he ended up in this place?

Him, the great Vincenzo, hailing from the most luxurious city in Italy.

The slight touch of Chiara's arm against his own reminded him, and he pulled away from her, repulsed. He remembered how he had reluctantly come down for a wedding of his cousin, who married a girl from this dismal region. He had not intended to stay for more than a night, but the liquor had been good and strong, and there he had met with a muddled mind his fiancée, Chiara. How could he have fallen for a waitress? But he had, it was one of his vices, falling in love, for it was always happened quickly, instantly, but never lasting. He now was convinced that Chiara had bewitched him with those stunning blue eyes of hers, for he had followed them religiously, like a surfer to the sea, like the citizens of Castelmauro to the blue statue of Mary. He had loved the sound of her voice, swollen and heavily accented with the southern sun, intoxicating him with her spellbinding words. He remembered how he had doted on her with a disturbing dreaminess, walking with her for hours through the woods that hovered above Castelmauro, far from her past and present. He remembered the taste of her intoxicating lips, like the sweetest grapes, and how her eyes had worshipped him, he could not resist this. Vincenzo might have been arrogant and wealthy, but he did not have many friends or lovers, for his tongue could be cruel with compliments and crueller with criticism.

Under the magic of her love, Vincenzo had asked Chiara to marry him, and she had agreed, and he was finally convinced that his unloved heart could be happy with her.

But then his idealized vision had faded as quickly as it had come when he met the disjointed characters of Chiara's life, and the fractured ruins of her home. He had been fooled into following the wrong Mary, for the Mary he had worshipped was full of dirty secrets and sins. He had then understood that Chiara was not the woman he had fallen in love with, and the lips he loved were now bitter, like the seeds within the grapes. But it was too late to retract the promise, for in marrying Chiara, he was marrying the town, who had quickly learnt to love and worship him.

Except one.

Domenico, that creeping, nerdy friend of Chiara's, who spent his days studying plants and insects as if they were a new-found marvel. He hated him for the power he held over Chiara, managing to see her in a light no one else understood. He hated him for the memories he shared with her, and all the days and nights that had come before him. But more importantly, he hated him for the connections he had with someone else, a man, who had despicably realised what he was and what he wanted.

Matteo.

Domenico's brother had been introduced to him early on in his time at Castelmauro, and he had been an acrobat of flirt and charm. The days he had not spent with Chiara were more frequently spent with Matteo, zooming in his beat-up red car to the coast, talking about all things new and old. They had swum in the sea, raced across the beach, wrestling each other, before tumbling to the sand, laughing and laying their tangled limbs around each other. Nothing had ever been said of that love in those moments, for neither could comprehend it, but both had felt the pulsing friction of desire, as they slowly, reluctantly moved away from one another.

It was absurd.

It was weird.

It was shameful.

But nevertheless, it was there.

One night, they had drunkenly staggered from the bar, bashing and brushing against one another, the night and drink making inhibitions free and sexual longings blatant.

They had snuck into a narrow alley, climbing a few steps to ensure they were hidden from all eyes. Without thought or question or worry, Matteo had pressed Vincenzo against the cold, damp wall of a deserted house, abandoning the longest, sweetest kiss upon his lips, and Vincenzo did not fight it. He played the game of secrets, sneaking his tongue into Matteo's mouth, and savouring the taste of everything he had ever wanted and would need.

But he could not have this, neither could Matteo.

They had talked days later about how this love was a match made to die, for both their parents were bound by the unforgiving and unjustifiable laws of God. If either set found out it would be the death and undoing of both of them, but a secret love could still exist in the sun's shadows and darkest nights. What was the harm?

Vincenzo's philosophy of love was a lot like his attitude to life. He was a material man, and he had always been given everything he could ever wish for, and if he was not, he found every way possible to obtain it. Forbidden and obsession were the same word to Vincenzo, for if he was refused something, he became maddeningly obsessed with proving he could have it and anything that came with it.

Vincenzo would marry his obedient wife, lavish her eyes with luxury, make her blind to any other love that existed outside of their marriage, and Matteo would marry a simple girl in the same way. Women meant nothing to Vincenzo. They were objects, like mirrors, used to deflect and reflect what men wanted them to see and hide what men did not want them to see.

As Vincenzo gazed at the head of Matteo, Bianca looked around and met his eyes, she meekly smiled and he quickly smiled, embarrassed by what she may have seen within his eyes.

He felt his fiancée smoothing her dress, a very annoying, nervous habit of hers, before she shuffled in her seat.

Bianca looked away with a slight blush.

Alessandro saw this exchange of glances between Vincenzo and Bianca, and his blood boiled, his heartbeat was angry and aggressive, for how could she fall for a man like Vincenzo? He had to talk to her after the service. He had to make her understand that Vincenzo would ruin her life just like he had done to Chiara. Why would Bianca sacrifice all her family and friends for a little, proud prick? He was useless, worthless, and completely selfish!

Vincenzo felt a throbbing growth in his groin and a pain in his heart as he recalled evenings tumbling with Matteo in the dry grass, their bodies hairy and unprotected against one another, whilst the grass cut their knees with their sin. He could even feel the tough grip of Matteo's hands on his hip bones. He could hear the grunts and groans, a melody of passion, which made his penis grow hard with the remembrance of this love. He could feel Matteo's fingers pressed into his thighs, and his warm wet mouth around his penis. He could taste the sweet rotten flavour of Matteo's lips corrupt his own willingly.

Looking up at the priest, Vincenzo felt revolted by his words, and by religion in general. What if Jesus had been gay? Would God have accepted him? Or punished him? What effect would it have had on religion and society? Would thousands of men not have been imprisoned for their love? Would thousands of "lawful" marriages never have suffered from emptiness? Would thousands of men not have been persecuted for their passions? Was Jesus tied to that cross for the sins of men loving men, or the sins of those who could not accept that love? He wished it to be the latter, but society had made it clear it was not this, and he felt fearful, frightened by the man he was and the love that filled him. But why should he feel like this? He had done nothing wrong, yet he would have to pay the price for this love. He detested the laws set out by a society ruled by religion. Why could a man not love another man? Why could this union of love not be solidified in the church? Why was there always constant judgement on the subject of love?

He hated religion. He hated society. He hated himself for the fervent fear Matteo provoked in him.

Love did not belong in a church, it belonged in the grass, the shadows, the sheets, and the silence.

*

Finally, the service finished. The bells in the tower were crashing with a frantic joy, and so were the families and friends spilling from large, dark oak doors. The pungent stench of the houses and the heat did not entice people to stand for long chattering.

The Fangos stood together, Domenico with his hand stuck deep in his pockets, Signoro Fango lit a cigarette, Nonna was talking to the priest, and Signora Fango slouched beside Matteo, fanning herself, like a queen. Matteo laughed with a few nearby friends, and Bianca stretched her legs, strolling away from her family and the stench, which made her want to vomit.

Alessandro watched Bianca moving away, and he called to his mum that he would be home by lunch, before chasing after his love. The chaos of the bells made his legs sprint quicker and quicker towards her.

Bianca could hear footsteps, despite the bells, thundering closer and quicker, like the pounding of her heart, for she knew whose footsteps they were.

She did not stop walking, and finally Alessandro found his step beside her.

They walked in silence for a moment, neither sure what to say, as if their words of the past had all been forgotten in a week.

"Have I upset you, Bianca?" Alessandro offered; his dark gaze fixed on her side profile. He saw the change in her face at this question, for her cheeks pinkened slightly, her bottom lip quivered, and her lashes blinked in quick succession.

She did not answer and merely shook her head, as if surprised by the question.

"I have not seen you this week. I was worried I had done something wrong. You know I would never do anything to hurt you, please say you believe me," pleaded Alessandro, his whole body turned towards Bianca imploringly.

Bianca stopped and looked up into his dark, loving eyes, which only reflected her own worried face.

"I believe you," Bianca responded quietly, for she truly did, but she knew their love had hurt them both, she was sure, certain.

"If you want to end our relationship, I will never stop you, though I might hurt the man who follows," joked Alessandro, yet his fists were already tightened into aggressive balls of fury.

"No, I don't, please don't say that," cried Bianca, as she finally saw the repercussions of her actions, for she noticed how much he had hurt himself with his own cruel imaginings.

Alessandro's tightened fists released at her words.

"Is there anything I can do to help, anything at all?" questioned Alessandro anxiously.

Bianca stopped and gazed at Alessandro's dark, smouldering eyes, and felt safe in his heart and in their future.

"Promise you will always be here for me, no matter how bad things are," implored Bianca, her dark eyes large and serious and fragile, like black glass. Alessandro could not understand her secretive eyes and words, yet he only wished he could. What was upsetting her?

"Of course, Bianca, I promise," stated Alessandro, taking Bianca's soft hand in his own scratchy dark hands, kissing each finger, as if they were the hands of a goddess.

A small tear slipped from her eye, yet a smile crept across her plump lips, making her whole face shimmer with the old beauty of her youth.

This promise was worth more than the "I do" of a marriage vowel, for they were not forced to perform by religion or society, only the natural instincts of love.

"Bianca where are you going?" bellowed her mother across the quiet group of chattering friends and families, who jumped at this brash voice cutting through the last of the dying bells.

"Just on a walk—"

"No, Bianca, get back here, Sunday is for family," barked Signora Fango with irritation.

People glared at Signora Fango, but she did not care, for she was embarrassed to see her daughter's display of affection for that man. The black sheep of the village, how embarrassing, she did not like him at all. Signora Fango did not like the way that man looked at her daughter or squeezed her hand or talked to her.

But in truth, Signora Fango did not like many things.

Bianca came and stood beside Domenico, who ruthlessly smiled at her, she nudged his ribs with mock annoyance.

The Fangos continued to chatter with the other members of the village, except for Domenico.

Suddenly, Vincenzo approached, sly and stealthy, like a snake, Chiara followed obediently behind with a dragging, desolate expression within her narrow face, like a moody teenager.

"*Buongiorno*, how are we?" greeted Vincenzo with a slimy joyful welcome, his smile unable to meet his vacant, green eyes.

"Very well, Vincenzo, very well, how are you? When are your family coming down for the wedding?" Signora Fango spoke attentively, for she wished Vincenzo had fallen for Bianca, saving the family from their poverty.

But in Signora Fango's mind there was still a chance to put things that were wrong, right.

"Yes, I am well, and yes they will be down in a week," answered Vincenzo with a gritted smile, sweat gathering under his floppy blond hair, and spilling into his neatly styled eyebrows.

"Wonderful, I bet they are excited, well make sure you come round for dinner with them, I promise I will seat you next to Bianca, who I am sure will look after you," stammered Signora Fango, smilingly, as she fanned her hot flushed face with her hat, exposing the greasy black hair and sparkling white dandruff.

Bianca rolled her eyes and stepped towards the shade, for the heat was unbearable.

Chiara glared at Signora Fango, what a spiteful, conniving woman, she thought.

Vincenzo chuckled slightly, before he said: "Only if Domenico is serving rather than sitting."

Signora Fango cackled exaggeratedly, before placing her hand flirtatiously on the strong arm of Vincenzo.

"He would be more useful serving, rather than boring your poor parents with plants," laughed Signora Fango, the wind of the fan unable to shift the matted, tangled dark hair around her shoulders.

Vincenzo and Matteo both grunted with laughter.

Signoro Fango flung his cigarette to the ground and stamped it out pretending it was the face of Signora Fango, the black tar stained the burning hot ground beneath, as his wife's words stained the wind with their worthlessness.

Bianca rolled her eyes once again.

Chiara moved her glaring eyes to Domenico and saw that he was smiling with a sarcastic disbelief at her.

She, too, smiled, for they did not know half the things Domenico could tell them.

"Matteo, I'm going to drive over to the next village for a drink, do you want to come?" Vincenzo asked cheerfully.

"Yes, sounds fun," Matteo replied casually, unable to meet Vincenzo's tempestuous green eyes.

"Wait, Vincenzo, you promised you would come for dinner this week as you missed last week, I have bought all the ingredients it would be a waste—"

"Don't harass me, Chiara, I shall do as I please," Vincenzo snapped. He hated her whimpering, whiny voice, it made his blood boil, causing an upsetting indigestion in his throat.

Chiara's face was swamped in a red flush of embarrassment, and she bowed her head demurely at his unnecessary cruelty.

"Don't worry Chiara, I will have him back before lunch, no need to worry your pretty head," comforted Matteo, patting her hot head patronizingly, like a dog.

Chiara shrugged him away. She did not like Matteo, his presence made her skin crawl and her stomach flutter uncomfortably. Whenever Matteo was kind there was always an ulterior motive, for ever since she was a child, he had bullied her with snide comments and derisive cackles.

"Happy now?" Vincenzo bit, his poisonous eyes flashed, like a snake, at his future wife.

"Yes, that is fine," Chiara agreed without choice.

Vincenzo and Matteo waved goodbye and sauntered off together.

Signora Fango regarded them with delight, for this friendship was a promising one. Maybe Matteo could convince Vincenzo to give up his engagement to the witch next door.

Signoro Fango began to amble home with Bianca, her arm threaded through his, like she did when she was a child, and his aching heart was soothed by her idle chatter.

Nonna limped home alone. She liked to be by herself after the service to digest the words of the priest. Words she had heard so often, but each time provided her with a new way to understand and transfer the old-world values to fit the new world, like bending the shape of a puzzle piece to fit the gap.

Chiara gawked at the disappearing men, partly annoyed, partly relieved that Vincenzo was not following Bianca from the church, and therefore his loyalties and love were still bound to her.

Suddenly, she felt Domenico slide his strong arm through her arm with a guiding protection and peace.

Gazing up at his face, Chiara smiled in response to his dimpled grin, and watched his silver eyes glittering like tinsel.

Glancing down on the smiling face of Chiara, his heart leapt in his chest, catching his breath brutally, as his eyes fascinated over her eyes, for they were strange in that moment. They were darker than usual, clouded by the cruel words of Vincenzo, yet there was a small rippling glint of wild blue, brightening her whole face with a broken beauty.

"Let's go home, Chiara, unless you don't want to walk home with me," Domenico asked.

Chiara drew her brows together, puzzled by this question. "Why wouldn't I?"

"I don't want to bore you with my plant talk," teased Domenico, his face shining with mischievous mockery.

"Too late for that," retorted Chiara as they began to amble home.

Domenico laughed, tilting his head slightly to the sky, Chiara could see his thin throat vibrating with the humour of this insult.

"I'm so sorry, Chiara, if I offended you with my boredom."

"It's OK, I think I will survive."

"Well, only if you're sure, I have a new theory about a certain plant in—"

Chiara put a hand over her mouth and pretended to yawn, her eyes closing, shutting away that blue magic, like flushing the sea away.

Suddenly, she felt a hand tickling her ribs, and she tore away from Domenico with gushing giggles, as she tried to breathlessly swipe his hand away.

"Stop! Stop! Domenico stop! I'm sorry," apologized Chiara between fits of giggles.

Domenico stopped laughing, yet his eyes still magnified their glee behind the examining lenses of his glasses.

They joined arms again and continued to bounce along the street.

"I am going down to the land before lunch, do you want to come?" asked Domenico, hopefully.

"I'm sorry, I can't, I need to finish cooking, I would have loved to," apologized Chiara sincerely.

"Is it because you are worried I will bore you to death?" teased Domenico.

"Was it that obvious? Anyway, all your stuff is too clever for me," sniggered Chiara, but she stopped for Domenico was no longer laughing, instead his grey eyes were clouded and disapproving.

"I hate it when you say things like that as you know full well you are just as clever as me, why do you put yourself down?" interrogated Domenico.

Chiara looked at the ground, downcast, for in truth, she did not know.

"Can we make a promise?"

"Yes?" Chiara asked eagerly.

"OK, if you marry this idiot, you promise me that you will never be bullied into believing you are less than him or anyone," Domenico stated, his hand held out, ready for the signature of her consent.

Chiara turned to face him, and placed her hand in his with an uneasy, achy heart, for he believed so much in her significance it killed her but...

...why could she not see that she was worth more than that man? Why did she let him control her brain? Domenico hated it, for he had known Chiara since they were children, and he knew that she was more clever than he could ever be. Her intelligence was superior to his, for she twisted her knowledge and insight to see things in ways he would never have been able to see them.

Her small, dainty hands became invisible beneath Domenico's large engulfing ink-stained fingers.

Domenico squeezed Chiara's hand with a heavy, soft pressure, as if he wanted to imprint the marks of her hand within his, so that she would never truly leave him.

They met each other's eyes, and the church, mountains and village fell away around them.

A promise was sealed between them. A silent promise of indefinite love, whatever form it should take, platonic or erotic.

Chiara gripped his fingers with the mourning knowledge that after her marriage they would be separated by distance and duties. They would never have those moments together. They would never hold the secrets of the future together, only the promises and pain of the past. She hated love, for love was ruthless in its benign brutality.

They walked the rest of the way in silence, and when they parted at their doors, Chiara ran to the bathroom and sobbed into her hands at the loss of her only true love. How could she be so stupid to love him? How could she have been so stupid to lose him?

SEVEN

The sun was at its hottest point of the day.

The countryside was barren with people and purpose.

The crickets blazed the countryside with a loud throaty noise. The only noise that vibrated the sparse collection of bushes and shrubs.

There was no one in this ungodly place and hellish heat, except for two people.

Beneath the olive trees lay the panting, naked bodies of Matteo and Vincenzo, hot and breathless and delirious. Their skin was speckled in the grey shadows of the branches, and the slick, sweaty patches of sunlit skin made those parts glitter like diamonds.

The leaves naked with protection, like the nakedness of their bodies.

The branches knotted in naked entanglements, like the naked limbs of the two men.

The heat off the ground was hot and alive with the fire of the sun, like the hearts and breaths of these two complicated lovers.

The sky was an endless blanket of blue, like the neatly folded trousers of Vincenzo.

The ground was dusty and dark beneath them, like the lips and mouths of these lovers.

Matteo rested his head on Vincenzo's shoulder, the strong collarbone poking his temple with a lovingly new familiarity.

Matteo never thought he could love another body which was not a woman's, but now he believed he could never again love a woman's body. He loved the elegant lines of Vincenzo, like a ballet dancer. He loved his long torso, and he could not resist running his fingers down the bony chest, bump over the ribcage, before massaging the slight swell of his belly, as if Vincenzo's very skin would heal him. And in some ways, it did, for it made him feel complete. But in what way did he feel complete? Was it a physical completeness? Was it an emotional completeness? Was it a spiritual completeness? Perhaps it was all three.

Matteo gazed up at Vincenzo, and he found so much fascination and fear within this man. He loved the way his Adam's apple moved inconsistently with nerves, like a snake digesting its prey. He loved seeing the little hairs he had missed with his razor. He loved his firm, unbending red lips, which scowled more often than smiled. He loved the strong, slim-line nose, and the hollow paper white cheeks which stretched from it. He loved the clearness of his forehead, and the way his blond hair flopped across it in sweaty strings of sexual relief, like string cheese. Yet in this love was his shame and fear, for he loved something that he should not.

It twisted his heart with a strange grief, for how could such great happiness come from such a sordid secret?

It did not matter, for in this moment Matteo would just treasure the smell and sound and sight of Vincenzo. Inhaling, he drew in the sweaty scent of Vincenzo, which always smelt so sweet, like coconut cream. He listened carefully to the heart, which thumped fast and hard against the barrier of his bald, lightly freckled chest. He looked upon the body, which was built and born from a life of luxury, for it was smooth and white, as if it had never been used for the hardship of labour. Maybe, Matteo should not have loved this, for his body showed a life of purposelessness and uselessness, yet there was a mystery about it, which drew him in and in and in, like the statue of David.

All of this felt strange, but sensational to Matteo, and he could only wish that things in their world were different.

Vincenzo traced his sticky, dirty fingers around the shadowy outline of branches on Matteo's hairy arms. His chest heaved with the weight of Matteo's arm, but he would not have moved it for all of the world.

How could he love this man? This man was ugly, a lowlife, a layabout, and the scars of this life were everywhere, from his bulging belly, his undefined muscles and his racing breaths. He did not understand how he was attracted to this man, for he loved women's bodies, they were beautiful and smooth, whilst this body was rough, unclean and undignified. Yet, in this ugliness there was a truth, unlike the false love he felt for the few women he had fucked. He loved running his hands over the thick-cut thighs, the hairs spiking with his movements. He loved the round, soft belly, which slumped heavily on his side. He loved the broad open chest, which would envelope him in those arms with a protection he had not found anywhere else. He loved the round face, which squished between his fingers, like clay. He loved the soft, round pink lips, which mumbled lyrics of lust, like a never-ending love song. He loved the dull shadow of his prickly stubble, which cut his own skin with its ardent abrasiveness. He loved the small, coffee-coloured eyes, especially when they made love, for they rolled around in his head, as if he had lost all control of his body to love.

Love? How could he say this was love when it was wrong? But how could he not say this to be love when it felt so right? He felt as though his body was being torn apart from within him, for he wanted Matteo with all his flaws and vices more than Chiara with all her goodness and kindness. Suddenly that overwhelming panic of confusion and clarity took hold of his heart, for he could not go through with this marriage. He could not lie to himself. He could not lie to Matteo.

Here, in this place, they both felt at one with themselves, like their truest identities were on display for everyone to see.

Yet no one could see.

The many apprehensions that had rattled their brains and corrupted their confidence were at rest, and they allowed the deepest secrets and insecurities to bleed from their bodies, like a disease being bled from a dying man. It granted them a peaceful comfort from those long days of wearing costumes which no longer fitted nor reflected them as they had once done. They were holding in so much love and passion, like a balloon about to burst, and so when they made love it was loud, combustible, and exhausting with the burden that popped and released.

Both felt at ease with one another like they had known each other for years, perhaps it was because they were both bound and trapped by their shameful happiness.

"Matteo?"

"Yes."

"When will this…? I mean what can… I don't know what I am trying to say," whispered Vincenzo, his croaky voice vulnerable and lonely in his thoughts for the future.

"I know what you are trying to say," broke Matteo, shifting his body higher, as he gazed down into the green, wealthy eyes of Vincenzo, like unripe olives.

"You do?" asked Vincenzo, his eyes searching those dark chestnut eyes for an answer of comfort.

"Yes, and I don't know how to answer. I don't understand why this has started or what's going to happen or if this will last, or, or…" Matteo's voice trailed away, sadly and quietly.

They were silent, mourning the mess they had made of their hearts and minds.

The crickets bleached the land with their endless noise.

"I can't go back to Chiara," Vincenzo admitted solidly.

Matteo rolled his eyes and rubbed his forehead with worry.

"Vincenzo, you need to go to her. This is the only way it will work—"

"Why should this be the only way it will work, Matteo? Tell me! It's the fucking 21st century, why are we still acting like we could get arrested for this?" Vincenzo shouted moodily, as he swiped his blond hair away from his face, so that it splayed in a tangled array around his head, like a lopsided halo.

"Look Vincenzo, we can't, there is a lot to lose, and it might make us hate each other, it is too risky, it is better this way, I'm sorry," Matteo spoke firmly, yet comfortingly, yet his throat felt parched with the dark, false future which engulfed him.

"I'm sorry too."

The church bells rang far away and forgotten, yet it still broke the happiness with God's reminder of their "sin".

Suddenly Matteo sat up, alert, as he flicked his eyes around the barren landscape, for he thought he heard the noise of a car engine, but it seemed to come as quickly as it went. There was probably no one there, besides they were quite far from the road.

Vincenzo felt the emptiness of Matteo's skin against his own, and his fingers slowly climbed his strong, tanned back, coaxing him back to his side.

Gazing back at Vincenzo, Matteo felt his heart sink, for this man was in a trap far worse than his. Vincenzo was webbed with the pride that comes from a wealthy family, marrying a poor woman like Chiara was bad enough, but loving a man who was poor and unsuccessful was a far greater problem with far greater punishments.

Bending over Vincenzo, Matteo allowed his lips to kiss and touch every part of his face, cherishing this chance he had at a real blissful love. He allowed his teeth to nip the line of his neck, tasting the salty sweetness of his skin, like popcorn, before his tongue skimmed the harsh jawline. He kissed softly the flushed, puffing cheeks, the corners of his lips, and the base of his jutted chin.

Vincenzo's body pulsed with an uncontrolled, blessed passion, and he hurriedly took Matteo's face in his hands, enjoying the feeling of his damp tender flesh on his thumbs and fingers, before kissing his lips hard and long.

Matteo's body snapped, stunned with the intensity of this lust. He quickly climbed his body over Vincenzo's, and kissed him again, yet this was deeper and darker in its danger. Their bodies were electric. Their penises grew bigger, breaking the seal of cum they had already released. They mashed their lips against one another, holding each other, like they wanted to become one.

The strange sensations of this secret were being pulled and pushed, pounded and released with each new kiss. The torment and fear of this love was in the goose pimples, which lit up their bodies with an energy that would leave them lethargic and lonely later.

Their nerves were alive.

Their hearts were manic.

Their breaths were rapid.

The grass crackled.

Rasping, gasping, breaking.

The grass crackled again, louder and closer.

Footsteps.

They stopped, frozen.

Snapping their faces away, they turned their eyes towards the road, which stood far, far away.

There was a figure framed in that barren dry landscape.

Blue and blurry.

Frozen.

They were all frozen rigid, watching each other, like a predator hunting an alert prey.

They all knew who was who, yet no one dared speak.

Slowly, the clothed figure turned away from the two naked men and walked towards the road.

They watched him go with frantic hearts until he disappeared, and the vehicle growled to a start, revving and zooming off quickly.

The pair did not move at first, until the sound had completely disappeared.

Neither spoke at first with the shock of this intervention.

They breathed hard; anguish had replaced lust in an instant.

"Will he tell?" questioned Vincenzo, his blood cold, and his face pale.

"No."

"Are you sure?" persisted Vincenzo, grabbing his clothes worriedly.

Matteo stared off into the distance in disbelief.

Firm and true, these words came to Matteo without hesitation: "Yes, my brother never tells."

EIGHT

Bianca coughed the last of the sick up into the skid-marked toilet, a slimy trail of bile covered the colourful sick in a shiny sheen. Leaning back against the cold, scratched marble bathtub, she closed her eyes, exhausted and trembling. Too exhausted to even wipe the smelly saliva from her lips and chin.

Bianca breathed hard, her lips as pale as the white toilet, her face a sheen of sweat, her eyelids sticky and quivering. She enjoyed the feeling of the cool white marble against her hot, sweaty head.

Her black, frizzy hair had been tied back, ready for the punishment of her sins.

She felt dizzy and disorientated, for she had not even eaten breakfast. The thought of food made her feel hungry, yet sick at the same time.

Her breathing shallowed and quickened with the fright of being sick again, or even worse, fainting, for it felt as though the ground was falling away from her and the room seemed to spin faster and faster, like a carousel.

Her mouth and throat burned with the acidity of her sick, and her teeth longed to be cleaned and rid of this smell, as if it would rid the whole mess of this situation all together.

She began to breath slower, for she was lethargic and exhausted by this stubborn routine.

Finally, her eyes peeled apart to reveal two pools of salty tears, like copper coins at the bottom of a fountain, yet stuck within the heart of them was a message of fear.

Bianca shivered, cold and scared and alone by the facts of her future.

The church bells sung out laughingly, tormentingly to the petrified ears of Bianca. She cursed herself for what she had done. She had been so stupid, so foolish, so irresponsible, and now she would have to pay a price, heavy with responsibility, confinement and no freedom.

What would she tell people?

Staring down at her pelvis, it seemed it was already changing and shaping with the growth of her mistake. Her hips felt wider, her breasts felt larger and tender, her back hurt slightly, and her head ached with all the anxious thoughts she had harboured for so long. Her nerves were tired, yet her hormones were alive and raging, throwing her into wild tantrums or abundant tears at nothing.

But how long?

How long was she gone?

Her last period seemed years ago, but it can't have been any more than a couple of months.

Laying a hand gently on her stomach, she thought of the thing growing inside her, sewn and nurtured by the seeds of love, she could not just cut it out, or let it die, for somewhere deep behind her guilt and worry, she felt almost happy. When she lay her hand there, it was quiet and unmoving, but she knew that there was something there, it felt like the sweetest and bitterest secret between herself and it. Sometimes, she smiled, her heart swollen with a protective love for this little creature, but at other times, she heard the voices of society cutting her out, isolating her from their circle, making her a figurehead of sin. But she hated society, for if she was alone on a desert island, she would not care what others thought, her whole attention would be happily captivated by the baby growing inside her.

Society dashed her dreams, and religion harassed her hopes.

Her greatest worry was not society, but Alessandro, and the tears cascaded down her face in rapid successions, whilst snot bubbled beneath her nostril, like washing-up liquid. How would she tell him? What would she tell him? Where would she tell him? How would he react? Would he be happy? Sad? Angry? Resentful? Disappointed? She could not face it, he would be furious, she was sure that he would blame her. She was convinced he would walk away from her and their child without looking back. She would be left entirely alone with only the child to permanently remind her of her mistakes and loss of her first love. She knew that if Alessandro left there would be no more love, whilst he could keep moving forward with a new lover, every night, if that is what he desired. Who would love a woman with a ruined body and soul? Who would touch the red, splitting stretch marks that would break her skin? Who would caress the leaking heavy boobs of her maternity? Who would hold her widened hips? Who would grip her sagging arse? Who would fall in love with a face tired and aged before its time? What man would ever see past these flaws? What man would ever accept her for her new ugliness?

Throwing her face into her hands, she sobbed loudly, taking advantage of the quiet house, filling it with the loss of her bright, carefree future.

What would she do without Alessandro? What would she tell the child? Would her future child be bullied for not having a father? Would he be made an outcast to the whole village? Would they have to move? Would people accept her as a single mother?

Bianca's sobs grew louder and more engulfing as she thought of all the things she would lose. Friendships would be the first to go, for what could she talk about with her friends? They would be talking about parties, boys and alcohol, whilst she would be talking about nappies, sleepless nights and first words. They would whisper her name around with disbelief and disgust, like a soap star. Their mothers would warn their daughters to be careful otherwise they would end up like Bianca Fango, fat, deformed and tired by her mistake.

Her mother would be raging with fury, for she did not even like Alessandro.

And her father, how would he react?

Oh God! Oh God! Oh God! Bianca moaned to herself, before the sobs shook her once again. Her head was pounding and pressured, as if it would explode. Her eyes were sore and aching. Her breathing was rapid and rasping.

Suddenly she heard a gentle thumping against the beige door, and the voice of Domenico asking if he could use the bathroom.

The sound of the noise shocked her for a moment, and she sat frozen, stilled by the exposure of her misery and panic.

Pushing herself from the cracked tiled floor with the help of the cream-coloured bathtub, she flushed the sick away as if nothing had ever happened.

"Bianca are you OK?" called Domenico with a slight urgency in his voice.

She ignored him, and ran the tap, before splashing her red, raw eyes and sick-stained mouth with cold water, leaving no trace of evidence behind. When she was satisfied, she rubbed her face roughly on a scratchy, old flannel, and interrogated her puffy, red face. The mirror mocked her, for her face was no longer radiant with youthful beauty, but nor was it the responsible calm face of a mother, and it was certainly not the happy, overjoyed face of a mother to be, she lamented.

Pushing the tube of toothpaste, a small plop of vibrant blue paste fell on her brush. Bianca began to vigorously clean her teeth, she liked the minty attack upon her mouth, washing away the rotten taste and smell.

"Can I come in?" pursued Domenico, tapping harder on the door, so that it made the towel rail rattle with its urgency.

"Nawh," she said through a mouthful of frothy toothpaste.

Bianca spat and washed her mouth out with water.

Placing her toothbrush back in the pot, she stared at the rest of the family toothbrushes, some more frazzled than others, Matteo's looked like it had never been used, and she began to relax at this familiar sight.

Bianca attempted a reassuring, calm smile in the white-toothpaste-splattered mirror, but it cried of despair. Her face was still red and unwell, her puffy eyes were still swimming with tears, and her lips were cracked and dry. She looked unnatural, unlike herself.

Everything will be ok, Bianca tried to convince herself, but it was unsuccessful.

"Should I get Mum at the shop?" Domenico suggested.

"No," Bianca almost shouted with earnest.

"OK, OK, open the door then," Domenico instructed more severely.

"OK, wait," she retorted, equally abrasive, as she unclasped the lock from its socket, and readied herself to quickly slip past Domenico before he could ask any questions.

The door opened and standing in the frame Domenico seemed to tower over her, like a guard. His face was grave and unsmiling. His eyes were narrowed beneath his thick-framed glasses, and they were severely silver in their calculations and theories as to why she had hidden in the bathroom. He did not blink. He just stared her straight in the eyes, as if his eyes were microscopes, analysing every flicker and fleck of her own red bug-like eyes, and for the first time she feared those eyes for what they saw in her. But when his results had drawn their conclusion, Bianca saw how his whole face slumped with sympathy and fondness. His eyes were no longer glaciers, but soft, silver pearls of kindness. Bianca knew he had just come back from the land, for his clothes were dirty with the dry soil and his hands were cracked and filled with soil, whilst his face glowed bronze with the early rays of the sun.

"What's happened, Bianca? Why are you crying?" Domenico inquired gently.

Bianca stood defiant in her secret.

"Nothing, I haven't been crying," she snapped defensively crossing her arms across her stomach, worried that she would be given away by the slight imaginary bump of her pelvis.

"Yes, you have," Domenico replied forcefully, unperturbed by her lie.

"No, I haven't, can I go?"

"Yes, you have," Domenico persisted unflinching.

"No, I haven't, what makes you think I have?" challenged Bianca, slightly regretting this question.

"Yes, you have, I heard you sobbing from the front door, your eyes are all red and you have used half of the toilet roll, I'm guessing to blow your nose," explained Domenico methodically, like a detective, his stubborn, incessant eyes started to become firm and suspicious again.

Bianca flinched at how obvious her sorrow was, but the toilet roll he was wrong about, as it had been used to wipe up the excess sick from the seat.

"It doesn't matter why I was crying—"

"But I thought you said you weren't crying—"

"OK, I was crying but it doesn't concern you," shouted Bianca, irritated by her brother's finickity ways.

There was a moment of silence, and Domenico leant his body against the side of the door, leaving a small gap for Bianca to escape from, yet she could not move.

"Was it Alessandro?" Domenico interrogated gently, his eyes flashing fierce with protection.

"What?"

"Did Alessandro hurt you, or do anything?"

"No, no, Alessandro has done nothing," mumbled Bianca, her feet shuffling nervously from side to side, as she felt Domenico's eyes cut into her head, like a knife, trying to pull the truth out of her.

"Then why are you upset?" Domenico repeated softly.

"Because, because, because I'm pregnant," Bianca burst out without thinking.

Quickly, she threw her hands over her mouth, and stepped away in shock of her own blatant, stupid and inconceivable words.

How could she have said it?

It sounded harsh, and almost unbelievable, which made Bianca begin to weep, for it was the cold hard truth of her present and future, and now it felt real. Very real.

Weeping into her hands, she had no idea of what Domenico's face displayed. Shock? Disbelief? Mockery? Fury? Suddenly she felt his large, sturdy hands guide her slowly into the bathroom, before placing her on the scratched rim of the bathtub.

She felt Domenico sit beside her quietly, steadily reeling off sheets of white toilet paper, before placing them firmly in her shaking damp hands.

There was not a sound in the house. The streets below were quiet and still, occasionally a motorbike would zoom past, but the only constant sound was Bianca's heartbreaking sobs, and every so often the sound of tearing toilet paper.

Domenico perched silently beside her, rubbing her back soothingly as he waited patiently for Bianca's tears to cease, and finally they did.

"Does Alessandro know?" Domenico queried, handing her the last of the toilet paper.

Bianca shook her head, unable to speak, as she wiped her wet, innocent eyes with the tissue, like a child.

"Do you want to speak with Chiara, she might be better to talk to," choked Domenico uncertainly.

Bianca nodded, sniffling. She noticed him stiffen with tension, for she knew Domenico had been avoiding Chiara since Sunday.

"OK, I will go and get her. Phone work and tell them you are sick," suggested Domenico, unmoving.

"OK," stuttered Bianca wearingly.

Taking her damp hands in his scratchy warm fingers, Bianca looked at Domenico, and saw that his face was kind, whilst his eyes were judgeless and encouraging.

"Don't worry, we will sort this all out. Try to be happy it is an amazing thing," supported Domenico, squeezing her small, moist hands, still so young.

"Amazing? If you mean amazing as a complete ruining of my fucking life," grumbled Bianca, rubbing her eyes tiredly with her free hand.

"No, your life isn't ruined, it's starting a new chapter, you've only ruined your life if you think you have ruined it."

Bianca stared at her brother incredulously. Why wasn't he angry? Why wasn't he disgusted? Why wasn't he disappointed? Why did he not want to snitch on her to their parents? How was he so calm when all she could do was cry freakishly?

"Right, I'll go and get Chiara. Be back soon," Domenico said, as he jumped to his feet.

Bianca listened to his heavy footsteps tumble down the stairs and away from her. She felt the loneliness of her situation take over once again, and she hoped Domenico would return soon without a change of heart.

*

Chiara checked her bag. She had her keys, her wallet, and her sunglasses, for she needed them on this blinding bright day.

Vincenzo had left a list of things he needed, and he had given her some money, casually saying to buy something for herself. He had been much more benevolent since his trip with Matteo, and she was beginning to believe he was finding his feet as her future husband.

Despite the absence of Domenico, her heart was elated, and pleasure was displayed from every inch of her face, especially her blue eyes.

Suddenly her thoughts were interrupted by a loud, urgent thudding against her door.

"Coming," she called, as she lightly smeared a layer of watermelon lip balm across her lips.

But the knocking continued more urgently, snapping her happiness.

Racing to the door, she flung it open, preparing to scold the person who clearly had no patience.

However, when she saw who stood by the door, Chiara gasped slightly, and the torrent of abuse was frozen, for Domenico stood beneath her with a face contorted with anxiety and perplexity.

Domenico felt the tension release from his lips, cheeks and eyes as he beheld Chiara, for now he felt things would be in control under her calm presence. Yet, he could not avoid the fury whipping her eyes into clouds of bright blue thunder and the firmness of her glossy lips. But surely, she would not let the past week stop her from helping him, she was not like this.

Chiara refused to acknowledge him, like he had done to her all week. She would not come crawling back to his side when he needed her. She was not some dog that could be pushed away and whistled back when needed.

Slamming the door shut, she marched past him and down the street, greeting the elderly ladies who sat outside their doors gossiping in the sun about this and that.

Domenico followed her, but she moved quickly, as if she did not want to talk to him.

Running slightly, he felt anger pounding through his veins, for how could she be so selfish, if she knew the true reason for avoiding her, she would be more grateful he kept his distance.

Suddenly Chiara felt his hot hand on her thin arm, gripping it tightly to stop her from moving away.

Chiara briskly shook it off. He was so selfish. He claimed Vincenzo abused her kindness, but Domenico did it even more, and what made it worse was that he knew he was abusing it.

"Chiara, please talk to me," pleaded Domenico.

She continued to stomp away, as if she had not felt or heard Domenico.

"Please Chiara, please stop," implored Domenico grabbing her arm again, and this time she felt his grip tighten and arrest her.

"What do you want?" she growled through gritted teeth.

"I need you—"

"That's funny, I needed you these past few days, but you have been nowhere to be seen. You have been down at the land, I understand, but you were there all last week and still found time to see me, so what has changed?" hissed Chiara, staring aggressively into the grey eyes, which listened intently to her, yet equally they seemed somewhere else.

"I'm sorry. I'm so sorry, but I can't explain. It doesn't matter. I don't need you, but Bianca does, please come with me," stumbled Domenico.

She felt him trying to drag her back to his house, but she refused to follow. He had pushed her too far this time.

"No, why should I?"

"Because Bianca has done nothing wrong to you, and she needs you, and—"

"Are you just saying this to make me come with you somewhere?" challenged Chiara, her blue eyes fierce and sharp, like sapphires.

"No, she needs you—"

"Why does she need me?"

Slowly Domenico leant his face close to Chiara's, and she felt his breath tickling the tiniest hairs on her face. His eyes grew and magnified, elongating his lashed and broadening his irises.

Domenico felt his heart skip, skip, skip, as he drowned in those electric blue pools, the lashes were blacker and wider, staring into the very depths of his soul, making him feel unsettled by what he might expose to her.

Chiara could not look away, but she did not want to.

"Bianca's pregnant," Domenico whispered, his breath smelt of coffee, the blackest and strongest espresso.

Chiara stepped away slightly in disbelief. He was lying, surely, he was lying. She couldn't be, she was only sixteen, she had said that she hadn't done anything with Alessandro, but maybe she had?

Domenico could see the shock and doubt fight between her face, for her mouth was slightly open, breaths catching in exchange with the hot air, yet her eyebrows were drawn tightly together in questioning.

"Look Chiara, I know you are mad and rightly so, but I don't know what to say to her, she is panicking and very scared. Please, just talk to her, even for five minutes," Domenico whispered earnestly.

Chiara had been examining his red lips, which moved quickly and frantically, and she found it impossible to believe him. Yet when she looked into those steel eyes, she knew he was telling the truth.

"Yes, take me to her," commanded Chiara, for she felt dizzy, weak and confused by this news, perhaps it was because she could not believe it.

Domenico sighed with relief, before taking Chiara's hand within his own, for she seemed dazed by the news, unclear as to what to do or where to go.

Eventually they arrived at the entrance of the bathroom, her mind had been in such a blur, she had not seen the watching and gossiping old ladies, or even comprehended how she had put one foot in front of the other.

Knocking on the door, a meek voice called for them to enter, and they did, Chiara in front of Domenico.

Chiara had not known what to feel, but when she saw Bianca's beautiful red puffy face, she went over and scooped her into her arms.

165

Tears and apologies leaked from Bianca uncontrollably, but Chiara just cradled her close to her chest, cooing words of comfort to this poor girl, as if she was a child. Bianca buried her face in Chiara's small shoulders, and breathed in her new, expensive perfume, which gave her comfort. The strong, stable structure of Chiara made Bianca feel safe, as her own body trembled and shook against her.

Chiara ordered Domenico to go and buy more toilet roll, and gave him Vincenzo's money, mouthing before he left "and ice cream".

Chiara watched Domenico leave, and she whispered to Bianca that they would come up with a plan.

And they did.

*

Alessandro sat quietly glancing between the two women's faces, for they both seemed tied together in the same thought. He could not understand what was going on. He had received a text earlier from Domenico saying they were going to his farmhouse. He had picked up the pizza and chips as usual and waited excitedly to see the three-wheeler turn up. But his heart had sunk when he saw the three faces within it, talk about a picture of misery, they had all looked morbid, as if someone had died, and they were all deadly quiet, as if they shared the same secret.

Alessandro had believed they had an argument, but when he tried to tell a funny story about his work, no one laughed, except himself. He concluded that perhaps he was the problem, yet he could not fathom as to what he had done.

Alessandro was sure something was going on, for Domenico drove slowly and carefully, yet he did not notice the scenery, as his eyes were fixated on the two women, who seemed so absorbed in their secret they did not even notice him watching.

Climbing from the vehicle, he held his hand out to Bianca, and she took it, averting her gaze, as if she was scared to meet his eyes.

She would not hold his hand on the walk down, but clung to Chiara with desperation, whispering words he could not hear, yet her tone seemed tight and fretful.

What was going on?

Alessandro tried to ask Domenico, but he only shrugged his shoulders dismissively as if he did not know. But he knew this to be a lie, for he had known Domenico since they were children, and he struggled to keep secrets a secret. He was not a snitch, but it seemed Domenico's brain did not have room for intense secrets, and their truth spilled across his face without his knowledge.

Finally, the sad group of four arrived at the farmhouse, a place that was once rich with happy memories, now seemed to mock them all. The farmhouse was darker with the evening shadows, and the chickens were quiet, nestled close to one another as they slept soundly, undisturbed by their approach. As they strode across the courtyard, Bianca noticed an eggshell, crushed and gooey with the destruction of the baby-to-be.

The evening was full with the raw, red sun. An array of colours descended from the ball of fire, raspberry dusted clouds collided with peelings of dull orange, streams of roses and lavender were strewn across, like forgotten headbands, whilst white smudgy lines of airplanes interrupted the deep indigo tapestry behind. The sky promised romance and reminiscing, yet the air was hot and close, promising tension and irritability. Luckily, the excruciating edge of the sun's temper was dulled by the wide concerned eyes of the silver moon and white stars. The town above watched this young carefree group become mature and tired with the promised responsibilities of adulthood.

They all stood awkward, for no one was sure what to do. Chiara glanced over at Domenico and motioned her eyes to the trails of vines.

"Right, I want to check the vines one last time before the evening is up, anyone want to come?" Domenico asked lightly, his large shoes kicking up dust and dirt, as he turned his body in the direction of the vines.

"I'll come. Only if I can taste," teased Chiara, attempting humour to soften the tension.

Chiara watched Domenico turn his face back towards her with a huge, radiant smile, splitting his cheeks with the deepest dimples.

Her heart heaved and her smile instantly grew, like a reflection to his.

"I'll think about it," Domenico compromised as he began to saunter away. The dust was like a ball of fire, as the red rays of the sun split across them, like laser beams.

Chiara squeezed Bianca's sweaty, nervous hand, and followed Domenico, her heart pounding for Bianca as the anticipated moment was now close at hand.

Alessandro and Bianca were alone, neither met one another's eyes.

Bianca fiddled with the tie of her black wrap dress, whilst Alessandro tapped his greasy fingers repeatedly upon the pizza boxes.

"Can we go inside, I feel a little hot and sick even in this evening heat," Bianca complained, but in truth, it was the anxiety of telling him the truth that made her sweat and want to be sick. Also, she felt too exposed in this dry, wild world to speak her secret, as if the almond trees were spies of the village.

Alessandro assented, and slouched ahead, holding the flimsy door open for her.

He knew she was going "to talk" to him, and already he could feel his heart breaking in anticipation. But he refused to not remain a gentleman, despite her savage words to come, which would undoubtedly leave him depressed for the autumn and winter to come. Yet he refused to have a woman caged to him, if she wished to fly, he would not pin her wings down and break her legs if she felt it was right to go, for whatever reasons those may be.

Alessandro thought of society, for it seemed women always needed men, but in reality, it was men who needed women. Men were lost without women, unguided and unsafe by their own insecurities, and Alessandro admitted he was not an exception to this rule.

The door closed behind the young lovers, and from the jungle of vine trees, Chiara could hear Bianca's high-pitched voice speaking softly.

"Hey you, don't listen to their conversation, you are as bad as my mother," Domenico joked, yanking her away from the house.

Chiara turned to him with powerful, denim-blue offended eyes: "I am not like your mother. I listen because I am worried, your mother listens because she is nosy and a gossip."

"Very true, I am deeply sorry for my mistake, Chiara," Domenico mockingly apologized.

Chiara smiled, and ambled closer to Domenico, their arms brushing against each other, prickling the hairs on her arm, whilst a warm thrill raced through her bones and blood.

She watched their shadows moving and slanting across the vines, but the shadowy hands remained clasped, unbroken and cemented. This is what she wanted, this moment forever, repeatedly. A realization that had always haunted her mind suddenly began to speak loud and clearly. She needed to tell Domenico how she felt, how she did not want to marry Vincenzo, how she wanted to leave her father, how she wanted to leave Castelmauro, how she wanted to study, how she loved him more than anyone. When they had been children, they would walk hand in hand to school together, trading secrets to one another, but now it seemed harder to...

...replicate this act was a futile effort, and so Domenico moved closer to a bunch of grapes, round and full with the juice of his success, yet he did not feel his usual contentment at his successful future. He felt lost, purposeless and uninspired by the vines, yet equally he feared them for the secrets they held and pulled from his own heart. Hope bound his body and blood together, just like the earthworms within

169

the soil, allowing him to thrive. He had always believed this hope was within the dream. The dream of the grapevines and studying. The dream of learning and conservation. But this was not the dream. Chiara was the dream, and his hope was within Chiara. She was the grapevines, and she was the future. This thought frightened him, for he had always thought this career success would be enough, but now he was not sure. He was not happy, he had felt depressed for a while, in truth, ever since Chiara had announced her engagement. But he had tried to push these feelings aside, yet now standing here with both his dreams so close, he felt that only one was his true…

…inspiration to speak her mind and confirm the mistake she knew she had made long ago when she announced her engagement.

"Chiara," Domenico spoke, interrupting her thoughts.

"Yes."

"I feel strange about everything, especially about leaving," Domenico admitted shyly.

"Why? You have always wanted to study and leave this town," reminded Chiara, tenderly watching his facial muscles twitch at the emotional strain on his brain.

"Yes, I know, but with my sister and best friend, and Nonna and you. I feel it is becoming harder to just take off and leave," explained Domenico, picking a grape from the bunch.

He burst the skin with his teeth and allowed the sweetly acidic juice to dry his mouth out, before crushing the pips, which released a bitterness that only matched the bitter thoughts he digested.

"I don't know what to say. I think you need to go; you are better than this town and this is your dream. You have worked so hard to throw everything away on sentiment. I thought you were made of stronger stuff," scolded Chiara jokingly, but heavily.

Domenico smirked, yet the laughter was not in his eyes, only sadness.

"Usually I'm not, maybe it's the thought of being an uncle, I don't know, maybe it's Bianca crying and all her hope that Dad will be fine with this, when I am certain he won't be and—"

"Look Domenico, all things, whether you go or stay, will still happen, and maybe you want to be there to comfort Bianca, but she will have Alessandro and me to help her, and you are only a phone call away," Chiara persuaded holding onto his forearms, facing him with eyes full of loving persuasion.

She hated that she said these words. All she wanted to tell him, scream out was STAY! STAY…

…STAY! Why didn't you tell me to stay Chiara? Why do you want me to pursue this…

…dream was more important, and she loved him enough to sacrifice her own feelings for his dreams and future happiness.

"Yes, there's another problem keeping me here," Domenico admitted, his eyes entertained by the rocks he unpicked with the tip of his shoes from the ground.

"What is it?"

"You."

A suspenseful silence followed, and Domenico removed his glasses, cleaning the lenses, whilst hiding the love which bulged and broke across his eyes.

"What do you mean?" Chiara asked, her heart beating rapidly and uncontrollably.

She wanted Domenico to meet her eyes. She needed to know his true emotions. Was he joking? Laughing at her? Was he serious? Was this how he truly felt?

"Well, I will find it so hard to leave you because… because—"

"I'm sorry Alessandro, please say something, anything," pleaded Bianca, her voice high pitched and crumbling with tears.

There was no response.

Chiara met Domenico's worried eyes, and she took his hand, dragging him back towards the farmhouse, as they heard a door slam and the soft cries of Bianca walk through the farmhouse.

They met her in the courtyard, and Chiara rushed over, drawing the trembling Bianca into her arms. Stroking the damp knotted hair of Bianca, she whispered words of comfort to her, and eventually her sobs subsided, yet the tears did not stop falling.

Domenico shoved his glasses back on.

Alessandro stepped from the farmhouse, and all eyes, except for Bianca's, viciously glared at him.

They all stood uncomfortably together, waiting for someone to say or do something.

Bianca felt sick. Sick with the pain of love. Sick with the pain of anger. Sick with the pain of shame. She wanted to go home, if she could still call that place that name.

Slowly, she heard Alessandro's clumsy steps stomp towards her, and Chiara moved away to Domenico's side.

An arm, heavy with its loving familiarity knotted around her shoulders, and held her close to his heaving, moist chest. A kiss was dealt upon her forehead, and he drew her into a hug full of safety and security.

"Bianca let's take you home," Alessandro murmured into her mangled dark brown hair.

Bianca pulled away with heavy wet eyes as she examined the face of Alessandro. It seemed sombre, depressed and serious. There was no mischief in his eyes. There was no flickering humorous twitch of his lips. There were no laughter lines framing his mouth.

"Are you mad?" Bianca urgently whispered.

He shook his head, and his eyes seemed to mist slightly, yet a slight smile crept across his lips.

"No, I just feel shocked and worried, but we will talk more tomorrow. I promise I will look after you, OK?" Alessandro muttered, his breath shaking with the very truth of these painful words.

"OK," Bianca sighed.

They smiled, but their smiles were aged and strained by the strained love within Bianca, and the strained consequences to come.

The age of youth and youthful love had ended with their new bundle of responsibility, marking a new milestone of stressful, premature maturity.

After dropping Alessandro off at his home, they finally arrived back at the Fango's house with aching heads and heavy hearts. The evening was drawing to a close, and the fiery dance of the sunbeams snuck away, the impending descent of the night overcrowded the hope of earlier, and even the stars seemed to sparkle less.

The last trial for the exhausted Bianca was her father, who usually at this time watched television, until he fell asleep on the sofa with a thankful excuse not to go upstairs.

When they entered the house, Chiara and Domenico snuck away, and sat on the staircase, listening with ears pressed against the wall, whilst Bianca quietly entered the room, disturbing her father's sleep, who fuzzily smiled at his beautiful daughter, for he was glad to see her.

The room was dark and baking hot, for the doors were closed against the cool night air, whilst the TV gave an inconsistent, blurry artificial light to the small, cramped room. Bianca could barely see her father, except when the TV flashed suddenly as it ran through the bright, robotic adverts.

"Bianca, are you unwell, Angela said you rang in sick this morning, do you want hot water with honey and lemon?" Signoro Fango offered, shuffling stiffly from his sinking seat in the sofa.

"No, Papa, thank you. I was sick this morning, but not because I am unwell," Bianca choked, a lump hardening in her narrow throat as she cherished her father's favourite remedy for any illness.

"Bianca, you know I don't like you drinking. Men are nasty creatures, and I know you are not responsible for their ugly ways, but I don't want you to get hurt," Signoro Fango warned protectively, squeezing her shoulder as he hobbled over to the fridge.

The dull orange light of the fridge lit up Signoro Fango's worn, line-ridden face.

"I haven't been drinking, I don't know how to tell you, but I'm…" Bianca trailed off into the shaking sobs from earlier.

Signoro Fango rushed over to his daughter, and held her close, stroking her long brown hair, as if she was still a child, yet she felt far from that. She felt wrong, tricking her father into believing she was a good person, when she had done something that would wreck this image in an instant.

"Bianca, you can tell me anything, except if you are pregnant or doing drugs," laughed Signoro Fango.

Bianca stiffened, and the atmosphere in the room shifted with the tension of this subtle movement. When Bianca pulled away, her father's eyes were menacing and merciless, and his lips were set in a rigid line.

"Which is it?" interrogated Signoro Fango, lurching away from his beloved daughter, as he pulled out his cigarette box.

There was a shy buzzing of a mosquito nearby, as Bianca tried to find the strength to speak.

"Well, which is it?"

Bianca gulped, as tears rushed into her eyes.

"The first one."

They stood in silence. Bianca watched her father's chest rise up and down with fury, his jaw noisily clenched and unclenched like a knuckle gripper, as he squeezed a cigarette between his inflexible lips.

"I'm sorry, I'm sorry, please forgive me—"

Signoro Fango ripped the cigarette from between his lips, twisting it between his finger and thumb, as he gulped loudly.

"Get out," barked Signoro Fango, abruptly turning his back on his favourite child with an icy fury.

Bianca stood there, tears dripping onto the floor in disbelief, and then she went reluctantly, her heart had now shattered completely.

Bianca met Chiara and Domenico on the stairs, but she violently shoved passed them, and ran quickly to her room, slamming the door behind her.

Bianca had collapsed as soon as her head hit the pillow, but she awoke a few hours later, muddled by the darkness and the soulless church bells, yet she was quickly and sadly reminded of the day's events by her unchanged clothes.

She undressed, and threw her pyjamas on dazed and dreamy, before she nipped to the bathroom to wash her tear-encrusted face. Yet, when she reached to turn the tap on, she stopped, and gripped the chipped sink to steady herself. She felt the sorrow return as raw as it had been, how could such a simple thing symbolize so much? How could such a simple thing ever be taken for granted? How could such a simple thing make her heart ache more than she could have ever believed?

Her father's toothbrush was missing from the pot, gone, as if he had never lived there.

NINE

"How is your father Domenico? Has he forgiven Bianca yet?" Chiara breathlessly asked, as they climbed up the steep, wooded hill together.

The sun was at its summer worst. It seemed closer to the earth, blazing the town and countryside with excruciating and exhausting heat, killing every little thing that tried to grow, except the olive trees and grapevines built to combat the heat. The pure, misty blue sky palpitated, almost melting like blue plastic under the heat. The humidity was unbearable, sweat seemed a permanent accessory to people's bodies, and the new favourite perfume of summer seemed to be BO, some more than others. People had developed new attitudes, some were moody and melancholy, others were irritable and idle, others were lustful and longing, like cats on heat. The village and countryside smelt different with the heat, stale and stagnant, like bad morning breath. Dust held suspended in the air choking those with weak lungs, but everyone craved a cooling breeze, a release, even the sweetest whisper of the wind would be a welcome relief. Many stayed indoors fearful of the sun's power. Exhausted by the heat, they slept often, but their dreams were muddled, uncomfortable.

Domenico and Chiara had agreed to take the day off and walk to the woods for the coolness and calmness of its shadows and secrets.

"No, he is still angry, well I don't know if he is angry, because he doesn't say anything. I feel bad for Bianca, he doesn't even acknowledge her in the street and, everyone's noticing and talking about her badly," Domenico puffed out, his red cheeks falling and rising with the exertion of his efforts.

"People are horrible, bless her, can we finish this conversation when we reach the top of the hill, I think I might pass out if I keep talking," Chiara laughed breathlessly, her calves aching with the steepness of the incline.

"Agreed," Domenico coughed out.

They climbed the rest of the way in a breathless silence, only the inhales and exhales filling the noise between them. They were right, the woods were much cooler. The air was balmy and sweet. The pine trees rose from the ground tall and protectively, shading them from the worst of the sun. Little pieces of the sun still trickled through the gaps in the trees, dancing and lighting the crisp, dark ground beneath. Leaves had begun to fall slowly, for it was now September, and autumn was fast approaching with its cold wet spells dreaded nearly as much as the sun. The woods seemed more alive, the dead leaves occasionally rustled with the work of mice or the evil slithering plans of snakes, whilst flies danced idly through the air, passing the time by annoying Chiara, who swatted them away lazily.

The air smelt and tasted different up here. It tasted of rich soil, untainted by the blasting rays of the sun, the scent was rich with nourishment and moisture. Fungus claimed some of the trees, moss bubbled like lava on the dead boughs, hiding scraggly squirrels and other woodland animals, who rustled around, busy in their preparations for winter, ivy wrapped and clung to the trunks of trees in a decoration of deceit.

There was not another soul in this place, which many people feared for its tales of wolves, bears and wild boars, who tore and ravished the ground beneath. But some people were scared by other immortal things, for many claimed that the wood was dark and crowded with ghosts, long lost tormented spirits of forgotten families, but on a day like this, it was hard to believe this to be true.

There was no breeze, and so every sound seemed magnified, their breath, the heavy treading of their footsteps, and even their thoughts seemed louder.

As Chiara trampled further up the hill, she felt liberated and free for the first time in weeks, yet a persistent worry still bothered her sleep.

The church bells called longingly to the mountains, echoing and rebounding on the rigid nerves of Chiara.

She was to be married in two days.

Two days from now she would no longer be a free woman, but strapped to a man, whose temper changed and fluctuated with the wind.

Over the past two weeks, the wedding preparations had been in full swing, and she had barely had five minutes alone with her thoughts. She had her wedding dress fitted and cut, arranged decorations, finalized the service with the priest, tasted the food and wine for the wedding meal, and finally, the worst of all the jobs, she had met his parents.

They were proud, poised and constantly pushing their wealth in her face, as if they were still trying to dissuade her from marrying their son. It seemed they tried everything to intimidate her, they wore the most lavish designer clothes, and expensive jewellery was strung around every exposed part of their body, as if the glitter and gold would blind the very eyes of Chiara. Vincenzo had not helped matters, for he never defended her or showed her off as a wonderful woman, but only joined in with their bitter defacing of her character.

But today, she vowed she would try to forget all this and enjoy her last day of freedom with Domenico, who would soon be leaving to study and shake away the shadows of this town.

Sometimes, she hated Domenico, for she envied his bravery and distance towards his family. He did not seem bound by guilt or obligation. He did not care who he left behind and who he might meet in the future. He did not care about leaving his family, or herself...

...but he was troubled by the thought of Chiara leaving him. He already felt a haunting hollowness within his heart for the day when she would be lost to him forever. Who would he talk to? Who would he walk with? Who would understand him as well as she did? Who would listen to him? Who would he depend on? Who...

...would she cry to? Who would understand her as well as he did? She glanced towards Domenico and felt an emptiness dig a place into her heart, like a grave. Chiara could already feel an oppressing grief, like a widower, suffocate her for the day when Domenico would be lost forever. It felt as though he was dying, and that day was his funeral, where she would finally have buried him away from her future, and his thoughts would be eternally extinguished from her ears. They would never laugh together, whisper together, hold each other again, and this thought terrified her, for who would she turn to? She believed she would go crazy with her own thoughts, and grow mad within her own body, just like Domenico, for his body was a straitjacket on his emotions. She could rarely read his mind, yet, despite this, she knew he would be her failing and falling to hell. After all these years, she was beginning to see how dangerous this friendship had become, for she entirely depended on him to survive, and without...

...her he should die, mad and alone, for he dangerously depended on her to live. The love between them was like the tendrils on the grapevines, the wood was pierced permanently within the soil, just like the love within his heart. Once, he had believed that Chiara, like the grapevines, had clung to this love as he did, but now, it seemed she was growing away from its toxic power with the maturity of another venomous love. Domenico would have done anything to protect her, for even though her love was distant, Chiara was still embedded within his skin, hair and heart, and she would be forever. Yet, one thing he could not shield Chiara from was the disease within Vincenzo, a deadly disease, one that would kill her instantly, like the phylloxera bugs turning the grapes black with their poison, and there was nothing he could do to combat this force, the only person who could was Chiara.

He peered over at her and noticed how red and tense her face was, her teeth were gritted together, her eyebrows were drawn tightly together, and her eyes squinted, yet he could not understand why she looked so upset. What was she thinking about? He loved Chiara for many reasons, but there was one which topped all others. Domenico found it hard to read people's emotions, but with Chiara he could understand her, like being in a foreign library and finding the only book which speaks your native language. Yet the nearing days of the wedding had made them distant, so that he struggled to understand her face, as if the book he had once understood had been cursed forever, unreadable. He wished she knew that her reasons for marrying Vincenzo were not based on love, but on the need to forget her past suffering. Yet, how could he show her? What…

…could she have become if she had allowed her mind to forget the past as her mother had done? Suddenly she wondered as to where her mother was, where did she walk? What did she do in her spare time? Did she work? Did she have a new partner? Did she think about her? Did she have half siblings? Did she ever want to come back and see Chiara? See what she had done to her daughter, how she had damaged Chiara's life with her selfish actions. But most likely she had forgotten her and the life she once had. Sometimes, Chiara believed it would have been easier if her mother had just passed away, for then Chiara could draw comfort from the heavens, rather than bitterness from her betrayal. Perhaps her father would have been different, braver with the bliss that his wife had not left because she wanted to, but because God wanted her to go.

What would her mother have thought of Vincenzo? What would she have advised? Would she have told her to chase her dreams or save her family? Would she have advised her to follow Domenico and study?

She could not say, for her mother was a complete stranger to her, and to predict her thoughts would have been…

…impossible to believe Chiara's mother would have wanted her to marry that vile man, for he would not set her mind…

…free from the longing for Domenico, and the pain this longing incurred. Within this last week, she had not seen much of Domenico, and subsequently she was learning to accept that the unrequited love she had for him was withering with the emptiness of her wishes. But now, with him beside her, that love erupted once again, and with effort, she tried to draw comfort from her imaginary new life as a married woman in Milan, free from all ties of her past. She held onto this false future, like a buoy to a drowning swimmer, for it promised her…

…a life of hellish entrapment, where her heart would die and her imagination…

…was running wild with the wealth Vincenzo promised.

This promise would set her free, free to live her own life as she wished it.

Smiling contently, she imagined herself promenading around the grand city of Milan, her arm resting in Vincenzo's as he guided her through all its rich history and richer shops, buying her expensive jewellery and clothes she would have once been ashamed to have. She could not wait to see the envy upon other women's faces as they gazed with jealous admiration at her bag, knowing it cost more than what they made in a year. She wanted to be…

…envied Chiara for she was smiling without a concern for her future. How could she be smiling when her wedding was in two days? He could not stop the knots of anxiety, which pestered him in the middle of the night, from returning now. Worry spiked his happiness, for she seemed happy, but why? He knew why, and she did not, this was the crucial difference. He knew what her future husband was, and the closeness of the wedding made him fidget with the guilt of his secret. Should he tell her? Surely, she would find out soon, but was this the wrong time? Yet, if she married him that would be even worse? He had not slept soundly the last week, for his mind had mediated and mulled over what he had seen and the impact it would have for Chiara. He did not want to hurt her, yet to withhold this crucial information was morally wrong. Why was love so complicated, so crammed with secrecy and lies? Was all love like this? If it was, he would be glad to live alone, and he thanked his body for granting him with a brain rather than beauty. He was thankful to study the biology of plants rather than the biology of a human heart. It seemed easier and less wearing on his energy.

Yet, when he looked over at Chiara, his heart ragingly needed her with a long brewing love which had never been dispelled or tasted. He wanted to know what it was like to kiss those lips, hold her naked body in his arms, trace his fingers over every place his eyes could see and not see, run his hands through her soft, straight locks, and kiss the pale space of her neck that never saw sunlight, and place his finger in the crook of her elbow before leading her into a dance.

Forget this, forget her, he tried to instruct his mind, but it was pointless, for this fire of love would only die when he should die.

Domenico hiked faster, desperate to extinguish this unsettling energy of passion, which made his mouth dry, his heart pound, and his penis throb with life.

Finally, they reached the spot which had welcomed them many times before.

Their calf muscles ached, and their chests heaved, but they both stood still, completely captivated and speechless by this place and the memories which haunted it. The first time they had found this place they had been ten, and it was the summer holiday, bored of the town and the other children, they had escaped. They had embarked on this grand adventure with backpacks stuffed with sweets and sugary drinks, and their imaginations wild with ignorance. They had scoured the intricate route of the woods for hours, until finally they had reached this spot with muddy, tired faces and scratched, dry bloody legs. They had spent the whole day there together, playing games and chatting as freely as the birds in the trees above. When they had both arrived home, they were punished severely for escaping, but it had been worth it.

Another memory that crowded their vision was when they were thirteen, they had sat in this spot talking of dreams and destinations they wanted to go, their minds already maturing with the black spell of adolescents.

Another memory was Chiara crying in Domenico's arms, admitting sheepishly that her period had started, but she had no idea what to do without her mother's help. But it was not her period which had made her cry, but the cruel way her brain could no longer recall her mother's image. Domenico had comforted her with the ruthless words of reality, which had caused them to argue. Yet, those words had been important to Chiara, for it finally rid the last speck of sad hope she had left of her mother's return.

And there was one memory, one precious piece of gold that neither talked of, for it had the potential to destroy the whole structure of their friendship.

"It's always more beautiful than I remember," Chiara breathed, her eyes and mind awash with the poignant prettiness of her past. This place was like finding an old, pressed flower in a dull book, reminding her of all the untroubled joy she once knew. She knew that no matter what happened she would always have those days to take to the grave with her, for they were imprinted in the blackest ink on her heart, like the eternity of a tattoo.

"Yes, I know what you mean," Domenico agreed. The picture of this place, the only reason why he wanted to stay in this dreaded town with Chiara beside him, the prickly trees behind him, the smell of the woody, sweet pines, the chill of the air on his arms, the delicate wildflowers, and this view of their small world before him.

Chiara threw herself on a fallen bough and pulled the water bottle from the side of her rucksack, thirstily drinking and filling her mouth with its coldness.

Domenico sat on her right as he always had done, and took the handed water bottle from Chiara, relishing the water with gratitude.

They slouched in the shade of the wood, gazing at the sunlit view without a word, their eyes, ears and senses all instructed by the beauty of that place. There were many places Domenico and Chiara had never been, but they would always believe this place to be the most beautiful.

The view was framed by a border of pines that parted at this exact spot, as if nature had intended without accident or coincidence to show off this irresistible view. The view boasted of high mountains, cluttered with gifts of bushes and trees, alight and alive with the ravishing sun. Below this, the low valley was shadowy and still, sparse, except for the knotted ribbons of vines and the frozen dancers of olive trees, like a secret dance floor. Further afield you could see the rows upon rows of smiling yellow sunflowers, their faces upturned to the sun, drinking its golden rays, like beer. The land was a rise and fall pattern, a patchwork of colours, greens, dark greens, yellows, browns and more, whilst some were dark and eerily grey with the shadows of clouds. And then finally the land declined and flattened, until your eyes feasted upon the dazzling turquoise of the never-ending sea, which today seemed to almost merge with the sky, like gravity had been tampered with, so that the very sea washed over their heads. This sight of the sea was the only knowledge of other worlds, and even the most desolate of souls could not end their life at this view, for it dreamt up adventures and new places to explore and escape to. This sight was alluring in its magic, bewitching their eyes with hope, for the sea looked so ideal and dreamlike, but as you drew closer and closer, these dreams were dashed, for the waves would crash and thrash them against the shore, like a wild beast.

Ripping a cereal bar open, the pair halved it and munched hungrily on the food, forgetting the view for only a moment.

Wiping her chocolatey mouth on her arm, and licking the melted chocolate from her fingers, Chiara stood to her sore feet and wandered closer to the edge of the mountain, her eyes treasuring the sight of the countryside and sea, the only small square of the world she knew and loved.

"Domenico, look, come here. I can see the Island of Tremeti, come here," cried Chiara excitedly, her left hand waving out to that place of great mystery.

Domenico pulled himself to his feet and followed the direction of her hand with a flickering, crooked smile.

The Island of Tremeti stood small, proud, yet mysterious, like a volcano floating on the water. This place had been a great mystery for Domenico and Chiara, for some days it was visible, yet other days it seemed to disappear, as if it had never existed. The volcano could have been a maddening thing for an explorer, for if you wanted to find your way there, you would be constantly fooled and misled by its disappearing act. They had created grand stories of this island; Domenico had believed as a child that the island came alive when someone was in distress and needed help or a place to flee. Yet Chiara believed the island showed itself because a woman had been banished there for loving a married man, and so it only appeared on occasions to remind her lover and his wicked wife that she was still watching and waiting for him. However, education had robbed them of these fairy stories, replacing them with facts on the weather being the reason for its visibility. Yet, this place still held a strong, mystical beauty in their hearts, for it was the island of dreams, the place you could escape and be any person you wanted to be.

"Do you think we will ever get there, Domenico? Like we always talked about?" queried Chiara, leaning her hot head against his cool shoulder.

Domenico stiffened slightly, for his emotions were delirious with the desire to be lost with her at that island, and in that moment, love seemed a strong, supernatural current, which, he believed, he could not defeat this time.

"Yes, of course we will. One day we will walk to the very top of that island and look back at the land laughing about how often we talked about it," Domenico muttered shakily.

Suddenly Domenico imagined standing on that island looking back on themselves, and how small and insignificant they would be. This thought made him think, for if he said or did something that he shouldn't, surely it would be insignificant to the greater world, just as an ant's doings held no consequence to his life.

"It would be amazing to feel completely unchained from anyone or anything," murmured Chiara, her lips moving against Domenico's arm, stifling his heart with a frantic passion.

"Yes, imagine walking along the beach with only the sky, and the sea, and the sand, and—"

"Do you ever think about that time when we were fifteen up here?" Domenico suddenly asked without thought.

Chiara pulled away from him with shock, for they had both agreed to never speak of that day. She carefully glanced up at his face, but it was focused solely on the view without a hint of emotion. What would make him say that? Why...

...had he said that? He was a fucking idiot! Oh God, this was going to backfire very badly, he dreaded.

"I... I... I don't know, sometimes, do you?" Chiara stuttered, her eyes fluttering here and there.

"Yes, sometimes I do, especially today," he admitted shyly.

Chiara's dry, pale lips trembled with the words of her next question: "Why today?"

Domenico cleared his throat, as if to buy himself some more time for his answer.

Turning his face on Chiara, he saw the panic and passion within his own heart in her eyes. His glasses became steamy, and he removed them, making Chiara's face become a fuzzy complication of colours and emotions.

"I don't know, perhaps it's the thought of things changing. Maybe it's because I feel I am missing out on something. Bianca has Alessandro, and you have Vincenzo, and I guess I feel alone," confessed Domenico, laughing slightly at his own stupid sentimentality.

He turned his gaze back on the view, and Chiara could see the sharp clench and unclenching of his jaw working as he stood silent and lost in his own thoughts.

Chiara did not know what to say, she felt shocked and astounded by the admittance of his feelings. Domenico never exposed how he truly felt, he always kept his feelings locked tight and far away from everyone, even herself. But with these words, she could see that he truly did feel abandoned and isolated in his cold relationship with science.

"You don't need to feel alone—"

"I know I don't need to, but I do, maybe it's this place with all its memories and history and…" Domenico's voice trailed away, and his eyes flickered and flashed across the view with melancholy, as he placed his glasses back on the bridge of his nose.

Chiara was stunned, speechless, what could she do? She wanted to help him, she wanted him to feel that she would always be there for him no matter how far apart they were, yet how could she show him this?

Suddenly that memory of when they were fifteen came back to her with such a sudden force, she felt almost giddy with its presence. Domenico had been there for her on that day, but also every day before and every day after.

"Domenico," Chiara whispered, the blood thudding through her ears, making her body pulse with its energy.

Turning his whole body to face Chiara, they locked eyes. He was astounded by her eyes, wide and open, the dark lashes curled right back to reveal their tragic and tantalizing turquoise, speaking a story he could not hear.

Chiara could not let go of those swift, silver eyes, and they were magnified, like stars through a telescope, burning, flashing, and dying without anyone's knowing. Those eyes, which had represented perfection, like neat silver cutlery and polished clasping cufflinks were tarnished, pinging apart this dishevelled truth.

Stepping towards him, she cupped his jaw in her hands, and placed a kiss as light as anything upon his lips.

It was tiny. Insignificant. The smallest meeting and parting of lips, yet all the barriers of control came down, and a chaotic confusion ran riot in their heads.

A brief silence followed, the noise of the woods was unheard by this man and woman.

"Why did you do that?" Domenico croaked, his lips so close to the bridge of her nose, if he merely bent his head, he could reclaim that kiss and never let it go.

Chiara did not move, for her aching heart bashed furiously against her chest, as if it wanted to escape. She thought she might die. All those weeks of holding her emotions of love and passion within her were all for nothing. She had released herself into temptation, and now she did not know the path back to the principled past.

"I… do you remember when we were fifteen in this exact spot you kissed me?" Chiara recalled, her blood racing and rattling around her body, as her hands softly slid away from Domenico's face.

"Yes, you were upset because the girls at school made fun of you because you had never kissed anyone," Domenico remembered, his red lips unfamiliar with the words of the friendship, forbidden secret.

"Yes well, I thought I would return the favour after all these years and to remind you that you are not alone," Chiara broke, her eyes fluttering nervously, whilst her fingers twisted and knotted with a strange discomfort.

"I know, I just, in all honesty I will miss you a lot. We have never spent one day apart, and it will be strange you not being there," whispered Domenico, his voice low and fragile.

Chiara gazed once again into those familiar spiralling, grey eyes, and she could see the hurt of their goodbyes already playing within his head.

Looking towards the view, she stared at the island of Tremiti, alone and isolated, full and crowded with magic and mystery and the dreams they would never share.

"Everything is changing so fast. When I was fifteen, I would never have imagined I would be getting married so soon, and that we would be parted," Chiara reminisced sadly, the view of Tremiti becoming hazy as her eyes became studded with tears.

"Neither would I."

"Thanks, glad to think you wouldn't have thought I could marry," scoffed Chiara attempting humour.

"You were my first kiss, I probably thought we would marry," Domenico joked, but the sentence fell flat and stale, tightening the tension already present.

Chiara moved away, tucking a loose strand of hair behind her ear as she thought about how different her life could have been and would be. She could have been happy, so happy. She could have been loved. She could have been respected.

She could have had everything, maybe not gold and silver, but a true purpose, a true love, a true home.

"I have a surprise for you, Domenico, I haven't showed anyone yet," Chiara spoke excitedly, trying to bring both minds away from the cunning cruelties of fate.

"What? Let's see," Domenico perked, as he went to stand near her, the crisp, early autumn leaves crunching beneath his shoes.

Chiara bent down, and unzipped the backpack, before she pulled from it a long, white dress. Holding it against her small body, she clasped it to her chest with shy excited giggles, whilst her cheeks flushed a soft pink with pride.

It was a wedding dress, crumpled and creased, screwed into a tight ball of unforgiving resentment and shame, like a hurtful letter crumpled up to be thrown into the fire.

"What do you think?" Chiara burst as she twirled the dress around, like she was dancing her first dance, dragging the hem through the stray, spiky pine leaves.

Domenico did not speak, for fury boiled through every pore in his body, as he watched Chiara's petite body became engulfed by this white sheet, like a funeral sheen. Suddenly he snapped, and he grabbed his backpack, hurriedly throwing it over his shoulder, before marching away without even looking at Chiara.

"Where are you going?" Chiara asked, startled by his response, lowering the dress from her chest with shame.

"I'm leaving before I say something I regret," Domenico growled without stopping.

"Don't you like it?" Chiara questioned; her pointy eyebrows clenched together with confusion as she followed him deeper into the shade of the woods.

Domenico froze and turned to look at her with a face dark with the shadows, and darker by its malice.

Chiara instantly stopped, slightly afraid of this new deadly expression.

"Yes, I like the dress, I just don't like the person in it," Domenico spoke, his voice cold and cruel, like black ice.

"What? What do you mean? How could you say that," shrieked Chiara, her fingers gripping the silky, white material.

"What is wrong with you, Chiara? What is wrong with your fucking mind?"

Chiara stepped back and stared at him with incredulous blue eyes.

"There is nothing wrong with me, but there is something definitely wrong with you—"

"Yes, there is, do you want to know what's wrong with me? Do you really want to know what's wrong with me?" shouted Domenico as he stepped quickly towards her, until he was as close as they were when they kissed.

"Yes, what's wrong with you?" challenged Chiara, unafraid of his close presence.

"You know what's wrong with me. I am in love with you, crazily in love with you, and I have been for a long time. And you are going to marry a man you don't love and who also doesn't love you and never will," exploded Domenico, his chest heaving with this expulsion of passion that tingled upon his tongue, like sherbet.

Chiara stared at Domenico in bewilderment, her mouth hung open, as if she wished to say something but couldn't.

Domenico flung his body away from Chiara muttering swear words repeatedly, before smashing his fist against the dark, scaly bough of a nearby tree. The bark cut the skin of his knuckles, causing blood to trickle through his fingers.

"You can't be," Chiara murmured after a while, as she moved away from him, her whole body numbed by his words.

"Yes, I can, and I don't care anymore because you will still marry that man and I will go and study—"

"No, I don't believe it—"

"What have I got to lose? You have got your plan all carefully picked and laid out—"

"No—"

"Yes, you will feast off his money and fortune, but you will never be loved—"

"Vincenzo does love me, don't say that—"

"Vincenzo does not even love women," shouted Domenico, his face bent and threatening over Chiara's shocked, pale face.

"What are you talking about, of course he does," Chiara stammered, her hands shaking as she held her dancing wedding dress weakly between her fingers.

"No, he doesn't, I saw him with Matteo, both of them were fucking naked and kissing a few Sundays ago—"

Domenico was suddenly silenced by the sharp slap of Chiara's hand across his face.

The wedding dress fell to the floor, as she covered her whole face within her trembling hands.

Domenico moved his hand to the red splash of colour upon his left cheek and stared at her with equal shock.

They held one another's mad gazes, like two wild animals released, savage and unsafe.

Domenico snapped his body around and marched away, but suddenly he felt two hands grip his backpack and pull him back.

"Tell me you are lying, tell me you are lying, tell me you are fucking lying," screamed Chiara, as Domenico tried to shrug her hand from his rucksack, but she clung on, as if her life depended on it.

"Let go, Chiara—"

"No, tell me you are lying," commanded Chiara, sweat trickling from her temple, clamping her hair to her face with despair.

"No, I am not fucking lying, Chiara, ask your wonderful fiancé, he might give you all the juicy details," sneered Domenico, his breathing was hard, and his eyes were blurred with tears.

"I am still going to marry him, so if you think this little story will deter me, you are wrong," exclaimed Chiara, bashing his rucksack brutally one last time.

"I know you will because you are weak and you have no courage, you are a fucking coward, you just want security, but that isn't happiness," laughed Domenico scornfully, shuffling his rucksack back to its original place.

Chiara stopped, her fist frozen in the air, for his words sliced her conscience deeply with self-repugnance and shame.

"I am happy."

"Yes, sure, and I can fly, have a good day on Sunday and a happy life with your future husband," Domenico snarled sarcastically, as he trudged away, and this time for good.

Chiara stood, vacantly watching her oldest friend move away from her forever, but she would not let him go so easily.

Domenico could hear the light crackle of footsteps following him, and he only prayed she would not follow him home and be a witness to his woe.

"Why did you tell me that? Why did you tell me you loved me?" Chiara choked feebly, her head swimming and the lump in her throat becoming larger.

Domenico stopped in his tracks and spoke to the faceless pine trees before him: "I don't know, I just had to."

"How long have you felt like this for?" Chiara asked softly, her steps treading closer and closer to Domenico.

The stooped posture of Domenico did not move, but Chiara could see his cheeks were wet, for the sun glistened upon them.

He coughed, clearing his throat of the suffocating sorrow.

"I can't remember, a long time."

Chiara's body shook, and the tears slowly crept back into her eyes, as her lungs caught the air with a snap, like she had been pounded in the gut.

They were silent, ears aware to the twittering birds in the trees above.

"All this time you have felt like this, and you never said anything. But today, two days before my wedding you decide to tell me. Why did you do this to me? Why? Did you think I would just run back to the village and cancel the wedding and tell him and his parents to fuck off back to Milan? I mean, why would you do this?" Chiara spoke, her voice hoarse and trembling, whilst tears uncontrollably jumped from her eyes.

Domenico turned around, for he recognized that voice, and it killed him to think he was the reason for her tears.

"Please, Chiara, I am sorry, I made a mistake, but I had to tell you—"

"But we saw each other every day for years and you waited until this moment—"

"I know, I'm sorry, please listen—"

"All this time, you tricked me with your friendship, and kept your distance, never saying a single word, why couldn't you tell me?"

"I was nervous, I didn't know when the right moment to—"

"And this is the right moment?"

"No, but I could not stop myself from saying it when you kissed me and then got that dress out, I just wanted to scream—"

"What did you think I was going to wear, my fucking underwear?"

"No, it's just that, I always thought when I saw you in a wedding dress it would be at our wedding not some idiot's," Domenico flung the words out without clarity or conscience.

Chiara struggled to speak, for grief clogged her throat, as she tried to comprehend his words, causing a long teal vein to strip across her left temple with the stress of her sorrow.

Her shoulders shook as she sobbed into her hands, her eyes hidden from Domenico's own misty gaze.

Domenico came towards her, but she violently pushed him away, repulsed.

"Get away from me, you are crazy," barked Chiara through her breathless sobs.

"I was only trying to help," broke Domenico, trying to hold her, yet she lashed at his skin with her sharp nails, like a vicious cat.

"Help! Help? I have waited all these years for you to tell me those very words and now you have done it at the worst time. I will be married in two days," cried Chiara, her face contorted with pain, whilst her blue eyes were a frenzy of insanity.

"I know, I'm sorry, please forgive me," begged Domenico, his lips and chin were trembling as he tried to hold her.

"I can't, I will never forgive you for this. I never want to see you again, ever, leave me now," Chiara ordered, her sobs suffocated for a moment, so that her words cut the woods with their clarity, which even silenced the birds in the trees.

He waited, examining her rigid, wet face for something, anything to change, but her eyes were set in her decision.

It was all over!

Domenico nodded and turned away. He ambled distractingly into the distance, not once looking back at his first true love.

Chiara watched his blurry figure, until he had completely disappeared.

She moved numbly back to where her rucksack lay, before falling to the ground, inches away from her crumpled, white wedding dress.

She wanted to tear that wedding dress to pieces, rip its lace with her very teeth, yet equally she did not want to touch it, for she was terrified by its black magic.

Bending her face to the soil, she cried bitterly.

After a while, she looked up, the sunlight slanted through the forest at a different angle, and the sky seemed even more faded than before.

Tremiti was now a brown blur on the horizon, vague and undefinable. Dreamless.

Yet, Chiara's attention was arrested by something else, the leaping flames of a field burning in the distance, frizzling and scolding the land with a loss of control.

Was this an omen?

To end everything here and now, and allow the flames to devour her, or wait for the fire engines to save her from self-destruction.

Caro Signoro Maestro,

I have not received any letters from you, not a phone call or any information reminding me there is still a world outside these barred, barbaric walls.

Are there still plants growing or withering? Are buildings still standing? Are people still travelling by car? Are people real or robots?

What time of year is it? It feels cold in this brutal box, but it has always felt cold.

Tell me, God, what is the weather like? What plants are in full bloom? Has olive picking season started or ended? Has the grass grown lush and green? Are the woods covered in snow? Is there heavy rainfall washing away the rare truffles? Is the sun burning? Burning the grass? Burning the skin? Burning the trees? Burning the flowers? Is the end of the world upon us? Have all those climate change talks come true? Is it no longer global warming, but global burning? Has it always been that?

Burning. Burning. Burning.

Signoro Maestro, tell me how much time has passed? Is my nonna still alive? Are my parents still alive? Has Bianca had her child? Or is she bulged and bursting with the child, like a seahorse? Or is the child already crying in her arms? Or maybe it is running down the streets? Was the child pushed away from the arms of his family for being a sinful child, like myself?

Ha, it is funny God isn't it? I don't even know what that child is, but I know we have something in common. It is a sinner just like his uncle Domenico, and when I finally leave this hellhole I might pass the child as it comes in to serve its time. It will be in here, I am sure of it. He is born from a place of sin into a place of sin. But I would never recognize my own nephew, for it would be a complete stranger to me and my crime.

God, explain to me how an innocent baby can be deemed as sinful as a murderous man? I have caught you out, haven't I? You can't explain this fatal mistake. 'Sin' is a made-up word, yet it has damaged people, shoved people in cages and killed them. 'Sin' was a word made up by those fat men who wrote the Bible to isolate and criminalise the weak. 'Sin' is a word made up in that bullshit we call the Bible, made up by those blokes with broken hearts, made up by those men, who feared lying dead in the ground. But God you have it all wrong, death has no sin? Those fears of death, heaven and hell, are in living, breathing and laughing. But those big boys with all their guilt and betrayal had to write a set of laws to make their sinful lives justifiable. Oh God, your book is a book of jokes, a set of board game instructions. Tell those who love without God's blessing to go to hell, tell those who top themselves to go to hell, tell those who love differently to go to hell, and those who tell shall go to heaven.

Reset your sins with lies. Reset your guilt with lies. Reset your mistakes with lies.

LIES! LIES! LIES!

God, if you don't believe me, go and speak to Matteo, he will tell you everything. But don't believe a word of it, he is a liar, lying in the grass, lying naked, lying with that man. That man. He had been there at the courtroom, both of them, defending their secret, their lies, their lust. Ha ha! God I am laughing, tears are rolling down my cheeks. It is funny, you, Matteo who was so confident was so scared, and I saw your fear like I saw it in the fields. I saw you begging me to not speak your lies whilst you spoke your own. I saw you shaking. I saw you paling. I saw you save that man over your brother. I saw you, Matteo, compromise the laws of legality for love, love, love, that damned word, that wicked word, that sinful word.

Do you know God, your rich disciples made a big mistake when writing the Bible, for when they talk of LOVE, in real life it translates as LIE.

Please God tell me how many centuries, months, years, weeks, days, seconds have passed? I entered this cell at nineteen years of age, but how old am I now? Twenty? Forty? Seventy? I don't feel any age, but I have a number, and this number comes with no measurement of time.

I see this number tattooed across the walls of my cell, on the foreheads of the prison guards, on the bed, on the toilet, and I can even see it burned into my own skin, like thousands of bloodthirsty fleas.

666.

This number excites me, for I know it well. Haha! God I can't stop laughing. I can see your face, and what a look of disgust. Why are you disgusted God? Tell me! Why are you angry? Why are you disappointed in me? Answer me!

Can you blame me for finding comfort in this number? You have been no help! You fucking useless layabout!

You might think I'm crazy, but I know Satan. I sit next to him all day, face to face. He watches my every move, and offers me advice, much more than you have ever done for me!

Satan does not take the form of man nor beast, he is these four merciless walls, hollering and harassing me, pushing each wall closer and closer together crushing, crunching my bones to dust, like a pestle and mortar. The prison guards, ha, they are Satan's disciples, whispering, softly, softly, shh, shh… the savage secrets of their boss.

But God, believe me when I say this, I am safe. I still have the crucifix of her guarding me from any evil spirits, but I am starting to believe she is the evil spirit.

She is a witch, hypnotizing me, bewitching me, killing me, cursing me.

She makes me smell the woody vines. She makes me taste the sweetness of the grapes. She makes me see the burning sun. She makes me hear her vile voice.

Her vile screams, screaming and screaming and screaming, until I scream.

Her eyes follow me, they are the eyes of Satan.

Big and blue, like the planet of Pluto, foreign and forgotten. They are a plague, a poison, a possession.

She is a fixation, a fantasy, a fiend.

She is the murderer. She made the fire start with her wine-tainted lips and hot hands.

She wanted to die, and she wanted my dreams to die too.

Yet, God, why am I still drawn to her?

She is gone, isn't she?

She is dead, a pile of ash blowing upon the wind, lost and unpeaceful. Is this why she haunts my nights?

I can hear her now whispering, teasing, laughing my name, and I call back to her, shout at her.

Where is she?

She is coming closer.

'...Other seeds fell among thorns, which grew up and choked the plants...'

She is speaking to me The Parable of the Sower. God, she is trying to tell me something. I can hear her voice desperate, straining, searching.

Say it again, Chiara!

'...Other seeds fell among thorns, which grew up and choked the plants...'

I UNDERSTAND, CHIARA, I FINALLY UNDERSTAND!

That man choked you to death, he strangled all the dreams from your heart, he stole all the happiness from your eyes, he bashed and broke all your love, like glass. He made your life unlivable. If it had been only the soil and seeds, you would have lived. Oh God, she would have lived happily, she would have lived unafraid, she would have lived as a girl should live.

God, do not reproach me for my tears, she could have been something, she could have lived.

Do not touch my shoulder, I don't want to hear your lame advice.

Stop touching my shoulder!

Stop!

Wait! I have made a mistake!

Don't stop!

Chiara come back, come back to me, forever.

God, Chiara is alive.

Alive.

She is singing in my ear. She is leaning over my shoulder as I write.

Oh stop, Chiara, I can't write that.

I am laughing God. I am smiling. I am happy, so, so happy because Chiara is here, watching me with her Adriatic blue eyes and whispering to me of the Island of Tremiti. We are planning a trip there soon, where no one will find us!

Life is good, God, I'll write soon.

Lots of love,
Domenico

TEN

Bianca waited.

There was no clock in Chiara's room, but somehow she could feel the minutes, slow and painful, move onwards and onwards.

Ripping a handful of tissues from the box, Bianca tried to squeeze her fingers between her sweaty cleavage, but it was tight and unmovable. Bianca felt even this small movement made her feel even hotter than before. She sighed and screwed the useless tissue into a ball, tossing it to the old, wooden floor with frustration.

She had not felt so heavy with her pregnancy until this day, for the dress was suffocatingly tight across her growing breasts, and the skirt did not flow as it did, but hugged her slightly bulging pelvis with mocking.

The heat also made her feel heavier than usual, for it seemed to make her fingers and toes swell, and every movement felt emphasised and exhausting.

Lethargically moving towards the nearby window, the sun was hazy with the humidity. The thick, sticky rays oozed through the threadbare lace curtains like lemon curd, only adding to Bianca's discomfort.

Running her hand beneath her swollen breasts, she felt how damp the material had become. Shit, she thought, this material was expensive, an emerald green silk sewn by the skilled expensive fingers of a Milano, and now it was ruined by her sweat marks.

With this thought, she yanked the window open and leant her melting face out into the street.

But there was no wind.

Not even a whisper.

The street below was deserted, and the sky above was empty with clouds, as if every form of nature had abandoned its posts for the day.

Suddenly Bianca turned her attention to a window ledge on the opposite side of the street, for this was the only sound she could hear. The bleat, bleat, bleat of three, no four, baby pigeons. Peering closer, she could see how beneath their layers of thick, raggedy fluff, they were skinny, and their mouths were open wide, begging for food.

Bianca's indulgent heart softened, and she felt her crazy emotions whizz around her body, making her want to cry at the plight of these small innocent creatures. They wanted help, but though people heard no one did anything, including herself.

Dabbing the corners of her eyes, she removed a thick, curdled lump of grey mascara. She leant her tired face against the window, closing her eyes, hoping she could shut away the future from happening, wishing she could travel back to the past, longing to live the life she once had.

She remembered that day when she had tried on the Maid of Honour dress with Chiara, and even now, she felt a smile curl her lips with pleasure. They had laughed so hard that tears had leaked down their cheeks, and their lips had ached. Bianca had twirled around in the dress feeling beautiful, like a movie star, clutching a glass of champagne, as she watched Chiara watch her with an envious eye. She had not seen that gaze since the news of her pregnancy, but what did she expect? Of course, no one was

202

jealous of her beauty now, for her eyes were as black as bruises from sleepless nights, her forehead was heavily lined, and her once velvet hair was black, flat, and thick with grease. She was looking more like her mother each new day, she thought depressively.

Suddenly, she was awoken from her thoughts by the creak of a door. Flipping her head around, Bianca gasped and leapt to her feet, forgetting her selfish melancholy instantly, for stood within the doorway was the bride-to-be, Chiara.

"Chiara, you look, you look, just wow, I don't think I have ever seen you so beautiful," exclaimed Bianca with tearful, excited eyes.

Chiara only shrugged her shoulders, as if this comment unsettled her. Bianca paid no attention to Chiara's reaction, for she had been acting unusual ever since her walk with Domenico, which she could only assume had ended on bad terms, as neither had spoken since.

Walking slowly around Chiara, she admired the finery of the dress, for it seemed like a work of art. White lace upon white lace cascaded over Chiara's body, the hems decorated with little white flowers, whilst little diamonds or crystals had been sewn neatly along the waistline. She looked like a fairy-tale princess, and Bianca may have been even jealous of Chiara if it had not been for her miserable, mopey face.

As she moved around Chiara inspecting the fine material and intricate lace work, she noticed a faded brown stain, but she decided to ignore this, for the veil seemed to cover it. However, this was not the only one, for as Bianca examined the back there were more stains, like it had been dragged through the mud. Peering closer, Bianca touched the material, yet Chiara suddenly flinched away, flinging the skirt away from her eyes with a glare.

Standing to her full height, Bianca stepped away and smiled gently, yet her brows were narrowed in confusion. Where had those stains come from? What had Chiara been doing? Why did she react to Bianca's touch, as if she had poked at an open, infected wound?

It was bizarre, but this whole wedding was a strange occasion.

"I'll just finish the last of your make-up before the car arrives," Bianca encouraged, clasping Chiara's damp, fragile hand, as she ushered her towards the dressing table and away from any further tension.

They both sat down carefully, mindful of their expensive dresses.

They faced one another in silence.

Chiara refused to meet Bianca's eyes.

What was she hiding from her? Why was Chiara so upset? Was it merely nerves or something darker?

"Chiara, do you mind if I put a little more mascara and lipstick on you, it has faded slightly," Bianca inquired softly.

Chiara glanced up and nodded, uncaring.

Bianca reached for the sticky, black smeared mascara tube and untwisted the voluminous, jet-black brush from the tube.

Leaning closer to Chiara, she carefully combed the black ink through her curling lashes, already clumped with the first layer of mascara, before swapping the mascara for lipstick. Moving even closer, Bianca began to paint the ruby red paste across her cracked, faded lips, yet she did this quickly, for Chiara's breath wreaked of alcohol. It seemed to plaster the tense air between them with a cry for help, a cry of desperation, a cry of save me, save me, save me. But these words did not fall from Chiara's false lips, and so what could Bianca do?

Leaning slowly back, Bianca watched Chiara's body jitter nervously, and something within her heart sank, was it foreboding? Was it jealousy? Was it worry? Bianca believed it to be all three. This was not the girl she had grown up with. The girl who had been courageous. The girl who had been independent. The girl who had laughed loudly in the fields. The girl who had let her hair fly free. The girl whose face she had only ever known of being naked and smiling. This woman, who sat before her, with her neatly ironed brown hair pulled tight at the nape of her neck, her face a mask of pale pastes and powders, her eyes thickly lined with black, and her glossy red lips unmoving and silent, was not the Chiara she knew.

This was meant to be her special day, yet Chiara seemed as though she would rather have been anywhere else, perhaps even dead.

Taking Chiara's cold, moist hands within her own, Bianca wished she would look at her, but it seemed her eyes were jumping, leaping across every corner of her old bedroom, like fleas. It was unsettling, even disturbing.

"Chiara, are you ok? You seem sad, look it's not too late to cancel, if that's what you want," implored Bianca desperately, her eyes fixed on the false, even ugly face of Chiara.

Snapping her hands from Bianca's, Chiara folded them tightly across her chest and glared at her.

"That is exactly what you would want, anything to stop them from talking about your mistake," snipped Chiara sourly.

They stared at one another for a long time. Bianca felt her stomach swoop and dive, as she examined Chiara's cold, vacant dark eyes, for they seemed lost and disquieting, like the eyes of the dead.

Bianca dropped her gaze and noticed how Chiara's nails seemed to sharply pinch the backs of her naked arms.

Suddenly there was a loud blaring of horns.

The wedding car had arrived.

Chiara stood up, and Bianca followed. Stepping towards the bride, Bianca gently tugged the thinly laced white veil across her friend's face, shutting her frightened mind away from the world, blurring the future she would have to face alone.

"I'm sorry," whispered a frail voice from behind the net of spiders' webs.

Bianca smiled, yet that voice pierced her heart with its fragility, as she handed her friend the drooping bouquet of white lilies, sad and limp with the heat, just like the bride.

"It's OK, you have been stressed, don't worry about it," soothed Bianca, as she reached for her own bouquet.

Suddenly, Chiara threw her arms around her in a drunken, desperate embrace, clinging to Bianca like an inexperienced swimmer to a buoy in rough sea. Bianca held her tightly without a care for the creases in their dresses, rubbing her hand across her back like a mother to a crying child.

"Bianca, I'm scared," choked Chiara, her voice strained and hoarse with the putrid alcohol she had consumed secretly.

Bianca held her closer and felt the fast thudding of Chiara's heart, shaking her body against her own, but perhaps it was her own body which trembled with foreboding.

"You will be fine, Chiara, I promise," Bianca comforted, her voice swollen with tears, for she felt as though she was lying to her best friend about a future she could not predict.

There was another heavy beeping of horns.

Bianca pulled away from her reluctant friend, squeezing her hand encouragingly, as they turned to leave the hot, suffocating room of Chiara's past.

*

Chiara's father waited within the small, cream-coloured car, agitated and sweating through his old, moth-gobbled brown suit jacket. He had not worn this since his daughter's christening, and it still held stains from that worthless day. Rubbing his bloodshot eyes, his stomach began to toss with the alcohol he had consumed, and he gripped the burgundy leather seats to steady his spinning head.

The heat pounded against his face, like a heavy heartbeat, like knuckles smashing against his face. It seemed close, strangling around his neck, climbing through the thin, threadbare walls of his shirt, melting him into a puddle of mess, like a snowman. The heat was in his ears, ringing and hissing and hurting his brain. The heat was in his mouth, like a vacuum, dehydrating and draining all the words from his tongue, like the sun on the soil, evaporating the very source of life from the ground. The heat sealed his eyes tightly shut, like wax, closing away all the things he did not wish to see, and all the things he wished others did not see in him.

He felt her close. Her strange hands lying on his, soft and safe, poisonous and painful. The brush of her legs against his, a gruelling gentle reminder of how she could easily run from him. And then her face came fast and furious into his mind, shooting electrical currents of cruelty through his blood. She looked beautiful, smiling and secure, but she was leaving him, turning away from him, running, running, running.

Suddenly, Chiara's father opened his eyes with a gasp, as if he had been choking, and he met the icy, frightened and curious eyes of the driver, who looked away instantly.

He breathed hard, recovering from the shock of his wife's face. Where had she gone? Why had she gone?

Gazing up into the rear-view mirror, Chiara's father met his own hollow eyes. There was no colour in the irises, but the colour came from the black bags draped heavily beneath his frazzled lashes and through the red streams of fatigue, which stained the whites of his eyes, like the blood running from a murdered body. His cheeks were hollow, unshaven and shadowy, whilst his nose was almost purple with the endless intoxication of alcohol. His lips were grey and cracked and scowling. Lines of aging regret and worry were carved throughout his face, deep and dark, permanent. His grey, fluffy hair had receded, hiding behind his large ears wisps of dark youth. He could not remember the face he used to wear, or the smile he used to hold, or the twinkle in his eyes, for they had all been taken away when his woman left him. She left him nothing. Nothing. Not even his own features and fantasies.

Suddenly, the short, ugly driver jumped from the car, talking gruffly and irritatingly to the two girls. Chiara's father glanced out of the smeared window to see a vague, fuzzy outline of white and green. He grunted with annoyance and turned his face back to the opposite window, where the old ladies, who haunted the houses opposite, stood throwing handfuls of white petals to the blinding hot road, shouting with delight and congratulations.

Chiara's father sighed and turned his gaze to his dirty, scuffed coffee-coloured shoes, as he heard the click of the door and felt the thick, heaving lace of a wedding dress brush his arm. He did not look up or greet the two girls, who seemed quiet and tense, but kept his eyes on his shoes.

The door slammed, clicking tightly shut.

The driver fell back into his seat with a thud. The leather squeaked and the girls' dresses rustled and rippled, like seagulls hunting through rubbish bags.

The driver turned the key, and the car engine fidgeted, rumbled, then stopped. The driver huffed and snatched the keys out.

Chiara's father glanced at the hands of his daughter's, the heavy, blinding diamond engagement ring, a signal for his freedom. But there was something strange in her hands, for her middle and index finger were knotted so tightly together it turned her olive dark skin, white. Was she praying for the car to start or stop? What was his estranged daughter thinking? What was she wishing for?

Suddenly the car jerked to a start, and the driver beeped, beeped his horn at the crowds, antagonizing his dull, dizzying mind.

As the car pulled away from their 'family' home, Chiara's father turned his fuzzy, intoxicated eyes to his daughter. She looked fucking miserable, he thought carelessly. Why was she miserable? Why were women so hard to please? Did they like being miserable? Was it a women's entertainment, misery? Was it a hobby they pursued? He could not understand it. Yes, he was miserable, and his anticipated dread for the day had been confirmed quickly. He hated leaving the house, for he knew people whispered and picked apart his past with combs and tweezers of spite. Turning his gaze back to the street, they passed old, sweaty women with mouths moving, and he knew they were hissing his wife's name and debating the downfall of his life.

He knew they were scolding his lack of parenting, and those smiles were mocking, mocking his dependence on his daughter to survive. Those loud, round mouths spewed laughter at his unsuccessful life, his lifelong sentence of unemployment, his cruelty towards his daughter, and then they finished their laughter with a conclusion. A conclusion, which grated and scratched at his mind, like a rat. His wife was lucky to leave when she had, that is what they concluded, that is what they believed. But what they forgot was the man he had been before his wife had left. He had been a confident man, striving in his trade, successful in his love, and supportive of his small child. Yet when his wife had left so suddenly, without an explanation or goodbye, his whole existence had been destroyed and devastated by the depressive doubts, which harassed his brain day and night, day and night. But this town had not taken pity on him or tried to save him from his nightmares, they only ridiculed his inability to exist as a man. But what was a man without a woman? What was it to be a man?

He could not look at these ugly, aging beasts any longer, and he wished they would crawl back into their houses to die quietly and painfully and alone, like he had been doing for years. Staring back at his daughter, his heart was not jubilant or joyous at the sight of her fine white lace and a veil, which hid many untold secrets that only time could unravel. All the memories of his wife were brought back to life. They could have been twins, mother and daughter. He felt as though he was in a time warp of his own life, travelling years and years back to the day that was the best and worst in his life. He did not like his daughter, he never had. She held the same strange eyes as her mother – wild, uncontainable and completely bewitching with their liberty. But this was a curse, for he knew his daughter would leave Vincenzo as coldly as her mother had left him, and he refused to save her from the ridicule he had endured. He would not pity or comfort her, but punish her, for these women needed to be taught obedience and the duties of a wife.

Ripping the tie from his neck, Chiara's father felt choked and hot with his disturbed thoughts. Tossing the tie to the floor, he quickly rummaged in his suit jacket for the cold, comforting flask which came everywhere with him, like a favourite toy to a child. Pulling it from his pocket, he unsteadily gulped a mouthful of something bitter and burning, as they jumped and jolted over the worn road. He closed his eyes and felt the heat from within fight the humidity of the outside. Sweat broke across his forehead, creeping down his temples, before rolling through his hair and neck, ridding his body of evil.

Gently, he felt a soft, manicured hand tug the flask away, and instantly his eyes burst open with panic. He turned his attention on his daughter, who gulped his precious poison away, her throat softly moving, as sweat also dampened her pasted face. What was she doing? How could she do this to him?

His daughter finished the last of the flask, licking her lips, before handing the empty, useless grey flask back to him without ever meeting his eyes.

Fury made him senseless, insensitive and savage, curses stormed through his mind; that fucking bitch, that fucking piece of shit, that fucking child, who had made her mother go. It was her fault. It was all her fucking fault.

Slamming the flask to the floor, it bounced and rolled around their feet, and Chiara's father stamped on it, as if it was on fire. He wished it was on fire. He wished it would set the whole car on fire. He wished for his daughter to die at the hands of its flames. He wished to die at the hands of its flames.

He wanted to kick those girls out of the car. He wanted to order the driver to drive far, anywhere, he did not care, as long as they got out of this fucking God-awful town.

But it was all too late, for the bells in the church were crashing and crunching their tuneless melodies across the square.

They had arrived at the church.

Matteo stood beside Vincenzo at the alter, alone, before all the eyes of the villagers. All these men and women crammed tightly together, like colourful sardines, radiating a human heat, which could be tasted upon the tongues, sour and rancid, like a mouldy orange. The unforgiving sun vomited the colours of the stained glass across the floor in a messy tapestry of light, like a toddler's painting. It was ugly and senseless, as was this wedding.

The bells within the tower rumbled through the walls, shaking the foundations with their relentless chant of marriage. The sound made him feel hotter, for it seemed as though the bells' melancholy tune was a weighted hammer, smashing his skull until all the regrets and guilt and memories were spilled across the floor for all to see.

Vincenzo looked fucking amazing. His suit was a dark grey, sewn to boast his body's beauty, tailored to complement his skin and hair, woven to hide the woe in his face. Matteo gazed at Vincenzo with a chest heaving with a hungry, heartbreaking love, for he wanted to remove these clothes, peel away the suit jacket, unbutton the tight waistcoat, and dust away the shirt, as if this day had never existed. He wanted to go back to the dry fields and hold those smooth hands within his own. He wanted to taste the exotic privacy of their love. He wanted to fill Vincenzo's days with fantasies of their future. He only wanted to love him, and love him until they were both buried deep in the ground.

Suddenly, he felt his eyes prick slightly with tears, a foreign thing for Matteo. He never cried, but it was because he had never loved anything as deep as he loved Vincenzo. Yet it was all going to be taken from him forever, and he hated himself for this fate. It was his fault. If he had not been a coward, he could have had the future he desired, but society scared him, frightening him away from courage and choice. He had messed up this love and life because of society's judgement. If he had lived anywhere else in the world, he could have been standing here with Vincenzo saying the words 'I do', but instead he would never have this tantalising chance.

He would never be even close to this dream.

He had to say something, anything. He had to stop this wedding.

Stepping towards Vincenzo, he placed a heavy hand on his shoulder, and instantly Vincenzo turned to face him.

"Vincenzo, you can't do thi—"

Slowly the heavy oak doors were pushed aside, and the string band began to plod their way through an insincere love song, as Bianca made her way down the aisle.

Matteo saw the fear and failing within Vincenzo's pale narrow face. Matteo felt the nerves shaking through Vincenzo's body, like an infection. Matteo could see the struggle of right and wrong in his swamp-green eyes. Matteo begged, pleaded, and prayed for Vincenzo to not look away, but he was slipping away from him and into the costumes of social propriety.

Vincenzo turned his attention to his bride.

Matteo stepped away with his head bent to hide the tears and trembling of his lips, for it was all too late.

As Vincenzo watched Chiara slowly and painfully stumble up the aisle, he felt as though his suit was becoming a straightjacket, arresting him to a future he dreaded. Why had he done this? Fear, it was all fear. Fear for what he wanted. Fear for what he had become. Fear for his parents' disapproval. Fear for the sneer of society. Fear for himself and Matteo. What were they going to do? Sometimes, it felt as though he should go back to Milan, forget Matteo, and start this new doomed life with this new dreadful wife. Yet the thought of this made him want to scream with irritation, scream with frustration, scream with hatred. But if he stayed how long could this secret with Matteo last? How long could he hide his true life from Chiara?

How long could he keep hurting Matteo and himself? He had never realised how deep Matteo's love had been until that moment. Oh, that action had cut him deep, for it made Vincenzo's mistake greater, his chance to be who he was a greater loss, and his longing for Matteo only seemed to grow stronger and stronger.

The sound of the strings made him feel sick, as Chiara's father let go of her limp arm, shoving her towards Vincenzo, as if he did not want to hold onto this burden any longer.

Chiara stood before him, and his regret only grew more powerful by her presence. Beneath that lace curtain, he could see how stiff her face was, like an ironed napkin. Her lips were shrunken and red, completely silent, her eyes were red, lost and flitting around every corner of the church, as if she was searching for something. Vincenzo knew what she was looking for, and thankfully he had not shown up.

He hated his new wife, detested her, for she was like a fallen tree across the road, blocking his path to freedom and love, and the only way to be rid of the fallen tree was to burn it.

Why had he married this woman, who was tense and full of spite? Why had he not sacrificed her to the humiliation of a non-existent groom? Why had he used this girl to cover up his true desires? Why was he such a coward? He was not ashamed of who he was, but he was afraid, really afraid.

But why must he be afraid? There was no sin or shame to love another man. His parents' generation were wrong in their laws, and in this wrongness they had wronged and wrecked the lives of their children.

The music ceased. The crowd aggressively flapped their programmes at their red, moist faces. A baby began to shriek. The heat made everything, everyone completely restless and irritable.

The weak, trembling priest began the service with one eye on the Bible and the other on Chiara's breasts.

*

The manager of La Parco della Stella made her way through the wedding party with trays of champagne flutes, as the never-ending church bells charged through the mountains. She already felt exhausted, for the heat was relentless and not relinquishing, whilst her staff were useless and unreliable. How could two of them call sick today? Out of all of the days, she needed them most now, what with the wedding, and the birthday party, and the restaurant remaining open, how would they cope?

She felt her chest tighten, her heart pounded, her back dripped with sweat, and her eyes fogged and fizzed with dehydration. She needed to sit down and breathe until she was calmer, but there was no chance of doing this, she thought bitterly.

Not only did the lack of staff and stifling heat annoy the manager, but the wedding party were impossible. For some strange reason they had decided to split themselves into two groups. The groom's family stood beneath the shade of the long winding white porch, whilst the bride's small family sheltered under the sparse shading of the dying trees. She felt like a messenger between two warring sides, her white shirt a truce for peace, and her tray of Prosecco a payment for that peace. Yet, in truth, she was an instigator to their anger, for her shirt was grey and transparent with sweat, whilst the Prosecco was flat and warm, a poor payment.

Marching towards the groom's family, they looked like dolls in a toy house, frigid and false, abandoned in a place they did not belong. Most of the ladies perched on the worn, metal chairs, their hair scraped painfully back to reveal painted faces pinched with disgust, perfectly lined drooping lips, like dead fish, and pin-like eyes prickled with prejudice. The men stood with clean shaven jaws clenched, hair slicked and styled with expensive gel, and cold eyes, which laughed and mocked the lowlifes standing beneath the trees.

They were mostly silent, watching, judging, misjudging, mocking, waiting for this ghastly day to be done with. The manager approached quietly, yet all eyes slid to her, critical and condescending. She had always believed she was a strong manager, yet beneath their gazes, she suddenly wanted to cry and throw a tantrum, for why should they judge her? She was nothing to them, yet they ridiculed her, making her feel the worth of her worthless, wasted life.

Sweat rolled faster and faster down her back, making the shirt stick to her, like cling film, as she rushed through the crowd of Milanos. She offered Prosecco to the ladies, who took the glasses with napkins protecting their smooth, manicured hands, as if she carried a deadly disease. Some refused any type of drink, despite the ravaging humidity of the day. They would rather dehydrate like a raisin than accept a drink from her hands, and so be it, she savagely thought. The men accepted the drinks with sneering smiles, before openly polishing the rims of the glasses with their money-dirty thumbs.

The manager raced away, her body squirming with their snobbery, as her black shoes kicked clouds of silver dust from the scorching gravel path that separated the two camps.

Moving towards the bride's party, she gazed above their heads and towards the beautiful view of the hazy, dry Molise valleys, her eyes rising and falling with the shape of the landscape, before it settled on the twinkling sequin blue of the Adriatic sea. She stopped for a second and narrowed her eyes, for she could vaguely make out the dark volcanic shadow of Tremiti, a creature as mythical as the Loch Ness Monster.

Chiara's father and friends gathered beneath the feeble shade of an old, dying olive tree, its branches and trunk as silver as a gravestone. The group were again eerily quiet, except for the occasional explosion of weaponizing words dealt abusively from Signora Fango to Alessandro and Bianca. Matteo, Chiara's father and Signoro Fango drifted absently away from the group, each man obsessing over his own thoughts.

But as the manager drew closer to these men, she could feel the different weight of each man's silence.

Matteo's silence was unnerving, for she knew how he flirted and flouted his confidence about, as if it was a prize. But today, he seemed distant and distracted by thoughts, which seemed to cause him suffering, for his face was sagging with melancholy, his eyes were lost and occasionally misty, and he bit his faded red lips, as if he was trying to comprehend his own thoughts. She gently offered him a glass of Prosecco, yet he shook his head, and slumped away from her.

Signoro Fango's silence was tense and fidgety. He chain-smoked cigarettes, as his eyes frequently darted towards Bianca. The manager had heard the rumours, and she understood the pain Signoro Fango endured, for she had been dealt the same fate only two years ago. His body was rigid with tension, his eyes were fleeting and flighty, and his fingers shook, as he drew the cigarette towards his scowling lips. His position only abruptly changed when he heard the barking of his wife's brutal voice. She politely offered him a glass of Prosecco, and he took one with a shy smile of thankfulness.

Chiara's father's silence was disturbing. The manager could feel his presence from quite a way, and she felt her sweaty body shiver uncomfortably, for she detested him. He was rude and vile, full of self-pity and complete loathing for everything and everyone who existed, especially his daughter. The manager had hired Chiara when she was only a child, and she had seen the true extent of her father's cruelty upon her body and in her sweet blue eyes, which were always plagued with fright. She offered the tray towards Chiara's father without meeting his eyes, and she could smell the stench of alcohol upon his clothes and hands as he helped himself to two glasses.

The manager hurried away, her skin crawling with his creepiness, whilst her mind became more alert to her surroundings, for she knew of his unpredictable madness, and she refused to let him ruin this day for his daughter.

The next half an hour was a time where the manager's ears were bombarded by noise, as she raced backwards and forwards between the two groups, each member's tongues becoming looser with the Prosecco. The band had begun to tune their instruments, yet there was one out of tune violin weaving its sinister, minor notes through the dismal wedding party. Children played, chucking the confetti at each other, screwing their noses up, and screaming of how it stank of cat piss. The fight between north and south had begun, and her mind felt close to overflowing with the insults they made of one another within their groups.

From the white, elegant porch to the scraggly olive tree, the manager's mind became a collision course of insults, a battlefield of the rich, eloquent Milano accents and the broken, brittle, bullying bite of the southerners. "They are ruining this country," moaned the northerners. "*They think that they can just take our land,*" barked the southerners. "They are a drain on our money." "*They think they are saving us with their wealth.*" "Why do we work so hard to support these lazy Terronis." "*Why should we give them everything we have worked for.*" "These southerners couldn't give a shit about how much we support their crippling governments." "*Those northerners have no idea what a hard day's work is.*" "The south is rife with unemployment, and they don't even care." "*The north talk shit of independence and freedom from the south, but they would be lost without us.*" "If these southern shits think they don't need us, we should let them go." "*They are arrogant, only concerned if their Prada leather shoes break.*" "They are dirty, unable to even afford to buy decent clothes." "*Look at their faces, pale as ghosts, you can tell they have never worked a day.*" "Look at their hands, filthy with mud." "*They are no better than dolls.*" "They are as useful as donkeys." "*They are liars.*" "They are thieves." "*Self-righteous arseholes.*" "Lowlives." "*Arrogant.*" "Lazy." "*Stupido.*" "Terroni."

The heat. Angry pale faces. Red hot faces. Sad olive faces. The porch. The swish of expensive dresses. The click click of expensive shoes. Laughter. Shouting. Children screaming and screaming. The out of tune violin. The olive tree. Empty Prosecco glasses. Pop, pop, pop of corks. Stumbling men. The barking of Signora Fango. Clouds of smoke. Scowling faces. The heat. The sun. The words. The pride. The prejudice. The porch. The politics. The wedding.

The squeak of the violin. The rumble of men's voices. The bullying. The hate. Hate. Hate. Hate.

Suddenly there was a loud blaring of horns, as the white wedding car approached, coughing black smoke into the blinding white drive.

The manager staggered into the restaurant, her head aching, her eyes fizzing, her mind spinning, her stomach flipping and her chest heaving, gasping for air, gasping for life.

Crouching behind the bar, she guzzled a glass of cold water, before laying the glass against her pounding forehead, as her breath slowed and her mind regained focus.

She wanted to cry. She wanted sleep. She wanted the cold. But there was no chance of these wishes coming true, as she anxiously heard the scraping of chairs and chatter in the restaurant.

The meal was close to beginning. The manager reluctantly left the bar with a shaking smile.

*

The meal was nearly over, and Signoro Fango was grateful. This wedding had been a disaster, especially the meal. Food orders had gone to the wrong table, one lady from Milan was sick after eating shellfish, between each course they had to wait what seemed like forever, the food was cold and unseasoned, and drinks were slow to arrive. The room was hot and humid, and the air was stale with the stench of sweat, alcohol, and garlic. The dozy manager had tried to make the aircon work, but it was useless. People were restless with the heat, men rubbed their sweaty foreheads on crisp, white napkins, whilst it seemed women's faces were melting, as their eyeliner and mascara smudged in grey clouds beneath their eyes. Children threw aggressive tantrums, screaming and stamping their feet, whilst other children slept drunkenly across their parents' laps. The band was tripping carelessly through various love songs, sometimes a beat behind, as they wiped the salt-stinging sweat from their eyes. Signoro Fango wanted to bash each of their instruments around their heads, for his head ached with their talentless noise.

Signoro Fango felt irritable with the heat, for though the room was as white as freshly laid snow, it felt as though the walls and marble floor were made from black leather, absorbing and harbouring all the heat from that merciless sun. He shuffled uncomfortably in his seat, before picking the skin from around his fingers.

He was depressed as he mournfully watched Bianca, his only daughter, enjoy the wedding without a care for his dismal state. She did not seem upset about their cut relationship, for she laughed and joked, as if she had never known who her father was. He had avoided her since the news of the baby, and his fury had only grown greater when he had learnt that they were not considering marriage to save the child. This was the final blow to his weak mind, worsened further by the urgent queries of elderly ladies, who tried to persuade him to persuade his daughter to marry and save her reputation. Day in and day out, he had to combat these random villagers, who covered his daughter's name in filth without any respect for his despondent heart.

Signoro Fango studied his daughter closer with cold sober eyes, and he felt his throat harden and choke with a lump of sorrow, for he missed her presence and prattle. He missed the way she looked up to him, as if his word was religion. He missed laughing with her, he missed teaching her things. He missed listening and comforting her when she faced troubles. Even today, she looked like the old Bianca, smiling and glowing with innocent beauty, chattering with Alessandro, as if nothing had changed. He knew he had lost his daughter forever, and he knew the only way to have her back was to bend to her laws of life. But how could he trust these new laws of youth? How could he even begin to understand them? How could he forgive her? Yet, how could he kill the pride in his heart? How could she show him no kindness or pity? He did not want to lose his independent daughter to a new future where he was forgotten, yet to be a part of this, he had to relinquish the old laws of society and accept the new.

He craved a cigarette, and a few moments of peace from the raving rants of his ugly, bullying wife.

Bianca stared at her father as he waded through the white, lopsided tablecloths, and squeezed through the thick, cream-coloured chairs with a perturbed sadness, but not guilt. He passed the daintily decorated table, which held the trophy of the day; the wedding cake, before exiting the building. But this cake was no longer grand and expensive, but sloppy and cheap. Curdled cream melted and dripped onto the white lilies beneath, the decorations every so often slipped off, shattering to the floor, chinks of sponge were left exposed, and the layers had somehow merged into one great, white mess, like a pile of gym socks.

This wedding was a disaster, and Bianca could not wait for the day to be over. But she was not the only one, for Chiara was miserable and silent, drinking her dread away in glasses of red wine.

Bianca glanced over at Vincenzo, who was ignoring his new wife, as if he was already bored by the marriage, joking and laughing with Matteo, like they were the two who had wed. She rolled her eyes with fury, and stared at Chiara, who slumped drunkenly and demurely in her chair, her lips stained purple with the wine, whilst her fingers shakingly fiddled with the gold band, as if she wanted to yank it off.

Chiara seemed dead and emotionless to the world around her, yet it was those alert, aqua-blue eyes, which brought a panicky life back to her, as she persistently searched the crowds for that face. Bianca's heart grew heavy within her chest, for Chiara seemed desperate in her search for Domenico. But he had not come.

Placing her hand on Chiara's thin arm, she drew her attention away from the crowds, and those drunken, dazed eyes met her own with sorrow.

"Chiara, are you OK?" Bianca whispered gently, as her eyes softened with concern.

"I don't know," Chiara responded with a weak, false drunken smile, which quickly turned to grimacing disgust as she closely inspected Vincenzo and Matteo.

"I'm sorry Domenico is not here today," Bianca comforted, stroking Chiara's arm with her thumb.

Yet Bianca noticed that something changed in Chiara at the mention of his name, for her body was suddenly tense, goosebumps rose on her arms, and her eyes rolled furiously back at her. Bianca could see injury in those eyes, a damaged pride, a pain, which she could not understand.

Snapping her arm away from Bianca, she shoved her chair away with a drunken fury, before racing from the wedding table without looking back.

Chiara stumbled quickly from the room, her ears overwhelmed by the loud tongues of Milanos, the loud, unsyncopated noise of the band, and the loud clattering of cutlery. Her nose was overwhelmed with the sickening scent of food. Her body was overwhelmed with the tightness of the wedding dress. Her eyes were overwhelmed by the loud crowds, who watched her closely, like an artefact at a museum.

She needed to escape from this hot room. She needed air. She needed quiet. She needed space.

She wanted to be alone, even for just a few seconds.

A few blissful seconds.

Stepping onto the veranda, Chiara moved through the smoking, drunken guests, ignoring their grating cheers with a small, false smile to keep their suspicions at bay.

Staggering further along the winding, white veranda, the crowds dissipated into the secrecy of lovers, their drunken bodies bent over the balcony, lips in a battle of passion, whilst their hands fought a fiery debate of desire.

Chiara bowed her head, and tried to ignore these experimental lovers, as if they were the plague.

Rounding the corner, she hid in the shaded darkness of that place, as she rested her hot, dizzying head against the coolness of the stone, white wall, untouched by the sun.

She felt safe, for no one would find her here in this place.

Breathing in and out, in and out, Chiara felt as though her lungs were trapped unable to expand and fill as she desired, for the dress was tightening, choking, suffocating her every breath.

With trembling fingers, she tried to unknot the work of threads and ribbons from their clasps, but they were unbreakable, like chains.

She could not escape. She was no longer free. She was stolen and trapped, like grapes picked from their vines, assigned to death.

Chiara felt a fool in her pride, ashamed in her sad egotism, and unloved in this new isolation called marriage.

How could she have married him?

But she knew the answers.

Greed and poverty had created a love, which managed to cover up all of Vincenzo's worst parts. It made her blind and deaf to all his hate and villainy. This love had lied to her, spinning her fairy tales of happy ever after, but now she truly knew this all to be a lie.

This marriage, that man, they wanted to change her into something unnatural, unlike her true self. He wanted to transform her into something that belonged only to him, like turning grapes into wine, shutting her in a bottle and stamping his name on the front; a warning. She was his possession. She was his poison. She was trapped by him.

The ceremony had been and gone in a drunken flash. A flash of falsity and fake smiles. Vows that meant nothing, and a kiss that was as formal and empty with love as a handshake between business associates.

Love, that very word made her feel sick, for it held so much promise, yet it only delivered punishment and pain.

Love was the game of fools.

Love was a black swamp of hope.

Love was the poisonous fangs of a snake.

Love was the empty sea, the treeless mountains, the buildingless cities, and the grassless countryside.

Love was the dead plants on her balcony.

Love was Tremedi. A thing of illusions. A thing of tricks and traps.

Chiara felt as though she belonged neither to the past or the future. She was nothing.

Her anxious mind was suddenly sober with the thoughts of escape. How easy could it be? How wonderful would it feel to sneak away from this place? How amazing would it feel to keep running and running without looking back?

Excitement activated her brain, as she calculated ways to make this dream happen. But it was impossible, by the time she reached the end of the drive, Vincenzo would be pulling her back with that invisible leash he held around her throat.

Tears bubbled hot and uncontrollably within her eyes, for it was hopeless. All those plans and dreams she had allowed herself to entertain were eternally dead. She banged her fists against the wall, imagining the face of Vincenzo, and the tears leaked, cutting her cheeks with grief.

Slowly, she stopped bashing the wall, her breaths uneven and trembling, as she wiped the black tears from her face. She would need to sneak into the bathroom, Chiara thought, for she was sure her face was a mess.

Turning to leave, Chiara stopped, her whole body frozen, her breathing shallow and her eyes wide in disbelief.

"Chiara," spoke the low, familiar voice of him.

She shivered, cold, despite the choking humidity of the day.

He was here with those strong arms draped in black, as his work-worn hands fidgeted with the wet label on his beer bottle.

He was here with his long body, topped with the curling dark hair she loved combing her fingers through.

223

"Chiara, I didn't know you would be here," he spoke, clearing his throat uncomfortably.

He was here with his sharp jawline and gaunt cheeks.

He was here with his dimple and firm red lips, like pomegranates.

"I'm sorry, I know you said to not see you, but I had to come. I had to know…" his voice trailed away, breathlessly, beautifully.

He was here with his soft, silver eyes, those eyes, which she had always loved.

He was here.

Three steps away from her.

"Chiara, please say something," he begged.

Was he real or false?

Was she sane or insane?

Was he truly here?

He sighed, and shuffled uncomfortably, nervously, waiting for her answer.

The silence suspended between them was strained and strangling, making them both suffer.

He would save her. He would make her free. He would keep those dreams alive, like he kept the grapevines alive.

"I'm sorry this was a mistake, I will go," he choked, as he reluctantly turned his body away from her.

Suddenly two hands gripped his arm, stopping him from leaving.

"Take me with you," ordered Chiara, her electric blue eyes wide and imploring and wild.

Domenico nodded, taking her hand in his, as he led her willingly to the three-wheeler.

Domenico was aware of the trouble which would hunt their journey to love and freedom, like a fire tearing through the valley, destroying the grapes and soil into ash. But he would have done it a million times to save Chiara, the love of his life.

ELEVEN

Domenico cut the engine with a jolt. He stepped out of the three-wheeler, slamming the door shut behind him.

Opening the door, he helped Chiara out of the low seat, her white dress overfilling the small cube, like an overflowing frothy bubble bath. Domenico did not know what to feel, was he excited? Was he nervous? Was he afraid? He could not answer these questions, yet within his heart it felt…

…Right. This was the right choice for her. Yet something within the back of her mind seemed to taunt her with doubt. Had she made the *right* choice? Had she done the *right* thing? Was this *right* for her?

She could beg Domenico to drive her back. She would not have been missed much in this small amount of time. She could return back to that life with that man and become that woman.

Chiara could not resist smiling, despite the panic picking her mind to pieces, like a crow over a corpse, for no amount of money or jewels in the world could convince her to return. She was free…

…and smiling and alive. As Chiara moved passed Domenico, he felt the fear evaporate with her ease, yet a new trouble awoke within him; love. Slamming the car door, he thought of all those years, weeks, days, hours, and minutes, he had spent dreaming of this very moment, and now he was here, he felt dizzy with euphoria and agitation, for what if he did something wrong? What if this long-awaited dream turned out to be a nightmare? What if she did not want this? He was sure another round of unrequited love would kill him off, but what if...

...he could not forgive her? What would she do? Where would she go? Sneakily glancing towards Domenico as they walked slowly through the blonde, naked countryside towards the farmhouse, she could not help thinking how they looked like husband and wife down a wedding aisle. A sudden sadness crept into her soul, for if only this had been the case, she could have saved her neck from being wrung...

...since they had left the church. But now, there were no church bells ringing, only the music of nature surrounded them. The crickets hushed their throaty hymns, the birds slept through their lyrics, and the dry grass crackled and snapped, as Domenico walked this well-worn path. Occasionally her arm brushed gently, so lightly, so delicately against his own arm, reminding him she was real, like pinching your skin to see if something so dreamlike could possibly be real. Domenico wanted more. He wanted to take her hand in his, enfolding all its fortune and fate into his own life, yet he was not sure if she...

...wanted him to hold her hand. Chiara could feel his smooth, black jacket rubbing against her silky skin, soothing her wary mind, yet she wanted more. She wished he would take her hand, and never let it go, like he had done countless times before...

...he would never have thought twice about such a simple action, yet in this place, in this moment, it felt wrong, for he did not want to take advantage of her drunken vulnerability. Trying to distract himself, he turned his attention to a large, fluffy bee bumbling and vibrating the air with its loud song, for...

…there was no breeze, no relief, no place for sound to hide. Every noise was exposed to her attentive ears, as she listened anxiously for the footsteps of their discovery.

Chiara saw no clouds interfering with the sun's energy. The sky seemed almost white with its raw power, and the…

…air was close, touching and moist with the humidity, making this small world of Domenico's look hazy and heavenly seductive, for the valley…

…was dry, flaking in clouds of white dust, as they moved, yet Chiara felt fresh and cool and wet with a reckless…

…lust was in her body, in her skin, in her eyes, in her soul, infecting the whole of this valley with its wickedly killing power. But Domenico was not afraid, for he had already been diagnosed with this infection many years before.

Chiara stopped, stumbling from her white heels, ungracefully, carelessly, freely. Domenico grabbed her hand, stabling her body, and she glanced up at him with those eyes, enchanting, enticing, as blue as a mermaid's love song. He quickly flicked his gaze to the thirsty fields, like the ash from a cigarette, desperate, yet unable to quit this…

…poison was in those silver eyes, like mercury, but it was not menacing, nor malevolent, it was dazzling in its danger and desire.

Her tight lips quivered with a smile, for she forgot how small she was standing beside Domenico, for he towered above her, shrinking her height, and diminishing the importance of this day. She loved feeling small, for it offered freedom in its invisibility, and comfort in its safety.

Suddenly her hand was emptied of Domenico's warmth, and she watched him shrug the black jacket from his strong shoulders, before throwing it to the ground, where plumes of scratchy white dirt tainted the expensive material, as if money made no difference to nature.

A lump choked her throat as she stared at the unknowing Domenico, for she felt almost sad with joy. Why had she waited so long? Why had she tortured him and herself for so, so long? Why had he never stopped loving her after all this time?

She thought she knew everything about Domenico, her best friend, yet this man was someone else, a figure she had known for a long time, but never managed to see, like a mythical spirit. She had never noticed the strength in those tilting shoulders, stomach and back, which made him stand taller and tougher than any other man. She had never noticed the dark chocolate curls of his hair, some blonder, bleached to death by the sun. She had never noticed the smooth, carefree movement of his limbs and torso, working efficiently, like a dancer. She had never noticed the pride in his jaw, the red, tenderness of his lips, and the narrowness of his cheeks. Yet only one thing remained the same; his eyes, silver bells tuned to her every emotion, no matter how great or…

…small, her slim body looked swamped in that undignified, ugly, false dress, which had become quickly spoilt with the dry soil, her netted trail was cluttered with the hay-like grass and the corpses of spasming flies and insects, trapped in her woeful web. She waltzed on like a pagan goddess, radiant and transient with the sun and flowers, and Domenico found he could not follow her, stuck by her striking beauty. Yet he had always seen this within her, even when she could never see it. No girl had ever compared to Chiara, for they were basic and unimaginative with their TikTok beauty, fake with their 'natural' foundation. Yet Chiara was different, even today with her black smeared eyes and melting powders, he could see the beauty of her mind and soul spewing from every pore like a fountain of light. He wanted to release her dull, brown hair to the sun's nurture, for it seemed to hurt her, tugging at her temples, unrelenting. He wanted to unravel those seams of red ribbon lipstick to reveal the true poetry rose-pink of her real lips. He wanted to slide his wet thumb under and over her eyes, removing the black paste, like a mourning hood. He wanted to swim deep in those spellbinding blue eyes, survive each wistful wave, and dive deeper and deeper into her dreams and desires.

He had to turn his gaze away from her, and his eyes searched for flowers to entertain his mind, yet they did not exist in this part of the world, for the heat had scorched them to death. The only plant thriving was the long, stretching vines, their branches heavy with the swelling, deep purple fruits. This path a temptation, like the Garden of Eden, but he wanted to indulge in this temptation, touching and sucking and swallowing the sweet, sweet juices, slowly and...

...recklessly, she prised the engagement and wedding rings from her finger tossing them to the floor, forgetting their price, forgiving their pain, for the past was free from her now.

The farmhouse was in sight with its old, familiar blue roof, exposed and naked, surrendering itself to the sun. The courtyard was empty, for the chickens slumbered in the shade of bushes. The door...

...was parted seductively, like a woman's lips bent for a kiss. The windows were dark and calling, beckoning and hollering for Domenico to take her inside, hiding her from the eyes of ...

...this world was alive with colour, but...

...the noise was dead, suspenseful, and silent...

...and it halted Chiara, for she suddenly felt nervous. What if Domenico did not feel these feelings she felt? But what did she feel? What did he feel? She only wished he would give her a...

...sign, a message, a code, anything, for Domenico could not understand what Chiara needed from him. Domenico lightly stepped around Chiara, opening the door wide, his hands trembling, for if she wanted to leave, she could turn away and order him back to the car. But if, if she wanted to stay, she might...

...enter, and she listened to Domenico's heavy-soled footsteps behind her with a sigh of relief. She led the way up the cold cemented...

...stairs, her feet silent and soft, as if she was a ghost of his imagination. Domenico felt he was offending the moment with the clomp, clomp of his black, thick-cut shoes. He tried to quieten his tread, as...

…she arrived at the only room upstairs, the bedroom, a place bland with the bare necessities. The harsh skein of gold sun cut randomly across the room, highlighting dust and damp and darkness. Chiara stepped aside slightly, as she felt…

…Domenico approach. He stood closely behind her, his breath tickling the wispy strands around her neck. Peering into the room, a shame crept through his body, for the poor room was unromantic and stank of loneliness. The mattress stretched…

…across the floor, grey and worn, a blanket discreetly covering the slight tears, whilst a limp pillow offered little comfort. A small, oak desk…

…stood in the corner, and Domenico slid past Chiara, as he went over to this small object of comfort and reassurance. He leant his body against its wobbly, broken frame, whilst Chiara…

…leant against the splintering wooden door frame with her arms folded and her eyes on the floor. There was nothing else…

…except them. Domenico began to nervously bite his fingernail, for he felt confused and anxious and ardent with love, which he did not know how to initiate. It was his first time, and…

…it was her first time. She did not know who was leading who…

…he did not know how to begin…

…she did not know what to say…

…or do…

…or act…

…Domenico knew what he wanted, but where were her loyalties? Did she feel she could not do this? Did she still feel under the power of Vincenzo? Domenico stopped biting his nail, as he listened to the rustle of Chiara's dress dancing closer and closer towards him. He met her eyes, full and wide, soft and sensitive, loving and lustful, calm…

…and curious, wide and wicked, torn and troubled, she wanted to be near him and show him what she needed. Her lips…

…were red and slightly parted, her breath shallow and slow, as she came to stand within the sun before him. *What's wrong?*

...I don't know what you want. Chiara tell me...

...Domenico's eyes were challenging, two silver plaques at the end of a race. They were not afraid, or scared, perhaps a little sheepish, but ultimately, they were confident, seductive with...

...the sun's power, turning her irises turquoise, like the untameable ocean shoreline, exotic escapism, yet unbelievably unpredictable...

...she parted his legs...

...he gulped...

...she placed her shaking, smooth hands on the creases between his thigh and hip...

...his penis throbbed, he felt dizzy...

...as she leant her body against his...

...mouth was warm with her whispering breath...

...I only want you...

...his mouth was sticky with the cloying, sexuality of her words...

...she wanted him. Oh God, she wanted him bad...

...his nerves were painful, ablaze with the long burning fire of love and...

...longing and lust made every part of her body throb, throb, throb...

...Domenico slowly slid his thick, scratchy hands up her silky, soft arms...

...his touch was deep, sinking every finger into her skin...

...her shoulder blades were poking and exposed...

...his fingers burnt marks in her slender neck...

...her breath was shallow and unsteady...

...his hands were splayed, steadily over her jaw and chin...

...she moved closer...

...his nose slid into the perfect gap beside her own...

...her eyes softly shut, as she felt his cool nose press into her hot cheek...

...he closed his eyes...

...her breath shook suspensefully, out of time with...

...his lips met hers, softly, subtlety, safely, like...

...when he kissed her in the cool...

...woods above Castelmauro when...

...they were only fifteen...

...he felt her hands tighten their grip on...

...her jaw, as the kiss dissolved and deepened and darkened into...

...something he had only dreamed of since...

...she could remember...

...he felt his lips were bruising, breaking...

...burning with the pressure and passion, she had to go further, all the...

...way, he had to have her, even if it was just for today, even if it was just...

...this moment. She pulled away, gasping, her mouth gaping, whilst...

...his lips tingled, every sensation alive, like sucking...

...a sun-filled lemon, obliterating any other...

...sense and logic were lost in her captivating, cool blue eyes, as she whispered...

...*Take my dress off*...

...he let his hands trail slowly down her wealthy dress, until...

...she felt him hold her waist, turning her body...

...around, he stood and pulled a pocketknife from his suit trouser, before...

...she heard a ripping, tearing, slashing sound, as...

...the delicate stitches gave away, like a poorly sewn wound, exposing...

...her back, which felt cold and sensitive to the touch of his lips, which...

...pressed kisses across the top of her back, as he shimmied...

...the heavy, swamping, tainted dress from her body, she stepped from its barrier...

...like a butterfly from its chrysalis cage, beautiful, bold, and...

...free. She felt tears stud her eyes with relief, she was finally free, except...

...for the slip of silky white, which still shielded her body. Domenico felt an urge to tear it from its place and rip it to shreds with his teeth, but...

...she felt his shaking hands tease the silky straps from her narrow shoulders. Her stomach flipped with excitement and anxiety, for what if he despised...

... her body was like a work of art, a poem of femininity, a hidden flower, making his blood pound in his ears, as the...

...dress flopped to the dusty floor, she shrank and slouched, embarrassed. She felt his fingers...

...carving and weaving down her spine, around her narrow waist and hips, his penis began to hurt with its desires, making...

...her whole body tingle, as she heard him inhale a breath, before he spoke...

...*I have never seen anything as beautiful as you*...

...Chiara's smile was wide, and a salty tear spilled down her cheek...

...*Have I hurt you?*

...*No*...

...*If you ever want to stop, or if I am doing something wrong, please tell me, and I will stop*...

...Chiara nodded, unable to speak, knowing she would not need him to stop, for...

...she meant more to him than sex or anything, and he would rather die than harm her. He loved her more than palaces and pennies, for in loving her was his luxury and...

...in loving him there was a peace greater than silence within her mind, and a fulfilment greater than wealth within her heart. She turned to face him...

...and he watched her remove his glasses, so that this perfect vision was blurry and bright, her body disfigured by the slashes of sun, which...

…warmed her pulsing body, throbbing breasts and throbbing thighs with a wild heat, like fire…

…his mouth was dry with his thirst for love, as Chiara…

…pulled clips from her hair, spilling her dark hair into ringlets, which stuck…

…to her flushed, moist cheeks, like swirls of dark caramel, and he was captivated, his…

…eyes burned her body, and she went to him, unpicking the buttons from his shirt, which…

…he flung off, unfocused, as he felt her hands fiddle and release the belt, chucking it to the floor with a clatter. He could barely breath. His tight chest…

… was nested and covered with dark curls, as it rose, and, fell, rose, and, fell, repeatedly with…

…rapture ruined Domenico's control, and he quickly picked her up…

…carrying her to the bed, clumsily, she was thrown upon the squidgy mattress, smiling, the scent of Domenico was all over her, sweet and sweaty and…

…thick with the sun. He lay his body on top of hers, and they fitted perfectly, it all…

…felt right. She took his face in her hands, pulling him closer with her lips, kissing and…

…groaning, he fiddled inexperiencedly with her white lace bra, and finally it popped from its…

…release. He stopped kissing her lips, which felt sore and sizzling, as he weaved the bra from her arms, before…

…his lips stamped a path from her neck to her chest to her breasts, her nipples…

…erect with this new arousal of lust, as she felt his teeth pierce and bruise her smooth skin. She grabbed and gripped his hair…

…pulling and playing, exciting his body, making him grunt, making him greedy, as he kissed her…

…long and deep and slow and deadly, before she felt him move…

…his dry lips down her chest, leaving kisses, like stepping stones, down her body, as she spread…

…her thin, silky legs apart, inviting him, torturing him, and he answered her, sliding his fingers around the…

…fragile lace rim, before he gently tugged the underwear from this place of…

…privacy and pleasure, yet he waited, alert for any sign of discomfort within her. Yet…

…Chiara spread her legs slightly wider, begging for him, and she saw his body droop and hunch, before she felt his tongue gently go to the place only her hands had been, and she moaned and…

…dripped, wet and warm, his tongue full with the taste of her. She moaned louder, her body writhing upon the mattress. Her thighs trembled slightly and…

…her vagina throbbed and throbbed, almost painfully with the pleasure. Suddenly he stopped…

…and kissed the inside of her thighs, torturing her, enthralling her, as her eyes rolled around in her head, her body rising and falling, clenching, and releasing, the only thing…

…steadying her was the pressure of his large hands on the side of her thighs, but he could not withstand this yearning any longer. He felt light-headed, as he…

…laid his hot body against…

…her hot body…

…her eyes were glowing…

…his eyes were sparkling…

…her mouth was red and wet, like a dewy rose…

…his mouth was shiny and pink, like ham…

…her hair was a messy, sweaty splurge of knots…

…his bark-coloured curls were black and flat with sweat…

…he rushed from her, ripping his trousers and boxers from his body…

...exposing his strong hard penis, possessed and alive with passion for Chiara...

...he crawled between her legs, panting...

...she arched her body to his, breathless...

...his lips hung close, so close...

...her eyes locked with his, frantic and feverish and fervent...

...*You OK?*

...*Yes*...

...He smiled, the dimple deepening into his cheek, before brushing her lips with a kiss more killing...

...than a bullet...

...Domenico pushed gently, moving slightly to adjust his positions...

...and then he pushed again, harder, and stronger, Chiara gasped...

...Domenico's eyes squeezed shut with a happiness that made him want to cry, for it was a love as healing as hell, a...

...love as murdering as a knife to the heart...

...a love so dangerous in its deep-rooted dependence, like the grapevines and soil, to kill one would kill both, and so...

...the act of love began...

...with only the sun, the grapes, their dreams, and the screeching of crickets close by.

Caro Signoro Maestro,

You were right, God. Of course you were right.

Signoro Maestro you taught me many things. You taught me the plants and the vines, but you also taught me love and dreams. You taught me to find them. You taught me to follow them. You taught me to hold onto them firmly.

And now, God, I am here.

"...I see with my eyes, hear with my ears, understand with my heart, and in turn, I am healed..."

Chiara is alive and well.

It was all a huge mistake. She was never murdered. She was never engulfed by flames.

She is the flame. She is the murderer. She is Satan.

With this power, she has been most kind, for she has ordered her disciples, the big, barking prison guards to take me to another room. This room is more secluded and alone, private, away from the prying eyes of her disciples. They cannot hear our conversations. They cannot see our kisses. They cannot feel our love.

This space is perfect for us. It is small and cosy. I mean I would never dare call it a room, for it is as wide as my outstretched arms, and as high as my height. It is sealed in tight with a big, thick black door, and there is a tiny closed window. They slide it open and shout abuse at me, but Chiara tells me they do this to quell my excitement and to not make them jealous.

I will do anything she says. I will do anything she wants. I will do anything to make her wishes come true.

God, this place, shadowy and stinking, is heaven. I just never saw it, until I saw Chiara.

I do not need the crucifix, for she is here, shining gold and beautiful before my very eyes. She is scolding me for writing such silly things to you. I burst with laughter, and it echoes, rebounding between the walls, passing my joy around, like a box of chocolates.

She is right, of course.

Chiara is whispering words softly in my ear, and instructing me to talk quietly in my letter.

Are you sure, my darling? Can I really ask this of him?

Yes, you seem so confidant, my love, but it is a huge task?

I will not argue with you Chiara, if you want me to ask, I will.

God, I speak quietly, for you must keep this secret to yourself. I know what a blabber mouth you are. Tomorrow you need to go to Termoli and collect two tickets to the Island of Tremiti for me and Chiara. We leave tomorrow.

Shhh, shhh, God keep your fucking voice down, it is a secret.

Stop talking, God, Chiara has it all planned out, for she has promised to speak to the security guards and explain about this silly mix-up, and then we will be free.

She promised, and you must promise to keep this hush hush.

How wonderful! How wonderful!

The future is bright and blinding and brilliant and blazing, like those grapevines in September.

Oh God, you should see Chiara, she is beautiful, dressed in that white wedding dress that she wore when I stole her away to the farmhouse on that fateful day.

But I would not dare take it off her this time, she promises me we will be married in Tremeti.

238

Ha ha, I laugh, for I have been married to her my whole life…

…yes I have, my darling, you just never knew it…

…yes and now you do want to marry me…

…How wonderful!

We have been talking God about the past, especially after she fled from that vile robot called Vincenzo.

Chiara is giggling that sweet, cynical melody, she agrees he was a robot.

A robot full of the blackest evil and the most killing lazers.

But he is away from us now, God, I killed him. I killed him with my bare hands around his neck. His face turned red then purple then blue then grey then white. His eyes popped from their sockets, and the noise, like the squeak of a mouse, escaped his dead lips.

And then there was silence.

A sensational silence of finality.

Forget this, Chiara cries, her eyes alight with my bravery and heroism.

But I can not forget this, my darling.

I have to confide in you God, Chiara do not roll your eyes, this is important. I have to tell you that those words, *The Parable of the Sower*, I understand.

"…other seeds fell on good soil, where it produced crops…"

I know the message you were trying to confess to me. I am the soil and she is the grapevine seeds, and when alone together, depending entirely on one another, we thrive, strive, survive.

It was him, that man, but now that I have killed him, nothing will kill us.

Finally I am back in those fields, following her wild, dark hair, tossing the sunlight around, like the flickering flames of a fire.

I wanted to touch these burning strands, and catch her smouldering body, unafraid of the death that would befall me.

It was all worth it. She was worth all my suffering, all my punishments, all my life. Every heartbeat I would give her, every breath I would surrender to her, every thought she could possess, every moment she could steal willingly.

It was all for her.

She was my queen, and I, her servant.

I can hear her dress scratching across the floor, like it had done in the farmhouse.

God, bring me back to that day, where actions and thoughts were hotter than the sun, where kisses were better promises than stamps, where touches burned, where hearts exploded, again and again and again.

I turn and she is still here, sleeping in the bed, her lashes clamped with mascara, sealing her dreams away.

I want to know those dreams.

I want to kiss those lips.

I want to hold her body.

I want to grip her skin.

I want to lick her fingers.

I want to fuck her.

I want to love her.

I want too much.

Too much.

Oh God, I want so much from her.

I want everything for myself.

Those grapes had been my dream. My dream to study, my dream to leave, my dream to succeed.

But it was a lie.

All my life I had studied those grapes, but really I had been studying Chiara.

She was the grapes which filled my thoughts, amazed my mind and questioned my questions.

She was the grapes I had dedicated my life to.

She was the grapes I ran to.

She was the grapes I pursued.

She was the grapes I loved.

The grapes I love and live for.

It is strange, God, for you would not believe a goddess clad in white would not belong in this place. But she did, just like she had done in the farmhouse. It seemed that whenever we were together it felt right.

But no one could see this. All they saw was religion, and with this, they only saw money and society. Religion was a form of punishment, not prayer. God, please make a note of this, for it will be very useful for the sequel, Bible Strikes Back.

Ha ha, you are right Chiara, I am funny when I want to be.

What a devil she is!

With her here, I am free, secluded and safe from our enemies. We don't exist, as if we had never been born.

Here, we are happy.

Chiara, we are happy, aren't we?

Chiara!

Chiara!

Don't go!

Don't leave me!

Where are you going?

Chiara, STAY, STAY, STAY!

She has gone. God, I wanted too much.

My girl is cursed.

My crime is hers.

CHIARA COME BACK!

God, she has left. She did not even turn to look at me and wave.

I must sign off and find her.

All my love,

Domenico

TWELVE

Signoro Fango marched through the town, his hands were tucked deep in his pockets, as he dodged the spotlights of sun. He felt itchy and fidgetty with the heat. He could not settle today, and Signora Fango had not helped with her overbearing abuse and senseless stupidity.

His bowels moved uneasily, a common symptom of his wracked nerves. He let out a few farts discreetly and carefully, yet his stomach still rumbled uncomfortably. Scratching his greasy, grey head, he was furious that this outside turmoil, which had nothing to do with him, was effecting him so badly.

Yet, it did.

Suddenly the church bells snuck upon the town with their eerie melodies, and Signoro Fango felt a sly shiver creep through his spine at the remembrance of that fateful day. The bell's song seemed to hang suspensefully over the town, unable to flee, turning their tune stale and distasteful, like the rancid smell of his farts.

His son had ruined many things for him, and these harmonious bells were another.

Sweat ran from his hair down to his neck and back, rolling and rolling, until he was unbearably sticky. His right leg kept cramping and his head was tense and aching. He had not drunk much water today, yet he was not thirsty.

The streets were empty and silent, and Signoro Fango was grateful, for he was exhausted with the questions and suggestions and accusations he had fended off for his family's sake. He was furious with Domenico and Chiara, for they had escaped to their isolated paradise, elusive and unoffended by this town, yet why was he paying for their mistakes? Why was he dodging the customers? Why was he feeling ashamed and guilty? Why was his body being abused by the agitation of their unforgettable disappearance?

He had heard tales of their disappearance, yet when one rumour rises another grows from it, like rabbits breeding and breeding. He had heard stories of suicide, Chiara's insanity, their elopement, their deaths, but he had denied all knowledge of their existence.

But it had all been lies, lies, lies, for he had seen them. He had seen that wretched three-wheeler drive away with the bride tucked in the front seat, and he knew exactly where they had gone.

The town was punishing in its silence, for the noises of that day rose violently in his own mind. The grinding of gravel, the chatter of guests, the sizzling of his cigarette, the church bells ringing and ringing and ringing.

He stuck his fingers in his ears, like a child, and itched them, hoping to pull the sounds from his mind, like the thick ear wax which coated his nails. When the quiet returned, he rubbed the wax on his navy trousers, as he turned up a hidden stairway. Doorsteps lined the crooked, grey steps, and the overwhelming smell of cat urine made him gag. The houses were ugly, unpainted and dark grey, like thunder clouds, and the raggedy lace curtains were closed against the bright sun, yet he knew behind them listened the prowling ears of the villagers.

He had to be careful, for he had not told a soul about their whereabouts. He would have taken this truth to the grave, if it had not been for that other rumour.

That rumour made him itch. That rumour made his skin crawl. That rumour upset his stomach and left him sleepless.

That rumour could rewrite the wrongs he had made Domenico suffer with for all these years.

That rumour was probably false, but it was a risk Signoro Fango was not willing to take.

Finally, he arrived at his destination, a small, narrow ash-coloured house with moss green shutters and bright pots of dying flowers cramped beside the front doorstep. Little floral scented drips fell upon his head and shoulder, and he glanced up to find a line of colourful washing drying in the afternoon sun.

He rose his hand to knock, but he shied away, for if he asked for help, he would lose this fight. Yet maybe this fight needed to end, maybe all these mistakes of his children had been caused by the lack of fighting. The lack of fighting the social system. The lack of fighting the reigning religion of this town. The lack of fighting the immoral morals of a trapping and torturing town. The lack of fighting the wrong.

These thoughts gave him strength, and he hurriedly banged his fist on the slender, beige door, before he changed his mind.

Waiting patiently, he began to hear the shuffling of footsteps behind the door, and finally the lock clicked revealing Alessandro's mother, Maria.

Immediately her round face turned from a warm welcome to a cold, critical and condemning expression. Signoro Fango squirmed beneath those dark, tough eyes, like shots, for he knew she did not approve of his cruelty and unkindness towards their future grandchild.

"What do you want, Signoro Fango?" she scathingly questioned, one eyebrow arched, whilst her arms folded tightly across her large chest with hostility.

Maria had a reputation no one messed with. Her parents had immigrated from Nigeria, and they had endured starvation, discrimination and suffering when they had arrived. Signoro Fango could remember her parents, for they were isolated, and if you ever looked them in the eye, they almost ran from you, as if you would beat them senseless. The only person who they had truly warmed to was his mother, and he had spent many days with Maria, yet they had grown apart after he married his monster. But he knew her parents' struggles had made Maria proud and stronger than any woman he had ever seen. She was the only girl in school who could beat the boys. Standing before her now, he felt an unfamiliar feeling of fear. He had only ever known her to be soft and kind to him, only witnessing her strength when others offended her. Yet, now he stood like those boys from school, cowering from that tall, tough body, and cracked lips, which contained words like whips and weapons.

"Can I speak to my daughter?" Signoro Fango asked politely, but his tone was icy and formal for addressing his rival grandparent.

Maria slid her dark eyes up and down Signoro Fango with disgust, as if he was a piece of dog shit. She scoffed, her nostrils flaring, as she began to shut the door in his face.

Luckily, he was quick with his wits, and before she closed the door, he shoved his foot between the frame, preventing the door from moving.

"Get your foot out of my house," commanded Maria threateningly, pushing heavily upon the door.

"No, not until I see my daughter," responded Signoro Fango severely, his weak stature as strong as a tree, unmoving and uncompromising.

"She does not want to see you."

"Well, let me hear those words from her own mouth," he growled, losing his patience with this defiant woman.

Maria glared at him, her despising eyes unblinking, but he held his own, despite his bony foot cramping painfully. Finally, that large woman rolled her eyes and called the sweet, angelic name of his daughter.

Signoro Fango could hear the crash of a door, and the light footsteps of his daughter tumbling down the stairs.

245

"What's wrong Maria? Have I done something wrong?" called Bianca, her soft, high-pitched voice instantly wrenching his heart with guilt.

"No, no dear, someone is here to see you," Maria comforted, her voice deep and husky with sympathy.

The door was pulled slowly away, and Signoro Fango's heart exhaled with relief and happiness.

At first Bianca stared at her father in shock, before slipping into suspicion, yet her pale lips quivered. She did not move, frozen in the door frame, like a painting. She was hesitant, biting her nail, her eyes flickering between her father and the stairs, as she considered her decision.

Finally, she tiptoed outside, the door shutting gently behind her with a click.

Suddenly her father's arms were around her, crushing her body to his, as he repeatedly murmured her name, as if they were words he had never used before.

Tears climbed into Bianca's eyes, as she held her father close to her like he was a child, fearful and anxious of the world around him.

"What's wrong? What's happened?" Bianca softly gurgled against his shoulder, as she inhaled the deep-rooted scent of his dirty cigarettes.

Signoro Fango pulled away, and faced his daughter, yet her face was not how he remembered, for it seemed to have changed since the last time he had seen her. Her eyes were dark, bloodshot, and hollow, her forehead was lined slightly, her cheeks were grey and slightly gaunt, whilst her hair was in a scraggly, messy dark bun.

Bianca had grown up quickly, her features maturing with this new-found responsibility.

"Bianca I need to tell you something, but it cannot go any further than us," Signoro Fango spoke quickly, as he sat on one of the steps, his knees creaking with age.

"Yes, but can I tell Alessandro?" asked Bianca, sitting beside her father, whose anxiety was spreading like a disease, for she was suddenly concerned by the burden that might befall her, and she did not wish to face it alone.

Signoro Fango considered this for a moment, but assented, he might be needed.

"I know where Domenico is," whispered Signoro Fango cautiously, before his eyes scanned the houses with paranoia.

Bianca sharply inhaled and closed her eyes with dread and bewilderment. Was he dead? Was he safe? Was he with Chiara? Had he found her? Please God, just let him be alive and safe, she prayed.

"How do you know where he is?" questioned Bianca sceptically.

"Shh, shh. Because I saw them leaving the wedding together."

Bianca stared at her father in disbelief, as a TV played loudly from a neighbour's house. She was uncertain whether she could trust her father, perhaps in the past she would have, but after everything that had happened, she did not know him as he was. Sometimes he seemed like a stranger to her.

"But he wasn't there, I looked out for him, and he was nowhere to be seen—"

"He was there, Bianca. I went out for a cigarette, and I sat on the rocks in the shrubbery by the driveway, and I saw his three-wheeler leave with Chiara," Signoro Fango explained quickly and quietly, his anxious eyes once again flicking wildly around.

Bianca scratched her head anxiously, for she knew her father was not lying. She had never seen him so wound up, so perturbed and paranoid by this knowledge, but why? So, he knew where they had gone? Yet, why was he so tense? There was more, she was sure.

"What? How come you didn't tell me sooner?" Bianca interrogated, her hand anxiously scratching her head.

Signoro Fango glanced at the ground and noticed the slight bulge of his daughter's belly hidden behind her pale blue shirt, and he held his tongue for the true reason.

"I didn't want to worry you," Signoro Fango admitted feebly.

"Why are you telling me now then?" Bianca hissed, for she knew her father's true reason and he would not go unpunished for his prejudice. She wanted him to look her in the eye and tell her he was wrong.

Signoro Fango sighed, flashing his eyes at Bianca, shocked by her harsh words.

"I… I am sorry, I should have behaved better, it is just hard to understand it all," apologized Signoro Fango. He was defeated by his daughter and the modern world and its morals, yet he felt a strange relief. He thought of his own life, and perhaps if things had been different, he would also have been spared his miserable marriage.

Bianca smiled and squeezed her father's rough, dry hands.

"Bianca, I have heard rumours within the town, this is why I came to you," Signoro Fango admitted.

"What have you heard?"

"The rumour is that Vincenzo is going to kill your brother, and I believe a bastard like that will carry his threat through, no matter what."

Bianca gasped and leant her free hand against the wall of the house to steady her shaking nerves. She could feel the colour draining from her face, and her long, curling lashes fluttered wildly as they tried to contain her stinging tears.

"Oh my God, is he at the farmhouse?"

"Yes, I'm pretty sure."

They were both silent. A fly buzzed dully around their faces, but they did not flinch.

Suddenly they jumped, as they heard the bang of a shot gun from the neighbour's television.

Signoro Fango began to roll a cigarette, but his mouth was too dry to seal the paper together.

Bianca's lips trembled as she leant her head against the wall, gathering her thoughts, mapping out a plan, but her head was blocked with the bruising of her father's words. Vincenzo wanted to kill Domenico. Kill her brother. Kill him. It was unbelievable in its believability, for she had seen Vincenzo's evil mind in action. He would make Domenico suffer. He would torture him so, so, so slowly that Domenico would wish for his death. What would she do? What could she do? Should she speak to him? Should she ask Matteo to speak to him? Should she go down to the farm? Should she kill Vincenzo? Before her pregnancy, actions never seemed to come with consequences, but now each new thing her life encountered was weighed with the invisible repercussions to follow.

She rubbed the gap between her brow and inhaled the comforting smoke of her father's cigarette.

She felt sick, scared by the pressure of this responsibility. What if it went wrong? Would it be her fault? Would people blame her? How could she live knowing she may have handed her brother over to death himself?

She needed Alessandro.

She needed a plan.

*

The journey felt longer than usual.

The road beneath felt less bumpy than usual.

The wheels of his sturdy car seemed to move slower and more cautiously down the winding path of the countryside road.

They passed the town's cemetery, and for the first time Bianca could see the lines of graves sticking from the ground, and a shiver ran through her body, ice cold.

Alessandro kept his eyes glued to the road, unsure of his ability to drive this narrow uneven path, despite being the passenger of its turns and twists for many years. This focus was a gift in this moment, for it took his mind away from the traumas which may await them.

Neither spoke to one another, unsure of what to say, both distracted by their own thoughts.

The car was deadly hot. The humidity pressed against their faces like a pillow. Suffocating.

Bianca kept her eyes turned to the red countryside around her, everything aglow with the red thundering rays of the sun, turning everything to crimson, as if the very trees were bleeding, the leaves weeping blood, and the grass red, like a murder had been committed.

Bianca placed a hand on her bulge, a prayer overriding all her thoughts of Domenico and Chiara. She prayed with her eyes closed that her child should always be protected and safe. That her child should live in a world more forgiving and accepting. A world where two people in love did not have to hide it, or be trapped by it, or be killed by it.

Alessandro peeked at Bianca, and he was thankful her eyes were shut. Across the road were the strewn remnants of clothing. He slowed slightly and peered at a mangled, black suit jacket, dusty and faded with the soil. Suddenly the car jolted, as if they were running over a rock, but when Alessandro glanced in the rear-view mirror, he was shocked to find it was a white high heel.

Bianca felt the car shudder to a stop, and her eyelids peeled away, and she found they were parked right outside the farmhouse.

"I didn't want you to walk too far, you look exhausted," reassured Alessandro, his worried eyes now fixated on Bianca.

Alessandro could see how fretful she looked, for her once youthful face seemed as old as a middle-aged woman's.

He turned his gaze back to the farmhouse, and for the first time in his life, he feared it. He feared the crimes which may have been committed here. He feared the dead bodies which might be within it. Squeezing Bianca's hand, he held onto it for a long time. He did not want her to go.

Bianca smiled faintly, and pulled her hand from his tight, sweaty fingers.

She knew he did not want to be part of the conversation that was to follow.

Stepping from the car, she took a deep breath, and crept towards the lonely farmhouse, uncertainly. She did not know why she was scared, for the farmhouse looked exactly like it had done a few weeks ago, when they all seemed young and untroubled by the future. It felt almost offensive that nature had not changed with the changes of their lives, as if nature did not care for who lived or died.

It seemed deserted as she neared the building. The chickens were nowhere to be seen and even the crickets were silent. There was no one here. There was not a sound, except for the creepy door squeaking on its weak hinges. Did her father get it wrong? Was he mistaken by what he saw?

Suddenly, Bianca stopped, paralyzed with panic. She waited. Her body numb, except her ears, sensitive and sharp to every noise. She was sure, certain, that she had heard the rustling of footsteps. Yet now there was nothing, perhaps it had been a mouse.

Tiptoeing around the side of the house, she allowed her fingers to run across the sharp brickwork, as she listened intently for a noise.

She reached what she thought was the vegetable patch, yet it was empty of vegetables. A few tomatoes were still sparsely studded across the vines, yet the rest were gone, stolen. Had they taken these things when they had fled?

Creeping closer to the cucumber stalks, she could see that they had been ripped aggressively away, tearing and damaging the rest of the stalk. It was useless now, for nothing would grow from it again.

"Bianca?" a voice spoke from afar, distant and dreamy, startling Bianca with the shock of its presence.

"Chiara, oh my god, Chiara, are you OK?" Bianca stammered, as she ran this way and that trying to find her friend, yet there was no one there.

Racing away from the vegetable patch, she saw her, peering around the side of the house, where she had just come from.

She stepped closer to her, examining the white, thin figure, who seemed unreal, almost ghostly. The light shone behind her, and it was hard to read her expression. Her face was a hollow ash-like shadow, like an angel sent from hell.

"Yes, Bianca, I am fine, what are you doing here?" Chiara asked peevishly, as if Bianca offended her by caring.

But Bianca was a strong-minded woman and she would not let this aggressive tone put her off.

She edged towards Chiara, yet she instantly jumped back, as if she was stepping away from her past and everything she knew.

Straightening her denim jeans, she looked Chiara in the eye and spoke with a firmness unnatural to Bianca: "You need to go home."

These words had the effect Bianca desired, for Chiara staggered slightly, whilst her cool, elusive attitude broke into fragments of panic.

"No, I can't," whimpered Chiara, her small fingers twisting into knots.

"You need to," Bianca persuaded, coming slightly closer to the friend she had always loved and cared for.

"No, I can't," Chiara spoke defiantly, her bare feet slamming towards Bianca with a sudden passion.

"You have to."

Chiara flashed her wild blue eyes at Bianca, all the calm and control lost from them. Bianca had never seen her eyes like this, so savage and sharp with anger, they almost seemed to belong to a different person.

But Bianca would not be made a coward by the mere glare of a girl who she wanted to help. She stared back defiantly.

"You know what Bianca, you can get off this land right now. How fucking dare you come here and tell me to come home. Out of all my friends I would have thought you would understand and would have at least let me enjoy this little bit of fucking happiness," snapped Chiara, her words tactless and tense. Her tanned face crazy and chaotic.

She stood, crouching and childlike, smaller than she had been, making her jagged collarbones jut out, whilst her boring, walnut-coloured hair was wild, pushed and pulled in all directions, like a bird's nest.

"Chiara I am saying this for your own good—"

"You are a fucking liar, Bianca, you are saying this for your own good because you are jealous—"

"Jealous? Really? Please explain that to me," laughed Bianca spitefully.

"Yes, you are jealous. All of your fucking life you have been happy, you have had everything handed to you on a fucking silver plate, a boyfriend, a good job, and now you won't have that anymore—"

"Why won't I have that, Chiara? Tell me?" Bianca retorted, her heart slow and quiet, awaiting to hear the predictable words.

"Because you have fucked up your life, you are going to have a baby and ruin all your plans, and now that your friend is finally moving on and finding happiness you can't bear it," Chiara shrieked, her arms folded to hide her hands, which violently shook.

Bianca nodded patiently, yet her mouth tasted bitter.

"You don't mean that Chiara and you know you don't," Bianca spoke firmly and monotonously.

"Yes I do."

"OK, but why the hell would I travel all the way down here to wreck your happiness when for months I told you not to marry Vincenzo? Explain that to me," Bianca commanded, her eyes a fierce match for those vile blue flames.

"I… because… well… why are you here? Why are you telling me to come home?" Chiara stuttered, her arms falling to her sides, defeated by this clearly pointless argument, yet her eyebrows narrowed suspiciously.

Bianca closed the gap between herself and Chiara, grabbing her hands, gripping the fingers tightly with anticipation for the words she must speak.

"Chiara, I…"

"What's wrong?" Chiara asked, her eyes unfrozen with the fright that girl instilled in her.

Bianca's usually smooth hands were cold and clammy, making Chiara snap her own hands away, afraid to catch her disease of dread.

"It's… it's… Vincenzo, there is a rumour going around that he will kill Domenico. People think that you could stop him by just talking to him, but I just don't know," Bianca explained, her voice strained and high-pitched.

Chiara stared at Bianca with eyes round with shock, the colour dilated and weak with an understanding she wished she could unhear.

The murky church bells rang menacingly through the valley, making goose pimples rise on the arms of both.

A crow gruffly barked from a nearby tree.

"Please say it is not true?" Chiara begged, her fingers knotting so tightly together it turned her dark skin white.

"I don't know if it is, do you think Vincenzo would do such a thing?" Bianca queried.

Instantly she knew the answer, for Chiara's light blue eyes darkened, flickering uncomfortably with the memories which struck her brain with brutality.

Chiara did not need to think about the answer, it was as instant and pointed as Vincenzo's violence.

"Yes he would."

Quietly, the girls sprinted to the black car, anxious to not meet Domenico. Neither wanted to disclose that piece of information to him, for both girls knew that even Domenico could be tipped to the violent scale of murder.

Their breathing was fast and panicky, as they heard the distant whistling of Domenico weave its tune closer and closer to them.

They arrived at the car, yet as Chiara opened the door, she heard the slow, crackling of footsteps upon the dry grass.

The whistling stopped.

Chiara glanced towards Bianca and knew in her face she had heard them too.

Her heart thudded with trepidation and her ears pounded with blood, like alarm bells

"Where are you going?" asked the deep, dark voice of Domenico.

Bianca turned around first, but her mouth fell open with astonishment. Her brother was not her brother. He looked like a different man, feral and wild. His dark hair was longer and curlier, sticking up in all directions, his face was darker with the sun bringing out those silver eyes. Many villagers never liked to look at Domenico's eyes, she knew that, but she had never been afraid of them. But now, she felt scared, for those silver eyes were magnified with madness, sparkling, and incensed, like the silver bloodthirsty eyes of a wolf.

"What are you doing?" Domenico asked again, each step crackled with the snapping of the dry grass beneath as he moved closer.

"Look, Domenico, I, we came to pick Chiara up," stuttered Bianca, her body and face stiff with panic.

There was silence, and Bianca watched her brother's face closely for any signs of sadness or anger.

But his face did not flinch with any feelings.

It was motionless with emotion.

"Why?" Domenico interrogated sharply, his eyes large and immovable behind the glass frames.

"Because, because—"

"Because I need to go back to Vincenzo," broke Chiara, her voice croaking, as she struggled to speak through the large lump blocking her throat.

There was a brief silence, and Chiara knew she had lost Domenico, for she could not hear his thoughts anymore.

The words of Chiara seemed to bring life back into Domenico's body. He shoved passed his sister and stood before Chiara with pleading, poignant eyes, as he desperately tried to reconnect to her like he always had done. But she was distant, faraway in her thoughts.

"Chiara, why must you go back? Are you not happy?" questioned Domenico, his intense silver eyes flicking across her contrite face.

"No."

"But then why must you go?" Domenico persisted.

Bianca noticed how he pushed a strand of Chiara's hair behind her ear, before his heavy hand fell to her narrow shoulders, gripping and massaging them, willing her to come back to him.

"Look, Domenico, I promise I will come back, but there are things I need to talk to Vincenzo about, like a divorce and where we go from here—"

"But my darling, you don't urgently need to get a divorce, I mean we don't have to marry," Domenico whispered encouragingly.

"Yes, but I still need to talk to him, I can't leave him without answers—"

"Yes, you can, he doesn't care and you won't need to see him about the divorce, we just won't marry," Domenico beckoned with a small, comforting smile, his dimple dug softly into his cheek.

Chiara could feel how close his face was to hers, for his breath was warm and tender against her cheeks, and the pressure of his fingers deepened into her skin. She wanted to push him away. He was selfish and greedy, if he really cared about their future he would let her go, she thought bitterly.

The car door slammed as Bianca got in, making them jump slightly.

Chiara's memories were jolted by the last four blissful days they had spent together in exile. She did not want to go away from this place. This place that had opened her eyes to a real life of happiness. This place where her veins had pulsed with passion. This place where her heart had been overfilled with love, like an overwatered flower. This place where her lost soul had found unity with another. She did not want to leave his kisses. She did not want to leave his touch. She did not want to leave his silence. She did not want to leave his conversation. She did not want to leave his dimpled smile. She did not want to leave his loving eyes. She did not want to leave this place where life and love grew with abundance and beauty.

She did not want to leave Domenico, her home.

However, after all their mistakes and miscommunications and lost time, she could not sacrifice this long awaiting love and happiness for Vincenzo's pleasure in persecution.

Their future, their love, their dependency, would be safe, if she could free them both from Vincenzo's game.

Staring him in the eyes, her thick tears blurred her vision, like a watercolour painting, making him look hazy and faraway, yet her red lips remained firm and unyielding.

"I have to go, Domenico, please understand me, you don't know what might happen in the future," she spoke strong and unbending, yet her lips slowly began to tremble.

"Yes we do, and marriage doesn't matter, please don't go back to him—"

"How do you know that I won't remarry? What if I meet somebody else," Chiara snapped, her eyes blinking fast, trying to hold her tears in, yet they fell suddenly and stingingly down her cheeks.

Those words seemed to impact Domenico more than she would have believed. His hands were snatched away from her shoulder, his breath was cold and distant, his feet crushed the dead nature as he flinched away from her.

His eyes were on the ground, his face invisible, his body and spirit isolated from her.

She instinctively regretted her words, and tried to go to him, but he jerked away, as if she was contagious.

"Please Domenico, please try and understand. I promise I will be back before the night comes, I promise. I love you," Chiara choked, as she tried to touch him and remind him of her love and trust, but he was defensive, blocking and shielding her away, as if she was dangerous.

"Please Domenico listen, I promise I will be back, it won't take long. I will be here in the morning to wish you luck for your exam and interview, I promise."

Chiara stopped talking as Domenico held his hand up for silence.

"What's the point in the interview? What's the point in anything—"

"Domenico—"

"No, if you go back to him everything is ruined. I will forget it all, the grapes, the dream, you. I might as well burn down all these fucking vines and pack up and move away. Forget about you and all our memories. You are my dream, and if you go everything is fucking worthless," Domenico stammered, his voice wobbling and trailing away with the extreme emotions of fury, sadness and disappointment, which raged within him.

"I have to go," Chiara cried, the tears spilling faster and faster down her cheeks, her lips trembling and tripping over her words.

But Domenico did not listen, and she knew she had lost him.

"I promise I will be back before the night comes," Chiara pleaded, her voice hoarse and cracked with tears, like shattered glass.

Suddenly Domenico looked up with tearless, emotionless eyes of steel. His lips were firm, and his cheeks were taut. The dimple had vanished.

"If you are not back before the night comes, I will be gone and all this will be over," threatened Domenico darkly.

He marched towards the house without another look or word towards Chiara.

Chiara watched his misty figure get further and further away from her until he had disappeared altogether.

He slammed the door, making the chickens scuttle and squawk, disturbing the feathers and dust from the ground.

Turning around, Chiara collapsed into the car seat, and leant her head against the window, breathing hard, as she took one last look at this haven. The sun was viciously red, turning the vines black with its heat, as if they were burnt, whilst the house was flaming and foggy with the amber warmth.

This small happiness was frail, falling through her fingers like sand. She was unable to hold onto it for any longer, like a vicious frost stunting the growth of the grapevines, killing them before they had lived.

She began to weep into her hands, hiding her face, for she did not wish to speak to anyone.

Alessandro started the car, and worked his way back to the town, distracted and disturbed.

He had heard Domenico's words, and they had sent his body cold. He felt something stirring in the air forebodingly, as if death sat among them.

THIRTEEN

The Fangos' house was eerily quiet, as if it had been abandoned in a rush.

As Alessandro's black battered car pulled up at Chiara's house in silence, they sat for a moment, all lost in their own thoughts and theories. Chiara's tears had dried, yet her cheeks were red and tight. Bianca's nail had bled from where she had bit it to the bone, red crimson droplets frozen on her thumb. Alessandro shivered, as Domenico's voice grew colder and crueller, the words replaying in his head, like a song he could not forget.

Suddenly there was a frantic tapping at Chiara's window making her gasp with shock, as Signora Antico stood silently close.

Unwinding the window, Chiara smiled weakly at her.

Signora Antico was stunned, for everyone had believed Chiara had either fled or died, but here she was, alive and breathing, refuting these rumors in a second.

"I'm sorry to bother you, Alessandro, is Bianca there?" Signora Antico asked, ignoring Chiara, for she could not speak to a woman like her.

"Yes, I'm here, Signora Antico, what is wrong?" Bianca questioned, leaning backwards to address her.

"I am so sorry to tell you this Bianca, but your *nonna* is ill, she has been taken to hospital, Matteo and your mother went with her," she spoke shakily, for the young girl's face already looked drained and distressed.

"What! What happened? How ill is she? Did she have a heart attack?" Bianca interrogated quickly, her mind racing in a frenzy of concern, as she imagined dark images of her *nonna* being tied to an ambulance, her lips blue and her eyes closed, dead. She felt Alessandro's steady hand stroking the inside of her thigh gently.

"My dear it is OK, I don't know the details, an ambulance turned up and took them away," Signora Antico said sympathetically, her soft hazel eyes glanced between the faces of Alessandro and Bianca, who both seemed aged and tired by life's trials.

"Where is my father? Did he go with them?"

"No, your mother wanted him to stay here to close and open the shop for tomorrow," she explained patiently and calmly, as she tried to hide her disgust at the recollection of Signora Fango fussing and shouting orders at everyone, including the paramedics.

"OK, I will go and see him, thank you Signora Antico," thanked Bianca absent-mindedly.

"That's OK, Bianca, I am sure your *nonna* will be fine, do not worry dear," reassured Signora Antico before she shuffled away from the car, leaving a small lie in its place. She knew that Nonna would not survive the night, and perhaps it was for the best. The family she knew had fallen apart, broken into fragments of immorality. What was this town coming to? How could she call this place home, when it was so stooped in sin and loose morals? These young people seemed to have no control of their wild natures and desires. It was a dismal future she predicted for this town.

It was her, that monstrosity of a wife and woman, who sat at the heart of this devastating, disheveled future. People had whispered the words of witchcraft, and Signora Antico had always given

261

Chiara the benefit of the doubt. But now she was sure that girl was a witch casting the blackest magic upon her beloved town, turning it into a playground for Satan and his disciples.

She thanked God that her husband was not here to witness this fall of propriety, and she only hoped she would join him soon.

Chiara watched Signora Antico walk away, as the church bells rang, severely reminding her of God's lessons, which she had blatantly ignored for love. Fiddling with the cross on her neck, her mind and body felt the impact and consequences of her reckless actions. No one trusted her and no one liked her. She was the black sheep of this village, bringing nothing but bad luck and misfortune. She now saw how the village viewed her actions, which only irritated her, for they did not understand the reasons behind her ways. The sad truth was that the villagers did not want to know her reasons, it would make no difference to their opinions, for once they had established a sinner it was law, despite the evidence for her.

"Chiara, are we OK to leave you here?" Bianca spoke, her voice tremulous and terrified.

Turning around, Chiara squeezed Bianca's shoulder reassuringly, though her heart cracked with agitation for what stood behind that door. She did not want Bianca to go and leave her to face her husband, her punisher, her bully, her murderer.

"Yes, of course, Bianca, I hope your grandmother is OK, thank you for everything," Chiara lied, as she struggled to hide her apprehension behind a sympathetic smile.

Bianca placed her hand on top of Chiara's and smiled faintly at her oldest friend. Both drawing strength from the warmth of their hands, for at this moment, both needed the courage, like the oxygen they breathed.

"Thank you, I'll come and see you tomorrow," promised Bianca.

"OK, thanks, see you tomorrow," called Chiara, as she clicked open the door of the car.

"Goodbye Chiara," shouted Alessandro, as she climbed out of the car.

Waving, she shut the door, and stood back, as the engine grumbled, and the car moved away slowly.

Bianca waved, and both girls could see the reflected anxiety in their eyes.

Chiara watched them sadly drive away as she stood alone, outside this place she could not call home, for it was a prison.

A prison of dreams. A prison of childhood. A prison of poverty.

She felt like an escapee being once again chained and locked behind the bars of a prison.

She did not want to go in. She did not want to leave the safety of the outdoors. Yet, Domenico's words from the forest shot down her fear, he had mocked her for not having courage. This was the time to prove these words wrong.

Knocking fiercely on the door, she waited for an answer.

No one came, not a sound.

She knocked again more aggressively, for she felt her certainty slipping away from her with each passing second.

A light came on, a thin strip of yellow crept from beneath the door, and then she heard the slow plodding footsteps of her father.

Chiara braced herself.

The door opened slowly, and she stood like she had done as a child looking up at her father with the same apprehension and pity.

"What are you doing here?" her father asked gruffly, his face dead with emotion.

"I came to see Vincenzo," she replied coldly.

"He's not here."

Of course he wasn't, thought Chiara, bitterly.

"Well, I will wait here for him," commanded Chiara, desperately trying to convince herself to go inside.

Her father did not flinch or respond, he merely stepped aside and let her pass.

Once she was inside, and past the alcoholic stench of her father, she raced upstairs to her hot, stale room and fell upon the lumpy, thin bed.

But this room did not belong to her anymore, this was the room of another girl. A girl who had feared her own shadow. A girl whose best friend was guilt. A girl who had been betrayed and bruised by bullies all her life.

Chiara was not that girl anymore, or so she thought.

It felt strange to be back in this place, for the room had not changed a bit, yet everything was tainted a faded scarlet colour by the setting sun. The same sheets still lay across her bed, like they had before she was married. The bottles of deodorant and perfume still stood with the caps lying motionless upon her dresser, like she had been there only that morning. The curtains were still closed. The flowers on her windowsill must have died, for the room stank, like cat urine. White shirts from work lay scattered across the floor, and the creased clothes she had worn to the woods with Domenico sat crumpled in the corner, all ghosts of her past.

Chiara knelt before those creased, colourful clothes she had worn that day, and deeply inhaled the scent of sweat, soil, and pines, it made her smile, for the fight now seemed truly pointless. Yet, without that fight, she might never have left Vincenzo, and may never have understood what it felt like to be truly loved.

Domenico had been right about so many things, but she wanted to prove him wrong about her lack of courage. Her thoughts were drawn to him. What was he doing? Did he believe in her? Did he still love her? Was he still angry? Would he leave without her?

Chiara wished she knew the answers. In a past lifetime, she would have, but now everything was unpredictable. Her life was a game for all to play, and the risk could leave you in reign or ruin.

The stench of the dead flowers was making her feel sick. Opening the curtains, the room grew hotter and redder with the powerful sun, and she unlatched the window, yet no breeze entered. It was still, the air dead and odorous. Leaning out of the window, she looked down at her plants on the balcony, and her heart sank, for they were dead, dehydrated and brittle with the heat. She would miss her balcony, but she comforted herself with the visions of a future balcony with more exotic flowers and herbs to nurture.

The world outside was silent, and the abandoned homes stared back at her, emotionless, like Domenico's eyes, and suddenly her eyes fell upon the window ledge of another house. The fluffy baby pigeons, which had bleated so noisily and sweetly, were dead. Their bodies had been ravaged by another animal, split open, bloody, their soft feathers scattered and stuck around them, like confetti at a wedding. Their little beaks were broken and open, silent, and their eyes were wide and unseeing, or hollow, picked apart bloody sockets, blind.

Stepping away, Chiara's hands trembled, for the death of these little, insignificant birds made her feel uneasy, scared by her courage.

Trying to forget these birds, she wandered around her old room with a strange feeling within her stomach, for nothing had changed. Her clothes were still hung neatly in the wardrobe, her sheets and pillows still held the marks of her old body and head, frozen. The bedside table still held the book she was reading and her mother's doll.

Chiara picked the doll up, and held it to her chest, praying for her mother to send her a sign or a warning of any kind to help guide her. A sudden memory of her mother crashed through her mind, making her heart thud. She remembered the night before her disappearance, her mother had perched on the end of her bed crying and apologizing, but she had never understood why at the time. Before she left the room, she had kissed Chiara goodbye, and she remembered how tightly her mother had held her, like she did not want her to slip away, and then she had kissed the doll, as if she was saying goodbye to her own childhood. This was Chiara's last memory of her, and she had not thought about it for a long time. She had tried to shut all memories of her mother out of her mind, for they hurt her with their happiness.

Those grey glass eyes of the doll stared vacantly back at her with a coldness that she had never seen as a child.

Curling on the bed, Chiara snuggled beneath her old sheets, smelling her old scent with nostalgia, even her old hair smelt different, like chemical clean conditioners, tidy and fresh, harsh and abusive, instead of the dry soil and woody vines.

Chiara held the doll in her hands, and closed her eyes, for after her tears, her eyes were swollen with the need to sleep.

It came quickly, and it brought the strangest dreams.

*

Downstairs, Chiara's father sat in a drunken stupor. He listened for his daughter's movements, but there was not a single sound. Maybe he had imagined her coming in. Maybe he was going mad.

Maybe he always had been mad.

He could not believe she had returned, why had she come back?

Why had his own wife never returned?

He hated Chiara. Despised her. That daughter of the devil was just like her mother, wild and uncontrollable.

She was selfish and severe.

She was cruel and conniving.

She was pure evil.

Taking a swig of brandy straight and neat from the bottle, it felt warm in his mouth, but it hurt his throat savagely with new memories.

He could remember his curse as clear as day. He could remember her dark curling hair, long and free. He could remember her smile, golden and promising. He could remember her body, small and neat, perfectly made for his own. He could remember her eyes, almost violet, rare and startling.

But no, she was mad, horrible, and cruel.

And slowly the image of her dissipated into something of myths. The hair was raging, poisonous serpents, the fingers were foxgloves, dangerous to touch. The body was riddled with disease and the eyes were the vilest purple venom of a snake.

They could kill you with one look.

They could suffocate you with just one touch.

They could paralyze you with just one kiss.

Yet even after all these years of torment she had reduced him to, he still loved her like it was the first day he met her.

His lifeless eyes lingered upon the objects in the kitchen. The painted yellow kitchen cupboards, the stained white counter tops, the black oven, the worn, dark brown floorboards, the fridge stuck with notes and pictures of cities torn from magazines, which she had always wished to go to, the mahogany table and chairs, and the daffodil tablecloth, unchanged since she had left. All these things were part of another life, which he no longer belonged to, for the ghost of his wife was within everything he saw and touched. She still held him hostage, unable to escape her, unable to be free of her, but he never wanted to lose her.

Suddenly the pain of her departure came back to him like a fever, as cruel as the first day she had gone.

He remembered returning from work, not a soul home, not even his daughter. There was no food on the stove. The table was not laid. The curtains were shut. The lights were black.

It had shocked him, but he had just pushed it away with the excuse of her chattering tongue. She would come back, and the child would be with her, he would even suggest they go out for dinner, so that she didn't have to cook.

He had waited an hour, and then two, and then three, but he passed the time watching television.

Finally, he had heard a knock at the door, timid and frail, he had rushed to his feet, galloping to meet his wife, his wonderful wife had finally returned.

Yet, when he opened the door, all that had stood there was his small daughter, crying bitterly, whining that her mother had not picked her up from school.

She had stood alone, like she had tonight, and his wife had vanished forever, leaving only the irritating child.

His palms were sweaty around the neck of the brandy, and his eyes twitched with the unrelenting agony of his wife's disappearance. The bottle slipped from his hand, smashing onto the floor, but he did not react.

We had been happy, he was convinced. He loved her, adored her, idealized her. He had never cheated, or hurt her, or anyone. He had always bought her presents on her birthday and her favourite flowers on Valentine's, yet she had still left.

To this very day, he was still flummoxed and astounded by his wife, and after her departure his life had quickly fallen to pieces. He did not care for anything or anyone, he found happiness in nothing and sadness in nothing. His brain had been blocked up with the inability to love and empathize, like cement.

All he ever felt in his cold, cold heart was hate. The worst kind, where there were no unbending excuses for hurting another, and no sentimentality for who it concerned.

But in truth, he had only hated one person, and that was his daughter. He did not care for her wellbeing or future. He forgot her birthdays and left her alone at Christmas. He hated how she tried to keep him alive when all he wanted to do was die, just like she kept those bloody plants alive on the balcony. Her constant fussing for money and food irritated him, for all he wanted was death. He would have done it himself, yet he was a coward. He hated the way she grew, each year looking more like her mother. He hated the way she looked at him with eyes full of innocence that slayed his heart with spite. He hated her voice. He hated her movements. He hated her cooking and cleaning the house. He hated Chiara and wished she had disappeared with her mother. He believed Chiara was the sole reason for his wife's departure, for he had been nothing but good to her. Chiara had driven her away from the moment she was born with her incessant crying or incessant giggling, or her incessant need to be fed or changed. All these things had made his beloved wife flee forever.

He would never forgive Chiara for what she had done, the only solace was when she announced her engagement to Vincenzo.

This was the first chance he allowed himself to entertain the dreams of death, dusty and quiet in a dirty house. He hoped no one would find his body, for if his wife ever returned, he wanted to repay her for the shock she had left him to face.

He did not like Vincenzo, but this man was a ticket to his death, and so he welcomed him to Chiara without hesitation.

But then, the wedding came, and he had seen Chiara's eyes light up like her mother's, full of selfishness and free will. He could have predicted she would run, perhaps not on her wedding day, but he was sure it would not have been long.

He laughed a lot that day, great spluttering and engulfing laughs that had made him feel sick with the sensation, for finally, after all these years, another man should suffer as he had done.

Chiara's father sniggered now, but it slowly faded as his drunken mind was drawn back to reality. Unlike her mother, Chiara had returned to her husband.

Slamming his hands on the sofa, he smashed his fists against it, pummeling the cushions, scratching the fraying fabric, like an animal, until the fire in his nerves cooled.

But it never could.

He hated her.

He hated Vincenzo. He hated how Vincenzo would be spared of this pain. He hated how Vincenzo had his whole life ahead of him with Chiara. He hated how Vincenzo had a wife. He hated how in control of his wife he was. He hated how the luck of life was always benefited by others.

He hated this house.

He hated this town.

He hated every street and alley.

He hated every face within those streets.

He hated the constant clanging of church bells.

He hated his life without his wife.

He hated his past with his wife.

Jumping to his feet, he stumbled around the kitchen, clutching the table, then the chair, which collapsed beneath his grasp. He ripped the tablecloth off; empty bottles fell shattering onto the hard floor.

He fell to the floor, glass crunching beneath him, as he lay there, hoping, praying death would come.

No, he needed to leave this place like his wife had done all those years ago.

He could hear her voice, soft and mellow, beckoning him away. He lay there in silence, listening carefully, her voice was outside, so near, yet far, calling to him to "leave, leave, leave".

Pushing himself drunkenly from the ground, he staggered and swayed towards the door with a new-found energy.

Throwing open the door, he stumbled into the street and staggered away in the late sunset, as the melancholy church bells rippled through the dense, warm air.

He walked and walked and walked away from everything he knew, hoping he would never know it or encounter it again.

*

Domenico mournfully marched among the grapevines, watching the sky's radiant colours diminish with the slow setting sun. The moon was brightening, and the stars were waiting for their cue at nightfall.

It loomed close by, and yet Chiara had still not arrived.

Picking a grape, he held the plump, juicy purple jewel between his fingers, the work of his dreams, the pennies for his escapes. The love he had laboured over for years, felt worthless in this moment. It felt soft, false, like Chiara's cheek, lulling him into a safe place of love, which had never existed.

Another week he reckoned and then he would pick them all, take them to the nearby press for wine, sell, and shoot away from this place. But now he was not sure, for she had betrayed him and run back to her husband.

Why had she done this?

Had she forgotten the past few days?

Had she never loved him?

Had she tricked him?

Why had she gone as if his love meant nothing to her?

He loved her, for every part of her was plowed beneath his skin and sown into the deepest hole in his heart, like the seeds of the grapevines within the soil. He could not just rid these memories of her, for he was utterly dependent on her love, and once, he had believed she was equally dependent on his love. Yet it appeared as though she had only used his love to grow away from him, reaching for something better, blossoming into something unrecognizable.

Why was he surprised by her actions? How could he have trusted her? A woman who had run out on her own wedding without a care. A woman who had slept with another man on her wedding day. A woman who did not know what she wanted from love nor life.

He had been a fool, the greatest idiot. How could someone like him, who was intelligent, have fallen for her tricks? How could love murder his sight? How could love murder his reasoning? How did love manage to change him into a man he did not recognize?

The sun was only just haunting the horizon, like the tiniest slip of light, like the smallest glimmer of hope.

She had still not come.

She would come, surely she would come.

She loved him, she had promised, did that not mean anything?

A slight breeze swept softly through the valley, rustling the dead leaves from the autumn trees, scattering them amongst the tangled grass.

Winter would be here soon, and he hoped he would not be here to see it through.

The valley was surrendering itself to the night, only the lonely sloping mountains were outlined by the sun's last flames.

Suddenly he heard a scratching sound from behind him, so subtle, but it was there.

Domenico smiled with his back to the sound, and watched the sun die away with relief. A sigh sunk his uptight chest with relief, and he felt every nerve within his body untwist with tension, as the colour rose from his cheeks.

He kissed the cross on his neck.

She had returned.

Chiara had come back to him.

Turning his back on the sun, he shouted with glee, yet his voice trailed away with the wind.

Chiara was not there.

Domenico stalked a little towards the farmhouse, dark in the night, like a residence for ghosts, as he scoured the land for Chiara.

Yet there was no one there.

Another scuttling sound broke free, and he moved in the direction of it.

But when he saw what it was his face dropped, and his heart pounded with a fierce, maddening fury.

A tiny, grey mouse rustled around content and calm in its mouse duties.

It stopped when it felt the thump of Domenico's feet, its little body panting with panic.

Yet, all the love and care Domenico held in his heart had disappeared. Quickly he trod on the mouse's pale pink tail before it could escape, and with the other foot he crushed its body.

Stamping and slamming his large foot repeatedly on the mouse, he took a crazy delight in the crush of its bones, the spurting blood, and squishy organs. Finally, he stopped and peered at the mouse, dead flat, its whiskers crinkled, its eyeballs hanging from its sockets, dark red with blood. It did not move, and Domenico smiled happily to himself.

Walking away from the crushed, dead mouse, Domenico grabbed a handful of grapes, crushing them between his fingers, the juice leaking from the lines in his palms, making his arms sticky. He did this again and again and again, but it did not quell his rage.

Stomping to the vegetable patch, he kicked the tomato vines over, ripped the cucumber stalks from the ground, threw the soft figs at the house, leaving stains of violet behind, before stubbing the chillies into the ground, and mashing the yellow courgette flowers in his mouth, before spitting them into the dry soil.

Nothing would calm him, all this destruction made him more incensed, and he marched to the house with three key thoughts.

Kill Vincenzo.

Burn his land.

Let those dreams die.

He would leave early tomorrow, for he still had his examination. His last chance to escape.

*

Chiara awoke suddenly with a start. She felt her heart pounding against the bed, the only thing moving in her frozen body.

There was a crashing and banging downstairs, and she knew this to be Vincenzo.

Slowly and quietly, she sat up in bed and rubbed her eyes vigorously, for she was annoyed she had fallen asleep. She still felt exhausted, for her sleep had brought nothing but cursed scenes and distorted visions of her reality, which made her shake, for it had all seemed so real.

What time was it? Chiara wondered

Glancing out of the window, the darkness was all around her, suffocating her. The only light came from a distant street light.

The full force of the moon hung in the sky, as if Domenico's very eyes were watching and taunting her. The stars flickered and pulsed far above her, like they were laughing at her misfortune.

She was too late.

It was all too late.

She had missed her chance.

Dragging her cheeks down with gripped brittle nails, she felt as though she had lost everything, and the despair fractured and diced her heart.

How could she have been so careless?

How could she have fallen asleep?

How could she have sacrificed Domenico?

How could she have sacrificed herself and her dreams?

Chiara felt like an idiot, guilt and irritation made her want to sob, as she perched on the edge of her bed.

But then she heard the noise of clean-cut, expensive shoes staggering unevenly up the stairway, all thoughts of Domenico left her, and fear found its place, as it always did.

She did not have courage.

She felt weak, trodden and frail with the years of fearing the unpredictable.

Her back straightened, rigid like royalty. Her feet were steadied on the tips of her toes. Her hands gripped the mattress. She could do this, there was still a chance to undo the mistakes of her past.

The footsteps clattered and thumped through the hallway. She could hear his body bashing and crashing between the walls, shuddering the very foundations of the building, making her body flinch at each sound.

She wanted this building to collapse, crush the cage of her childhood, and let her fly free like a bird.

"Chiara! Chiara! Chiara! Where are you?" groaned a slimy, drunken voice, her name sludgy with Smirnoff.

Chiara's body shook.

Suddenly the door of her bedroom crashed open and, in its frame, stood Vincenzo, drunkenly swaying from side to side.

Chiara glared at him, her teeth gritted, making her jaw hurt.

Vincenzo stood in the darkness, only his unshaven face

was lit weakly by the flickering street light. He was smirking a sardonic smile, his intoxicated green eyes irritating, his hair white and flat.

He looked at his wife, who seemed to rock side to side, like a boat. Her hair was rough and wild, her body was scrawny, like a little bird, her face was pinched, her lips, a thin, disapproving line, her eyes were sleepy, yet savagely sober. But it was hard to know if this woman was his property, for she was shadowy with darkness, only outlined by the slight slip of the street light outside.

"My beautiful wife, you have returned, you have returned. Victory is mine," shouted Vincenzo with a sarcastic triumph, attempting to stabilize his body against the wall, as he stumbled and slipped further into the room.

"I have not returned, I only came here to talk to you," Chiara growled, her hands gripping the mattress hard.

"Oh, my sweet wife, don't look so sad, your husband is here now," yelled Vincenzo, drunkenly laughing at himself.

"No, he isn't. You are not my husband and never will be," Chiara shrieked, her eyes blue glaciers of fury.

Vincenzo continued to laugh, mimicking her words over and over again, like it was a joke.

Chiara felt her blood boil. His voice was loud and bearing down on her heart, like a fox upon a mouse.

"Can we talk?" Chiara questioned defiantly.

"Sure, sweetie, what do you want to talk about? How you ran out on our wedding?" Vincenzo snarled; his humour destroyed by this last question.

"I don't care if I embarrassed you, and I don't care what people think, I love Domenico, not you," Chiara spoke fiercely.

Suddenly Vincenzo was upon her like a hyena, she shrieked as he grabbed her hair and pulled her towards him. The stench of alcohol making her feel sick.

"Well I do care. You fucking embarrassed me in front of everyone. You are my fucking wife, and you will do what I want,"

Vincenzo bellowed, his spit flying across her strong, unyielding face.

"I am not your puppet that you can do what you want with, and I am not your wife," shrieked Chiara, as he tightened his grip on her hair ruthlessly.

"Really? I think the fucking church would disagree with that—"

"I am not your wife."

"Yes you are, you fucking witch. You fucking whore."

"You don't even love me," Chiara argued, trying to pull his hand from her hair, but his sticky fingers were clamped in a deathly grip.

"Of course I don't—"

"Then why do you care? Why did you marry me?" Chiara screamed, her body twisting and fighting, as she tried to run from Vincenzo.

The room was roasting and unbreathable.

"Because you are obedient and very very quiet, and clearly very easy," laughed Vincenzo.

Chiara kicked him aggressively on the shins, repeating this action, despite her husband's shouts of pain.

Finally, he shoved her away, and she staggered unstably from him with her hands outstretched, as she tried to regain her balance.

"Why do you care if I'm easy or not? You wouldn't want to fuck me anyway," cried Chiara, a cold sweat breaking across her forehead.

Her head humming with pain.

"Why not, my sweet wife?" challenged Vincenzo sneeringly.

"Because I'm not your type—"

"No, but you have all the bits and pieces I need to satisfy myself."

"Do I? Are you sure about that?" retorted Chiara inspecting Vincenzo's vacant face. Did he understand her words?

"What are you talking about, witch?"

"I know Vincenzo, I know about you and Matteo," confessed Chiara, her voice cracking with this burst of information.

Vincenzo stared at her, his eyes and mind sobered by her words. He glared at her, callously, challenging the knowledge she possessed. She did not know, how could she? thought Vincenzo.

The heat was scalding, it made him light headed.

"What about Matteo?" smirked Vincenzo.

"I know that you are in love with him."

Chiara's words hung suspensefully in the scorching air.

"You are a fucking liar—"

"No, I'm not, tell me that it's true."

Suddenly two large, brutish hands grabbed her arms tightly. His breathing was like a savage animal as he flung her on the bed.

Chiara screamed, trying to fight him off with her hands and feet, but he was too strong.

He flipped her onto her front, pushing her face into the bed, stifling her cries.

His knees held her down on her back, crushing her spine.

His right hand flung the doll to the ground.

She heard it shatter, and the head lay in broken pieces on the floor, the glass silver eyes broken, watching, uncaring, ignorant.

"Tell me you are a liar," Vincenzo threatened, pushing, pressing her into the bed pitilessly.

"I'm not," cried Chiara, tears creeping from her eyes with this new force, this new fear, that had never threatened her before.

Suddenly he climbed off her back and dragged her legs closer to the edge.

He ripped her underwear from her body and pushed the white wedding slip into a scrunched-up pile above her bum.

Chiara screamed and tried to toss her body from left to right with a frantic panic.

A sickening panic.

A death-like panic.

"I'll fucking show you, I'll fucking show you that you are a lying whore," grunted Vincenzo.

"No! No! No!" screamed Chiara through crackling sobs.

Chiara heard the unzipping of his trousers.

Vincenzo split her clamped legs apart, and shoved his body between the gap.

The heat of his body blistered her naked skin barbarically, brutishly, blindly.

"Please stop, please," Chiara begged, trying to shake him from her body.

But it was too late.

Too late.

She screamed as her vagina was torn open with the force of Vincenzo's revenge.

He pressed her crying face against the bed.

Chiara closed her eyes shut.

Screaming, screaming, screaming.

But it was all in vain.

No one could save her.

It was all too late.

FOURTEEN

Domenico was awoken by the loud shrieking of a bird in the almond tree.

His eyes snapped open, as if he had never been asleep. He felt awake and alive, despite only catching a couple of hours' sleep. He had struggled to find sleep, for his mind had writhed with the memories of her. That woman, who had tantalized his imagination. That woman, who had driven his dreams, and quelled his nightmares. That woman, who had stood by his side, working and supporting his every thought and question. That woman, who had stirred his sexual yearnings. That woman, who had completely captured, captivated, and condemned his heart to eternal love.

But that woman was gone. His imagination was dead. This new woman now stunted his dreams and navigated his nightmares. This new woman now mocked his work and support from a silent distance. This new woman now turned his love to loathing, and his sexual yearnings to violent willfulness.

Domenico had not cried. He found tears did not come in the face of this brutal betrayal, and only anger swelled and stirred in his body, racing and running through his veins, wanting to explode with its energy, yet what could he do with this anger? Who would console him now?

He felt mad, incensed, yet powerless without her.

Walking to the window, he rubbed his stubbly chin and scared the peaceful bird from the tree with his wild waving hands, still sticky from the grapes.

It flew away in a fluster towards the weak-coloured sky, the darkness of the night was an ombré of blues, purples, and blacks. The moon still hung suspended in the sky, but the stars had become diluted by the dull light of the sun. It had not yet crept over the mountains, and so the valley still lay in the pale shadow of dawn. The trees were calm and still, yet active with eyes and ears that knew everything that humans did not.

A new day, but all the melancholy of yesterday had not melted with that new sun, like the evaporating morning dew.

Domenico leant on the windowsill, and watched his farm awake, fresh, fertile, and alive with hope. The chickens clucked and chattered in the courtyard below, pecking their beaks at the ground. The leaves were uncurling with the light, their dry faces looking to the sky with a prayer for water. The grass untangled its dry limbs, revealing and releasing the dusty moths to the air. The crickets had silenced their croaky song, leaving the valley peaceful with the distant twittering of little birds, discussing the items of the day. Flies sleepily buzzed through the stale air, landing tiredly on the windowsill to rest.

Domenico had a desperation, a despairing need to leave this place he loved so dearly, for it did not belong to him anymore, but another man, who had fled in the night with all his hopes and dreams.

He knew it was early, and he decided he would walk to town to pass the time, and then he would wait in the cemetery, where he could draw comfort from the grave of the old man, who used to own the land. Perhaps, he might find peace in the quiet thoughts of Signoro Maestro.

Pulling his eyes away from the view, Domenico searched the dark room for his clothes. Bundled in a pile were his black trousers, now patched with dust, and his white shirt creased and grey. The jacket he knew was still strewn in the bushes from that day, and there it would remain. He found his black shoes and socks scattered amongst the dark room. Once all those items were collected, he piled them on the bed and gazed at them, his lips tensing with anger, whilst his fists curled with a passionate fury, for the memories attacked his mind like a pack of hyenas over a dead carcass.

Domenico tried to fight away these memories of the past with thoughts of the future, and it helped. His practical mind decided that when he arrived at Bari, he would buy a new suit and shower there. He would have plenty of time to kill, so he did not need to worry about that.

Sliding his arms into the cold shirt, he buttoned the front slowly, and suddenly all his thoughts were drawn back to her small light fingers. He remembered how she had unpicked each one quickly, eager for his love. He pulled the black trousers over his strong legs and searched for his belt, which had snuck beneath the mattress, like a snake in hiding. He tightened the belt around his pelvis, and he thought of how it had suffocated him when he had seen her body, naked and beautiful and all his.

Pushing his feet into the crusty black socks, and then the tight black shoes, he felt trapped and uncomfortable, for the last few days he had paraded freely with bare feet.

Glancing around the bedroom one last time, he collected a science textbook to read for the journey down.

He did not look at the wedding dress that sat in the corner of the room, sunken and soft in its depressive state.

He refused to look at the bed that had held their bodies, tangled and trapped in a spellbinding love that he thought would last forever.

He shook his flushed face, embarrassed by his naivety and stupidity, for his love would always be unrequited.

Clambering down the stairs, he left the little farmhouse, closing the door behind him with a final click, a closure on his memories.

An instinctive urge to inspect the vines gripped him, and he obeyed this command, for it could do no harm, and he had plenty of time.

As he trudged towards the vines, the chickens raced away from him fearfully, the trees seemed to shy away, and the animals were silent and still, as if nature was frightened by this new man.

Ambling carelessly down to those vines, a maze of memories and magic, he became engulfed by her.

Her bright, breathtaking blue eyes flickering through the gaps in the vines, as she watched him work, never leaving him.

Her red lips parting for the taste of the grapes.

Her dark hair waving behind her like a flag.

Her fingers and hands tenderly touching the light leaves and dark wood, as if this place was a grave of her own dreams.

Her body silhouetted by the flames of a sunset, drifting away, his own body caught in her elongated shadow. He was her shadow, following her every move, dependent on her for his existence.

Her voice seemed to be everywhere, in the grass, in the trees, in the very grapevines themselves.

His footsteps fell in the places her own had fallen, and his eyes looked at things her eyes had seen, and his nostrils smelt the nature she had smelt.

But his hands did not touch the grapes or leaves, for this was his last dream, his last opal of hope, and to touch them could taint everything he had left.

He was delirious with sleep and sorrow, for he found himself beginning to believe she was actually here.

Slowly, his eyes were drawn to the havoc of flies squabbling in the bushes nearby. Walking towards this, the flies flew away in a frenzy, disturbed by the earthquake of his steps. And then, he saw it, the squashed mouse from the night before. Its little mouth open and its eyes eaten away by another animal.

He felt nothing, not a care or pity for this little disfigured creature, made to suffer by his own power.

He stood still for a moment, for his feet were already rubbing and blistering within the shoes.

Suddenly a golden-brown mottled snake, long and sneaking, appeared from the grass nearby. Domenico did not breath or flinch, afraid of this body that could poison and paralyze his nerves in a heartbeat.

The snake did not seem to see Domenico, its long, flickering tongue seemed excited by the dead mouse, as if it was licking its lips. It slowly slivered towards the carcass. The last remaining flies scattered away with fear as the snake approached. Its mouth opened as wide as the diameter of the mouse, engulfing the body, cutting its bones with its fangs, until the mouse had vanished.

Domenico watched how the small body of the mouse deformed the thin form of the snake, who widened and morphed, digesting the body brutally. It lay there, motionless, full and satisfied with its morning breakfast.

Slowly Domenico crept away from the snake with a childish fear.

The church bells banged in the distance, before finishing with four monotone rings, calling all farmers to their land.

It was four in the morning; the workday had begun, except for Domenico.

This man, who had worked this land since a child and cared for its nourishments, walked away without another look.

*

Signorina Morderna was awake as usual. It was early, but not unnatural for that lady of the night.

Sitting by her window, which looked out onto the square and Signoro Fango's shop, she nursed a cup of hot espresso, sipping it with a sleepy desire, despite the coffee burning her lips and mouth.

Staring at the reflective window, she saw her face, it seemed aged and wrinkled with the cruel hands of time. Her eyes were bloodshot and slightly misty with her sleepless night. Her chestnut-brown hair stuck up in all directions making her appearance seem messy and disheveled. She could see the creeping strands of grey hair, discolouring her youth. She wore a close-fitting red, silky nightdress, which rounded over her curvy hips and slightly loose belly. Her hardened nipples studded the dress below the lace trimming. She saw her chest spotted and bruised by the sun, and her neck hung loosely with the lessening of tension on that piece of skin.

Tucking her swollen, crusty feet below her thighs, she took another sip of coffee, warming her mouth and staining her teeth with its powerful aroma.

These mornings were always filled with self-loathing and regrets for how she'd lived her life or hadn't. She could never sleep on nights where her bed was not filled with another body. The loneliness of that huge bed kept her awake with self-doubt. Had she lived her life wrongly? Had she spent her years of lust badly? Should she have spent these years filling her house with children? Should she have spent these years with a bed filled with a husband, who she could have loved and loathed in equal measures? Should she have spent these years despairing over her saggy, worn boobs, black tired eyes, and a belly scarred by the frightful experience of childbirth? Would that have made her happy? Would that have filled the hole in her heart or made it grow?

It seemed strange, for most women were normally filled with self-loathing and regret after having spent a night with a random man, yet she was the opposite. When she awoke with a stranger beside her, she felt content, loved, and fulfilled with companionship. She always slept better when she knew there was someone else beside her, for though these men did not care for her, the companionship tricked her into believing that she was not alone or unloved.

Signorina Morderna knew most of the women judged her actions with the harshness of the Bible's scriptures, but they did not understand her need to have a man beside her. These strange men rarely ever satisfied her sexual needs, for most were filled with a selfish greed for their own satisfaction, but it did not matter. It never had mattered, for what she truly craved was the attention of another. Sleeping with men was not a mission of sexual pleasure, but a need to be idealized and loved by another. She had heard people call her a slut, a whore, a woman who had no discipline over her desire, a woman who shirked marriage and morality, a woman who was a bad role model for the town, and a woman who should be kept away from tainting the minds of young girls. She knew her name was used as a bad example for the teenage girls of the town to learn from, but it did not bother her.

She respected herself, and she didn't need the false compliments of other women to make her feel grand and good. She knew she was better than these petty women of the town, for she never judged anyone else's life. When she heard of Bianca's pregnancy, she did not want to condemn that girl, but offer her help. When she heard of Chiara's wedding escapade, she felt oddly proud. Sometimes, she felt women were a greater evil to women than men. Of course, men took what they wanted from her, but equally she took what she wanted from them. Yet these spiteful narrow-minded women, who preached kindness and friendship, were frauds, for they tore down girls who loved in a different way, and you would never see their holy hands helping a girl who had stepped outside of God's law.

Sipping the last of her coffee, she stopped, for her eyes had been attracted by a strange movement in the street. Standing up, she placed the coffee cup on the windowsill, and leant with her nose pressed hard against the window, as she watched the figure limp through the street.

She gasped as the figure grew closer, misting the window.

It was Domenico, who had been lost from this town for nearly a week.

Yet as she stared carefully at the moving figure, he seemed different.

285

This man, who had once presented himself with a clean-cut accuracy, was a dusty mess, ragged and worn and bedraggled. His curling dark hair was quite long, licked and flicked in all directions, his clothes crumpled and dirty, and his movements unfocused and frantic.

What had happened to this prosperous young man?

He looked homeless, a wreck of his old self.

She viewed him suspiciously as he came towards the family shop. He seemed to take a key from his pocket, and slot it in the door.

Yet, he did not turn it.

She observed how he pushed the handle down and the door gave way, as if no one had locked it the night before. It was probably Matteo, Signoro Fango often moaned of how careless his eldest child was, and she could easily believe it.

But Domenico seemed to be fixated on investigating the lock, yet she could not see what troubled him.

Finally, Domenico went in, closing the door behind him.

Signorina Morderna could see no more, but she thought it was strange he should be sneaking through the streets at this time in the morning.

Yet her thoughts were quickly distracted, as suddenly from the corner of her eye, she saw a figure running lightly down her street. The figure wore a slippery, silky white dress, but she could not identify anything else, for this spirit seemed frantic, tripping quickly down the steps beside the newsagent.

The little head bobbed quickly down the steps and ran fast, sprinting out of her sight.

Signorina Morderna blinked, and when she opened her eyes, this white figure had vanished, as if it had been a ghost.

A shiver slid like electricity through her spine, goose pumps rose from her skin and her mind pounded with questions.

Who was this young girl?

Was it a ghost from long ago?

She had heard the slurred tales of drunks, who on their walk home, had seen ghosts of lost relatives. Had this happened to her?

But, surely not, it could not be, this figure had seemed too alive to be a spirit. Yet, why had this young girl sprinted through the streets at this time? Why had she seemed so desperate to get away? What was she running from? Was she escaping something? Or was she running towards something? Was she safe? Was she crazy? Was she trapped?

No, Signorina Morderna commanded her thoughts. It was a figment of her tired imagination, and her sleepless eyes had confused things that were real and false as one.

Yet, secretly, Signorina Morderna was sure she had seen something, a ghost, or a living girl, she could not say.

Suddenly her eyes flickered back to the shop where Domenico was emerging, yet there was nothing in his hands. What had he been doing in there? she wondered suspiciously.

She watched Domenico shut the door behind him, and amble away in the same direction as the white ghost, but he would never see or catch up to it, for that ghost had moved fast and urgently.

She found it strange that he had not locked the door, for his key stuck out, like an invitation for a thief. Why not? This was not in his character, usually this young man had been meticulous and precise in his duties and responsibilities of the shop. She knew he was the only one who mopped it and gave the accurate amount of change. Something was wrong with Domenico, he seemed careless and distracted, shaking his responsibilities and family reputation to the hands of criminals.

Should she call Signoro Fango? Let him know of his son's mistakes? No, she would not, for it was not her responsibility or her business to intervene in.

Domenico had disappeared from the scene, and the street lay silent like it always did at this time in the pale morning. Yet Signorina Morderna felt troubled by the figures and actions of this place, and this was reflected in her paling face and anxious eyes, which stared back at her.

Moving away from the window, she turned her back on the street and reached for her coffee cup.

She took a sip, but it was chillingly cold, offering no comfort or warmth to her cold body.

What should she do? What had she witnessed? Should she even feel concerned?

Signorina Morderna stood at the foot of her bed, one hand clasping the dark, ornately decorated bed stand to steady herself, and the other weakly holding the coffee cup.

She would shower, and if after that, she felt it necessary to confront Signoro Fango, she would.

But mostly, she needed the shower to not only cleanse her body but clean her mind of the scenes that had been acted upon the streets with a strangeness that sickened her heart.

*

The rolling church bells chased her, reminding her of that day, making her run faster and faster and faster.

Her breath was gasping and tight across her chest, as if every step was crashing through walls.

Dong.

Her legs wobbled.

Dong.

Her heart throbbed.

Dong.

Her feet crashed against the stone.

Dong.

Her head, her mind was numb with only the screaming, shrilling words of escape.

Dong.

She needed to escape.

Fast!

Her legs and feet did not ache with the penalty of her freedom.

The bells died away. It was five in the morning.

She could feel nothing, except for the agonizing pains shooting through her pelvis and vagina, like spikes and swords of the grossest and cruellest crime to a woman.

Yet her body, weak and exhausted, hungry and thirsty, began to give way.

Slowly her footfall staggered, and her body bent over her aching pelvis, completely breathless, dizzy without oxygen.

It was early and she had snuck away from her prison as soon as she had known her captor was completely killed by the alcohol of the night before.

Before the murder of her mind.

Before the slash of her sanity.

Before the butchering of her femininity.

Before the, before the, before the…

No, she did not want to remember. She wanted to forget, she wanted to die, and let those memories die with her.

Yet, they flashed and frightened her fearful mind and heart, like the rattling of thunder to a mouse.

She wanted to scream, erase those malevolent memories.

Blur the brutality. Mist the madness. Fog the fear.

Suddenly between her breaths, she heard footsteps, long, slow, and mournful following her own path.

She turned her head, yet there was not a soul in sight.

Holding her breath, she listened carefully and alert to every sound.

Thump, thump, thump.

Footsteps.

He had followed her. He had found her escape.

He was going to punish her again, like last night.

He was going to take her.

Trap her.

Blind her.

Mute her.

Poison her.

Dread devastated her heart and rocketed her veins with adrenaline.

Morbid adrenaline.

She needed to hide, quickly.

Along the road, shrubs grew sparsely, but it was her only hope, her only chance to survive.

Sneaking behind the shrubs, she fell and lay on her front, motionless, like a dead body.

She buried her face into the dry, dusty soil, which choked her breathless lungs and tickled her nostrils, like a tormenting tease to make her sneeze and expose her hiding place.

But she held her breath.

She bit her lip and began to taste blood oozing from that place.

The footsteps thudded closer and closer and closer.

This man, that man, that monster would catch her, string her up like a prized hunt, before tearing her down and ravishing her with immortal delight.

She was not a woman anymore.

Gender and sex, what were they? Name tags for the hunters and the hunted. Names to hurt and harm. Names of prosecuted clarity. Names that did not belong to her anymore. She was neither man nor woman. She was neither human nor object. She was neither found nor lost. She was invisible, like air.

He had taken everything from her. He was the winemaker, and she, the grape. He had ripped her from her vines. He had pressed the skin from her body, leaving nothing of herself behind. And then, he had crushed the last of her memories from her body, pressing, pressing, pressing himself upon her, squeezing every last drop of her happy youth from her body.

The footsteps rose in volume, violently pounding and punching her very heart with the wounds of the night.

Her hands shook against the dust.

Her black curled lashes did not blink the itching dust from her eyes.

Sweat cloyed her bloodied thighs and groin, making them alive and real like the night before.

He was coming for her.

He was going to attack her.

Vandalize her body.

Kill her.

And for the first time in ages, her eyes dimmed with tears, splashing onto the soil, soaking that dry dead earth with life, as if her grief grew the crops for the next season.

Suddenly the footsteps faded and then vanished, as if God was finally, ultimately answering her prayers.

They seemed to walk in the direction of the graveyard.

Relief flooded and overwhelmed her assaulted body and mind, as if it were food and drink to a beggar.

Tears and sobs were coughed from the deepest parts of her body with the release of adrenaline.

Suddenly she bent her body over and threw up, acrid bile trailing from her lips to her chin.

Her heart still pounded madly.

Her vagina felt more acute with its agonizing pain, sore from the sacrifice she had born brutally.

Chiara curled into a tight ball around that place which promised the gifts of life, but only punished her with the death of herself.

No position could cure that pain.

Reaching her hand to that place, she could barely touch it without the need to moan with the merciless pain. Removing her shaking hand, blood streaked her fingers, sneaking beneath the nails and discolouring them.

She could feel the sticky syrup of sweat and blood cling her thighs together.

She could smell the dried, metallic blood on her white silky dress.

She could feel the bruises of his fingernails.

She could feel the smashes of his hands.

She could feel the lead weight of his body.

She could feel his ruthless love infecting the rest of her body, until she was riddled with fright and disgust and destruction.

Suddenly she jumped to her feet, renewed with an energy to flee, to forget, to fly away from all this hurt.

She began to run, run, and run, away from that town, that house, that dreaded, detestable man.

She knew where to go.

She knew where safety stood.

She knew where love lay.

She knew where kindness called.

She knew where wisdom walked.

Down in the farmhouse with Domenico, in the dry valley bursting with the ripe vines, this is where she must go, her last chance to dream.

*

Signoro Fango was irritated by the loud, damaging rings of the church bells. Why did they have to ring so early? At six in the morning, those who were awake did not need to be awoken, and those asleep were useless.

He had slept terribly, and so he opened the shop early, if only to give him something, anything to do.

He worried about his mother.

He worried about his son.

He worried about his shop.

Luckily, Bianca was with him.

A few customers ticked away ingredients for this and that. Their thoughts meaningless and worthless to him.

Signoro Fango stood at the cash register with his daughter, lamenting and lingering over the subject of his mother, her grandmother.

"*Buongiorno* Signoro Fango, how are you today?" inquired Signorina Morderna, her eyes heavy with fatigue.

"Yes, *buongiorno*, my morning has been bad," grumbled Signoro Fango, chucking her groceries carelessly into her bag.

Signorina Morderna sympathized with the exhausted, heavy-lidded eyes, scowling mouth, unshaven cheeks, and uncombed hair of Signoro Fango.

"I'm sorry to hear that. How is your mother? Any news?"

"No, they say she is awake, but only just, whatever that means. But on top of that the shop was broken into this morning," explained Signoro Fango, rubbing his creased forehead with anxiety.

"Oh dear, how awful, did they steal anything?" she interrogated, her eyes wide with the secrets that surely had to be shared.

"No, it is so strange, I cannot understand it, why would someone do it? It seems pointless and you know what, I believe Matteo or Signora Fango must have come back this morning because they left their bloody key in the lock. Not that it matters because the lock had already been snapped, but why didn't they tell me? Anyone could have stolen something seeing a key lying around. It is stupid," he raved, slamming the numbers of her items into the till, his raging eyes flicking between price tag and till, his lips as thin as ribbons.

Signorina Morderna inhaled sharply, so it was what she had seen, even the ghost could have been true.

"It was not them," Signorina Morderna spoke, her voice low and grave.

Signoro Fango's dark eyes snapped open with shock, which quickly diluted into suspicion. His gnarled fingers were suspended over the till, frozen by her words.

"What?"

Bianca looked up from organizing the sweet counter, staring at her in disbelief.

"It was Domenico," she answered quietly.

"Domenico! No it couldn't have been," cried Bianca, grasping the woman's arm with damp hands.

"How do you know this?" interrogated Signoro Fango, his eyes narrowing, his nostrils flared with a temper not to be touched or tampered with.

Signorina Morderna hesitated for a moment, unsure of her place in this play of madness.

"I don't know who broke into the shop, but I couldn't sleep, and so I was just drinking my coffee when I saw him try to unlock the door—"

"Did he come out with anything?" Bianca almost shouted this question, her eyes wide and fearful.

"No."

Bianca and her father exchanged a look of confusion and misunderstanding. Neither could comprehend why he had been there. Maybe for food? But he had come out with nothing.

What had he taken? Bianca wondered.

What has he planned?

*

Chiara collapsed to her knees, exhausted, eyes swimming and drowning in her silvery, salty tears.

A smile flickered with relief across her cut, gritty red lips.

She had arrived.

She was safe.

This place was home, for Domenico was home, and always had been.

Dragging her body to its feet, Chiara gazed around the sunlit farmhouse, calm and collected in its shabby array.

Yet, something felt different as she neared it.

There was an eerie quietness about this place, as if no one lived here.

Wandering around the perimeter of the house, the chickens chased her ankles, the vines stood in their usual place, undamaged by Domenico's threats, as if they were untraceable. Yet as she moved around the corner of the house, she found the vegetable patch demolished. The tomato vines had been viciously dismantled, the remnants of fruit and vegetables were strewn across the ground, tomatoes were slashed and squelching beneath her feet, whilst her eyes inspected the purple stains, like hickeys, marked upon the pale wall of the house.

What had happened here?

What was he playing at?

Where was he?

He must be here, for his three-wheeler had stood outside the gate, untouched and unmoved.

Quietly she called his name through the windows of the empty house, which echoed her feeble voice back to her, reminding her of her weakness and instability.

No one answered her quiet calls.

She moved away, confused and suspicious, yet perhaps, he had gone for his exam early, he would not have left her alone.

He was not that sort of man.

Retracing her steps, fear still held her mind captive, and she snuck through the door, and quietly tiptoed up the stairs without a sound.

Chiara saw the bed and fell upon it, hiding her body under the blanket and her eyes away from the wedding dress. She drank in his scent, like the finest wine, absorbing his safe mind and secure hands, like a sponge, holding his heart close to hers.

It was the only thing that gave her hope.

It was the only thing that she had left to save and keep.

It was the only small, magnificent thing holding her love and life and dreams together.

*

The shop was empty and quiet, only filled with the clanging, chaotic bells. Signorina Moderna had left about an hour ago with her groceries and guilt, for the secret she had spilled not only confounded

Signoro Fango and Bianca, but angered and worried them in equal measures.

As Bianca filled the conditioners up, she thought about her brother, so filled with prosperity and promise, now degraded and devilish in his secrets.

Why had he come here?

What had happened to Chiara?

Had she gone back to the farmhouse?

Maybe he was innocent in his actions, maybe Signorina Morderna had seen something wrong. Maybe he had never been here.

But Bianca knew in her heart it was all fake theories and excuses, for after her confession, they had rung her mother, who had been offended and full of rage by the suggestion of this sneakiness, whilst confirming Matteo had been by her side the entire time.

Bianca wished she could say her mother was a liar, but one of her mother's only credits amongst her many vices was her harsh honesty.

But why had Domenico made the trek here to only go back to the farmhouse?

Had he killed Vincenzo?

Had he killed Chiara's father, for he had vanished from the town in the night, like a ghost?

Suddenly a loud growl of an expensive engine startled to a stop, and a car door slammed.

The shop door crashed open, banging a nearby display as it shut.

Bianca jumped, especially when she saw who it was.

Vincenzo, alive and fierce with rage.

This man who persecuted the streets in his fine clothes, looked like a wreck. His clothes were the same as the previous day, and his blond hair was tossed in sweaty clumps in all directions. His lips were dry. His eyes were cracked with red blood vessels. His cheeks were pale. His hands shook.

Yet, when he greeted her father, he spoke with his usual arrogant, smooth tone, as if it was another day, ordinary and ineffectual.

"*Buongiorno* Vincenzo, what can I get you?" Signoro Fango asked through gritted teeth, his mind desperate for the taste of nicotine.

"Two packets of my usual and a packet of matches," responded Vincenzo haughtily.

Signoro Fango nodded and turned his back on this evil man.

Opening the cigarette cabinet, he grabbed Vincenzo's usual. Signoro Fango's crooked knees bent to the bottom shelf, and his eyes fell on the matches shelf with perplexed panic.

The matches, usually stacked in neat rows, had been pushed and shoved in a scatter of mess, like someone had been in a rush to grab the packets.

But why?

Moving the matchboxes back into place, another realization struck him.

Two packets were missing from their usual stack.

"Excuse me, but I am in a hurry, so do you mind sorting your little shop out when you are finished serving me?" demanded Vincenzo, his voice smeared with arrogance.

Signoro Fango inhaled sharply, craving his cigarettes more earnestly as he meekly stood to his full height, his knees cracking with this exercise.

Punching the numbers into the till, he read the total and exchanged money for the purchases with a coldness from both parties.

Before Vincenzo left, he stalked up to the ignorant Bianca, who continued stacking the shelves in the soft morning sunlight, which streamed through the smeary windows.

"Bianca, can you do me a favour?" Vincenzo asked, his slimy hands touching her shoulder.

She shrugged his hand away, keeping her eyes on the shelves.

"No."

"Its not hard, even a simple village girl like you could do it," Vincenzo mocked.

"No."

"What a shame, Chiara will be disappointed," Vincenzo falsely lamented, flicking dirt from beneath his fingernails onto Bianca's head.

Bianca froze in her actions, at the name of her dear friend.

Her heart began to pound quickly against her chest.

Was she safe?

Surely, she was at the farmhouse, Bianca prayed.

"Why will she be disappointed?" Bianca asked casually, biting the bate she knew she would regret.

"She wanted me to give Domenico a message."

"What message?" Bianca bit, her lips trembling with anxiety, yet she kept her eyes away from Vincenzo, for she feared they would expose too much. No information was safe in the hands of this vile man.

"To wish your clever brother luck at his university exam. She would have done it, but she was tired, being married means a lot of late, late nights, but you know what I am talking about," explained Vincenzo moving his eyes creepily towards her slightly swollen pelvis as he raised an eyebrow, before he continued: "I thought it would make sense for me to deliver the message."

"I see," Bianca spoke unblinking.

Did this mean Chiara had not gone back to the farmhouse?

Had she sacrificed her brother for that man?

Was she trapped?

Or were all of Vincenzo's words a cruel trick?

"I can give him the message myself as I'm sure you won't remember, where is he? Has he already left?" queried Vincenzo, opening his packet of cigarettes, chucking the clear plastic to the floor thoughtlessly.

"I don't know, I haven't seen him in a long time," Bianca responded, lifting her eyes to Vincenzo.

Vincenzo smiled poisonously and tucked a cigarette behind his ear.

"Don't worry, I know where he is," smirked Vincenzo, and with that he left the shop.

Bianca stood speechless with shock, as she heard the foreboding engine growl with money, before it moved away with a purpose, with revenge.

A revenge she knew all too well.

*

Chiara flicked to the next page of the book. The sun's rays were brightening with their torrid torture, melting her cold, tense bones and making her head ache, as she squinted at the words, which she struggled to absorb.

She knew their meaning and matter, but her mind was vague with fatigue.

Snuggled under the blanket, she smelt the book and a vision of Domenico came to her mind. She saw the dirty thumbprints and placed her small thumb on top, their DNA bound together. She whispered the sentences underlined by his wobbly hand and read the side notes, like a speech, feeling his tongue and voice in her own mouth. She unbent the corners of chapters and thought of his eyes drifting into a deep sleep full of science.

The book comforted her beyond all measures, for it felt as though Domenico was here, protecting her, holding her heart, and clasping her hand in a solid embrace of love.

The heat fermented the whole room with its vicious energy.

There was not a sound in this tranquil place, for the treacherous sun had banished all creatures to sleep in the shade or die within the flames.

It was a comfort, yet a curse.

Her mind still heard the screams, shrieks and groans that had erupted from her own mouth only a few hours ago.

Chiara rubbed her temples shakily, her mind weakened by the attack and her body unforgiving to its torment.

She did not dare close her eyes, for the merest darkness brought back the brutal barbarity of that man.

But she was strong. She would beat that man. She would not let him trap her ever again.

A promise she had made in the quietest place of her soul.

He might have taken her femininity. He might have taken her body. He might have smashed her mind. He might have killed her dreams.

But he would not take her love, for it was a root so deep and strong that to break it would kill her heart and steal all the breath from her body.

She sighed as she heard the bells chant loudly and disruptively from the town. It was eight in the morning.

They made her shiver.

They made her wretch.

They made her afraid.

He was still close, close enough to find her, and therefore close enough to hurt her.

But the church bells also comforted and calmed her heart, for soon Domenico would be on the bus and then he would be back.

They would go to Tremedi, she was sure of it.

Suddenly a tickling sound of grass caught her attention.

Chiara closed the book and listened closely with a pounding heart.

The sound came again.

The crackling of the grass, the rustling of the bushes, the sound of heavy movement.

Slowly, without a sound, she lifted her eyes just above the windowsill and glared out to the glaring sunny landscape.

She could not see anyone, but the sounds still murmured through the window.

Suddenly, she saw the blur of a blue shadowy figure in the distance.

Perhaps a farmer, her mind tried to console.

Perhaps not, her heart argued.

The shadow moved through the vines, like death, elongating and distorting with the sun.

It was coming closer and closer and closer.

Chiara whispered a prayer, her lips moving against the wall with urgency.

Who was down there?

What did they want?

Finally, the figure and face of that shadow came into focus.

Chiara gasped, and her heart stopped beating.

The man who stood there she knew well.

But not like this.

Her mouth dried, her eyes watered, her heart plunged and panicked.

A sinister chill crept and crawled slowly through her spine.

Her whole body shook and trembled, dead cold.

This man she thought she knew well.

Dangerously and disturbingly well.

*

Giacomo waited at the bus stop, drumming his fingers against the wheel of the bus, leaving sweaty fingerprints upon the worn black wheel.

Sweat tickled the backs of his ears and gathered at the nape of his neck, for the heat was suffocating and stifling. The light blinding and bad.

Where was Domenico?

Giacomo sweared beneath his breath, before glancing at his watch for the hundredth time.

8:47am.

Seven minutes late and counting.

He could hear the passengers grumbling, as they glanced at their watches or phones with huffs of annoyance.

Gazing out of the window, he surveyed the countryside, but it seemed almost misty and foggy with the extreme heat.

Peering closer, he thought he could see smoke in the distance. No, surely not.

"Giacomo why have we not left? I have an appointment in Termoli, which I will be late for," moaned Signora Antico clutching her purse, her voice strict and severe, like a schoolteacher.

Giacomo held one of his hands up in surrender.

"I am sorry, Signora Antico, we will be off in a moment," apologized Giacomo through gritted teeth.

She went away, annoyed further by his words, as he heard her whine to another passenger.

Come on Domenico, Giacomo's mind pleaded, for his prideful career was under attack by this mob of morons.

Another minute crept by, and Giacomo sighed, irritated, he could not wait any longer without damaging his reputation.

Closing the door, Giacomo switched the ignition on and adjusted his mirror.

Suddenly there was an urgent rapping on the door and Giacomo glanced up to see the face of Domenico or who he believed this man to be.

Opening the squeaking door, he heard his audience sigh and swear at yet another inconvenience.

Domenico stepped onto the bus, and Giacomo gaped at this wild man, who had once held himself so well, yet now stood messy, breathless, red-faced and disorientated. His dark curling hair was greasy and limp, his cheeks were grey and unshaven beneath the red. His eyes he could not meet.

Giacomo could not help but stare, shocked and uncomfortable by this unusual image.

Domenico appeared agitated, nervous, almost guilty in his stature, he nervously shuffled his feet, making his stooped posture fidget fretfully before Giacomo's cubicle. He thanked

God that he was safe and locked away from this strange man.

"Are you OK Domenico? You look tired," hesitated Giacomo, almost smilling at this understatement.

"Yes, yes, I am fine, how much do I owe you?" Domenico muttered coldly, his hands shaking as he delved into his pockets.

"€5," Giacomo responded cautiously.

Domenico pulled the money from his pocket, the note trembling and fluttering in his soiled hand as he gave it to Giacomo.

"I should have charged you extra for making me wait nearly 10 minutes for you," joked Giacomo, sliding the damp note into his box.

But no humour or laughter crossed Domenico's grey, unsmiling lips.

Giacomo saw the restless flicker of his eyes flitting in all directions, vague, yet alert to something he could not see.

That face, from boy to man, had always been calm and intelligent and kind, but now Giacomo could see it was dead, emotionless, and dumb with thought.

And those eyes, oh those eyes, they evoked the same fear as that landslide from his childhood. His silver eyes were wild with their wicked, unpredictable power, like the wet, bestial soil, moving sickeningly, like an avalanche, completely capable of destroying every single grapevine within the valley.

Domenico walked away and took a seat by the window.

What was wrong with him?

Giacomo took his foot off the clutch and began to maneuver the exhausted bus from the curb, slowly and carefully.

Suddenly a red sports car cut past him, causing Giacomo to break suddenly, startling the passengers and himself.

Giacomo slammed his hand on the wheel, the horn blaring across the empty street.

Fucking idiot! thought Giacomo, for he hated the young man who owned that car, he had heard this man was a wealthy Milano.

Of course he was, for all those northerners were all the same – arrogant snobs, trampling the people of the south with their expensive designer shoes, like they were rubbish.

They did not care, for they believed that this land was their right and power. They believed their money was sown in the countryside and cemented between the bricks of these houses, for they had this belief the south was indebted to the north.

Giacomo shook his head and drove through the town, his fierce, political thoughts fading as they returned back to Domenico.

Poor young man, he was probably worried for his exam and had probably overslept after a night of studying.

The bus left the town and Giacomo passed the IP garage, beeping the horn to catch Alessio's attention, but his back was turned to him. Giacomo could see traffic building up along the main road, he was confused, for there was never traffic along this road, especially on both sides.

People were jumping out of their cars chaotically, but Giacomo could not see what caught their attention, as he passed another bus.

Suddenly the bus erupted with gasps and cries, Giacomo stopped the bus with shock at the noise.

What was going on? All he wanted was a peaceful day.

And then he saw it.

The fire.

People were racing through the traffic, a standstill on both sides. People were screaming and children were crying. Men shouted and women shrieked, grabbing children from the edge.

Cars were emptied and the owners and their passengers stood on the roadside above the valley.

Domenico was the first to the door, begging Giacomo to open it, and he did without feeling or thought.

Hell, that was the hell of his imagination, red and alive and hot. Scolding hot.

Domenico tumbled from the bus and ran to the edge of the road.

His farm was on fire. It had not yet spread any further, yet it was only a matter of time.

The flames were a rebellion against the earth, slashing and smashing everything in sight.

The vines were ravaged with red flames.

The grass smoked, black and burning.

There were a hundred shades of red, orange and yellow rising from the valley, like looking inside the mouth of a volcano.

The heat was terrible and toxic.

The noise was like an earthquake, rumbling and roaring, decimating the land, like a beast.

Even from this distance, the chickens could be heard screaming.

But no, it was not the chickens, but a girl's voice.

Screaming.

A white figure stood by the little house surrounded by a circle of uncontrollable flames.

Red fire engines spilled down the side of the valley with an ironic slowness.

Collapsing to his knees, Domenico watched the scene unfold.

The white figure ran into the house.

But the flames destroyed every inch of space.

The courtyard was engulfed by the fire, but the flames were still hungry.

They were upon the house, climbing the walls with ease, crunching and crumbling and cracking that building.

"Chiara!"

"Chiara!"

"Chiara!"

Domenico shouted and shouted and shouted, but it was useless.

The fires held the power, and all that girl's suffering and sorrow was nearly at an end, like witches burning at the stake.

Finally, the faint church bells could be heard, and Domenico bent his head to the ground, his body shaking with a grief that killed him instantly.

The screams were silenced as the flames engulfed the blue roof. The very same blue as the eyes of that girl named Chiara.

Caro Signoro Maestro,

Chiara has not come back to the cell.

A man spoke to me. He wore a black suit. He said someone else had killed her. There was a mistake. She was dead.

I was so sure she wasn't dead. She was here only a moment ago.

She was killed, he said, by her father.

But we all killed her.

All three men who she loved trapped her, killed her, ravished her in flames.

The cell is on fire.

The world is one great fire, killing, burning, burning, burning away, dying and I will die with it.

The Parable of the Sower is a lie.

The crucifix is not her anymore, it is Jesus.

Cold.

I've been waiting for her, sharpening and filing and perfecting the point of the cross.

The point is sharp.

I carve her name into my skin, piercing, cutting and slashing C H I A R A.

My arm is thick and full with blood.

Drip, drip, dripping onto the floor.

I grind the point into my veins, hacking and engraving her name into my blood.

C H I A R A.

She won't be taken from me, never again.

I lie in the bed, the blood soaks into my clothes and seeps through the dirty sheets, like the flames.

The bed is red, like crushed grapes.

I am red, like red, red wine.

The bed is on fire.

I am on fire.

Death will come.

Chiara and I will go to Tremedi, together, never parted, never separated.

We will walk with the sea and the sky and the sand and